The Weird
Colonial Boy

The Weird Colonial Boy

PAUL VOERMANS

VICTOR GOLLANCZ

LONDON

First published in Great Britain 1993
by Victor Gollancz
An imprint of Cassell
Villiers House
41/47 Strand
London WC2N 5JE

A catalogue record of this book is available
from the British Library

ISBN 0 575 05325 9

Typeset at The Spartan Press Ltd
and printed in Great Britain by
St Edmundsbury Press Ltd, Bury St Edmunds, Suffolk

For the B'Spellians,

another reason to be cheerful.

Contents

'*In the great crisis of our life, when, brought face to face with annihilation, we are suspended gaping over the great emptiness of death, we become conscious that the Self which we think we knew so well has strange and un-thought-of capacities.*'

Marcus Clarke, For the Term of His Natural Life, *1874*.

'*Gr-r-r-r! Ouph!*'
Ibid.

One

Fish on a Bicycle

Nothing is as simple as it looks, except a chicken. Chickens are as thick as speckled brown river pebbles.

Yet even chickens have changed men's lives.

When Nigel called the tropical fish shop old Blither curtly informed him that because Nigel had not shown last Saturday the price for the Fool's Gold swordtails had risen. Again. Of course it did you no good arguing over the phone. You borrowed five dollars from your mum. You crossed town by treadly to save on the tram fares. Fine: the morning was cool enough and there were three gardens on the way to Balaclava. But as Nigel stood to pelt up the big hill toward the city his right pedal gave out, dropping him smack on to the crossbar and into a vivid new world of pain.

Lucky thing Nigel had such long legs.

He left the bike spinning in the gutter and sat on the kerb, head between outsize knees. Now he would have to freewheel back down to Collingwood and climb on top of the garage for his father's ancient Raleigh and cannibalise it in a flat rush – all for a 75 cent cotter pin. He fingered the tears from his eyes and struggled to his feet. He wheeled the bike across the happy holiday traffic. From above a nearby Greek restaurant the Sex Pistols deconstructed his ear-hairs with 'Pretty Vacant'. He would have smiled to hear it, except that he felt his gonads were twin peach-pits driven into his belly.

*

The cotter pin was the wrong shape.

He thrust his hands deep into his pockets, as he usually did when worried. With an effort, he pulled them out and set to work.

He smoothed the pin on his father's bench grinder but it still didn't fit, so he hammered it with a centre-punch until it bloody did. By the time he had finished his shirt clung wetly to his lean body. His breath pushed through clenched teeth. The sunlight *leaned* on his hair, telling him it was close to shop-shutting time and that it wouldn't be a pleasant garden ride after all, but a race against Blither's arbitrary pricing system.

This was Nigel's idea of the wicked excruciation of hell.

He absolutely had to have those swordtails. Nigel had slaved in his father's factory like some ancient Roman dude, washing gunk out of drums and feeding noxious chemicals into the gloop under the despicable Todd's direction for a whole month, merely to pay the deposit. He would have all the delicate little mutants in the country if the government maintained the import ban. Then he would triumph where everyone else had failed utterly. He would breed the beasties. So what if they were mostly sterile because of dumped pharmaceuticals? They bred in the wild didn't they? He had lain awake dreaming of the little footnote in tropical fish-breeding history that might be his: *Xiphophoras helleri donohoei*, named after the twenty-two-year-old genius who'd first fixed its line, Nigel Donohoe.

As he gingerly remounted his bicycle the thought of it made him shudder with delight. Then his depression slammed back twice as intense. He couldn't bear to think of how much he stood to lose. Blither had told him he never kept fish for more than a month. Just a ploy to raise the price, naturally. But what if it weren't? What if he sold the swordtails to someone else?

Nigel leaned on the right pedal with some force. It clunked forward an inch and he wobbled dangerously close to a semi-trailer for a moment, but the pedal held at that position and he was able to right himself and dodge back toward the kerb. He gathered speed and was soon sprinting through East Melbourne down to the Yarra River.

If you want to make a mark on the world you have to suffer, thought Nigel.

He could never have imagined how much suffering those swordtails would bring.

The sign above the decrepit Victorian shop-front read: *AAAAAAA Premium Tropical Fish Procurer's*. Below that, on a piece of warped masonite in erupted Letraset: *And 'Registered' Chicken-sexing Agency*. Nigel discarded his bike against a lamp-post and ran for the door. Blither's scientifically tanned face lurked behind the door's filthy pane; he had one hand on the sign which read: *CLOSE*.

At the sight of the soaked and shaking form of Nigel Donohoe, Blither paused, calculation narrowing his eyes. An unspeakable evil skulked in those slits of blue. Calmly, he flipped the sign all the way over and disappeared between the violet-lit fish tanks. His white slacks were the last visible part of him; it was as if a pair of disembodied legs floated into the dinge.

You could not put a Donohoe off so easily. Nigel hopped cursing from foot to foot with hands in pockets in a kind of worried hornpipe, yes, but launched into resolute action mere moments later.

Blither's hapless chicken-sexers, armed with plastic wallets of pinky prophylactics, determined the gender of surprised baby birds on the outskirts of town for a miserable pittance. They didn't last long. Blither was forced to train squadrons of them, schoolboys usually, which meant chickens on the premises. Perhaps out of paranoia about miscegenation Blither maintained a chicken-versus-fish apartheid. This meant a separate door . . . which might not be locked! Nigel danced sideways to his right. The door was open. In his glee, Nigel stumbled through the 'reception' area – a desk and a payphone – almost colliding against the screen which hid the fledgling sexers from an innocent world. He diverted his forward momentum to the left and stomped to a halt behind Blither, who was back at the door wondering why his bargaining tactic hadn't worked on Nigel.

Blither turned. Nigel started, nervously, as he always did when confronted by the old Nazi.

'Ah, Mr Donohoe! I am afrait we are clost.'

Nigel managed, 'I've cucome for my ssswordtails, Mr Blither.'

'That's *Blit*-er,' the unscrupulous importer corrected. 'And which sworttails are these?'

Nigel sighed. Blither was one of the few who could revive his stutter. He had a deathly calm that put you on edge. Despite the heat from the tanks Nigel's sweaty clothes made him tremble. Or perhaps it was his allergy to the little chicks beyond the screen; he could already feel his nose dripping, his glands beginning to swell. 'Mmmy swordtails,' he said.

Something of Nigel's desperation must have penetrated to Blither because he said, 'A small joke. Come this way, my friendt.'

As they walked past the aquariums of exotic rarities to the tank for illegal imports Blither continued, 'You know my rules, my young friendt, I have fet and nurturedt these telicate specimens for you over a month and this is expensive for me – not to mention risky. I am afrait I will have to charge you a small fee for this.' He stopped at a tank holding pygmy purple *discus* and took some pink flakes from a canister to prove his point. 'These are very hungry little specimens, your swortfishes. And not fit, either. Three have tied in the last week alone.'

'But you said they were fine!' blurted Nigel.

'Those which are living, yes. But my sources in Central America tell me everything in the pollutedt stream from which they came have perishedt.' In the coloured light he turned eyes that shone pink upon Nigel. He shook his head sadly. 'So you see, my young friendt, I have labouredt like

Achilles just to keep for you these specimens alive.' He drove his final words home, 'And this is no cheap feat.'

He walked on, brushing the flakes from his fingertips as if they bore some distasteful recollection.

Finally, in a back corner dominated by two fizzing salt-water tanks, they arrived at Nigel's swordtails. Blither stood aside for the younger man to admire, one hand spread like a minimalist showman.

The breathtaking sight of these small fish brought out the mother in Nigel. Their darting forms actually appeared to glow. In a shoal of about fifteen they swam the limits of their mingy tank, a restless cloud of poignant salmon and fragile blue glitter flecked with black and slashed with bloody red. Most were male. None of the females showed the precious gravid spot which proved a live-bearer fertile. Behind the glass of the aquarium to the right a small hammerhead shark butted blindly toward them. Nigel was ready to offer all his money and the bike as well just to free them from this place. Their tank had plastic sand! He was prepared to break the law to have the fish today, prepared to maim, to kill, to wriggle across hot coals in a yellow rubber mackintosh.

He was even ready for harsh words.

'How much?' he asked. His throat seemed to have bloated. His palms felt like two cold oysters against his fingertips.

Blither named a figure way outside Nigel's means. Nigel boldly halved it. The ex-*Einsatzgruppenführer* rolled tortured eyes and set a figure twenty dollars higher than last week's. Unusually, Nigel let some of his impatience show; not even Todd at his father's plastics factory made him this mad. Now he felt as if he might any moment foam at the mouth and bite the goateed war criminal's throat out.

The look in his eyes shocked Blither, who had known Nigel for years as the kind of fish fan shy to the point of dementedness. He was just about to accede what he reckoned was a fair bill for all the care he had lavished on them (they *were* a danger to his import licence) when Warren Cauley emerged in his white polyester coat leading one of the chicken-sexing students by the arm. On the student's other arm, apparently stuck to his pinky judging from its cheeping, was a fluffy yellow chick.

Blither moaned. 'Again. *Mein Gott* you punish me.'

'Every time we try to pull it off it squeaks,' Warren whined, 'like it's in real pain?'

'Of course it is in pain,' snapped Blither. 'It is not a happy picnic in the Rhinelant to have the finger of a giant clot up its rectum, however petite your fingers are. Here –' he grabbed the student's forearm. 'So. It is tone.' He thrust the chick into the student's other hand, which he closed firmly but not unkindly around it. 'Now go away and to not bother me here again. You know I to not like the birts here with the fishes.'

The student, a gormless pimply creature in grey school trousers and the regulation *AAAAAAA* ill-fitting coat, perhaps in awe of Blither's easy chicken command, let the bird fall to the lino as soon as Blither released his hand. Warren dived to his knees. In his frantic efforts to nab the chick, which was hopping and slipping about in a sprightly way, he scooped the bird up far too forcefully. It catapulted through the dimness, and bounced off Nigel's forehead into the salt-water tank.

Said the gormless student in reverent tones, 'Look at the shark!'

The hammerhead had stirred itself from the tank wall; now it rose positively coyly toward the chick's kicking legs.

'Urrrghgh!' went Nigel in horror. Before he could think about it he had flipped the chick into the air above the swordtails' tank and caught it. The bird's bowels gushed a greeny liquid between his fingers, which dripped into the water.

As he handed the startled, lucky chick back to the student (who was frog-eyed with amazement now), Nigel noticed one small female swordtail make a dash at the faecal string and worry off a tiny morsel and swallow the thing.

All he thought of this at the time was: *yuck*.

In another age, Nigel Donohoe might have become a great explorer-taxonomist. Or at least one of the great goat-breeders of his time. Although he had read little of Darwin or Banks beyond the usual high-school obituaries, whenever such names were mentioned he became a little more dreamy-eyed than usual, a little livelier in his foolish lope afterwards. He had a mind as full of junk as a farmer's loft, but he loved all living creatures – even his pre-Jurassic co-worker Todd, sometimes, when he wasn't making sexist or other fascist remarks, and wasn't scratching his bum-crack. This dreamy potential, this hint of prodigy mutated into a bedroomful of aquaria, worried Nigel's father.

It didn't worry Nigel. He punched the air and whooped like a *Tour de Poisson* winner as he rode home through the cooling spring afternoon.

But when he got home there were complications. Nigel's mother greeted him in the doorway with the news that his father had glued himself to his secretary with Experimental Adhesive 69 again. And both of them had been glued to the TV set in the office as well as to the sprinkler-system outlet. Not only were they in danger of drowning and electrocuting themselves, the Prime Minister was being interviewed at length and they couldn't change channels.

His mum was in her dressing-gown, a hideous beast of orange acrylic fur; she was due at the football club to referee the 'Grand' Raffle First Prize a Trip for Two All Expense's Paid to Eden. In her worry she'd let her pink lipstick seep into the cracks around her mouth and had stuck a false eyelash to her cheek. Could Nigel take a can of the EA 69 solvent down on his bicycle for her?

Nigel held up his bag of fish in dumb protest.

'Ah, new are they? Lovely colours. There's a good boy – just twenny minutes, right? If you get his hands free he should be able to do the rest hisself.' She plucked at one of the curlers in her mauve hair; her hand shook from lack of drink. 'It's not as if it's a Doberman this time, is it? Thanks Nigel, you're a love.'

She shut the door in his face.

You didn't merely dump tropical fish in a tank and watch them swim around. Unless you were a moron or a heartless fink. You had to take extraordinary care not to *shock* them with different water conditions. Nigel supposed he could let the bag float about in the new breeding-tank for a while, just to get them up to temperature. He'd have to do that anyhow. He hoped Blither had put enough pure oxygen into the bag to last them. He almost prayed.

He leaned the bike on the wrought-iron fence and made his way down the path of trampled weeds at the side of the house to his bedroom.

Thankfully, it didn't take as long as it might have to free his father's hands from Mrs Pimlott's shins. Closing the office door on the gluey, geometrically improbable scene, Nigel spotted Todd closing the factory exit. As the only full-time worker besides Nigel's father, Todd's hours were his own. 'Just so he gets the work done,' Nigel's father always said. And Todd usually did. You had to give him that.

Todd had showered, changed and coiffed; he was ready for a torrid date with Melinda, his equally charmless sty-mate. He wore a white ruffled Bri-nylon shirt, a venerable brown leather waistcoat, pea-green plimsolls and tight purple leather trousers which featured a blue denim crotch. Hyper-virile curly black hair spilled over his shoulders. On sighting Nigel, Todd's face bloomed with an unnatural array of teeth. In those dark eyes glinted something immeasurably repulsive, his copious nostril hairs and rampant moustache gleamed like evil itself in the sunset. On top of all this he had a fat nose.

'Where have *you* been?' asked Nigel, attempting not to stammer.

'Up me auntie's fanny – where do you reckon?' Todd dropped his massive bunch of keys into his shoulder-bag and turned his broad body to face Nigel square-on.

'You know my dad's been stuck in the office,' Nigel managed to say.

'Great. Good on him. Where else is he supposed to be?'

'No – I mean stuck there with EA 69. I just now got him free! You must have heard him calling to you.'

Todd's easy insolence clouded with guilt. He wasn't really an evil man, just obnoxious. 'Heard someone *grunting*, if that's what you mean.' He forced a cackle, and tried to distract Nigel with his wit: 'I thought he was trying to race off old Pimlott. Can you credit it? "Ah Jack, give me ya love bullets all over me twinset, Jack. Oh yes! Hold on while I undo me girdle Jack!"' He caressed his hair and gave a pelvic thrust. 'What a ripper!'

'Oh come on,' said Nigel, close to his limit. 'When I got there they'd been stuck to each other and to the sprinkler and the telly for half the afternoon. Mrs Pimlott had to phone up my mum with her nose!'

Todd stared for a second. Then he stuck his thumbs down his trousers and roared with laughter; he held on to his belly as if about to give birth to some horror Todd-creature, doubling over and clutching the brick wall beside him. 'I'm not even gunna *ask* how they did all that!' He laughed some more. 'Here.' He made it to his feet and fished in his bag. 'I'm not gunna need *anything* tonight.' He turned and staggered off down the street, still racked by gales of oddly feminine giggles. 'Dialled the phone with her nose . . .' he muttered as he disappeared round the corner.

Nigel listened to the laughter fade. Whatever you thought of Todd, his laugh made him more human, almost likeable. Nigel inspected what Todd had given him. Two tabs of acid, called *Happy Turnips*, and a small bottle, the label of which read in silver italics on purple, *Adoration 'Finest' Liquid*

Incense. NOT TO BE TAKEN INTERNALLY. Amyl nitrate. He shoved the gifts into his jeans pocket and made for his bicycle. Bloody hippie, he thought. Then he smiled.

Now at last he could get back to his fish.

They were all right, the little beauties. Nigel knelt on the stool before their tank and counted them. Fourteen Fool's Gold swordtails, skitting and glimmering in a cloud. Funny, he thought. He had previously counted fifteen. He shrugged. He let the plastic bag slide from his hands into the tank-water. He got to work.

There was plenty to do. First he dripped a measured dose of violent blue fluid into the aquarium. (A week ago he'd treated the water against every disease but whooping cough but you couldn't be too cautious with the dreaded whitespot.) Then he checked the acidity, which was fine; he hunted wetness all over the tank's seals with a cotton bud, although he had made the deep all-glass two-footer himself so he needn't have worried. Both the under-gravel and power filters were functioning perfectly, the twin air-stones continued to give out pretty sprays of champagne bubbles in either back corner, the snails and loaches had the algae under control, the plants (tropical eel-grass and Amazon water-lettuce as well as a canopy of what Nigel called brain-weed because of its luminous red network of filaments) had all been planted a month before and were flourishing; the carefully washed river rocks held no rogue insects and had settled firmly into their roles as terrace-edges in the beautiful layout so they wouldn't be dislodged by some adult nosing after youngsters, there were no fungal dead to remove, and this was after all the best position in the whole glassed-in back verandah for a sunny (but not too warm) display.

In short, everything was hunky-dory.

Then he noticed it.

He was humming Patti Smith's 'Redondo Beach', his fingers were fiddling with the bag's seal, he was bouncing on the stool with anticipation at how his new buddies would positively revel in this superb microclimate, when he saw *an extra swordtail pop into existence out of nowhere.*

It was a smallish female. Rapidly he counted them again . . .

Fifteen!

Nigel blinked amazement. The fish were hovering in trepidation at his slight sloshing of the bag. As they do, the shoal suddenly shifted positions, and again were still. Nigel counted them once more.

Fourteen.

Was he going bonkers? He would have to release them soon or risk their oxygen starvation. It would make them more difficult to count.

Well, he had planned to ogle them half the night anyhow. He'd watch them every bit more closely now. He broke the bag's seal. He allowed a little tank-water to flow over one edge. He counted them another time.

There were fifteen swordtails present this time.

Gradually, he let the bag fill with tank-water. He counted and recounted, but the number of swordtails remained constant at fifteen. He examined all the smallish females. There were three. He named each of them according to their looks. There was Rainbow, whose red was not mere stippling but a definite band below her pink and blue back. There was Speckles, who had quite a number of black markings. And there was Carmen, who looked almost exactly like Speckles except for her way of constantly rippling her tail-fin seductively from bottom to top.

Nigel tipped the bag all the way to one side.

Tentatively, the swordtails emerged. Rainbow and Carmen hung together, and so were easy to track, but Speckles darted off into a thicket of water-lettuce as soon as she found herself free. One of the larger males almost immediately began his backward shimmy of love around a large female. Ordinarily this would have thrown Nigel into ecstasies; now he hardly noticed it.

He could feel his ears redden, his heart belt, his toes curl.

Every sense was heightened. He could even smell his mother's lemon pelargonium in the backyard and Mrs Major's parsnip pie next door. He saw the three females down a tunnel, outside which everything was a blur. He tried to memorise every fin-shape, each scale of the three.

What had the fish done? Could it pop out of existence and back in again at will? Perhaps it was some kind of mutation which went transparent when threatened. They had lived in a chemical cocktail in South America, after all. But surely you'd see its eyes. It seemed most likely that Nigel had imagined the fish suddenly appearing, had mis-counted – he was still utterly rooted from his ride up the hill to Balaclava, and he had not eaten all day.

For hours, until he went boss-eyed, Nigel stared at Rainbow, at Carmen, and at Speckles when he could find her. But nothing happened. He told himself for the eighty-seventh time that nothing had happened. When at last he rose from the stool to make a sandwich and find a beer he discovered his legs wouldn't work properly. He stumbled past the fish-tanks along the back verandah which served as his bedroom, to the kitchen door.

As he balanced the tall pile of peanut butter and blackberry jam sandwiches on his way along the narrow space between his tanks, Nigel sighed. With half a can of Vic Bitter down him rational explanations for what he had seen abounded. Fish moved fast. He had caught smaller fish in the creases of their bags before. One had been right behind another; a simple twist of the bag would spin the water inside a little and reveal the one behind as if by magic.

He planted himself on the stool, parked the plate on his thigh, and tucked in. Absently, he looked around for Carmen and Rainbow and Speckles. All there, all fine. Although Carmen had a strand of brain-weed snagged on one pectoral fin; he would have to cut her loose if it hung on.

Boy, am I hungry, he thought. The unimaginative tea made him think of where else he might have dined on a Saturday night, had he known anyone who'd go out with him. Somewhere in Melbourne there lived a bold and beautiful woman who didn't mind acne scars as bad as Nigel's. Staring at Carmen's rippling tail-fin, he decided he'd take his imaginary someone to a Spanish restaurant. They'd drink red wine and tango and she would find him manly instead of bumpy . . .

He noticed Carmen was having real trouble with the weed: it was an unconnected strand, but she didn't appear to know it and tugged on it as if it were fixed to something. Then he noticed that a piece of brain-weed about a foot away from her was jerking each time she shifted her piece.

And yet the pieces were not connected.

Or were they? Nigel put his plate and beer on the floor and cast about for a tool. A surgical clamp he used for planting caught his eye. He dived down the aisle for it. Breathing hard and fast he carefully dipped the clamp into the tank and snipped Carmen free. Then he tugged at the weed himself.

Sure enough, the piece of weed about a foot away moved as well. Trying not to shake, he released the weed and withdrew the clamp. He bounced across the bed for the box of odds and ends he kept under it. 'Ah-hah!' he cried.

Back at the tank, he unwound about a metre of fine trout filament from its spool. He snipped the piece of brain-weed still joined to the main plant and tied the length of filament to it. He then clamped the piece on which Carmen had snagged herself and, ever so gently, tugged.

The brain-weed with the nylon tied to it shifted. He fed some fishing-line into the water. He tugged again. The tied strand seemed to disappear along its untied end at exactly the same pace as he was pulling the clamped strand toward him.

They were attached to one another. They were not separate strands at all. Yet, when still, they appeared to be two ordinary pieces of brain-weed with at least one foot of clear water between them. Slowly, he continued tugging. At last he had the entire length of brain-weed on one side of the tank and he had the filament attached to it on the other side. He gave one more, teeth-grindingly delicate, pull.

He had done it. The trout line was through. He shifted the clamp to the end of the filament still knotted to the (now provably single) strand of brain-weed, and jerked. The filament on the other side jerked as well! He took either end of the fishing-line between thumb and forefinger, then moved it back and forth like a saw. The line obediently moved.

But it had a gap in its middle of over a foot!

Nigel opened his mouth. He shut it again. He tried to think his discovery through.

This must be a single length of fishing-line, he thought, but now it's a foot longer than it was and invisible for over a foot. Or, it's going somewhere else then coming back, like there's holes there, a gap through which the line has passed except that *to it* no distance (or at least very little) separates one hole from the other.

Carmen somehow found these holes and popped through them from place to place. No, that was silly. All the water would run out into wherever the holes led. Carmen made the holes somehow and they closed up after her. What a piece of work was Carmen. What a piece of luck that Carmen had snagged on the weed and prevented the holes from closing.

He gripped both ends of the filament in one hand. Then he dipped the clamp between the apparently snapped ends of the line. Nothing in between. Nothing up my sleeve! he thought, and giggled.

He took the ends of the line in either hand again and drew them apart. The line formed two diagonals, taut. He tried to raise both arms. The wet line threatened to slide out of his grip so he wound it around a couple of fingers and tried once more.

It was like cutting invisible cheese with a wire. At any moment, he imagined, it would come out the other side and he'd see the line whole again. But no: the 'cheese' was infinite; his 'cut' sealed itself as the line rose. First he pulled up, until the two points where the line entered (wherever) were above the water. Next he pulled forward, so the entire thing, filament and two points in the air where it disappeared, was clear of the aquarium. He tied the clamp to one end of the filament and the wooden fishing-line spool to the other. For a moment both objects hung still in the air, the taut lengths of line above them extending about half a metre vertically before giving out. The clamp, heavier than the spool, gradually sank toward the floor. Just before the spool reached its highest point, Nigel grabbed it.

So where did the line go when you couldn't see it? By tying fish-hooks to the line at measured intervals, Nigel discovered that in fact nearly ten centimetres of line was held wherever the hell the line went and that the large fish-hooks could disappear as easily as a thin thing like filament. What accounted for the other good ten centimetres which didn't appear to exist in this world? There was a discrepancy of over twelve centimetres here.

Nigel tugged the jangling hooks back and forth as he mulled it over.

And as fish-hooks will, one of them snagged on something. Something on the other side.

Nigel wound the line around one hand and tugged. It was a bit like when you got a snag whilst fishing: you didn't want the line to break. However, this time he was more than keen to find out what the snag might be. He tried a steady pressure, short jerks, giving some slack then tugging suddenly, and moving the whole line up and down holding tight on to both ends.

Just when Nigel was about to give up, the snagged hook leapt free. It surprised him so much he let go of one end. He flailed for it, slipping sideways and on to his knees. He caught the last hook before it vanished and held on, scratching his index finger but careless of himself in his panic.

It was only when he had fully regained his balance that he managed a good look at what he had caught with his line.

Dangling from two hooks at once, torn and dirty, was a girl's handkerchief. There was even a mess of snot fused to one corner. It was not this which sparked Nigel's curiosity, however. What attracted Nigel Donohoe and was to cause him so much trouble, what eventually changed his life, was the embroidery on another corner of the handkerchief:

C.A.S.

A chicken had set off all of this, although Nigel was not to figure out that part of it until much much later.

Two

The Other Side of Nowhere

On his way to collect his mother from the Social Club, Nigel was attacked. The nearby Excelsior Hotel had been named in a recent survey as the place in the Southern Hemisphere where you'd be most likely to have a plastic chair broken over your head. But as a local Nigel had never seen the need to avoid it. Normally, besides one another, the Excelsior drinkers attacked only council dog-catchers and, for obscure historical reasons, Argentinian tourists.

It wasn't a very determined attack. His assailants seemed to have trouble with simple tasks, like walking and talking, let alone highway robbery. Their swaggering across the road from the pub was anaemic, they looked about as dangerous as wet Vienna loaves, and their threatening gestures were more like the death throes of decapitated skinks. They did have a weapon: a Collingwood Football Club sock which actually seemed heavy, although it sounded as if filled with pistachio-nut shells.

'We want your *dosh*, pal,' said the taller one. He thwacked the sock into his palm with a crunch. 'Whaddya reckon we want – a couple of milk shakes and a *souvlaki*?'

'I wouldn't mind a souve,' said the one with the Safeway name-tag still pinned to his shirt. He rubbed his palms on his jeans in anticipation.

The taller one shifted from foot to foot, more like he had a small toad down his brown cords than out of impatience. 'Yeah. You hear that? Me mate's ready to clock ya one if you don't hand over ya cash.'

Nigel thought he had missed something. What was the significance of marinated lamb? He explained to them again, this time with apologies, that he hadn't a cent on him.

'Honest?' asked the Safeway worker.

'Honest, Terry,' said Nigel, reading his tag.

'Me name's not Terry,' he said, too quickly. 'It's — Knacker-Eater. I eat bull's balls for brekky.'

'Yeah,' said the taller one. He spat almost professionally beside him; it landed on Knacker-Eater's platform shoe. 'And I'm Fatguts.' He slapped his flat, black T-shirted stomach.

Nigel blinked. 'Howareya,' he said.

'Howareya,' returned Knacker-Eater automatically.

'Anyhow. I don't believe ya,' said Fatguts. He rubbed his cropped blond hair. 'I don't believe anything.'

'God is dead!' said Knacker-Eater.

'Eat the rich!' said Fatguts.

'NO FUTURE!' they both yelled.

Fatguts returned to his theme. 'You've got dough,' he said. 'Why are you on cocaine if ya haven't?' he observed astutely.

Perhaps they were rogue psychiatrists, Nigel speculated, out for a night of wild Neuro-Linguistic Programming and free association. 'I'm picking up me mum from the raffle?' he said incredulously.

'He's picking up he's mum,' said Knacker-Eater, helpfully.

'Yeah,' said Fatguts, 'so don't get any funny ideas, right?'

Nigel had long since conquered his fear. He decided he liked these two suburban skinheads. He would have invited them for a drink had he not the gnawing mystery of the snotty handkerchief to satisfy as soon as he got home. He thought he might explain it to them; Fatguts at least looked as if he might deal well with the irrationality of it. Just as Nigel opened his mouth, though, from the side-street behind the muggers came a dark, three-legged creature.

It slavered. It wheezed horribly. Its single eye rolled up to show a diseased-looking red tracery in the orange streetlight. It looked as if something had gnawed half its black tail off.

It was Buttercup the Labrador.

Buttercup lived in the Victoria Park railway yards, near the Football Club. Somebody plainly loved her, although nobody was sure who. She was fat and healthy, aside from her obvious disabilities and stone deafness. When she scared the primary-school children away with her friendly barks and attempts at tail-wagging, she would cock her head in perplexity to see them run. Perhaps her scariness came out of the children's tribal sense of guilt, for the story went that her disfigurement had been caused by a past generation of the school's students. She was said to be nearly twenty years old.

Fatguts and Knacker-Eater turned at the sound of her clatter on the pavement. They took one step apart from each other, wary.

'Skitchem!' called Nigel, inspired. 'Go on girl, rip their ears off. KILL!'

Buttercup stood jerking the grisly remnants of her tail from side to side, watching the skinheads retreat. She cocked her head.

'You're nowhere!' shouted Fatguts hysterically, as if betrayed by a good friend, running backwards.

'Yeah. Fucking Corn Flakes!' called Knacker-Eater, equally hurt. 'Nowhere!'

Perhaps this was how they found friends, thought Nigel. He waved goodbye. The two skinheads spat and ranted incoherently then turned and ran off into the darkness. Buttercup threw a happy woof in their wake.

Saddened, Nigel turned to her. 'Thanks mate,' he said, ruffling the loose skin on her saddle. Buttercup panted and grinned. She had perfect teeth.

Nigel stifled his pang of loneliness. He set off down the side-street toward the Football Club.

Back home, Nigel decided to take some decisive action about his discovery. He had yet to decide what kind.

He'd abandoned the line in the middle of his verandah-bedroom, with equal weights tied to either end, floating before his now-forgotten aquarium of precious swordtails. He left his mum making a cuppa for his dad and Mrs Pimlott (free at last). 'Off to bed,' he told them. He placed a stool by the strange hooked assemblage and sat down to stare at it in the yellow light which spilled from the row of kitchen windows behind him. He lost himself in its mystery; the backyard crickets rang airs through his thoughts.

After a while he tugged one of the lead sinkers, which had risen about two inches in as many hours, down to the level of its mate. The other sinker rose, as if an unseen pulley were concealed in the air above it. Nigel turned to the handkerchief on the foot of his bed. He fingered the clean, starched, embroidered corner for a minute. Then galvanised, he put the handkerchief between his teeth and turned back to the sinkers and tugged on the line until the two holes were vertically aligned instead of horizontally. He placed the top sinker on the fish-tank lid behind it and snipped the bottom one off. Then he fetched a little plastic scuba-diver from his odds-and-ends box and tied it to the filament's lower end. It dangled there like an executed Jacques Cousteau.

A glorious plan of innovation and discovery had swept across Nigel's brain. He had the technology. He had the know-how. He had the will. There was a future after all.

He stood, stuffing the handkerchief into a back pocket and spitting absently. After a lingering stretch of his lean and permanently tense frame, fists clenched in the air, he clapped both thighs and went quietly to the back door of his room, and stepped out into the vibrant night.

*

The birds were waking. A sallow pall of Sunday gave into his room from the backyard. Nigel examined his spectral form in the window, as well as that of the contraption beside him. Both he and it looked better that way. In the sharper reflection of the fish-tanks Nigel's skin resembled a cold rice pudding's. And when you stood back from the object of his night's work, it looked just like what it was: a conical *mélange* of plastic barrels glued together by an insomniac amateur.

Not a spacecraft at all.

Yet, if everything worked out it would not have to last more than seconds in the vacuum, and only its nose-cone at that. If Carmen the swordtail could flit from place to place then Nigel's craft could be pulled into one of the holes she'd made, for a look-see. Providing he could get in. His craft was so full of struts to prevent the exposed part exploding from its own air-pressure that he had to stand with his bottom and chest stuck out, head on one shoulder, one hand held by the other ear.

In truth, he had not begun with the idea of building a spacecraft in his father's garage. All he had wanted was a block and tackle to lift him till his head poked through one of the holes in the air. During the hours it took to build this from scratch, his sleepless mind had substituted dreams with imaginings of what *lay on the other side*. The handkerchief he had dismissed as a red herring early on, for who weaned on *Star Trek* could believe that a hole in space led through a laundry basket? No, the handkerchief was space-station debris from the future. It was odd to the touch. He could just as easily have snagged some futuristic Coke can or a misplaced positronic brain.

Thus the capsule. When he jerked on the string (ignition) it would pull the pin releasing (actuating) the rusted Valiant engine (power unit) suspended from a pulley (vector converter) on the tripod (gantry) outside the window (window) and its controlled fall (de-elevation) would pull on the rope that led via another pulley into the top hole (discontinuity) and out the bottom one hauling the cut-and-glued plastic drums containing Nigel (lightweight capsule plus astronaut) the necessary few feet into the air so both the clear top (nose-cone) of the craft and Nigel's head (neural redundancy network) would enter the cold clear vacuum of the infinite.

Space.

A fluttering began in Nigel's lower abdomen as he pulled the flap of the capsule to and sealed it with EA 69. Contorting himself further, he checked his equipment; Polaroid camera; kitchen knife (which eliminated the need to emerge from the second hole since he would fall back to earth when he cut the rope leading through the nose-cone's tip past his nose to the vehicle's floor); binoculars; waterproof matches and first-aid kit and oxygen tank (just in case); and a saw with which to hack his way out after touchdown. His fingers shook as much from lack of sleep as from nerves while he examined all the seals for the fourth time, his heart seemed to want to purl out of its cage. No leaks. He made sure the can of EA 69 was sealed. He was ready.

No putting it off now son, he told himself. This was what his life had been leading toward for twenty-two years. Ever since he and the doctor had gone flying across the delivery room with that sudden enthusiastic break from his mother's womb. He had run into walls from that date forward. Well, he'd had a gutful of that. He wasn't a stupid university drop-out who didn't even have the gumption to move out of home. He wasn't the awkward, at times stuttering, acne-scarred young bloke who at clubs stared fondly at the pale ones with outlandish clothes and bizarre hair, who longed to bounce and crash and judder around to the latest most degenerate chemical-driven black-clad punk trash in an undernourished nihilistic frenzy. No. No, no, no.

Nigel was the proverbial modest innovator. He would set up experiments, document them thoroughly, and like the inventor of the silicone breast, change the shape of the world.

He wormed an arm through the maze of thick plastic struts to the ignition string. He tugged. The rope connecting the floor of the craft to the car engine outside suddenly went taut. He felt the capsule rise towards the ceiling as the engine dropped from the tripod's apex to the ground. He heard the pulley above him turn and the joist above that creaking as it took Nigel's weight. Through the translucent hull he could see the faint line of the stout rope moving steadily into the first hole, then from the higher hole in space to the nearest pulley, then through a set of heavy screw-hook guides to the second pulley on the tripod beyond the window. The clear tip of his craft disappeared as it entered the void. In only seconds Nigel would make history.

There was an abrupt jerk. A sickening scream of wood. The capsule dropped half of the two feet it had travelled.

Something was wrong with the tripod.

A massive piece of metal clattered on the hull and thumped the floor. Nigel pressed his face to the plastic but all he could see was the rope skewed against a bright blur of morning through the window. He checked beneath the clear capsule floor.

The pulley. The pulley had come out of the ceiling.

Then what was holding him up? The rope must have caught in a guide, he decided; not much support there. His first thought was for the fish-tanks he had moved out of the way so carefully – if the capsule dropped and tumbled it would certainly hit one.

He felt helpless. At least his fluttering had gone. He watched the floor swing slightly a foot below him. If the rope had caught in a guide, then suddenly pulled through, the tripod might have shifted. That would explain the pulley ripping out and the jerk. And if the tripod had shifted the only thing keeping it from falling over was the lumpy rope getting caught in the guide again. And if that gave . . .

If the rope slid through, the tripod would tumble.

And Nigel would rise. But not just a few feet.

Into space.

'No,' said Nigel, as he began to rise, slowly at first, then with a stomach-dumping lurch, all the way into the hole, 'nonononononono. No. NO!'

To an outsider Nigel's makeshift capsule would have seemed to disappear from the tip down as the tripod, the second pulley and the old engine were released from their tilt and toppled and rolled into the garden, right on top of Mrs Donohoe's turnips. Then out of the second hole in space and through the window on its way to the tripod flew the end of the rope. It was not attached to the spacecraft – well, not to all of it. The EA 69 had done its job well but the plastic drums which formed the capsule were old and brittle: a piece of jagged translucent plate about the shape of Tasmania was the only evidence of the spacecraft that anyone would see in this world again.

Three

Transportation

He had never blacked out before. Unless you counted the time he and Mario Denuncio had smoked seven heads of dried lettuce in the cellar of the Casa Denuncio and almost died of smoke inhalation. That had produced the faint outlines of Deanna Durbin against a grey background spotted with plastic lemons, which he had always described as a 'trip' to Mario. Now, however, a true raven blackness enveloped Nigel; he had no idea of a body or location or time. Was this like death? Nigel had never known anyone who'd died, never seen the look in their eyes which might have given him some clue. Never felt grief.

And gradually, the blackness resolved into a hard clear dark around glittering points of light . . . Stars.

He was in space.

So why wasn't he dead? He now remembered the rope ripping from the spacecraft's floor and whacking past him to the nose-cone before it splintered the hole in the cone's tip and escaped. He remembered a moment of weightlessness before the dark took him. Through the clear remains of his viewport he had glimpsed a fiery splash of colour – sun? – then he'd sensed he was falling.

Finito benito. If he were in space his air would have rushed into the vacuum, he would have been a raspberry-ice explosion by now. Horrible.

Perhaps he'd been rescued by the space station, perhaps he was in some decontamination chamber or preservation unit . . .

But his back was wet. He could feel most of his body now. He was cold. He lifted one hand, stared at its grey shape trying to see the blood he could feel encrusted on his knuckles, and let it fall beside him.

Rock. He lay on a damp, mossy boulder which curved away, presumably to the ground below. He couldn't get rid of the unbidden image of himself as the Little Prince on an asteroid. Cartoon simple. He plucked up some moss to examine but couldn't see anything clearly in the moonless night. It was slimy between his fingers, not like terrestrial moss in the slightest. They didn't even have moss in cartoons.

Surely he was on some alien shore. He had been transported to another planet.

Taking a deep draught of brisk, fresh air, he struggled to a seated position and tried to make out some of the features of this new world. The silhouette of a forest spread across the horizon's glow beneath him. I must be quite high up, he thought. Lucky for me. I'll be able to check for signs of alien civilisation when the sun rises. Or *suns*.

Then he noticed something strange and at once familiar to his city-bred nose.

Frantic, he patted the stone around him, disappointment striking heavily into his gut. He held what he had found before the glow.

It was a gum-leaf. The smell was eucalyptus smoke, unmistakably. He was still in ordinary boring old Australia.

He swore and lay back on the cruel, wet stone.

He awoke chilled stiff on his side, aware of bruises that hadn't troubled him the night before. A blinding light seemed to fill the whole atmosphere; it was some minutes before he could sit up and look around him for a clue to his location. It was uncompromising light.

If the hole in space had not transported him to an alien planet it had certainly taken him out of Melbourne.

Yet he obviously wasn't too far from civilisation. Close enough for Nigel to have touched it in the dark was an out-of-date petticoat of coarse fabric, probably the discard from a costume drama for TV. At the foot of a whitened tree, the fragmented boulder's only remnant of vegetation besides the moss and some damp dead weeds, lay a handkerchief which matched the one he'd snagged with his fish-hooks, a clean one this time. Above, more broken granite sloped steeply into the sun-bleached sky. Its shadows seemed totally black, without half-shades. No hope of escape there. Below, a woodland of scraggy gums led into the distance as far as he could see.

From the familiar climate Nigel judged he had landed in Victoria. Although it was harsher here. Probably an effect of the open countryside. Since it wasn't the far west, if he skirted the rocks he might find a road. A highway couldn't be too far off; he'd hitch to Melbourne.

Wherever he was, it was still incredible that he wasn't in his back room at home.

The thought gave him a little more energy; he got to his feet. And where was his capsule? It was still more amazing that he and it should have gone separate ways. Or was it? He winced to remember thinking of it as his spacecraft and himself as an astronaut not so long ago. However, he had achieved something with his experiment, something almost as wonderful and perhaps more useful than his romantic dreams of alien planets. Science and history demanded he repeat his exercise. To do so he would need the tools he'd left with the capsule. Enough romance. Most probably his capsule had hit the rock, split throwing him clear, and bounced to the ground below. He'd need the Polaroid to record the location for posterity. And if he lost the house supply of the tricky and expensive-to-make EA 69, his father would kill him.

The matches and that might came in handy anyhow, he thought, if I'm not so close to a town as I reckon I am.

Nigel clambered down into knee-high dried grass. And while the dew immediately soaked his jeans, and his head felt like a herd of wildebeest had trampled one side, the magpies called liquidly from the woods, the sun began to penetrate his hide, the air smelled clean for a nice change and he had not, after all, perished in the frozen depths of space. His spirits lifted further out of his shame at the previous night's foolishness. A little foolishness was a good thing. Amazing scientific discoveries never got off the ground without a dose of foolishness – hadn't Einstein said that? (Or maybe Boris Karloff . . .) As he picked his way around the massive collection of rocks he actually looked forward to a day's adventure in the country.

After tying the luggable goods into the old costume petticoat (the matter-transportation vehicle had held up quite well apart from a kind of Nigel-shaped hole in its side), whistling softly, Nigel photographed the crash site as well as the prototype vehicle from several angles, then he skirted the rocks for the better part of an hour in his search for a road. Straying around the odd clump of stringy-barks or climbing over a part of the grey fortress of warming stone to avoid getting lost where the forest blocked him, he hummed a recent Barry White hit in spite of himself and pondered Carmen the swordtail.

Her mutation had been caused by the pharmaceuticals and heaven-knew-what-else which had been dumped by the fish's native river. Of course. Perhaps she saw space-time the same way she saw the surface of the water. The length of her leap through the air here was about the same as a normal leap above water might be, and it would be driven by the same thing: fear. If something scared her she'd break the universe's surface tension and leap to another place, then when she was about to drown in the air and fall into the dust out here the fear of death would drive her to snap those space-time bonds again under some homing compulsion. Possibly all the action of a gland.

Fancy thinking she went into space, Nigel thought, smiling. What an idiotic theory. Carmen would have exploded. Pfft, dried anchovies.

He'd leave the theories to the scientists. It would cause a revolution. Famous physicists might leap from windows or shoot themselves with their super-colliders, their lives' work destroyed. But truth was more important than one man's existence. Once he got home he'd see if he could thread some holes again, then he would take a trip out here by more conventional means to take a video of the fishing-line from the other side. Never mind himself going through any more. His life was naturally fair game like anyone else's when it came to serving scientific history, but *someone* had to tell the world about this wonderful achievement.

He strolled through the pleasant morning deep in the concoction of ways to harness Carmen to a hair-thin filament without shocking the poor fish into multiple jumps through the ether out of fear. You could make a teensy-weensy lasso, then when she felt it grab her she'd break a hole in space and the line carried through behind her would prevent that hole closing up again, and of course you'd have to snip the line after she had made another hole and returned to the fish-tank. But what would you make lasso from? Human hair? Vermicelli? It was a tough one. So total was his concentration on this vital issue, he didn't notice the clanking of metal against stone until he almost fell over its source.

It was a chain-gang.

The short rise over which the untidy group of labourers appeared proved an ideal place to hide. Lying flat where he had belly-flopped, he peeped over the crest at the twenty-odd men and their overlookers. He was not so much interested in the men, at first, as in the whereabouts of the cameramen and director and crew.

Only after a long bout of cunning observation did it register that these might be real felons, sent perhaps by some prison farm for the uncontrollably violent and devious (and ugly). Their motley was too well adapted to Australian conditions by genuine ruin to be a TV designer's wet dream. Their bodies and limbs and faces were burnt deeply by a long time outdoors and shadowed by a sorrier despair and emaciation than any complacent actor chappie's. Well, he could still ask directions. Even if it was uncomfortably real.

He bobbed up for another look. The wind shifted and Nigel caught a faceful. This was more than real: the men ponged like dead mayoral candidates in the sun. What Australian prison would let that happen? He had never been inside a prison, so he didn't know. He remembered the binoculars in his bundle. He swore under his breath and extracted them as he slithered up the rise. Teeth clenched, he inched them over the peak then moved his head behind them.

At last Nigel let himself slide back down the hillock. He rolled over to stare into the milky glare for a good long worry.

A true chain-gang. Men whose ankles were fettered by thick iron bands connected to three large links of chain which were bound by a cord to the waist. No Cool Hand Luke clearing this road. Nothing remotely like a prison as he knew it. These were miserable wretches working at a pace so slow that there could be no reward for them but more toil the next day. Yes, they had muscles, a stringy, weary set of ropes which had never seen a gym in their lives. Several eyes were cataracted, plainly uncared-for by medicine. Many displayed self-inflicted tattoos of black or blue in strange places as they dug, the sort which only the most degenerate punk might carve on an arm or hand, under the influence at that. Those wearing torn shirts revealed a criss-crossed hide of whip scars on their backs, the work of a barbarous hand of punishment. Nigel had noticed missing digits; two men had hands severed.

The convicts confused Nigel. Anachronisms, right down to cuts on a mass of scar tissue where the ankle fetters had rubbed them raw. And their stench had intensified: a funk of urine and faeces and rancid fat carried continuously now on the slight breeze to where Nigel sprawled, dumbfounded.

Had he gone back in time to the Georgian colony they

used to scare little kids with at school? It was the only reasonable explanation. It was lucky he had hidden from the imagined cameras so quickly. Who knew how the soldiers on guard would react to a man stumbling out of the forest? They might think him an escaped criminal and put him to work, or at least chuck him into gaol while they checked his identity.

He had to plan rationally. If the chain-gang and soldiers had arrived by cart and were working on a road there must be a road near by. He could either wait for them to leave and follow them (at a distance) or skirt the group through the woodland until he came across the road. Once there he could find the nearest town, work out where he was, get back to Melbourne, and –

And what? Get a job in a video arcade? The presence of convicts put him at least a hundred years in the past. The pre-pinball era. The hole Carmen had created in space had closed when the rope attached to his time machine had broken free. Unless she made another couple of holes right in front of his face and dragged some more brain-weed through to keep them open he was stuck in the nineteenth century, about as useful to anyone here as a ballet-dancer in a brick factory, separated from his fish, his mum and dad, Collingwood, the Cure, electricity, his fish, chocolate-chip biscuits and ice-cream, Phantom comics, the dole, indoor toilets, his fish, telephones, his bed, the Buzzcocks, his fish – *everything*! Out of his total reading and viewing about the era the single outstanding feature was an existence more brutal than any he could ever have imagined. Undoubtedly, he would die here.

Every part of his body trembled with shock as the thought sank in. The sky and trees close by seemed to swim, alarmingly for a moment, until he realised his eyes were full of tears. He turned his head against the rough grass and released the binoculars still clutched in his hands and curled into a tight ball and, as quietly as he could, sobbed.

Soon he felt much better. Bright thoughts penetrated the demented riff of self-pity in him. After all, he wasn't the

average stupid Georgian peasant. He had his fair share of the
typical modern Australian virtues: dauntless courage, a body
honed by rugged outdoor life, a fine education, and above all
an ability to hoodwink the gullible. Like Bing Crosby in that
musical about King Arthur he could wow the locals with his
twentieth-century know-how. He could go to the gold-fields
in Ballarat before anyone else and pick up a fortune off the
ground. He might write a future history which would prevent
depressions and world wars. Yes, and to make a living he
could become an inventor.

But he could not go home.

He would have to live with that. No use bawling. A new
world lay out there past the trees awaiting discovery. Finding
a town remained his first task. Employment and a bed came
next. With some kind of secure base he could carefully map
out a course for the long term. Nigel Donohoe was not about
to simply walk into trouble like they did in the movies, give
himself away, maybe burn at the stake, nope. Not him.

The sound of clanking was an uncomfortable reminder of
such mistakes. Nigel gathered his tools (he could sell some for
a meal) and slithered down the slope on his back. He put
himself well out of earshot before he dared stand. As he
headed for the blessed cool of the trees and where he guessed
a road might lie he picked leaves from his hair and brushed
the grass and droppings from his clothes. He told himself that
in no way whatsoever was he the itsy-witsiest particle
hungry, and he was not. Full of pride at this feat, he pointed in
a definite manner at where the trees seemed to thin. He set off.

During the hour he spent lost in the woodland he
distracted himself with a story which explained his odd
appearance and lack of local knowledge. He debated the pros
and cons of amnesia, but in the end rejected it because it
might get him institutionalised. The sun made fragrant pools
of heat here and there, pleasant on the skin and vital for
orientation in this seemingly infinite stand of mottled cream
and grey trunks carpeted by dead gum-leaves. It was some
time before he clued into the unique shapes of the little

clearings, however, so delighted was he with his idea of pretending not to know English and of having been robbed. It only clicked that he was hopelessly off beam when he spotted the huge stack of rocks once more through the trees ahead.

He shoved his hands in his pockets.

'Right son,' he said aloud, 'back again, and this time pay attention to where you're going.'

This was not so easy. It took Nigel another hour by his digital watch just to find the road which cleaved the forest. By then his head was hammered by images of crows eating him alive whilst he gasped and flailed, too weak from hunger to fend them off. For some reason he craved spring rolls. Chiko rolls. When the trees were abruptly replaced by a swathe of waist-high stumps and a fresh – no doubt convict-built – road scrunched underfoot, Nigel broke into a silly grin of achievement, widened by the sight of a crossroad not far away. With signs.

He ran toward them full tilt, stumbling twice, kicking up gravel and dust out of joy as he neared them on steadier feet.

The sign read, *Milton Keynes 7L.*

Milton Keynes? No place in Victoria had ever borne such a silly name; to Nigel's knowledge, no place on earth. He shrugged. He was not exactly Vasco Polo; he hadn't pored over every square inch of every map. It was probably a ghost town in 1978.

He set off whistling a Stranglers' song. Confidently he tramped down the road which meandered through scalloped fields of what looked like oats into the rounded distance. Remember son, he told himself, you're a foreigner. You don't speaka da English. He stopped for a second, to try out his language on a fat black crow perched on a stump. 'Aktivite, ramalan, barishnykov toy boy?' he asked politely.

The crow sharpened its beak ominously on the stump.

So close to Milton Keynes, Nigel held no fear of death. He shrugged. 'Kremlin pignog,' he dismissed the bird. 'Ramalan shoo-be-doo wah-wah.'

'Luck,' said the crow.

'Ta,' said Nigel, nodding. He rubbed his hands together briskly and turned back to the road.

'Ay mate! You bound for Milton Keynes?'

Nigel looked up at the buggy's driver with an uncomprehending smile. He was a compact customer, in his forties, Nigel judged from the peppered hair. The hands that gripped the leather reins were thick from work, the face looking down on him in an open, expectant but not stupid way was as dark and gaunt as those of the convicts down the road. He wore a floppy grey hat, with a band which looked like plastic but must have been polished leather, cocked back on his minuscule head.

Nigel's gaze met the man's friendly eyes for some seconds before he found the wit to answer as planned.

'Seiko elastoplast meshugga?' he asked.

'Foreignator, ay?' the man answered. 'Don't get many wokkies round here.'

Nigel continued to smile fatuously as if he didn't understand a thing.

'I SAID: WE DON'T GET MANY OF YOU BLOKES ROUND HERE!' he boomed. It was a large sound for such a small head.

'Ah?' said Nigel. He nodded vigorously. 'Veznuzz nuzzle nick faldo!' he said, as if explaining the secret of why lighting a cigarette makes your bus come on time.

He appeared to have done so, and more. 'UNDERSTAND BETTER THAN YOU CAN SPEAK AY?'

Nigel nodded again, still grinning like a galoot.

'GOING TO MILTON KEYNES?'

'Nick faldo, nick faldo,' said Nigel affirmatively.

'POOR THING! IT'S A BLOODY NIGHTMARE!' yelled the buggy-driver. 'HOP IN, I'LL GIVE YEZ A RIDE.'

When Nigel hesitated, the man shouted, 'DON'T WORRY MATE. WE DON'T CASTRATE FOREIGNATORS NO MORE!' He laughed. 'I MEAN – THIS IS

NINETEEN SEVENTY-EIGHT!' And he roared at his own joke.

Nigel, half-way on to the back of the buggy, tripped and fell painfully against the wood face-first with the shock of it. There was no mistaking what the man had said, the pinhead seemed to have bellows for lungs.

With a cluck from the man and a rattle from the harness they set off for Milton Keynes at a trot. Nigel rolled over, looking up at the back of the driver's neck. The criss-crossed scars of a convict's flogging corded above his collar; Nigel followed a stray one right to the back of his ear.

Nobody flogged anybody in 1978. Yet this was Australia, there were convicts, so where the hell was he?

'WE'RE ABOUT THREE LEAGUES OUTTA MILTON KEYNES,' shouted the driver over his shoulder.

Yeah, but where's that? wondered Nigel. He sat up, casting confusedly about him at the pleasant farmlands, his brain a curdled apprehensive moosh. A couple of hours passed. Nigel remained too mooshy to think of questioning the driver until it was too late. As they approached – then began to encounter – the bustle of the obviously sprawling town of Milton Keynes, he became less and less eager to find out where he'd landed after all. The driver was right: Milton Keynes was indeed a nightmare. Nigel was sickened by what he saw.

I want to get *back*, he wailed inside, I just want to get *out* of here. This is *not* 1978. This is *hell*!

But this was not hell, nor was he out of it. The cart crunched over real gravel, the screams Nigel heard came from real agony, the howls from undeniable anguish, and beneath the ordinary aches and bruises and scratches about his body Nigel found within him the dreadfully mundane certitude that around him lay not even another reality but the only one that had ever been possible. The horrifying had become the norm. His own world was a dream – and the dream was finished. He was awake.

Four

Lumps on the Head

A sinister lurching set of four wooden wings, and blood and triangles, and blood . . .

The microcephalic ex-convict took one look at Nigel's blanched features and stopped at the nearest inn. Unfortunately this was not so far into Milton Keynes as to muffle the screams much. With one of the buggy-driver's hands on his back guiding him into the cool of the Fez and Turban, Nigel noticed a man putting in wax ear-plugs before he left the inn. A few steps down and behind stone walls the cries of the flogged grew faint.

The buggy-driver enquired in a kindly bellow as to Nigel's means and when Nigel shook his head and offered his father's saw the man tested its edge and put some coins in his hand, then left with it. The suspicious characters seated in the varnished gloom around Nigel stared at the loud transaction with brazen familiarity. Nigel crossed to the bar. He put his bundle down and his hands in his pockets. The noise of punishment was audible again in the fresh listening silence.

'What's your pleasure, sir?' the barman asked, winking. 'Habitual?' He looked a dour little man, not given naturally to winks.

Nigel looked around for the person the barman was actually addressing.

Conversation resumed hastily. There was nobody at the bar but him.

'Beer,' he said, dragging his hands from his pockets by main force. 'A pot.' He emptied his palmful of coins on the granite slab.

'No arak?' asked the barman, disappointed.

'All right, a pot of that.'

The barman beamed. It gave his frown-lines problems. He served Nigel a large glass of clear liquid and fingered a small coin away from the pile, then retreated with a rag to a table occupied by a couple of nuns.

Arak. Now where had Nigel heard of that before? He sipped the drink.

When he could see and breathe again, Nigel found the barman back, grinning.

'Good?' he asked with a couple of eager nods. 'I got it from up north just today. Smooth, ay?'

Nigel managed to nod. 'Can I have beer as well, please?'

For some reason this amused the barman greatly. He retreated once again to cleaning tables with his filthy rag, and Nigel could have sworn he heard the man say, '. . . Donohoe wants a beer, good one . . .' but otherwise completely ignoring Nigel's request.

There was something odd about the statement. Feeling warmer and a little more secure amidst the low chatter, Nigel took another tiny sip of his drink. It tasted less gastric now, almost fruity. He gave the bar-room a couple of sidewise glances.

The pair he had taken for nuns appeared more like military women in yashmaks, with white patches on their shoulders covered in gold braid. Perhaps they were a visiting sultan's wives. But they did have large crosses between their breasts. Nigel was cheered to notice deep acne scars all over one of them; she even had a couple on her hands.

On the side of the inn closest to the street, at round tables beneath a botched horseshoe-arch window, sat an assortment of gamblers, alcoholics, thugs, and combinations of those types. The nicest of them could have eaten a child's toys just to watch it weep. In the short time Nigel spent looking at them one gambler, who looked as if someone had compressed her with a mallet at birth, nodded one of her chins at Nigel.

When Nigel did not react, the bald fleshy concertina of a woman rose and waddled over, took a seat by Nigel and breathed whisky all over him, checking the top of his head, for lice perhaps. She had a tattoo on her left shoulder of a bearded man, 'Mithra' scrolled below it. Nigel tried not to flinch and sipped his arak just to keep from throwing up, still hoping she would not speak to him after the health inspection.

'Mark my terms,' the thug said. She sounded exactly like Orson Welles.

Nigel silently debated the dangers of continuing to ignore her.

'Sir,' she whispered, full of sarcasm.

Expecting trouble, Nigel fortified himself with another sip of arak. He was getting to like it.

The blancmange gambler went on:

'You have a vacant head so I believe your intentions are good but you can't go on trampling over the *good citizens* of the Colony of Alfonso, they will not stand for it, Mr Donohoe . . .'

Colony of *Alfonso*? And how did she know Nigel's name, let alone the status of his brain? He didn't recall introducing himself to anybody. (Although he did not remember all the details of coming into the bar any more, he had been in such a funk, and the arak had fuddled him somewhat since then.) He turned away from the gambler. He turned back again. Too suddenly. The bulging eyes on the pump-handle in front of him veered too close, it seemed. He felt hot; he needed a drink.

'. . . get in the way of the likes of some and their coalitions in this town who enjoy revenge a little too well and it'll be the dance or the pickle for you, son, mark my terms: the dance or the pickle.'

Pickle. Pickles to me! he thought. A giggle broke from him. They talk funny here, Nigel decided. Pickles. What the hell did that mean? He laughed, and again, louder. He took a drink of the pleasant, warming spirit. He swung back to the big pasty woman beside him, who seeing Nigel's happy face broke into a gummy grin herself and shook her head.

'There's no talking to you, is there? Anger in your eyes . . . you're either a very brave man or a cull, no doubt about it. No doubt!' she said, and slapped Nigel's back.

'Oof!' went Nigel, spitting his drink on to the scarred bar surface. This broke him up entirely, and he laughed and laughed, he whooped and took a drink and laughed some more for the sake of it.

The night went by like a fish on roller skates after that. Some time later he found himself dancing with the big woman while a couple of her friends played a reedy pipe and a sitar-ish instrument beneath a window filled with leaping orange light. Was this what she had meant by talk of a dance? He learnt she was a bullock-driver. All an unmarried woman (not a lady) could become, besides a prostitute or a nun or a slave in a female factory. Past the whisky and dust she smelt of cloves. Still later (or perhaps before), deep in conversation with the nuns he declared:

'I've got an affinity with nuns. Nuns are hons. Ha. Me and nuns go way back, to when I was nothing but a worm. I *was* a worm you know. A wriggly – miggly, wormily worm.'

The nuns nodded. The thin, hawk-nosed one confided, 'I know where you're happening. I wanted to be a reflexologist when I was young, but do you think the order would have me? High and mighty traditions. Go back to the Alexandrians they reckon. Course they do. It's *all* they do! Nah, it was the best thing that could happen to me; I had to join a *fissi* iridology order and it made a woman of me. Adversity does it. Now I get to do my own work with no interference from above because we don't matter in the game. Too small. The only way to do things, stay small. Trouble is, as soon as you really get anything done you're fair game for the big porkings. Politics. Better to help the people you can and keep out of progress . . .' Perhaps he danced with the nuns as well.

Very late in the proceedings, with the nuns slumped snoring upon one another across the table beside him, he sat, depressed, and watched the bullocky being helped out by her two other dust-covered companions, and what he had held off all night crashed back into his memory, sharpened by the alcohol.

A dozen men at least on flogging-triangles in a blood-stained yard. The gore had splashed, whip, grunt, flap, wail, splash, over the scourge and the other tormented felons and the doctor and priest and even a small child there God only knew why. It had a perverse beauty in the low sun, like a Goya painting, something inherently evil in the way the priest leaned towards the suffering, a ruined European windmill revolving spastically like the flapping of a pair of monstrous wooden birds dying as they rolled in the golden light and red dust, magnificent terror in colours picked out more vibrantly than any he had seen in his known Australia. Whip, grunt, flap, wail, splash.

Nigel sat and meditated on the sneaky way memory managed to hit you when you were down. It did not occur to him to wonder what sort of Australia whipped its people right up to the late 1970s. In a short while nothing much occurred to him at all.

A gentle hand cradled his head. Cool wetness trickled down his throat. Sweet God was visiting, he was raising Nigel from the dead with this miraculous liquid. He swallowed greedily, his returning strength surprising him. His eyes opened, the pannikin disappeared, God's trouser-legs shuffled backward on to the street respectfully. No, not God, not with gumboots on. And that was water on his lips. Nigel got up out of the gutter. With a knuckling of the eyes and a crackling flex of the back, he decided it was not Judgement Day.

His rescuers practically fell on him in their joy. They overwhelmed him with relieved heartiness. They pummelled his torso, squeezed him, pinched his ears roughly, all the while nattering on in their native tongue as if he were a hero returned to their village from years of perilous adventure. Luckily, this gave him time to think.

He boomed, 'WAIT ON, CHINA!' right into the ear of the scar-faced brute molesting him at the time. 'THERE MUST BE SOME MISTAKE HERE!'

The fellow leapt back in shock and stuck a slender pianist's finger in one misshapen ear.

'You blokes foreign?' asked Nigel.

The five men immediately fell into a ragged military line, terrified at their error, changing and rechanging their order until the smallest of them, plainly the boss, was satisfied. He barked at them as though it wasn't his fault as well, then stepped forward, plastic cap in hand, knotted swag in the other.

'I am sorry kind sir for this stupid wrong,' he managed in surprisingly good Australian. 'We think you are an injured countryman from your white shirt and swag.' He nodded ingratiatingly. 'It is first day for my men with no guards. We make no offence.'

Nigel glanced at his shirt. Nothing special. He looked the fellow over, aware they hung on his words, but still too numb to make much sense. He cleared his throat. As his hangover began to fade, part of the previous day surfaced in him once more: *a dozen men at least on flogging-triangles in a blood-stained yard*. He scratched his ribs. He hitched up his loose jeans and sniffed.

The man before him was pint-sized in all respects aside from a bulbous head. Although not quite a dwarf he had the bowed legs of one. His black beard hung scraggily to his chest. The puzzling plastic baseball cap was matched by unaccountable plastic buttons, unexplainable belt and mystifying wellingtons which shone so they made his worn grey prison outfit seem nearly smart. His sycophantic grin showed toothless gums. He waved his swag by his knees, patient about Nigel's response.

Nigel gazed above the man's head at the sandstone buildings across the street. They, too, had decidedly weird touches, such as pointed oriental arches above the doors and *old* wrought-iron supernatural faces along the verandahs. A domed tower glinted behind and above them. Otherwise this conformed to his idea of a quiet colonial street. He looked down again. Dimly, he realised that these men would do anything he wanted – what any turkey-fucker in supposed authority wanted. They craved Nigel's approval. And what am I? he wondered A gangling, fat-lipped inner-city alien in jeans. He had never dreamed of telling anybody what to do.

A vague idea coalesced, coupled with the irresistible urge to be the turkey-fucker for once.

'Left – *turn*,' he snapped.

They did it! It seemed the correct signal. Or perhaps a wink and a nod would do.

He quickly checked the passers-by: a group of barefoot children chased a square ball a block away; two veiled women entered a pungent bakery; an old man muttered in his sleep on the Fez and Turban's verandah bench. Ordering prisoners about was normal here.

'Forward – *march*!'

And off they went. Nigel watched them go for a moment, then ran to catch up. The street continued with its business.

Despite the loss of every certainty (and sudden near-terminal hunger), success elated Nigel, but the possibility of a challenge from whoever actually knew what work the men were meant to do soon sent dread through him. When in panic he turned them off the main street into a genteel residential quarter his fear deepened as gardeners and governesses stared at the ragged felons footing it through their suburb, tucker-bags bobbing, foreheads shiny. Fortunately, Milton Keynes finished here. The string of water-holes along which Nigel marched his hijacked prisoners marked the city limits. Beyond, rolling wheatland spread between hills; further lay the indigo promise of mountains.

Nigel had found the least populated part of town: the cemetery. He arranged his men around the foot of a river red gum whose roots split the grassy slope to the creek-bed. He sat opposite on a rock, legs outstretched.

Sprawling, wiping sweat on their sleeves and fanning themselves with their caps, they grinned down at Nigel.

'Now,' he said. 'I want you to tell me some things.'

'Yes,' said their little spokesman. 'Yes. We tell you. Anythings!'

'All right,' said Nigel. 'Where are you from?'

The biggest of them, the most hairy palooka Nigel had ever met, spoke up. 'His Majesty's Penal Station Number Seven hundreds and six,' he rattled off.

The short leader hit him with his cap. 'Serbia,' he announced with pride.

The others clapped hands over their mouths and cast theatrically about as if for spies. The short man nodded in acknowledgement of his defiance. 'Yugoslavia,' he said.

Nigel nodded. Partly because he couldn't think straight when the Serbs began to untie their swags revealing salt beef and bread, he swallowed hard and frowned. They froze. He chose his next words carefully. 'I'm a newcomer, like yourselves. I have been far away and heard no news. If you have time, I would like to ask you many questions. Simple questions which would bore most people. Do I take you from your work?'

'Yes please,' said the huge one.

'No,' said the little one, and beat the other again with his hat. The rest looked confused. 'We must come to Emu station for tomorrow morning,' he explained. 'It is time to walk there for tomorrow.'

The others caught on. 'Mm,' they went.

'Holiday now,' said the thin one with the horrible scars.

'You eat?' asked the other scar-faced one. He held out his loaf.

'Here,' said the hairy one. He proffered his beef. It was greenish and filmed with something soft and white.

Nigel had to stop himself from grabbing it. He tore off a hunk with his teeth. It tasted only almost putrid. He grinned. 'Fine,' he told the giant lad.

They hoed into the food.

The light breeze blew cool green smells from the water-hole. Birds quarrelled and wooed in the trees scattered around the gravestones. Nigel recalled an evening he'd once spent in a cemetery. He could almost take all this for normality, imagine he and the Serbs had driven up from Melbourne for a picnic and a swim. Then the flogging-grounds on the town's outskirts intruded and he gagged on his beef. He stuffed a piece of bread into his mouth. When your next meal is so uncertain, you force yourself to eat. His Melbourne was gone. His whole Australia.

What had taken its place?

The Serbs were called (in ascending order) Pixie, Doug, Charlie, Johnno and Wal. Their guards had found their real names stones in their mouths and forced them on pain of flogging to adopt new ones. Wal, at seventeen, was the youngest and Pixie the eldest. They were prisoners of war from the most recent tangle between the British Empire and the European Community, Charlie explained. He was a slight, rabbity, olive man with thoughtful, minimal gestures. Apparently, the Australian Penal System did not see them as a serious threat to the law-abiding populace, more the misguided pawns of an evil government. The five were thus Assigned Workers on the lowest scale of security, now their probation was over.

Wal butted in, around a mouthful of food: 'Mwe froyloy twaffle if mwe show –' until Pixie hit him with a loaf. He swallowed. 'We freely travel if we show our passes, we have luxury of assigned quarters and privilege of twenty-five hours' work in a day for seven years – and then we get ticket.' He smiled, his eyes cherubic in the sea of hair.

'A ticket home?' Nigel asked.

He meant a ticket of leave, explained Pixie, grey eyes wistful at Nigel's notion. 'It is not freedom. There is no freedom here.'

Leaning towards Nigel from the tree-trunk, the thoughtful Charlie continued his explanation of their status. The Serbs' (or at least Charlie's) attitude to their captors was difficult to explain. England, on one hand, had formed the Dominion of Yugoslavia. The European Community, led by the infamous and ancient Adolf Hitler, had used their nationalistic Serbian fervour to great advantage in the war, turning them against the Empire. But the Serbs had no doubt that England was a land of saints; it was not England they had fought but the local, corrupt branch of its Empire. They saw the EC as evil too: in their area of the world it was one evil force against another with the Serbs (and most Croats) as helpless cheese and onion in the sandwich (the Croats, of course, as onions).

To that extent, Charlie told him, they had won their war. His Majesty's Government had intervened with a Royal Commission led by Lord Carrington after the protracted, ultimately stalemated, conflict between the Serbs and Croats. The latest news was the resignation of Yugoslavia's Governor-General, Sir Oswald Mosley; some of his closest cronies would stand trial. The five Serbs had not betrayed their people for nothing.

'You see,' Charlie spread his large-boned hands, 'we fought on the Croatian side.'

'You never!' said Nigel, remembering Serbs he had met in his Australia and their attitudes to Croats.

They all nodded sadly. It was the only way to get rid of Mosley, Charlie explained; he would not die. Wal told him fiercely that he would do it again if he had to. 'We had a separate brigade,' Pixie told Nigel, 'or we would not have done it.' Johnno moved his head fractionally in agreement, his torn lips thin, his dark eyes intense.

'And we were desperate,' Charlie finished. 'Now the brigade – we are all here.' He patted the root by his leg.

'God save King Rupert of England!' cried Pixie.

'God save the Empire!' chorused the others.

King Rupert? wondered Nigel.

'And now you,' demanded Wal, good-naturedly.

Nigel glanced around at the five. Pixie grinned knowingly, a gummy man of the world. Doug winked in his exaggerated, childish way. The networks of scars on Charlie and Johnno's faces made them appear ferocious but by now their gentle, if intense, ways had won him over. Wal reached down the slope and with one gigantic fist gave Nigel's shoulder a tender blow.

Nigel picked himself up off the grass and sat on the rock again, fishing in his imagination for a suitable story. Yet, how could he lie to these generous men?

He decided to tell them the truth. Even if they believed him who would they tell? Things were decidedly weird here in some fashion he could not fathom, but these were essentially good-hearted people, never mind their part in Adolf Hitler and Oswald Mosley's war. They'd certainly want to help.

At first they smiled and nudged one another as if to say, 'When does the punch-line come?' Nigel's account, with its exotic fish and seemingly magical door into another world, entertained them well enough.

'. . . I turned away from the big windmill and I saw this long, low building,' said Nigel. 'In front were these wooden frames, and tied to those were about a dozen guys – being *whipped*, for crying out loud.'

Nigel looked up at his listeners. They nodded, impatient for something amazing to happen, a little disappointed at this lull into convict reality but too polite to show it.

'The blood streamed all down their backs! It'd spattered everywhere. Across the blokes whipping them, their guards

– everywhere! There was a great *pool* of blood on the ground under each of them!'

The Serbs nodded gravely. Like flaming monkeys.

Nigel slapped the grass by his rock, ineffectually. 'Don't you see? Where I come from they don't *do* things like that.' He shook his head. 'Well not in civilised countries, anyhow. Well not so obviously.'

They stared at him. If they didn't do that where he came from, what did they do? How could you maintain order? they seemed to imply. The men you saw must have been bad people, said their eyes, and bad people will go on being bad unless you teach them otherwise. Nigel cast around the green verge as if ideas lay in the leaf-litter amongst the graves. 'Look,' he said. 'I come from a different world to you guys. This place is called Victoria, not Alfonso. The king is a queen – I mean, she's Elizabeth. In my world, Yugoslavia has been a communist country since World War Two – the war with – since 1945.' He thought hard. 'It's behind what we call the Iron Curtain. You can't get in or out.'

Now he had them again. They obviously thought the Iron Curtain was like the Great Wall of China. Well, so had Nigel until he was eighteen. 'It's a socialist federal republic governed by – um – General Tito.'

'Tito?' whispered Charlie. His ravaged face lit with religious fervour. 'Saint Josip?'

'Joseph Tito,' said Nigel. 'Yeah,' he said, thoughtfully.

'And he rules Yugoslavia?' asked Wal.

'I think he's the president – has been for thirty years.'

'Saint Josip – president?' said Pixie.

'God save the King!' shouted Doug.

'God save the Empire!' they all cried.

Then they laughed, rolling around. They hadn't taken him at all seriously. So much for his career as a turkey-fucker.

Nigel had an idea. He fetched the knotted petticoat from where he'd dumped it and teased it open with clumsy fingers. He whipped out the Polaroid camera, aimed up and took their photo. He liked group shots and so seldom found the chance to snap any but those of fish. This was a lovely one, right down to Doug pulling a stupid face at Wal.

His antics amused more than startled them. Nigel pulled out the shot. He thrust it into Charlie's hands – he at least might stop to watch it appear – and on the verge of a repeat, checked himself. He had only one spare pack of film; who knew what need he might have of it later?

As the others joked amongst themselves in Serbian about Nigel, he carefully wrapped the camera into the petticoat, studying Charlie studying the photograph. This backward world had possibly by some fluke come up with plastic, so that wouldn't surprise Charlie. Yet: the man's slightly hooded eyes widened as the image swam out of the dark.

'Fucking fuck!' said Charlie.

It had the desired effect. The others turned.

'I *told* you,' said Nigel, as one after the other snatched the photo to peer at it. 'I am from a different world. We can do so many things you guys have never in your craziest dreams imagined. It's why I absolutely have to find out every single little stupid thing you can tell me about your world. People sound different. It is different, but why is it different? How? Even the problems in my world you won't have dreamt of. F'rinstance, since I was just a little guy I've had dreams of atomic mass destruction. The whole planet – poof! – into dust. Probably it's why I'm such a hopeless dole-bludging wanker really; I've thought, What's the use? We're never gunna see the century out anyhow . . .'

They still weren't listening. He wasn't fool enough to think of them as simple Serbian peasants – they could well be artists and scientists for all he knew – but there was a *definiteness* about them, the way they were gathered around obviously unanimous about the wonderfulness of the Polaroid, which depressed Nigel profoundly. Nigel had never been definite about anything, never certain whether to use pyjamas or sleep in the nude and compromised by wearing the top or bottom of a Superman outfit his mother had made for one of his high-school pantomimes. (It was warm.) Yet he would have bet his prize piebald kissing gourami, these blokes had no doubts on the subject – whatsoever. None. Zilch. What a world.

The last shred of sun rode a cleft between two hills, giving the undressing men titanic shadows which slipped up the slope toward the cemetery from their swimming-hole. Except for Johnno, the Serbs showed obvious relief at their freedom from HM Penal Station 706. This took the form of mud-fights. Charlie turned out to be the group animal. He began by showing Wal how to squeeze mud out of his fist in a short, sharp ejaculation. They amused themselves for a while with exclamation marks against the sunset, then turned on their new-found friend like little boys. Their *naughtiness* impressed Nigel. Soon they were scampering Jackson Pollock people. Pixie copped it from everyone at once and laughed and laughed, hands on his thighs, unable to raise an arm against the others. He became a little chocolate man.

The sun's disappearance turned everything serious. Wal kept on for a dying minute while the others panted in the shallows and began to sluice their arms, but shortly even he was impressed by the violet sky, the emergent stars; tomorrow held more work, new masters, the first day of the next six years. The night recalled their criminality.

Out of whitened branches, Charlie wove an intricate base for the fire. Nigel regretted that he'd lost the matches with which to Bing Crosby them, but then the Polaroid hadn't done what he had wanted. Perhaps it'd soak in later.

Firelight drove back the moody dusk. Over billy-tea and damper the questions did flow. Nigel found no need to ask directly about their world: their questions revealed so much.

Even if it was another world it wasn't another *world*. It had the same physical laws and geography as far as he could tell. (The place where he'd crashed had to be Hanging Rock or therabouts, which would put him close to Melbourne.) What had altered history here began in people's minds. And as the night and conversation drifted by under ragged clouds which whipped across the Milky Way, Nigel started to see in their stories exactly what set these guys apart from him.

It had to do with evil.

Johnno was a toy-maker. He hadn't learnt this from his father (who was never mentioned at home) but from his grandfather, possessor of a long white beard and strong yet nimble fingers. Mostly, he sculpted toys from wood. The sort that snagged young Johnno's imagination, however, were kites. Johnno's grandfather made the best kites in the principality. The secret, he said, was flying them yourself. To this end he showed infinite patience with the boy. He rescued kites in trees, entertained Johnno's incompetent friends and their fleeting enthusiasms, bound up the fingers Johnno cut carving frames, and generally behaved more like a young father than an eighty-year-old man toward his only grandchild.

The kites the two produced resembled stained-glass cathedral windows. Angels flew on the spring breezes, saints and whole Bible stories soared in rich translucent colours. By the time of the first war against the British, Johnno's grandfather was nearly ninety and could scarcely hold a string, much less guide a blade down a birch length. He sat and watched the teenage Johnno try the newest designs, or he helped pack the kites in their panelled boxes for the long trip to market each month at Dubrovnik.

(Johnno paused here. In the firelight his twisted features ought to have seemed ogreous. Instead, the memory of his childhood made a whole of his jigsaw face.)

So close to Crotia, the folk of Johnno's village had seen many conflicts. In this, though, they found themselves against their own country. The Empire wanted to unite Yugoslavia, but the man they'd put in charge was as menacing as the traditional enemies from the West. Still, no one dared oppose Mosley yet. That wouldn't happen for a few years. It didn't mean they would willingly fight for him, though.

'You will not go to war,' Johnno's grandfather told him

on their way back from the village meeting, where the councillors had announced conscription of the eldest boys. 'Better Serbia becomes German than serve those swine in Beograd. Hitler may be dead already – nobody has seen him for years. We will not submit to *devzirme*!'

Johnno wondered if he had the courage to resist this press-ganging by Mosley's secret police, but never dreamt of disobeying his grandfather. Months passed, Dubrovnik was razed to the ground, the war went well for the English. Johnno, tugging the silken string of a blue tumbler one summer's afternoon, thought they might have forgotten him.

Of course they had not. The next morning Johnno woke to pounding at the door. His grandfather had not slept. He sat at the fire with his shotgun across his lap.

'Open the door, son,' he told Johnno.

And rubbing his eyes as the door swung in, the boy recognised, in the black shorts and knee-boots of the secret police, hair slicked back in the city style, armed with whip and pistol, his own father.

'Old dung-muncher. You have brought up my only son as a coward and a traitor,' accused Johnno's father, stepping over the threshold.

'Let us hope he has not inherited your propensity for rogering frogs,' replied Johnno's grandfather.

'I was just a boy. And you had me coated in beeswax and nettles and pelted by the whole village with herrings.'

'It is the traditional punishment for those who abuse amphibians.'

'Is it also the tradition to possess the spine of a mouldy turnip?'

Johnno's grandfather whitened visibly. It was the direst insult to compare a man with a tuberous root. 'You are the lackey of criminals – and nothing you can do will force me to send my daughter's son to die for them!'

Johnno, who'd been staring in a kind of trance at his father's head-shape, came to and shouted, 'No! I will not fight!'

Johnno's father raised his short whip to strike at his son's face. Johnno's grandfather warned that he would shoot. The secret policeman laughed. His whip came down and Johnno's grandfather blasted his son-in-law into the street. Before he had time to reload a second blackshorts entered and whipped Johnno all about the face to mark him as a coward. He whipped the old man until his arm ached from it.

The war ended in victory for the English before Johnno reached the front. The King granted an amnesty for conscientious objectors and Johnno returned to his village to bury both his relatives.

He did not let the undertaker close his father's coffin until he had felt the top of the dead man's head. His own head had the same bumps, though not as pronounced. Bumps of evil. It was not a sure method of telling the good from the bad – you might be as round as a coconut and totally corrupt. But from that time forward Johnno waited to find himself drawn to evil.

In the next war, he was.

Nigel lay staring into the embers long after the Serbs had begun to snore. How could people still believe such balderdash? His sleepy mind drifted from the flogging in Milton Keynes to Johnno's story, to the way people seemed to recognise him in the bar, and back to the flogging. Did bumps on the head separate his world from this one? He recalled a detail from last night's drinking: the woman who had mentioned dancing and pickles (must ask the boys about that one) had stared at the top of Nigel's head before uttering her warning. Nigel had thought it part of these people's mistaken familiarity with him. He remembered accepting that. He had needed company. He had accepted Pixie's eager invitation to travel with them as far as Emu station for the company as well. Whatever they told him about themselves, the Serbs were good blokes. And he did not want to be alone here. It scared him witless. It was a good thing he wasn't witless to begin with. Then he'd *really* be in deep bananas . . .

Five

Principia Lumpologia

When in the gentle twittering dawn Nigel awoke to find himself still surrounded by self-confessed Serbian war criminals, he fell back on to his log pillow with a painful thump. He felt blood seep into his hair. His comrades' fairly normal grunts, farts, splashing and groans, yawns and hawking and piddle, gained a strange new power. He lay staring at the blue flecks in motion between the gum-leaves. He reckoned the bump rising on the back of his head would match the Serb's criminal stigmata.

Phrenology. Something out of a Cole's Funny Picture Book. The science of reading personality by a person's skull-shape.

He yawned repeatedly, trying to rid himself of the instant nervous tension produced by the idea. While it was pleasant to smell the pungent nature and last night's camp-fire it didn't put the world back together again. He reeled inside at the way every object stood out separate and complete in itself and never resolved into the happy picture of a whole, sensible surround.

Shock, he decided, I'm in shock.

At the same time he tugged his shirt back below his chest, having pulled it up in the cold pre-dawn thinking it was his bedsheet. Even if his world had been going nowhere altogether too fast, he thought, at least there you had the logical conclusion to a civilisation based on rationality. There seemed no rationality in this world whatsoever.

He struggled with the tasks of tucking in his shirt and

getting to his feet, made clumsier by the questions spinning through him. Why were these people so backward? Was it related to the extremeness he saw in them? How? Is it innate or was there some point in history which tipped their traditions this way? He was close to hysterical. It was too early in the morning for this. He shoved his shirt-tails between his belt and trousers; he scratched his thumb on his belt-buckle and swore.

So he startled the gentle Doug, when the man had merely asked if Nigel wanted tea, with: 'Tea? What on *earth* is tea? We've spent millions – billions! – getting to the moon and you're going to light a fire, boil some water, chuck in some dried plant bits (and I bet a gum-leaf as well) and then give it to me to *drink* for *breakfast* with sugar I suppose? TEA!' he shouted. 'Tea? Why yes I'll have a cup of tea. Zounds, man! A cracker of an idea. Tea!'

He giggled, stumbling backward, tripping then rolling in the grass chortling in a kind of fit.

Doug scratched the blond curls on his chin. 'We have no sugar, Nigel,' he said.

At which Nigel stopped, groaned piteously as if it were the tragedy of the age, and began to cry.

Out of the sky came a Boeing 747.

There are times when an aeroplane blasts you so suddenly, so strangely, and fits your paranoia so perfectly, that you think, 'It doesn't matter what peace we have, this is the end, I wish I had my teddy with me.' An instant later, since the bombs haven't dropped, you chide yourself and carry on with your life. This instant passed for Nigel simply enough. Near-whiplash followed as he looked up again.

This is not happening, he thought.

He was still in a cemetery outside Milton Keynes with Pixie, Doug, Charlie, Johnno and Wal, convicts on their way to work. They were still walking to Emu station today.

And indeed, when he looked up once more, it was not happening. The sky was a pre-pubescent blue with clouds like sheep's thoughts tumbling through it. He had been losing it. He took a very large breath and walked down to the creek, telling himself to take it easy.

Following a breakfast of weevily damper, an ingenious kind of steamed curds out of Doug's swag, and tea sweetened some by native honey Wal had found downstream, the group set off for Emu station.

Nigel lagged behind. He remained plagued by speculation about life and progress here. Without a handle on the place he felt unsettled. Perhaps he'd always be an alien on this planet. Yet a waltz into the simplest situation unaware of what drove these people was as dangerous as playing billiards with a snake. Should you try, it would sink its fangs into your hand and you'd wind up writhing on the table in agony. Even if you put corks on its fangs, not only would you miss the ball, nobody would play with you – in fact you'd probably not be allowed into the billiard parlour in the first place. If you did get in it'd probably shed its skin in the middle of the game . . .

It was no use. He lengthened his stride to catch up with Doug, who politely did not prod about this morning's outburst.

Cheeses were his business. If cheesemakers were volcanoes, Doug would be a lactic Krakatoa. Actually, the stocky blond Northerner was a minor aristocrat, descended from Kraljevic Marko, *zupan* during the wars with the Turks. But his ancestry meant nothing when compared to his pride in his *kecak*. He had an unbeaten reputation among cheese-worshippers from the Italies to Greece. Otherwise he was a simple man, almost as short as Pixie, but without Pixie's effortless sophistication and wit. He was also rounder than Pixie. In fact, Nigel could see no pointy bits to him at all; his very elbows were round.

Charlie dropped back to join Nigel and Doug. As the sun-roasted crops moved by, Nigel heard how Charlie's scars had also come courtesy of Mosley's infamous blackshorts. It was not so dramatic as Johnno's story, he told Nigel. The guards had made Charlie a routine example for daring to speak out of turn at roll-call. They had sent him to the front with suppurating wounds; it was the reason he limped, he explained in his deadpan way.

Nigel had guessed right about his thoughtfulness. The son of a village handyman, he had a passion for taking things to bits. He asked to see Nigel's Polaroid. 'We'll have a look at it together. Later. Together,' said Nigel.

As the march wore on the company amused one another with songs and riddles. They had fine voices, apart from Nigel and Johnno. Johnno never sang. Wal and Pixie between them knew hundreds of songs, Wal because he was a goatherd and Pixie because he had worked as a spruiker with a travelling troupe of actors. Wal's voice, though, far outstripped his little friend's. It piped high and clear into the warming air, incongruous, coming out of a seven-foot walking rug. At one point, Wal and Pixie dropped back to conspire together. The others made lewd jokes about the two: Wal loved Pixie to the point of stupidity – although he wasn't the shambling cretinous hulk from *Of Mice and Men* and he had a volatile temper.

The happy abuse gave Nigel an idea.

'Hay, Charlie?' he said, matching step with the handyman.

'Nigel, *Sihi*.' Charlie smiled slyly.

'What does that mean?' Nigel asked him.

'The Mighty.' His grin grew wider.

Nigel gave a laugh. It wasn't such a bad world. 'Hay Charlie? How do you say "bite your bum" in Yugoslavian? I mean – in Serbo-Croat – in Serbian?'

'Chyrian.'

'Okay, Chyrian. Bite your bum.'

'I want to bite your –' he pointed '– arse?'

'No,' said Nigel. 'Like – when someone makes a stupid suggestion, here – where I come from – you say, "Ah, go bite your bum." Meaning, piss off.'

'Bite your own bum.'

'Yeah.'

Charlie tried it. He laughed. 'It's impossible!'

By now Doug and Johnno had joined them. Nigel explained what he wanted to say. They also tried to bite themselves. Even Johnno smiled, slightly. 'It is not possible,' he said.

'That's the whole point,' Nigel told them.

'Fine,' said Doug, in his simple way. '*Ugrizi moi dupa*' – and cackled to himself.

'No,' said Charlie, 'that is when you want someone else to bite your buttocks.'

'*Idi ugrizi svoi dupa*,' Johnno said. He shrugged his narrow shoulders and repeated it. He gave a snort. 'It is not *possible*!' he said. His tight skin wrinkled into a grin, revealing short, almost black teeth.

They began to chant the words. This brought Wal and Pixie back. When the novelty of the phrase had worn off, the convict leader said, 'Gentlemen. We have a small offering for our new friend, Nigel.'

The men applauded.

'Here, for the first occasion in these Australian Penal Colony, from one year from the Commonwealth of Yugoslavia and much acclaim from the goats there, we bring you all, on this road to Emu station, in middle of two oatfields . . . *Budimir Kliment Bogdanovic*! Otherwise known as *Wal*!'

More applause. Lots of whistles.

'But first a joke. Three pigs come to a country inn for sleeping. The boss pig *guyub* he says to the innkeeper, "I have only three legs, what will you take for the night, how about my friends they have four legs each will you take one of theirs for your stew?' And the innkeeper, he slaughters all three pigs and roasts them for his guests in the evening!'

The Serbs stopped and staggered about the road crippled by merriment. Soon Nigel found himself joining them, but still mystified by the joke. After the dust and laughter had settled, Pixie said, 'Very well. We walk again. You listen,' he told Nigel.

And Wal began to sing:

> I roam the valleys in my search of my goats,
> With my staff of oak and fur for my cloak.
> If I find them I beat them to death for running away,
> Because my father he beats me also.

The song went on for several verses, with a chorus about churches blowing over in the autumn wind and crushing old ladies. Pixie had made no attempt to make the traditional goat-song rhyme or scan, and this sometimes played havoc with the melody, but Nigel was touched by the effort. No one had ever sung to him before. As a child his mother's lullabies had made him wail.

Life here seemed to be working out quickly and simply, for the best.

Of course if everything were so easy we'd all be eating candied popcorn and living in yurts.

Emu station was a low brick farmhouse, red-roofed and surrounded by verandah. There was not a sign of emus. Several long stone sheds served as dormitories for the Assigned Labourers. Large stockyards and shearing-sheds lined the creek downstream from the living-quarters. It was more or less what Nigel had expected, aside from the animals.

Even for sheep they were miserable. Even from the road you could tell the heat obviously tortured the pathetic beasts. The feed and other conditions here must have disagreed with them as well. They disturbed Nigel. Previous sheep acquaintances had gone, 'Aaaah,' as though everything was much of a muchness to them. These went, 'Aiieee!' in continual distress. Perhaps it was merely their accent; the humans sounded different here, why not sheep? But the noise haunted him, distracting him throughout his explanations to the overlooker. Why had he accompanied five convicts from Milton Keynes? Gazing out the window at the sheep, he mumbled some tosh or other.

He'd read somewhere that before merino sheep could

thrive in Australia's heat, Macarthur had cross-bred them with other, more vigorous breeds. Were these sheep pure merinos? What had happened to Macarthur? Every Australian knew Macarthur had been a bastard. Perhaps someone had found lumps on Macarthur's head and he had never become regimental paymaster in the New South Wales Corps here. Perhaps he had never been born. But why had nobody else cross-bred the merino? It wasn't merely lumps behind this retarded development.

However, Nigel's thoughts went no further; the overlooker was on to him.

'So yer from a newsing paper,' said the overlooker. He scratched his grizzled chin with disapproval, glancing at the window by which Nigel had been gaping. 'What did yer say youze was scribin' about?'

'Um – I didn't.'

'Well?' People were as direct in this country as in his own.

'Convicts on assignment,' he rushed out. 'Ah – foreign convicts – from the war?' He tried a joke: 'We don't castrate 'em any more round here . . . I mean it's 1978!'

The overlooker stared at him.

The Serbs sat happily about the rest of the refectory table, sipping sweet tea from tin mugs, going, 'Hmmmm,' and nodding at whatever Nigel said. Nigel wished they would stop; it made his fibs sound positively conspiratorial.

'So. Yer from a newsing paper,' the overlooker repeated. He narrowed slate-grey eyes that were slits to begin with. 'What paper did ye say yer worked for?' He stood with one hand on the pump-handle by the window; in the blaze of light it was impossible to track the man's opinion of Nigel. The sun seemed to burst into the room and die in the cool dinginess.

'The – the *Sydney Morning Star*.'

'Sydney? Carn't say I know it.'

'It's new.' A safe bet. Sydney had to be hundreds of miles away. Nigel looked up from his fingernails at the man with what he hoped was a winning smile.

'Yer not a ticket-of-leave man, are yez?'

Ticket of leave? Ticket of leave? He still wasn't sure what one was. He *wished* he could recall his history. He wished he had quizzed the Serbs with some care but they only did that in films; real life (which didn't include his memory) was distressingly bitty. Bittiness could kill. He took a punt:

'No.'

'No,' said the Serbs.

The overlooker nodded. 'Thought not.' He batted his hat on his thigh and strode across the room on heavy heels toward the door. 'Too soft.' It was not an insult, merely a fact.

Nigel gathered up his courage and his teacup with both hands. 'So can I stay?'

'Not up to me, chum.' He drew lips as thin as anorexic worms back from his teeth, with real distaste now. 'The *boss*'s up in town and won't get back till tonight. Whatta yer reckon you'll be doing, anywar?'

'Well. I want to live and work with the boys here for a week, do a sort of inside story of the life of a convict. How they settle and that . . .'

The Serbs nodded vigorously.

The overlooker twisted his lined face into a mask of heart-stopping shock, as if the ways of journalists were a plague which might strike him dead one day. 'You don't wanna do that!'

'No,' said the Serbs.

'What in Baal's name for?' demanded the overlooker.

Nigel knew he had made a slip. Everyone in this country must have enough of criminals every day, he realised. He cast a desperate glance at the Serbs but they showed either badly veiled alarm or daft smiles, depending on their grasp of the situation.

'Um –' said Nigel.

The Serbs leaned toward Nigel in anticipation.

'Um –' he said again.

The Serbs leaned further, craning half out of their seats. The overlooker put his hands on the table and leaned as well.

'I'm a science reporter you see,' he explained in a rush, hoping the terms were used here. 'I'm going to measure the bumps on their heads before they start work here and then after two weeks of honest toil at Emu station I'll measure their bumps again and that way I'll prove what a good stint on an Australian farm can do for even the most desperate criminals.'

Oh my God what have I said, thought Nigel hysterically. What a ludicrous idea! A reporter doesn't go around doing that kind of thing even if people do believe in utter crap. His muscles tensed ready for reckless flight out the door. The memory of men tied to posts and covered in blood with cats-o'-nine-tails whacking their backs returned to him with a bout of nausea which pumped the bile to his gorge. Oh, he wailed silently, I'm a dead man. I'm a dead man.

'Ah!' said the overlooker, straightening. 'Why didn' yer say so before? It ain't a bad idea!'

'Mmmmm!' said the Serbs, nodding. Relieved, they leaned back into their seats, taking up their tea and sipping noisily.

Nigel grinned stupidly as the overlooker approached, hand outstretched. The bloke must be having him on. There was not a hint of sarcasm on the gnarled face, but Nigel remained ready to flinch and bolt.

'I don't hold with reading m'self,' the overlooker explained as he took Nigel in a surprisingly gentle grip. 'Anywar it's good to meetcha. Nigel, ay? Like I say, I'm off to the other side of the station and the boss won't be back till after tea, but yer welcome to wash up and have a down in the guest-room till then. Houseproper'll show yez where everythin' is.'

He released Nigel. 'Now,' he rumbled at the Serbs. 'As to youze motherless dogs, yer comin' with me. Get up and get out of the house. This is the first and last time yu'll see the inside of here.'

The Serbs nodded. They stood.

In seconds, Nigel was alone in the cool, dim, servants' dining-room. His shaking took some time to subside.

Six

A Woman's Work

'I will *not*! He reckons he can thunder about treating every one of us like his convict do-bundles, simply because he's a man and by sacrist blessing happens to be my older brother. Ever since the King gave him that grotesque toe-clipping knighthood thing for good deeds – to sheep of all things – he's been utterly repulsive. I've got a mind to go and shout the lot of it from the prayer tower or at *ejek*. The things he forces you to do. Deny it, go on! It's your fear of his bloody coalition in town that keeps you trapped here. I'm telling you: I will not stay and rot to unholy *biggle* with those disgusting animals of his!'

Nigel sat up in the bath. Only minutes ago he had mastered the arcana of the brass taps at his feet. You had to pull and turn at the same time and tug the chain to release the cold, but not too hard . . . After dousing himself in cold water then scalding his feet, he lay back in the tin tub and twiddled his reddened toes, determined to relax in spite of the rather one-sided argument raging down the hall.

The younger woman wanted to attend a Melbourne school. The older one reminded her of her robbery and near-rape by bushrangers during her last journey there.

'I needn't stop for a picnic this time. I promise to stay in the carriage with the blinds drawn until we reach the hotel,' said the younger woman. 'I am twenty-one years old, Melinda. I have survived bushfires, the pox, the local school, two convict rebellions and one *pikun*, and most of all I have survived my brother. I tally I'm in more danger here than on a simple Avis carriage to Melbourne.'

'The carriage ride is only a small part of the danger! Your brother is quite correct when he says Melbourne is a pit of downloaders these days. His Majesty has doubled the convict and wokkie transportations since the war and the authorities there cannot deal with such numbers.'

'My brother ought to know what a pit of downloaders it is – he's downloading there often enough. On every trip he and his gang find it necessary to kill for some slight or other. Don't you ever wonder about the depravity of *that*? It's grotesque, his thirst for revenge. And you're wrong about the war. The King's astrologer told the King there would be another Scottish Uprising and it has driven him further out of his mind than was previously thought possible.'

'Catherine!'

'Well it's the truth. With the criminal classes stuck here or in Arkansas the population of England is pure as the driven *santan*, so he must be moonstruck if he thinks some Celtic Jimmy Carter will rise and declare a republic. At the foot of it all, Melinda, you can't stomach anyone else escaping this *biggle*-hole because you're matched prime to him and'll only get out of here by dying.'

'That is very unkind, Catherine.' The older woman sounded hurt, undeservedly so, judging from her gentle tones.

'Oh . . . we all know what he does to you,' said Catherine. Compassion thickened her voice. 'You can't hide a thing behind the thin walls here . . . Melinda, I want to get out. Both my parents died here, and my mother never travelled past the river Barry. She never saw Melbourne, she hardly ever saw Milton Keynes. She had such a talent in her, and never sang for an audience. I want to find what I can do . . . oh, don't cry, Melinda . . . I'm sorry, I didn't mean to bring up your – you know how selfish and excitable I am . . . don't cry . . .'

A silence fell. Nigel found himself listening hard. He

thought he could make out a sniffle. Then came a hooting nose-blow. Nigel wondered if they were both in tears. He looked around for soap but found none. He scrubbed himself with his hands and got up. The towel the house-keeper had given him was as rough as a cocoas mat. He scraped and blotted himself dry, and he did feel cleaner and fresher as he dressed again, although the argument had distracted him too much for relaxation.

Tentatively, he pulled the door toward him. He made his way down the dark green plastic grass in the hall, flattening his hair with his fingers, hitching up his jeans. At the kitchen door he hesitated. The fine stubble on his chin sounded loud against his fingers in the silence. He pushed the door further open and went in.

The woman who sat with her back to him, arms spread wide and flat against the scarred hardwood table, one full cheek pressed awkwardly to a gingham sleeve, breathed quietly and evenly. Determined. This had to be Catherine. Only occasionally did her rhythm break with a sudden suck of air, a release. Nigel stood without a move or a word for two minutes, transfixed.

But not by the woman. On the handkerchief clutched in her right fist, he read the initials:

C.A.S.

Eventually, Nigel recalled where he had put the hanky that had helped maroon him in this alien Australia. He groped around to his back pocket, tugged it out and found the matching embroidery on its corner. Now he stood staring at this instead, rubbing his thumb across the letters. A long time seemed to have passed since he had first wondered about the hanky's owner. Small universe, he thought.

'Excuse me.'

He looked up. The young woman had straightened and turned in her seat. Her speckly blue eyes demanded an explanation of himself, of his whereabouts, of his liking for tangerines – the lot.

'Sorry. Hi,' said Nigel. 'I'm Nigel.'

'Charisma to meet you.'

Her small mouth, darker than most people's without the help of lipstick as far as Nigel could tell, twitched sardonically. Her broad face, lightly freckled, challenged. She stood.

'The overseer said I could take a bath and wait here till the boss got back from town,' said Nigel. He broke into an inane grin. He realised he still had the handkerchief in front of him and shoved it back in his pocket.

Her large eyes followed his hand.

'And you are . . . ?'

'I didn't tell you and I may not. You have some business with my brother, I tally?' She eyed his filthy clothes (and, Nigel thought, his skinny legs) with scepticism.

'Ah – yes. Sort of. I'm doing an – a phrenological experiment on the convicts who just arrived. Penal reform, you know. Proof of –' he waved a hand '– of the good system here.'

'Ah.' The word expressed cold reams of disapproval for 'the system'.

Nigel very much wanted her to like him. With her long thin hands on her plump hips, feet planted apart on the plastic grass, round and slightly upturned chin cocked at him, it didn't seem as if there were any possibility of that. As usual. But for once he thought he would try anyway. Irrationally, he felt tempted to blurt the truth to her; she looked as though she might receive it better than his cobbled-together codswallop. She looked strong and full of sense. He decided that at least he'd tell her as few lies as possible. This meant saying very little. Yet he ached to speak to her.

'Nigel Donohoe,' he said. He offered a hand.

'Catherine Samuelson.' Her hands remained on her hips. She was really much shorter than Nigel, but it didn't seem so at the time.

'I'm originally from Melbourne,' Nigel offered. He paused.

'Yeah. Well. When I finished university I thought I might move to Sydney, but my dad had – has – a business there and he offered me a job – I've never been the adventurous sort, so I took it.'

Why am I telling her this? he thought.

'Oh,' said Catherine. She sounded disappointed.

He said quickly, 'I'm certainly choofing around the joint now!' He laughed. 'You should meet these Serbs I came up with from Milton Keynes; they've got some amazing stories to tell. Really great blokes . . .'

That puzzled look, which the Serbs as well as the overlooker had given him, crossed her face. He knew he had said something which sounded weird.

She smiled. It was a beautiful sight, even so mocking a smile. It made her eyes twin chinks of blue. 'You don't think I'd be in herbal danger from them? They're not depraved members of the criminal class?' she asked.

'No, no. They're lovely guys. I mean – for criminals, you know, um, for traitors to the Empire, they're lovely guys. Wouldn't hurt anyone. Terrific. Hardly, ah, herbal at all. You've got to get to know them to reform them, don't you think?' he said as though at a cocktail party. (Not that he had ever attended one.)

She turned away from Nigel and went to the hob, rattling off in a high voice quite unlike her own, 'Where *are* my manners, you've come all the way to see my brother with a bunch of criminals – *lovely* criminals I'm sure – and I haven't offered you a cup of tea,' meaning not a word. 'Do sit down. I wonder if Melinda's baked some scones today. Shall I call her?'

Nigel felt he had lost what small ground he had gained but he wasn't sure why. 'No, no,' he said. 'Don't want to be any trouble.'

'You're right,' she said with a big false smile. 'Don't want – trouble, mm? I shall make the tea myself and we shall have a nice chat before my brother returns. In the sitting-room. It's very pleasant there at this time of day. That's down the hall and to the left at the end by the *kulkul*. I'll see you in a moment. Yes?'

'Okay. Yeah, fine,' said Nigel.

Catherine shooed him out. 'You do have a funny turn of phrase.' What had he said? 'Now let me get on with my woman's work,' she told him, full of artificial colour and flavour. 'You know what they say! "A woman's work is —"'

'"never done."'

'No.' She cocked her head and gave a genuine snort. '"A woman's work is to sweat blood,"' she told him. 'Rhymes with "mud."'

Nigel turned and left her to it.

In an overstuffed sitting-room chair, Nigel, clueless as to Catherine's sudden shift in behaviour, returned to the sheep problem. It was a pleasant room, carpeted, filled with flowers and mirrors, with a gentle light filtered through lace curtains and with busts of what Nigel guessed, from their bulging eyes and snarls, were classical deities or pederasts. Or composers. He found he could think here. She certainly gave him enough time to do so. Perhaps she was fetching scones after all. It was fine by Nigel. He'd eaten no lunch.

History had never been of the slightest use to Nigel. Once again he wished he knew a little more. He remembered Bacon's *New Atlantis* and Isaac Newton and the Royal Society had been important for the Industrial Revolution, somehow. He wasn't sure what the idea of a 'criminal class' had to do with that, though. The idea of an England full of saints reinforced the use of scientific method. Then again, perhaps not. He'd never met people as simply *good* as the Serbs (which might just be his limited experience) — was England really more virtuous? Did it mean a speedier progress of science into the intangible areas of the human mind than was possible in his own world? But how did it jibe with Australia as a concentration camp? His mind rebelled at the notion. And people didn't seem simpler in this world, merely more virtuous – or ready for greater cruelty ... Okay, take England as being chock-a-block with Tweety-pies, for the moment. So what did the discoverers of his world have in common besides maybe intelligence and luck? In Macarthur's case, the man had tried to stage a coup against Governor Bligh while in gaol, he had been a scheming, self-serving snob. Surely Isaac Newton didn't have much in common with Macarthur. In the cartoons, Tweety-pie always defeated Sylvester, but that was because the bird was actually a devious unprincipled rat of the first water. In real life the meek did not inherit the earth. Might be you should have just a few lumps on the head to go it alone against ignorance, and they crack down on lumps here, so no progress.

He seemed to remember Australia's wool industry had also required a gap in the market caused by a trade embargo somewhere. I'm probably mistaking cause for effect, he thought. Or Tweety-pie for Isaac Newton.

Sitting back in his chair, he gazed idly at the harpsichord by the window and wondered what had become of Catherine Samuelson. The harpsichord had little gargoyles carved into the black keys ... He checked his watch. Almost half an hour had passed. He sat and speculated about the scientific community here. The science history he'd studied as part of his philosophy course had left him with some funny-sounding names and not much else: Lakatos, Kuhn, Popper ...

Does virtue equal stupidity?

He needed someone friendly to talk to.

A fat pink book open on a lectern by the fireplace took his attention. He leapt out of his chair. It was the only book in the room, and hand-bound. There was no title. The first page showed woodblock prints of a baobab tree, a cluster of bearded faces, and a chihuahua. Beneath appeared the mysterious initials, 'W.S.'

Turning to a page at random, he read:

'And if a man have broken these commandments, which are the LORD'S, I will abhor him.

'And *he* shall not find forgiveness.

'These *are* the statutes and judgements and laws; which the LORD gave unto Ed in Clacton.

'And though he give years in repentance he is evil and until he dieth and faceth the LORD in *biggle*.'

The low flowing script was difficult to read. What he understood merely brought more confusion. He waited for Catherine with growing impatience, dipping into a book that covered every aspect of life, yea unto cleaning one's toe-nails in seventeen different ways. It was generous to many life-styles and forms of worship, but once you stepped outside its bounds – blam, the dreaded *biggle*.

When Catherine finally did arrive with the tea, she was transformed. Her plain, long-sleeved gingham dress and practical brown boots had been replaced by a knee-length hoop-skirt of a rough woven indigo plastic, white hose, patent leather hook-ups and a white blouse with leg-o'-mutton sleeves of pale grey silk. Her long black hair was now pinned in an elegant bun. At her cleavage she wore a sapphire cameo which bore one of those bug-eyed visages so popular here. To Nigel's disappointment, crude make-up covered her freckles. On the other hand, her perfume, whiffed as she rustled past him to lay the silver service on the table, was electric.

The strange plastic skirt made her look like *Scarlett O'Hara in the Twenty-fourth-and-a-half Century*. But the overall intention was obvious – and successful. Nigel was flattered. And winded with lust. She looked up from the table to catch him ogling her breasts.

Oops. He cast frantically about for a white lie.

'Now,' said Catherine Samuelson, a touch too much breath in her voice. 'Shall we have tea?'

She nattered on about how the weather had been decidedly

mild or not mild did Nigel think it was hot? and not waiting for an answer went on about the difficulty of getting buttons and those fiddly things you polish *otots* with (it appeared these were orange with lots of furrows) and on about how there is always *one* more thing to do when you want to play the banjo and about how they never had visitors at Emu station because it was too far off the main road to Carthage (which seemed to be Sydney as near as Nigel could make out) and on and on and bloody on. It made Nigel quietly furious, but he tried not to show it because he sensed a messy pain lay behind her words, a fragility. He was all the more infuriated because, besides the pleasantly warm fug of lust that made his loins quiver as though happy little creatures were playing house in them whenever she leaned towards him to pour a cup (still talking) or walked fragrant and soft beside his chair – besides this, he *knew* she was a witty and sensitive and powerfully intelligent woman who if she chose could have made Nigel laugh and in the long term really enriched him. He longed to meet that tough, self-contained, determined woman. The one to whom he had listened in the bath with a grin on his face. But she wouldn't let him near.

He sat watching her talk. She had a way of dipping her right shoulder forward when she made a point. He imagined what it might be like to wrestle her, a good clean childlike game, on the carpet between them. What it would be to get carpet rash from her! There was something apart from her natural fragile caution holding her back. He sat and puzzled, but he had bumped into too many puzzles lately.

About half-way through the afternoon, and on his twelfth cup of tea, the reason for her falsity began to soak through.

She was afraid of him.

And something else: she either wanted to keep him here (who could possibly run with a gallon of tea sloshing inside him?) or she was hiding the fact that there were no other men in the house. Or both. She kept excusing herself to answer imaginary calls from a stern and violent 'Uncle Jack', but in his boredom on the fifth occasion Nigel had examined the room and noticed a deep blue eye at the keyhole which, when he waved, widened and vanished.

He decided he was in desperate strife. The police had been summoned, or worse. At the first opportunity he would confess his whole strange story. The trouble was, she kept breaking off with mention of her great thighs-like-pillars uncle and rushing out!

'Wait,' he said at last. He took her by the forearm. (It was muscular and hairy and softer than anything he had ever touched.) 'Just a minute.'

She recoiled from him.

'I'm not what you think I am,' he told her, desperately.

To his amazement, Catherine began to weep great big tears. 'I do not know *what* you are!' she thumped him hard in the chest, then after a frozen moment of terror, fell away from him, out of his grip, and backed toward the harpsichord as she spoke. 'You come here and sneak in behind me and tell me a pack of lies . . . who would travel with convicts and not carry a gun? Where are your bags? And why do you have one of my monogrammed handkerchiefs? I am –' she pushed away from the harpsichord – 'I'm going to get my *uncle*!'

'You don't have any uncle to get!' shouted Nigel. 'And I *found* your handkerchief – on a rock!' He'd grown fierce in his panic.

'I don't believe you,' she said. 'You're one of the men who robbed the Melbourne Avis last week. You wore a mask but I recognise you . . . you took my luggage and kept my handkerchief and now you've come to finish your filthy bloody job!' She leant on the harpsichord and sobbed.

'Oh I hate myself . . . I really am good for nothing, just like my brother says . . .'

She straightened and faced him, vehement. 'Look at me!' she cried, raising her arms melodramatically. 'I'm a woman alone with an escaped felon who will definitely burn away his life after he's had me, who's less than the miserable sheep in the paddocks, and what do I do? I cry, I bloody cry.'

She took a step closer. He could smell her tears.

'When I was four my father lay . . . in this house lay dying of the smallpox, and he called me to him and told me nothing mattered, life was vain and foolish and ended in dust, no wheel of reincarnation or sacrist heaven – dust. I should never have children, he said, never learn what I might do or make in the world, because ultimately all a woman's work, everyone's work, is wasted. He gave me a phial of poison –'

She tugged a silver chain at her neck to produce it, an innocent pink glass dewdrop, made lambent by her throat.

'– I still carry it? I still carry it. And why – because I cannot – shake the idea he may be right. I am twenty-one years of age and I have not done a single thing in my whole existence I could be proud of . . .'

She spun, a natural actress, stepped back to the harpsichord, and stood stiff-backed facing the window.

'Take me,' she whispered. 'It's all the same, you see. I don't care. *Take me* and be done here you bastard.'

'*I am not going to attack you*,' Nigel shrieked. 'Okay?

'Look,' he said, more gently. Her story had begun to register, appalling him. 'If I were a – a bushranger, I would have a gun, hm? Wouldn't I?'

'I don't care. Anyway, it's too late, I've sent my sister-in-law for my brother, his overlooker and the police.' She turned, cut short a sob and scrubbed the tears from her cheeks with a fist. 'So there.'

'Please' said Nigel. 'Please sit down and let me explain what's happened to me. Please?' Now he was really in trouble, he thought he might as well tell her everything: it wouldn't make any difference anyhow.

His desperation affected her. She came forward and sat.

'It started with this fish,' he began. 'Carmen, her name was. Anyhow, I bought these really beautiful tropical aquarium fish and this one of them did something absolutely unbelievable . . .'

*

The police hadn't come. The overlooker hadn't come. Her brother hadn't come. Her Godzilla-type uncle hadn't come. I could have escaped by now, Nigel realised.

But he felt better for having shared his predicament.

Whether she believed or understood more than the Serbs was another matter.

'You are a very weird individual, you know that,' said Catherine. 'What you say sounds true but it's obviously the raving of a diseased mind.'

Catherine Samuelson was a lot cooler now. She clearly found Nigel's story enthralling. Though not, Nigel reflected, because it made the slightest sense to her. More because it didn't and she had a craving for the unusual.

'How can I make you believe me?' he asked. He wondered what she'd think of the Polaroid. It was, however, with his things in the bathroom and it would throw her back into panic if he got up. Anyway, it had wowed the Serbs, but they had reserved judgement on his story.

'I don't know,' Catherine answered him. 'I suppose you can't.' She smiled.

Nigel smiled back. He felt the presence of his acne scars acutely. 'I suppose not,' he admitted.

They sat in silence for a moment. The evening magpies began their wistful melodies. Even the crows on their way to dead sheep sounded sad.

'What will you tell your brother when he gets here?' asked Nigel.

'I don't know,' Catherine confessed. 'You don't appear dangerously insane.'

'I'm not.'

'No.'

Again, they smiled at one another.

A far-off rattling grew slowly louder.

'Your brother?'

'Yes.'

The sounds of men in boots running around the house on the gravel and then on the verandahs filtered through the windows. At a shout the doors burst open at both the front and the back of the house.

'LAY DOWN YER ARMS,' came a shout from behind the sitting-room door. 'YER POSITION IS HOPELESS SIR!'

I know that voice, thought Nigel. Where have I heard that voice before?

'WE ARE COMING IN NOW SIR! ATTEMPT NO VIOLENCE TOWARD THE LADY OR IT WILL GO HARD ON YE!'

'I know that voice,' Nigel told Catherine.

'You can't,' said Catherine, 'not if your story is true. That's my brother's voice.'

Nigel nodded.

But when the door was flung open, Nigel looked at the face behind the pistol levelled at him, and although he felt a chill of fear as chilly as ever had chilled him all his life and cringed away from the gun, Nigel had to fight the impulse to get up and say to the face which he had endured in his father's glue factory for over two years:

'My God. Todd. Yes, your last name's Samuelson! Todd Samuelson – you old bastard.'

He didn't say this, of course. The man was ready to pull the trigger – would love to, by the look of the grimace wedged in his virulent pointy beard. One move would finish him. Maybe not even that. So Nigel sat and quaked. Looking at Catherine's guilty face, still feeling the pain in his chest where she'd thumped him, he longed for one minute more of life in which to explain. But he expected to die.

Seven

Pistachiosity

Yet what could he explain? The same story as before? That he'd followed a fish here from a place where if you knew your position you didn't know your speed and if you had your speed you couldn't tell where you were and when you tried to find out for sure you got a recorded message? The gun in this other-Todd's hand looked primitive, like no gun he had ever seen, like a turnip in fact, but it was, no doubt, deadly.

'Get up,' said the other-Todd.

The breath he'd been holding escaped all at once. He was not going to die, just yet. Nigel grabbed the seat-arms and slowly pulled himself to his feet. He began to notice how this Todd differed from his own Todd. Their dress senses were appallingly similar. This Todd wore platform riding-boots which were nearly practical; his hair was every bit as voluminous and surly, although filthy; not only did he have a handlebar moustache, he wore an evil goatee which gleamed in the remains of the day; his orange leather riding-trousers sported blue cotton stripes down the side, his shirt was white and frilly. However, the Todd here looked stronger, more of a side of beef than the Todd Samuelson Nigel knew. And his eyes glistened with as much cold inhuman horror as his beard, as if he wanted to shoot *somebody*, and Nigel might have to do, failing the presence of cute furry animals or small children.

'Come on lag. Make a move! Over there.' He waved the gun toward the fireplace. Would Nigel be burned alive? 'Move, damn ye! Do ye want me to shoot ye *now*?'

'Don't shoot him,' said Catherine.

'Why not? Y'identified him didn't yer?' demanded Todd. 'Trespassing alone gives me the flawless right to blast whomsoever I wish.'

(He has better grammar than my Todd, thought Nigel, abstractedly. Positively affected.)

'Well, the overlooker let him in.'

'Don't tell me ye've taken pity on him. Baal save me from women and *santan*. The man is a dangerous criminal, do not forget it.'

The thought seemed to alight upon her as if fresh. Nevertheless she persisted. 'Well . . . I'm not sure he is what we think he is any more.'

Yay, Catherine!

Todd tutted with digust. 'Catherine. Y'send up the alarum alone in the house with this highwayman, but when yer rescue arrives y'are as always prepared to argue with me, out of sheer contrariness. This is not the sort of behaviour which will persuade our uncle to allow ye to face the downloaders of Melbourne. Act responsibly, and I shall do my best to assist ye with him.'

So there was an uncle! Nigel wondered helplessly about his thighs.

'Ye would argue with Baal Himself if He came to collect ye,' rumbled Todd at his sister's silent fury. 'At the expense of yer mortal soul!'

This was definitely not the Todd Samuelson Nigel knew. His own Todd had read the *Bhagavad-Gita* from cover to cover and kept the *I Ching* in his shoulder-bag. He never spoke like a pirate giving Bible lessons. *Or whatever the hell that pink book really was*. 'Um – can I explain?' he said, while Catherine fumed.

'No ye may not. Y'll have yer time in the machineries of justice. I have all the proof I need – or do ye deny our little encounter in the town this morning?' He showed Nigel his amazing teeth.

'I've never seen you before in my life,' Nigel said, not very convincingly.

'Oh, come, come. Are ye or are ye not still tender in a certain delicate part of yer anatomy?'

And with his left hand he grabbed Nigel's goolies.

Nigel yelped. In the part of his mind separate to the excruciation, he remembered his bicycle accident of a couple of days previous. 'How do you know?' he gasped.

'Because I kicked ye there old fellow!' Todd let Nigel go, and sniggered at the two troopers flanking him as Nigel slid down to the hearth. 'I suppose ye will deny the large lump on yer head now.' He lowered his pistol, put one paw on his broad plastic belt.

'Oh my God,' groaned Nigel.

Catherine, whose alarm had grown with his torture, now registered betrayal. She had wanted to believe him, he realised. If only he had had more time.

The two troopers were smiling at Nigel's virtual admission of guilt.

'I had a cycling accident yesterday,' Nigel whined. He looked back at Catherine. Her blue eyes had hardened; she didn't know what he was on about. 'You know – a bicycle?'

Blank stares all round.

'Two wheels, spokes, pedals? Anyway, I was going up this big hill and one of the pedals karked it and I fell on the crossbar.' He held out both hands. 'You've got to believe me.'

'You said that before,' observed Catherine, coldly.

'Two wheels,' said Todd. 'You want us to believe ye play with children's toys? You cannot go *up* a hill on a bicycle. Yer wanted for robbery under arms and attempted violence upon my sister, man. Though she did not see ye clearly, others did and ye were captured this morning. Y'may feign insanity but ye cannot deny our struggle this morning – I have a dozen witnesses who will recognise ye. Take him away.'

As the troopers took his elbows and shoulders and began to shove him to the door, Nigel blurted, 'There are too many discrepancies! I don't belong in this world! When we get to court you'll see. You might think I'm crazy but you'll know I'm not capable of any robbery. *Catherine you must believe me, ask the Serbs!*'

'It's not my sister y'shall have to convince, bold Jack,' said Todd. 'You see – I am the local magistrate.'

With that, Nigel was shoved through the doorway.

This was worse than the Old Melbourne gaol. It was aggressively filthy. Of course this was hardly a tourist attraction.

Nigel had visited the gaol as a schoolboy, seen the place where Ned Kelly had at the end said, 'Such is life.' Small things had conspired against him, too – who knew what would have happened had Curnow not informed on the Kellys at Glenrowan? Nigel's Curnow was a pair of sore knackers and a lump on the head. He remembered the last man hung in his Australia, Ronald Ryan. Nigel had been quite young at the time, but he recalled his nausea at the moment of Ryan's death. Some had approved of the act, no doubt. But where was the virtue in taking a man's life, even a murderer's?

He sat with his back against the cold, slimy wall of his cell, wondering if he might be – what did they call it? – 'turned off'. As in the movies, there was a beautiful woman involved, but she would not visit him. Certainly she wouldn't come wrapped in black velvet in the dead of night to free him so he might lead a revolution against the corrupt Sydney Greenstreet aristocracy. Ned Kelly had wanted a revolution . . . what if he'd won? No, it was another cracked notion. He was full of them. Catherine had rightly not believed a word of his crap. *I* don't believe me, most of the time. So I'll be convicted. Everyone seemed to think so. That wouldn't stand up in his own world, but he didn't know a thing about the law here. They might do anything at all to him . . .

The cell was tiny. It was more than cold. It was almost totally dark, aside from a single slat of light which fell from the door's observation crack to his cot. Nigel knew he'd feel better if he got up and wrapped himself in the greasy blanket, but he couldn't be bothered. Between warm and miserable and shivering and miserable there seemed not much difference.

Nigel sat up for the whole long night and went over his life.

He had never had things bad. His mother might have been an alcoholic but she loved him. His father might have been hopeless at business, hopeless in general – a complete and utter berk, in fact, but he had never clouted Nigel even when he had deserved it.

His parents had met on the Ferris wheel at the 1955 Barupyerbutty West Agricultural Show. His mother had thrown up all over his father from above. She had offered to wash his clothes, they had gone back to her parents' place, her parents had hated him, so she had married him. The two had endured poverty while Nigel's father had studied chemistry in Melbourne because he was an orphan and her parents thought he was sent by the ever-present agents of Beelzebub owing to his Harley-Davidson and ducktail. In his defence, he told Nigel, he really had loved that duck. When questioned about his possible satanism, he never denied it. But he had always laughed.

Nigel's first words had been, 'You stink!'

His mother had told him that much about his early childhood, but little else. For years he had fought paranoia about some infant misdeed; perhaps he had put a puppy in a blender or something. Then, during a row with her husband, his mother had let slip the real reason for her avoidance of those years: a stillborn younger sister when Nigel was about three. Afterwards, Nigel had guessed at the sadness which sometimes dulled his mother's eyes. It was partly why he had never moved out of home.

Nigel remembered his father's motor-cycle days. He recalled speeding down poplar-lined country roads behind his father, his face full of rushing air and the smell of his father's cracked brown leather jacket. He recalled a sandstorm on the beach when he was about five, his screams when the leaden atmosphere cut at his legs, his father's swearing when they reached the bike to discover it clogged with sand.

His childhood had passed in reasonable happiness. He had come away from school with three skills: pure mathematics, baseball, and dreams. After punishment for zooming far ahead of the maths class (he'd borrowed a simple text from the library and worked his way through the entire primary syllabus in a month) he had concealed his ability, plugged away with the rest of the class at long division while at home he tackled algebra and boggled at the concept of integration. Excellence at baseball had been no crime – merely useless. Cricket and football took up most of sports time. Baseball had been one of several games taught and discarded. By the time Nigel reached high school he had perfected the art of following the lesson with his mind and dreaming about his fish with his heart.

Then acne had struck. Like a bus in a box of soft chocolates. He did not remember waking up one morning with a mass of pustulant knobs on his face. But he did recall catching his reflection in a car window on his way home from high school and thinking it was someone else. Someone horribly disfigured by a nuclear accident. At one point soon afterwards his zits grew so bad his mother made him visit the doctor. Doctor Tape quizzed Nigel about his personal hygiene; he would not believe Nigel's nervous answers. The cream prescribed stank; it felt like yoghurt on his face. Nigel felt more of an outcast than ever, covered in this gloop. And it did not seem to work. During a game of spin-the-bottle at his first unsupervised party at Mario Denuncio's, the girls who got stuck with Nigel to kiss would do anything at all to get out of touching him. Nigel accumulated favours that way, but it was small consolation for the whispered negotiations held not exactly behind his back. He knew himself to be personally responsible for two girls' loss of virginity without having touched either of them.

His pimples alone did not cause his stutter. In fact it worsened after his rampant acne had passed. Nigel raged against his stutter. He hated first himself, then the people who made him speak, then his parents. It did no good. Vowels became impassable gorges down which he plummeted to claw his way blindly up the other side. Plosives were news of hurricanes; he would blink over and over and try his best not to overwhelm his listener when the consonantal storm arrived but his attacks were invariably worse in public or important situations where to turn away didn't do. Following the pressure of his Higher School Certificate he thought his stutter would subside. Instead he found himself in city bookshops lurking near copies of *How I Vanquished My Crippling, Ugly, Dangerous Stammer in Only 99 Days*, or *Articulate Yourself!* His father saved for therapy, which Nigel accepted gladly.

He did benefit from this, held in a comfortable consultation room in South Yarra with a smart young Englishwoman whom Nigel lusted after miserably. It was an incident at university, however, that served to nobble his ferocious disability. One summer's afternoon, seated in the Union Caf, a young nun from his philosophy tutorial approached with a tray and asked if she could share the table.

Nigel eyed her two or three meals and dessert, then the slim figure of the nun, and nodded, amazed. She plonked down the tray, seated herself opposite more gracefully, and began to mow her way through pasta, a plate-sized steak, and finally a salad enough for half a dozen bulimic wombats. She was not round in the face, yet not thin, perhaps in her late twenties, with little bow lips when she wasn't hoeing in, and she possessed a gigantic, suggestive hooter, softened by large ice-blue, lavishly lashed eyes and delicate cheek-bones.

On the verge of dessert, she spoke.

'My name's Anna.'

'I know,' stammered Nigel. 'Robbo calls you that in tutes.'

'And you're Nigel.' She smiled. It was the first time he had been smiled upon by a nun. Did they all have this angelic intention? Nigel couldn't help but smile back. His eyes fell from hers to the crème caramel.

'Would you like some?' she asked.

'Oh no, sister. I've just finished my lunch, thanks.'

'Go on.' She pushed it toward him. 'Don't want to make a pig of myself. Call me Anna.'

Nigel held up both hands.

She held his eyes for a second, considering something. Again, she smiled. 'I suppose I'll have to fit it in.'

It took a flat minute for her to devour it.

'Now you must have some coffee with me,' she commanded.

Half-way through the cup and part-way into a discussion of Nigel's aborted effort at comment on Hegel in their last tutorial, Nigel realised with a start what lay behind her eyes.

She was cracking on to him.

The only person who had directed such a look at him was Geraldine Ferguson, in form four. A month, it had taken him, to click, and by then she was rooting Tom Hambopoulos.

Well, Nigel thought, why not? It wasn't as if you went numb, just because you took Orders. You didn't follow them up, though. As his panic subsided he began to feel flattered. She was intelligent and attractive and she certainly wouldn't give him the mind-crippling tension he normally suffered. And she took his side:

'. . . the individual's ideas when in conflict with the universal may *be wrong* as long as those morals rule and *become* right afterward? Later generations will see the state as wrong and the individual as right by hindsight, ay, but that isn't a true understanding. I know it's a truism. But it means you have to fully imagine how every part of your life

would have been affected by previous beliefs. Is that what
you were trying to get at in the tute?'

Nigel frowned, carried by Anna's enthusiasm. He
couldn't really recall what he had stuttered about in the
tutorial. Her ideas on Hegel seemed even less informed than
his. But the argument gripped him. Soon they were on their
way through the green university grounds to a leafy corner
table outside one of the quieter student pubs, waving their
arms, interrupting one another. Nigel hadn't felt so good
for months.

Perhaps *Caligula* had done it. She held that Camus's play
explored the connection between the poetic, the absurd and
amorality, the dangerous ground where to question turned
into evil or where transgression and scatology could
become cultural and physical progress. Nigel said that
Nietzsche's humour could not be measured or defined or –
as was usual – ignored. She developed a gleam in her eye,
which he thought meant she wanted to get back to Camus,
but at the first pause she blurted her question, cold.

She moved her hand through the city of empty glasses
between them. She placed it in the palm of his.

It felt cool and dry. Her fingers were long, pink; they
rested on his large bumpy brown ones like a bird on its nest,
perfectly at home.

During the silence he decided he had imagined her proposi-
tion. Her hand had landed on his because it was appropriate
to their developing friendship. She smiled at him so
wholesomely. How could you even imagine a thing so
crude? he chided himself.

And he relaxed. They began a conversation about the other
personalities in their tutorial group. The sun began to set.
Not a sign emerged to show the subject had surfaced, except
if you counted the way she patted the back of his hand now

and then. He thought, I am a little pissed, yes, or I wouldn't have imagined such – stuff.

'We should have a meal,' he stammered.

'Yes,' she said, emphatically. 'Yes we should.'

'I don't know what sort of wage a nun gets –'

'I've got enough for both of us.'

'Oh no,' said Nigel, 'I was just trying to work out what we could both afford.'

'But I want to take you to a really nice restaurant.'

'I couldn't –'

'I want to take you out. It's not like paying you to fuck me; I like you. I want to do things for you.'

'Pardon?'

'When you didn't answer before I assumed you wanted to mull it over.'

'Um, yes, possibly – for years – for several decades.'

'What, it's a thing you'd like to think back on in your dotage? I really wish I'd fucked that nun?'

In vain, Nigel cast around for other drinkers, or the publican or a policeman – anyone! 'How can you say that?' he demanded, half strangled.

'It's not the sort of thing I do often enough to plan.'

'You mean you've done it *before*?' Careless, he sprayed her with spittle.

'No. That's not what I meant.' Tears rose to her eyes. 'That's not what I meant at all. I had to say it now or I'd never get up the nerve to say it – to anyone. Ever.'

Despite the emotion in her voice, Nigel couldn't help but comment, 'So it isn't me you want; you just want to find out what it's like.'

'No! Well, it's part of it, yes. I've toyed with it. I've never met the right man before. Now I think I have. You.'

He calmed. She licked a tear from her upper lip and sniffled. She wiped the spit from her brow.

'Let's walk,' he said, with hardly a stutter at all. He rose. He offered her his hand.

*

A good summer can be a selfish time in an urban culture; it means hedonism. So Australia, notwithstanding the thickness of thieves handed on by convictism and rural adversity, can be as selfish as a box of blind kittens. Not with money, that'd be crass, but with a depth of commitment. Has the sun bleached reliability from us like the pigment from a surfer's hair? Or have we peroxided our souls with our own brand of Californian glibness?

Whatever, the truth was at nineteen Nigel had no close friends. He saw in Anna the drive to get past the superficial kind of friendships he saw as common. In this he wanted what she wanted. More than anything.

If only he could talk her out of banging his ears off.

The sunset that evening was the sort to make a real-estate agent believe in God. It made things worse for Nigel. He explained his ideas on friendship to Anna as they strolled through the Melbourne Cemetery, petrified a priest might any minute pop up from behind a gravestone with a machete and – whack! – send him to Judgement. This was Nigel's idea of Catholicism at the time.

'We're not going to get killed, you know,' said Anna, spinning a long sedge-stalk between her fingers. She eyed him sidelong. 'Lots of people leave their Orders.'

'How did you know I was afraid?' Nigel veered away from a gloriously lit stone angel, directing Anna by short, annoying tugs on her cape.

'Oh they teach us to read minds in Loyola. *The Spiritual Exercises.*'

Nigel stopped and gawped at her.

'You're not that stupid are you?' said Anna. 'No of course you're not. Give us a kiss?'

Nigel gave a frenzied sigh.

'There's no one around.'

'No . . .' he mammered.

'Please?'

Miserable, Nigel kissed her. Her little lips were bouncy,

as if unused, except perhaps in a religious fashion (he wasn't sure how). Nigel wondered, kissing her again, if his lips felt the same. He wondered if he looked as pug-ugly to her as he did to himself when he kissed the mirror at home. She looked *naughty*. Close up her eyes looked bluely, manically . . . naughty.

She led him to the nearest gravestone. They sat amongst the little yellow flowers.

(The gravestone read, *My Loving Nestor 1925–1947. Why did you eat that banana?*)

'Nigel,' Sister Anna told him, 'I am not a nun. Don't think of me as a nun.'

'Then why do you dress like that?'

'No!' She placed his right hand on her groin. 'I mean I am a nun but I'm a human first. A woman.'

'That's not the way it goes, is it?'

'It is when you give it up. Do you want me?'

'Huh?'

'Look, feel how much I want you, Nigel. I could pin you to this gravestone and fuck your eternal soul free of its moorings if you just said the word.'

'And what's the word?'

'*Yes!*'

'Remind me not to say that word.'

The cemetery gates had been locked for an hour now. She had forced him back across the gravestone. The word 'banana' burnt itself into his memory for ever. Would he be raped by this nun? She was stronger than she looked. His traitorous body adored her hands. She hadn't yet touched his penis, but he knew that when she did – soon – he would not be able to resist. His breathing was ragged, his body tense; he was ecstatic, and as wretched as he'd ever been.

Abruptly, she stopped. She collapsed across his chest and made the strangest sound, a zizzing, like a persimmon in a fire. Then, more conceptually, 'Fuck, fuck, fucking fuck the fuck, fuck . . .'

It went on for a while.

He held her and whispered drivel to her while she cried. Her muscles felt like whipcord and steel. She must swim, he thought, imagining lanes of nuns free-styling in their capes, veils and multiple caps . . .

Gradually, her sobs passed. They remained so for a while: he seated awkwardly, she sprawled, her breathing so deep and even that he wondered if she might have fallen asleep.

'Anna?' It sounded loud in the graveyard. 'Anna,' he whispered, 'don't worry, I won't ever tell anyone about this. Nothing.'

She rolled over, fixing him with glistening eyes. 'What? I don't give a shit about that. Don't think of me as a nun. Never. I'm not a nun!'

'You already said that,' Nigel told her, mildly.

'I know. But I'm *not* a nun. I'm really – not a nun.'

He could not believe her. She'd attended nine months of lectures and tutorials in a habit. Beads, piles of fabric, cross, funny hat – the whole schtick. True, she didn't live in a college, so she wouldn't have to eat or watch telly or (possibly) sleep as a nun.

An ugly thought occurred to him, one he couldn't help but visualise, to his chagrin. Perhaps she dressed as a nun to get her rocks off. What a tawdry idea. He was ashamed of himself for thinking of it. Yet it might well be the truth.

He stared appalled into her big wet eyes as if he could extract information through them direct.

'What? What are you staring at?' Anna demanded.

This brought on Nigel's worst stuttering fit ever. Worse than the time Jeffery Snelling had exploded all those rabbits with penny bangers and tried to blame it on him. Worse than the time he'd been cast in *Mary Poppins*. The words rushed up his chest and found a log-jam in his throat, his tongue squirmed like a buckshot slug to no avail. *Perhaps my head will explode*, he thought.

Anna's consternation grew worse as she watched his face redden.

Nigel began to make wheezing noises. He waved his hands about, almost clocking Anna one as she struggled back to a sitting position.

'What's wrong?' asked Anna, taking him by the shoulders.

She was covered in spittle. He moaned and gave up, collapsing disconsolately backward on to locked arms.

Anna did not let go. 'What — is what you want to say connected with that I told you about not being a nun?' she asked.

Nigel nodded.

Anna guessed. 'Do you disapprove of it in some way?'

Nigel said nothing.

'You do,' said Anna, dismally. 'I've wrecked everything,' she sighed. 'I'll tell you why I did it. I did it for you, Nigel Donohoe.'

The night had begun to set in in earnest. The magic of the unimaginably huge made tiny penetrated both their glooms: the stars soothed. They let her talk. They let him listen. Side by side, the pair sat facing the vast black bowl instead of one another.

'See, when I rolled up for orientation day I'd just been in a car accident and I was shaken up, speeding. I guess I shouldn't have been there, but I was pretty idealistic and I thought it was important.

'Anyway, I seemed to see you every place I went. You were doing all the same courses as me. You never noticed me? But I thought you — you were the most spunky thing I'd ever laid eyes on. I couldn't stop staring. I started to follow you around. It was almost *spooky* that you never noticed me? Because I never made much of an attempt at hiding myself. In fact that was the only thing that kept me from speaking to you, at first. It was like I was invisible?

'Then I heard you speak. You don't remember me? I was standing right beside you at the time. There was a maggot or something in your lasagne and you wanted to return it. You hardly got a word out, you were so nervous, and I watched the cafeteria staff's heads turn, then the eyes of the woman you were speaking to . . .

'After that I couldn't face you. I know it's dumb. I dunno why – I suppose I thought it would break my heart or something if I spoke to you and you tried and couldn't speak back to me. Remember, I *was* all shocked-out from the car accident – you know, adrenalin, and although it wasn't serious, intimations of mortality. Huh.

'So I was taking things pretty damn seriously. All the way home on the tram and then the train and right through the night I mulled it over. I couldn't sleep. Not even masturbation helped – as a matter of fact it only made me think of you more.

'Well. Anyhow, it was early in the morning, must have been two a.m., when I came up with what I thought was the perfect scheme. I didn't want to come on anywhere near as strong as I felt about you. I wanted to strike up a purely platonic relationship at first, and the nun's outfit was the perfect thing. Anyway, my flatmate, Maryanne, helped me make the outfit and concoct a background and that, and she thought it was a bit of a joke, although she disapproved of it, really. And then a weird thing happened.

'I thought I'd just take a couple of weeks and get to know you and eventually reveal all, sort of, and we'd have a laugh about it, but when I wanted to approach you – I couldn't! It was like the cozzie had taken over, the cross and the *guimpe* and so on, as though, I dunno, my motives were wrong. Not pure, like. I mean I'm not even a Catholic! My mum'd have a fit if she knew.

'After a while I couldn't just not wear the cozzie without any explanation. I got myself in a knot. I thought up all sorts of stuff. When I actually did speak to you, if that didn't start something I was gunna speak to a couple of tutors, tell them

I was undergoing a spiritual crisis (well I was), tell them I needed to take a holiday, then leave. When I came back I wouldn't be a nun any more. And I'd come back to you as a – as a human being.

'I suppose I'll have to do that now.

'I don't know. I fucked it up. It all came out at once, months of holding back . . .

'I wanted to do so much for you, be so much for you.

'Now I can't be anything for you, can I?

'I didn't think so.'

She hadn't given Nigel any time to answer. She'd forgotten about his stutter, perhaps. Not that he'd tried to speak, for a time. What she had done out of love for him would rob anyone of words. Either she was a *great* actress, or she was telling the truth. She had dressed in a hot, unpractical, ridiculous outfit, forgone a heap of behaviour natural for a young woman – possibly she had gotten into all sorts of complications with her friends and family – for him. Nigel Donohoe.

Nobody had even blushed for him before, let alone done a thing remotely like this. He felt as though his brain had turned into week-old avocado dip, with a crust on top, so if someone were to poke the top of his head with a tortilla chip they'd wind up with a nasty mess on their shirt. And when that idea passed, he felt his whole body was hollow, windy, and what mattered in him was shrinking to a point somewhere below his chest. Was this what death would be like? He felt the node of his self concentrate into a hunger and shrink past that until it was the size of a peanut, no, more like a pistachio, the kind from which you can never remove the shell without smashing it.

Funny to think of it that way, his soul: a salty-shelled green nut.

Lucky thing for Nigel it didn't shrink any further, or he would have had a truly cosmic experience, perhaps as a poppy-seed.

As it was, he did have a revelation of sorts. Later, he wasn't sure whether his partial cure was connected with his altered state. But, he decided, even if he hadn't been cured it was still nice to know.

His revelation was this: for most of his life, Nigel had not inhabited all of his body. Now that he'd practically parted from it into a state of pistachiosity, he could sense the parts he'd departed from were not as large as his body. In other words, he'd always thought of himself as smaller than he really was.

Two police horses passed the cemetery wall. (Either that, or two extremely tall policemen were walking past going, 'Clip-clop'.) Gradually Nigel returned. Seeing as Nigel resembled a chicken whacked by a spade, Anna sat sadly gazing at the stars for a time.

He suddenly said:

'You were asking what you might do for me.'

She turned to him. With the caps and bands off, her hair was downy and peroxided.

'There is something we can do together, something very pleasant for both of us which we won't regret,' Nigel told her.

He had no stutter.

This wasn't unknown, but it had grown worse with university and his sexual torments once a week with the therapist didn't help a bit. Now, though, here, in a difficult situation which had aroused intense emotions, he should be clucking and spitting and twitching like a nudist in a hailstorm!

'What's that? What can we do together, Nigel?' She never did notice he'd lost his impediment.

'We could be good friends.'

In his prison cell, Nigel recalled how the idea had panned out. Her feeling for him had cured his stutter, by a kind of shock process. Pistachio treatment. In the unlit chilly night's confinement Nigel looked up (might as well look there as anywhere) and smiled. 'Thank you, Anna,' he whispered.

The two of them had spent half the night in the cemetery, much of it with Anna in tears. She would not accept 'just being friends', as she put it. He put it other ways. Anna, before they parted, agreed.

'I've got to, don't I? Can't very well rape you.'

A week later she left the university.

Nigel received one postcard from her:

Dear Nigel,
I'm really glad that
we went through what
we did together. I have
grown as a person a lot
as a result. This postcard
is just so you won't get too worried about me. Because
I know you would. I don't think I can get a friendship
with you to really work. It'd drive me nuts. I shall always
remain,
*your loving sister, Anna*XXXXXXXXXXXXXXXXXXXX
                                    XXXXXXXXXXXX

There was a picture of a penguin on the other side.

Nigel thought of her in his prison cell, thought, *I'll die a virgin, and I needn't have.* That galled him. His death did not seem real, but his virginity – he could get a firm hold on it.

For the first time without coercion, muttering or bafflement, he prayed.

Then he continued to ponder his history on earth. He turned his existence over, and over. Luckily, it filled more than the hours of darkness. Otherwise he would have been really peeved.

Eight

The Goatee in the Machine

A cock crew. Although Nigel had little doubt that he'd be sentenced to death this morning, the rooster's obnoxious harping filled him with a sense of universality, a love of all things, large or small, cute and cuddly or obscenely prune-faced, covered in feather-dust, mites, lice, bad-tempered and not even fit for eating.

Staying up all night can seriously warp your judgement.

Throughout Nigel's furry cheese and stale bread and tainted water breakfast the cock maintained its strangulated screech. Nigel didn't care. He kept his mind on the prospect of seeing Catherine Samuelson again. If she had thought about it overnight and went for Nigel's story instead of Todd's simple proofs via bruises and head-bumps he might have a chance. Not much of a chance. But even roosters could strut and gasbag in the promise of a new day and they were psychotic and disgustingly scaly. So Nigel could at least try to hope.

Why they had brought him here a good two hours before proceedings began, he did not know. But now Todd was here things would surely get going soon. Nigel sat listening to the rooster, staring at Todd. Todd qualified as a disgustingly scaly creature; his shoulders were white with particles of scalp: they cascaded down the triceps which threatened to pop seams, they covered his knees in a chronic blizzard, the ears poking elegantly from beneath the wig looked so full it was a wonder he could hear. The only place they did not infest was his beard, an oiled and brushed refuge from this scalp revolt.

Nigel sat astonished that someone so vain could tolerate head-rot as repugnant. It hadn't been as bad yesterday . . . perhaps they dabbed it on him for court. In heavy manacles and leg-irons, Nigel's love of everything was springing leaks. He sat on a crate, placed thoughtfully in the prisoner's box, branded on the one side with *British Nuclear Fuels, plc*, which made Nigel worry about bottom cancer until he read on the other side, *Your Peat from the Empire's Nucleus*.

He tried to keep his mind on a simple, at least fractionally credible version of the story he had told Catherine. He looked up eagerly each time he heard footsteps. It was never her.

The cock remained in as strong a voice as ever. Or there were several roosters working to a rota. It began to scrape Nigel's sleepless nerves. His love for everyone drained completely away. His back itched. Sharp nips in the armpits and pubis convinced him he'd picked up fleas – at least – from the cell. *Where* was Catherine Samuelson? Surely she had to show, as a witness. Irritably, Nigel cast around the courtroom.

It was an airy place. Its panels appeared new, light and polished, possibly of some European wood. Its windows were high, and while none too flat were clear enough, when not illustrated with mythical beasts and faces, to catch the gorgeous day outside. This was the kind of room which took filling to muffle a footstep's resonance, coughs and whispers. It was nearly empty today. Robbery and attempted rape must be common in this Australia. On the pew-like benches which went back a dozen rows to beneath the gallery, eight people sat. One was asleep.

Catherine Samuelson didn't turn up. Didn't look as if she would. On the other hand, the trial wasn't about to begin soon either. Todd, after settling himself on the bench, unfolded a yellowed, large-printed newspaper. He snapped it open and turned the pages with some ritual. A clerk dusted the dandruff off each page. Nigel read, 'HITLER STILL DEAD, SAYS PRINCE OF SOUTH AFRICA.' None of the articles was more than three lines long and none made any more sense than the headline.

The bailiff seemed to be boring for crude in his brain via his nose with one thick finger. Nigel was transfixed by the way his hooter moved around on his face like jelly under the violent finger-agitation. Then the bailiff uncrossed his eyes and caught Nigel's stare. He peered sternly back, indicating that as the Sovereign's Representative here it was his duty to fish for green globs. And perhaps it was, Nigel thought. The studiously inefficient manner here might have been lifted whole from elsewhere; it had the air of a bad copy of ossified traditions.

He guessed he would never know.

The cock gave up its throttled yodelling. Nigel breathed relief. Then it began again. Its rhythm was relentless. Nigel, past annoyed, began to imagine it announced his coming doom. It nauseated him slightly. He sighed again and, as much as he dared, sat back on his crate, breathing deeply of the dust-and-leather courtroom fug.

The minute he told himself Catherine had not felt as sympathetic as she'd looked, that he'd nurtured a mere flicker in those speckly blue eyes until it was something a sister or a lover might have given, soft as honey in the sun, the minute he wrote off her beauty as a trick of the light, she entered.

Maybe he wouldn't have fallen in love with her had he not been in the dock. He wasn't really in love now, just struck a glancing blow by an ocean liner. A part of him knew, yet it also knew today might be his final look at lunch-time and so it made that knowledge small, about the size of the gherkin you leave in the jar till last, and it sat the jar in the back of his mind, near the memories of watching clothes tumble in the laundromat. Nigel took mercy upon himself and called this the love of his life. He swooned.

Thus Catherine looked radiant. In fact, she did. Her cheeks glowed, shiny and round. Her breasts heaved powerfully. Her hair had come adrift, and lay about her right ear in a pile. She had been running.

For me! thought Nigel. For me.

He watched her halt, force herself to measure her steps toward her brother, and continue up the aisle with her chin pulled down. Soon she'd look up at him. Hers was the sort of face which seems alert even in sleep; her high-arched brows and rapid colour and sudden neck all spoke ardently.

To get Catherine's attention, he coughed. And again. This tickled his throat, sending him hacking and spluttering for some minutes. He must have caught some chill in the cell.

Well good luck pneumonia. She did not look up. Catherine had reached for her brother and the two whispered emphatically, her broad back to him. Nigel hadn't a hope of overhearing because just then the man asleep in the third row chose to snore. Heads turned. People giggled. The noises reverberated around the room.

At last Todd said, exasperated, 'Very well, my dear.'

Catherine straightened. She passed Todd a letter. Nigel knew she could feel his eyes on her back. She had come to plead for him but she couldn't let the townsfolk know. She loved him as he loved her. He might be sentenced to gaol for a while in spite of her testimony but she would visit him – oh, he could see her, clothed modestly in sombre colours before the bars, a lone sunbeam dappling one eye and the tears held there bravely until she walked away. She'd bring him a pie, a tin of biscuits, tobacco (although he did not smoke, he would for her), a blanket; and he, he would write her poems with the pencil-nub lent by a sympathetic guard, a verse for every square inch of that beautiful freckled skin, the deepest, saddest thoughts he'd ever think. And when at last he was let go, blinking into the dew-filled springtime, they would weave the tight embrace that had burgeoned in his long and solitary hours; he would kiss away her tears, her sweet and almost fragrant tears, hardly salt at all; they would wander down a road through wildflower carpets, toward the rising sun.

The words *for ever after* actually made their way across his fevered mind on a kind of magic carpet of the soul.

Someone nudged the stertorous gent in the third row. The cockerel tag-team had finally clocked off for the day. A lustrous silence seemed to rule for a second, into which Nigel sighed, an extended romantic near-warble. And Catherine turned.

Nigel's magic carpet developed threadbare bits, reeled, caught on the rusty nail of reality, spun and flopped, a pile of lint before the cruel machine of Justice.

One look from Catherine did this.

Fire reigned there. Hate. Betrayal. Unmistakably. But how had he betrayed her? She could not mean it. He searched for a spill of compassion from behind those eyes, but found not a sausage. Not a gnawed bone of pity. She had not come to plead for him, she had come to testify against him. She tore her gaze from his as one would avoid porn or a politician.

It drew a cry of pain from Nigel. A surge of dizziness. He fell forward on to the body-polished wooden rail, his crate dropped from under him on to its side. When he sat back into his despair he sat, appropriately enough, on nothing. He wound up inside the box, queasy, staring through the dock's wooden bars as Catherine strode back down the length of the room.

Out.

He grew aware of a large weight on his shoulder. It was the bailiff's snotty hand by his cheek. He looked up at the face grinning beneath the fancy red fez, and puked.

It was a short trial. Nigel's only experience in a real court was when he had witnessed an accident caused by Mario Denuncio's duck on Punt Road (yes, the court had found the duck had done it), but this was unlike any court he had heard about, barring an African tribal meeting in which the gods spoke through members in a trance-state. It began with an elaborate prayer led by Todd, who moved through the aerobic gestures perfunctorily whilst rattling off a series of questions-and-responses in some Middle-Eastern language. He then mumbled several phrases in Latin. Was he also a priest? Was England still Catholic? Some hybrid of several religions? In any case, if there had been no Reformation, was that why the Industrial Revolution had never come? Possibly they were both stifled by the same thing. The strange justice system and the second sacred language would support his hunch.

The snorer in the third row was roused completely now. He stood and tottered to the bench. He and Todd had a short conversation, during which various papers, including Catherine's letter, changed hands. A five-minute adjournment was called. Nobody moved.

Nigel had hoped for legal counsel. Toward the end of the break a bedraggled old man – greasy hair plastered across his pate, toes peeping from his boots, and owner of the most convolutedly crooked nose Nigel had met – shuffled wheezing down the central aisle and up to the prisoner's box, where he grinned toothlessly and lopsidedly at Nigel. From deep in his rancid shirt a metal flask was produced. He proffered it to Nigel. Chest-hairs stuck to it.

Everyone was grinning at him. The elderly snorer glanced up from his papers and nodded. Nigel smiled briefly. Another ancient ritual, filled with meaning he was sure nobody understood. He took the flask. It was silver, he saw, beneath the body-oil. He managed to unscrew it and sniffed its contents. Model-aeroplane glue. His nausea returned for a second. Since the court clearly expected him to drink, he raised it to his lips and lowered it.

The court applauded.

The old man snatched back the flask and shambled back down the aisle. It was as close as Nigel came to support for his case from the state.

As he had suspected, the man in the third row turned out to be the prosecutor. From an ornate hatbox he took a mask. Combined with a voluminous robe, the mask transformed him from limp frailty into whirling incandescence. His prosecution consisted of a reading of the charges, of Catherine's testimony – and a frenzy of stylised movements that made him either the greatest improviser of all time or a master of an intricate and rigorous discipline so accomplished it was impossible to fault. Naturally, knowing what the movements depicted would have helped. The branch of performance must have been so ancient that a twitch of the slender fingers or a wriggle of the elegant toe signified reams. Like in Balinese dance. There were gestures Nigel could identify. Sexual ones. Perhaps these referred to the rape Nigel was supposed to have attempted.

I'll never know, he thought.

This culture seemed very similar to one out of his own history, on the surface, but beneath it lay thousands of years of divergence. Nigel had tumbled to that much. As the prosecutor danced toward Todd, who swayed as if mesmerised by the stamps and claps and gyrations, his little pointed beard a metronome for the beat, Nigel regretted that he had blown his tourist chance here. He found himself humming along with the rest of the court's drone, thinking: Why? Why did I attack the coach to Melbourne, masked and armed, when it carried so little money and I was driven off before I could have my way with the woman?

What am I thinking?

He fought an impulse to leap to his feet and confess to his crimes. He was as mesmerised by the old man's dance as Todd. But why should it make him confess?

Well, the accusations sounded very convincing when read aloud in this manner.

Everyone is so sure I did it. Todd was so sure it was me he

kicked in Milton Keynes. For that matter, others in Milton Keynes had recognised him.

I did do it.

No, he told himself, shut up Nigel. But perhaps, in a way, everybody was right. Perhaps, like Todd, he had a double. *Or am I the wicked duplicate Nigel – was I born here?*

NO!

The dancing prosecutor bent over backwards, reaching some grand finale, in which Nigel was sure he was meant to contribute with his confession. How could he dance and speak as well? From side to side, the old man swayed his torso, brushing the polished floor with his fingertips. The pop-eyed mask he wore seemed less ferocious upside-down, the little golden people carved around its margins beckoned him. *Tell the truth*, they whispered, *it's the only way you'll save yourself.* Nigel leaned toward the gleaming fangs, the pulsing eyes, the muscular exaggeration of it. The mask's expression changed from warm and charitable to ruthless and stern, then back again, as the shadows of its features slipped across it. In its beauty he saw promise, of open fields and ripening crops, of hammocks by riversides and babies dandled on knees; in its ugliness he felt the crunch of the blade as it hacked through his neck, the eternity in darkness of the cell, he felt passers-by spit on his face as he hung at the crossroads, lifeless. Here was the mask of Justice, and he must answer it with Judgement from his own mouth.

He slipped towards confession.

The prosecutor finished his speech but not his dance:

'. . . and furthermore, the accused maintained he is from another world, where tiny men walk on the moon, and clothes may be cleaned without water. This is the testimony of Miss Catherine Samuelson, who has declined to appear today for fear of the accused, notwithstanding the irons binding him hand and foot. He is a desperate and dangerous lag. He has invented pathetic lies to cover his actions, and his punishment must be more severe for that. I plead with the court to pass the maximum sentence of tickling,

flogging, flaying, and hanging . . . NIGEL DONOHOE,
WHAT SAY YE TO THAT?'

The dancer fell quivering, twitching to the floor.

Nigel rose, opened his mouth to confess – and could not.
The dance had, at the same time as it offered the community's judgement of him, constrained him to the truth. His
thick lips stood open for a time, and at last the court hung
on his words. He wasn't sure he could say anything.

'I am not guilty!' he shouted hoarsely, at last.

The court made as much furore as a dozen men can.

Where people are either good or bad and the bad are
obvious you'd think the courts would be filled with decent
people. A part of decency is to do something for the safety of
others. In our society we all face the dilemma of what we
can best do for our planet. Generations as they emerge
yowling into the sunlight find themselves concerned with
everything that's wrong. Faced with so many dire situations, each with interlocking and confusing arguments
world-wide, a lot throw up their hands and give in. For
those of us who did not give up, the biological necessities of
growing older offer us two alternatives: we make a
profession of our virtuous efforts or we confine ourselves to
smaller efforts such as living as correctly as we can and
bringing up our children in a world improved by our
example. Either way we may be sucked into the hypocrisy of
compromising our earlier efforts in order to get on.

You would think that in a world where you could tell the
nice from the not-nice by feeling for bumps, where no
amount of moral argument championed by think-tanks or
novels or academics could convince us that Einstein was a
chicken, or a dog's other leg doesn't scratch in sympathy, or
that lawlessness offered freedom of choice – you would
think here people would not be accused falsely, or if they
are, not convicted, or if that, not sentenced viciously.

Nigel thought so.

Not immediately, of course; he hadn't thought through
his mild conclusions about this other Australia. As soon as

he was sentenced, though, with the dull weight of Todd's words upon his head and shoulders, his spine and scrotum, he clicked to the strangeness beyond his personal wronging. He had not thought, after the prosecutor's truth-extracting dance, that he would be 'turned off'. He had bested the wild face of tribal justice, still alive within the stale rituals of the court. Surely everyone believed in the mask's power? Todd had been every bit as entranced as Nigel. Hadn't his beard waggled? He *knew* Nigel had spoken the truth when he had denied the charge. And yet Todd had condemned him to – consigned him to –

It rushed in upon Nigel: what was a sewerage slug-sucker like Todd doing at the heart of the local justice machine in Milton Keynes? He was plainly a hypocritical rat of the first water! If evil always had bumps here this one had bumps on his bumps. Like the Todd back home he pretended light and life while really enjoying backyard sadism. Although he mouthed the sixties stuff about an ounce of dope a lentil burger and thou, he'd chop your fingers off if he caught them near his stash. He reserved the right to subtly torture his girl-friend Melinda because dabbling in the forbidden meant progress. He reserved the right to moral dodginess in the name of a new and ill-informed age. The Todd Samuelson here was merely writ large: his had a moustache, this one a goatee. And bumps meant nothing or Todd would have shown some and never become a judge. He had softened the sentence because Nigel had managed not to condemn himself, but he almost certainly had an erection when he announced the punishment.

So what did it mean when in a world like this an out-and-out bastard could sentence an obviously harmless dill like Nigel to be hung by the neck until he was dead?

(Not only that, Nigel would be whipped, two hundred lashes, beforehand.)

It meant the bad guys had their hands on the levers.

Nine

The End of Whatchamacallit

'Yer gunna die.'

Nigel said nothing.

'I said: yer gunna die. Perish. Kark it.'

'I know that.'

'So yez won't want the bracelet.'

'Hay?'

'That bracelet. You won't want it, give us it.'

'What if I don't?' Nigel looked up from his watch.

The gaoler shrugged. 'I'll get it after, prob'ly. But I'll have to fight the *tooky* for it.'

'Hay?'

'The tooky. You know. From the court.'

'No I don't know.'

'You know,' the gaoler explained slowly, impatiently, 'the bloke did the Dance of Solemn for yez in court.' He shook his head. 'Still pretending to be thingy, cracked ay? Yer gunna die anywar – why keep it? Yer body'll rot away, the flesh'll go like jelly and bugs and maggots'll fill yer up, eatin' at yer eyes and lips and comin' out ya nose –'

'Stop it.'

'– and o' course yer dick and balls are nice and juicy for them, they munch up yer whats—'

'Stop it!'

'You cause a fuss ya know an' I just call the trooper and you get lashes on the spot.'

Nigel stared at the gaoler.

It was one of the most beautiful afternoons Nigel had ever

seen. This was probably another ancient ritual, like the tooky's dance, that Nigel should be bound hand and foot to a huge lump of granite by a stream a league out of town. The journey here had seemed stilted, part of a routine. They must do a lot of these, thought Nigel. He sat in the shade of a colossal river red gum provided with food and water and wine, good food for a change. While this night ritual seemed like a ridiculously easy situation from which to escape – had he any friends – he had noticed several armed troopers at the edges of the clearing; and of course as the gaoler had pointed out, each had a cat-o'-nine-tails.

'So go and get him,' said Nigel.

The gaoler turned to go. Nigel's pulse thudded in his head, he stuck his hands in his pockets. You may have hidden reserves, he told himself without conviction, some way of coping with the pain. The gaoler's steps across the dry gum-leaves sounded like a forest fire to Nigel.

The gaoler stopped, and turned back. 'Ah,' he said. 'You don't wanna be like that.'

'Yes I do,' Nigel told him, his voice high and quavering. 'It's a pretty low thing even for this god-forsaken place to want to rob a condemned man of his possessions. I'd rather be whipped.' Nigel turned away. The stream rippled over weedy rocks. Sand-trout (*Pseudaphritis urvilli*) flicked over the gravel, their thin shadows rippling behind them.

'Ah. I was olnly somethinorother, jokin', mate. It's – part of the tradition round here to have a nasty joke or two before the dance.'

'The dance?'

The gaoler grinned and mimed: spinning gruesomely with his head to one side, he jigged.

Oh. The dance was the hanging. His. So that was what the woman in the bar had meant. And what else had she said? He couldn't recall now. It didn't matter.

'A tradition,' said Nigel. He turned back to the stream.

'Yep.' The gaoler stepped around Nigel, bobbed low to

catch his eye, and smiled. So far in this world, only Todd and Catherine (damn them both) had shown him perfect teeth. And now the gaoler. He said, full of smarm: ''Course – if yer gunna give that bracelet as a parting *gift* to anyone, I'd appreciate it.' He skipped spryly out of Nigel's reach and sat beside him, a little further downstream. 'Lovely spot f'yer last one.'

'Mm.' Nigel sat also.

The stream rushed by.

His name was Clarry. What made Nigel wonder about this world was not the oddnesses – he now expected things to be different, that was just one more veil torn from his eyes – it was the similarities. It was easier to communicate with this man than it had been with the Serbs because Clarry's English was better, marginally. But he wouldn't answer Nigel's fairly basic questions. He had to convince the man he really did believe he was from another universe first, and was not simply pretending he was gaga in some misguided hope of a reprieve. After a rerun of the story he'd told Catherine and the Serbs he looked into Clarry's eyes and, seeing a twinkle in the pale hazel, almost gave up.

Then he had an inspiration. What had he to lose?

'Refrigerator,' he said.

'Hay?' said Clarry.

'REFRIGERATOR!' he shouted. Nigel rolled his eyes so far back in his head it nauseated him.

'Ha.' Clarry lay back against his side of the tree, next to a line of red bull ants, scratched the white beard that sprang from his jaw-line alone, pulled his cap forward over his bald head, and snuggled down as if to sleep.

'This malignant bread dough comes pebbling dried moss in my bird-bath, on the fevered lipstick arrangement,' Nigel explained, anecdotally. 'Rhapsody, I wrinkled them! Will you marry me? Rhapsody! You bowl a karma riot and some geek dibbles your coal-mice door as streamlined

as you like. But it's latent salamander time in the hoosegow,
if you ask me.'

'Huh?'

Nigel was careful not to look at Clarry, but out of the
corner of one eye he saw the gaoler sit up to watch, breaking
into a smile.

'Parsifal Redsox bought me a conundrum, which I bleat
and bleat till I was Charlie Chaplined,' said Nigel, as though
honoured. 'I shimmied down my prerequisite tomato, so the
swordtail slept in my thigh. Super-ego *now*, saggital
gymnast! Plant snowflake regattas with me.' Nigel tugged
on his chains, careless of the chafing at his wrists and ankles.
'Better frizz a vegetable wisdom than inseminate inscrutable
pillar-boxes. The graces of timid sunlight lollipops patter us
all, pert sieve. Pert, pert, sieve!' He waved to a passing
blowfly as he might to a good friend. 'Seventh laundry fluff!'
he yelled passionately.

He had all the gaoler's attention now, but he really didn't
give a snip. Snared in his own invention, he struggled to his
knees, baying at the rock he was chained to and begging its
forgiveness for having polished bald heads. 'Winter gardens
were my sole preservative!' he explained. 'Martyrs to the
talk-show of rabbits, pilchards of joy . . . I WENT OVER-
BOARD INTO THE KINDNESS ONLY *SEALS* WILL
GIVE!' he cried.

Real emotion caught him as he crawled on top of the
rounded boulder. Awkwardly, he straight-armed himself to
a crouch. The chains reached just high enough for Nigel to
clasp his hands together above his head. He told the tree:
'You know my aunt once died of jazz–rock fusion. I
couldn't mourn her, really, she was left-handed most of the
time with me, and a real cunt for the rest. I only candied
aviators as a diversion, at first, it was when I found my
fortune I became addicted. They say that Tuesday corrupts
absolutely – well, I had pearls lined up on the mantelpiece
gorilla, blim blam blom. My mother liked a drop herself
when she felt a case of the parking inspectors coming on. I

don't know. It's municipal. You try your hardest to milk the mice every morning and what do you get? Flares. It isn't as if I didn't *vote* or something, I elected my whole body every morning like it or not, it's just –'

Nigel saw a ribald purple light everywhere. It was nowhere near sunset. He toppled sideways off the stone.

'Oof! – just evening-time that gets me, with its vibrant economies and union leaders coming home to roost in the caucuses. Every time I slip a gargoyle I regret it. Every time I snigger in the trees. Please don't sublime me the everlasting advisory positions on women's affairs. I personify you, please. I am, as I told you, a poor waistcoat in the service of the twin-tub . . .'

He raved on. It was out of control now. Scrabbling to his feet on the dry gum-leaves, stones and furious ants, Nigel brought one foot to his mouth and did his best to shove it in. It was irresistible. As if this were a signal the horizon flared an unnatural lilac which made the trees across the river into spindly silhouettes. A fizzing began in his ears, like the amateur efforts of a thousand crazed CB operators devoted to static. It was an extreme version of what he'd felt when he had awakened in shock in the cemetery with the Serbs. But now his limbs felt too large, and responded to this by shrinking. The gaoler's voice seeped through the fizz now and then from a distance. Then the lilac faded toward its centre and in the clear patch there appeared stars.

Thousands of the bastards. A hole might have been punched through the atmosphere. The sun might have set in that spot alone, except a part of Nigel knew there were still hours to dusk. A further, deeper blackness spread from the middle of the stars. And then, partly obscured by trees, Nigel saw it.

Civilisation, he thought.

It was the Excelsior Hotel.

It was huge. Its lights glowed kindly on to the road before it. A fight raged inside. Even that seemed kindly. The door opened and a man was (kindly) thrown into the darkness.

Like the space-ark of a benevolent race of beer-swilling aliens come to rescue him from the gallows, the Excelsior drifted above the horizon, huge and – kindly.

For a brief and truly insane moment Nigel, dreamy-headed fish-keeping drop-out, faced a violent *conviction* that he would be rescued from the lash and rope set for dawn, by his local watering-hole. Not via pot-bellied aliens but maybe by the two skinheads who had tried to mug him, or someone else with a little kindness in their soul. He could *feel* the crusty vomit-coloured carpet underfoot, *smell* the hoppy-pissy tang of the place, *see* the orange laminex table-tops scattered about in the lime-painted lounge. Mick, the barman, calmly stuck his fingers into glasses and whisked them out of the way of colliding bodies, waiting for the cops to pull up outside in a divvy van. Nobody but Arris had his shirt tucked in. All the women were down the Club playing bingo. Nigel had raved on till this point but now his lips moved for a moment and gave up the ghost; he was breathless and much more than homesick.

A cloud slipped between Nigel and the sun. A wind rose up off the creek and died. The Excelsior Hotel, a place he'd always despised, faded backward into the blackness bringing a pain like rope-burn in his heart, which, as the blackness was replaced by stars and the stars by lilac glow, faded as well. No aliens, no skinheads, not even Buttercup the Labrador. By the time ordinary (harsh) blue sky was back the little cloud over the sun had moved on and the breeze had dropped, and Nigel's pain was a blunt certainty:

The next morning everything he knew and felt would be gone.

He discovered himself on his feet by the stone with chained wrists held up as if hoping against hope for the hotel to return and break his bonds by some side-effect of the fight, perhaps a chair thrown, or an ashtray.

It didn't come back. He didn't really hope it would. What did they call such hysteria? Denial? Whatever it was he shoved it towards the mess at the back of his memory; it had passed, and Nigel stood a step closer to death.

Afterwards, the gaoler gave him no problems with simple-minded questions. He'd answer the silliest things earnestly, respectfully. He had seen nothing in the air above the trees; he was a little afraid of the intensity in Nigel's eyes during the private experience.

Nigel thought little more of the episode. Why should he pain himself when this was the end? It didn't matter if he was cracked, he'd be dead soon, equal to everyone who had ever died.

Lucky, ay.

Apart from a few timid questions from Clarry about how often he had such thingamybobs, when did they begin and so forth, he forgot about it. Simple as that.

'Youze like a bit of a dance then?' asked Clarry.

'Dancing? Oh – you mean do I like to see a hanging? Never really did it back home. We don't go in for that kind of thing.'

'Nah. I mean dance dancing. You know!'

'Oh. Well, we do go in for that, but I never. Bit of jumping about on me own when I was really pissed. No. Nobody really wants to dance with a face like mine.'

'Like what?'

'Cratered and so on. I used to have bad acne.'

'Thought it was the pox.' He peered at Nigel, his eyes twinkling for the sake of it. So close, he smelt vaguely of potatoes. 'Now ya mention it, it doesn't look like the pox, either.'

'Have you had the pox?'

'Thank Baal, no.'

'Don't have it any more where I come from.'

'Ah yeah. Good one.'

'No really! We get vaccinated against it when we're little. See?' He rolled up his grimy, tattered sleeve.

'So ya have had the pox?' Clarry leaned across the tree-trunk and poked the small scar on Nigel's arm.

'Sort of. I think what they do is they have a really weak strain of it and they give it to you. You get one scab but after that you're immune.'

'They give it to yez.'

'The bug. It's caused by a little – a very tiny bug too small to see, and they put a dead one in so your body's got the chance to work out ways to kill it, to cure itself.'

'I don't get how they catch the little bastards if they can't see them, but it does make a sort of sense in a cack-handed way.'

'What do your doctors do?'

Clarry laughed, a fruity snorfle. 'They used to steam ya.' He rubbed his heavy brow with one thick hand. 'But now they have crystals. If it's not one thing it's another.'

'You swallow a crystal.'

He cackled. He mimed trying to stuff an apple-sized rock into his mouth, and cackled some more at his own vaudeville. 'Yer not the olnly one that can act crazy y'know.' He gave a shy smile.

When Nigel didn't react Clarry said, 'Didn't mean to offend yez,' surprisingly gentle. 'Sorry.'

'Don't think about it,' Nigel told him. 'I'm not. What do they use the crystals for? How do they work?'

'I used to know them things. Used to be up on all the bulldust. Believe it or not I was a philosopher m'self, before I enlisted. Chemical philosopher. How they work, I will prob'ly never know now. But they use them for everything. Fashionable, I hear, in Londinium. That's all medical philosophy is, ay – fashion?'

'Not where I come from.'

'Mm. Anywar, it used to be a heresy for the rich (we have other heresies), people were burnt at the stake for putting one under a sick man's pillow. But there are so many heresies these days, olnly ones that whosiwhatsit do yez harm, get you fried.'

'Hang on. Are you a Catholic?'

'Mate, isn't everyone? Anywar, the crystals are supposed to focus yer prayers or summat. First, all the crystals were from the Holy Land. Now they come from anywheres. Still expensive, the best ones. Most people perfer the traditional cures to cheap Korean imitations. My mother . . .'

Clarry went on.

It made sense that the Church of England had never broken away. Everything he'd seen pointed to a vast sponge-like church. But why should there be heresies when the church was so accommodating, so – catholic? He broke into Clarry's rave to ask. The question stopped the old philosopher dead. He'd been humouring a madman, he thought: the naïve quality of Nigel's query almost convinced him of Nigel's story, you could see it on the man's weathered face. Blinking, stunned.

Clarry scratched his bald head, examined the dead skin beneath his finger-nail, and answered.

'I dunno anythin' about history mate, but it's plain to everyone what happened since Pope Caligula. Well, if you wanna get technical, between Pope C. and Mohammed the Conciliator there's still a steady process of absorbin' and jiggermacallit, see. But after that, pfft –' he cast a token glance over either shoulder as if an inquisitor were holed up in the tree '– the church is full of crooks.'

'How can that happen? In the church they'd be found out, wouldn't they?'

'Get out of it. The *good* stand out like dog's balls. I reckon there've been good popes and bad but *I've* never seen a good pope. I've never seen a pope, mind yer. Then again, y'don't haveta. They haven't lasted long since the big M, though, so there's always the idea in people's scones that the next one'll be orright. Maybe it's happened. Regular. See, the church is the spot where ya scumbags and ya holy men get together to do battle. Always has been.'

'They don't last long because it becomes obvious to everyone they're evil once they get into power.'

'Yep. But olnly then.'

'And they declare things heretical.'

'Yep. Reason I got out of chemical philosophy. Any result they don't like – boof. It's the end of whatchamacallit. Just when I'd think I was gettin' somewheres – boof. Some ideas pop up by accident and spread before the boofheads can give 'em the stomp, like when yer plasticky muck was invented by yer mad washerwoman in a tar-pit. But they're hen's teeth. You can't do science like that. Might as well pack it in, I thought. So many schools o' thought and every one of 'em competing for the church's favour. You never know where you stand. Different lot get fried with each change, caught with their retorts down, so's to speak. Till a pope gets promoted they're just another mullah or whatever so's you can't tell. What's happened, is the ones who do the selectin', the whoosisthingy, their numbers are usually stacked in favour of the military. And you know the military . . .'

'No. I don't.'

'Hmm. Everyone *else* knows – to be a good fightin' man you haveta be rotten. Now, they work out who's in charge by entirely different ways. Pure as the driven doodad. Good families and that. Trouble is, yer don't get on in a real war against real baddies like say the German SS unless you learn to be rotten.'

'I think there's similar pressures where I come from. But they don't corrupt your soul completely.'

'How's that? It's impossible isn't it?'

Nigel tried to think of a famous general who was decent. De Gaulle? Eisenhower? He didn't know enough about them. He did know the military had influenced science in his world, and that it wouldn't take much to tip the balance away from progress. His world might not be very much different to this one at all. 'You're right,' he admitted, yet the words didn't ring true. And perhaps he'd found the essential difference between his world and Clarry's. Hardly any statement rang completely true in Nigel's world.

Clarry examined Nigel's uncertain face, his own features definite in the sharp afternoon. In his book either your soul was corrupted or it was not. But the Todds of this world were not held by that book.

Those here who were held by the all-embracing church found a less exclusive and so more irresistible set of values than they did in Nigel's world of confusing diversity. Even those as apparently cynical as Clarry felt little temptation to exercise their imaginations to produce other ways of life. Nigel would have bet his life there were no novels here. The only transgressors in this world were committed to manipulating values to their own ends within the monolithic church and empire. Forget absurdity, laterality, forget all but religious art. To ordinary people such as Clarry, doubt equalled evil. It meant Clarry's change from chemical philosopher to gaoler must have been slow and painful. So did the adherence to a corrupted church come entirely because of an all-brands belief system or was this lack of doubt in some people genetic? He'd have to go over thousands of years of history and even then he'd never find out, no matter how much he quizzed Clarry. You couldn't read a world like a book, you lived it. Or died.

'You know I'm right,' said Clarry. 'Sure as the doohickey is purple.'

Nigel grilled him, but never did find out what in this case the doohickey was.

They chatted companionably through sunset and dinner. It was the first meal Nigel had enjoyed since his night with the Serbs. And it was the most nutritious meal he'd eaten since dinner at the Café Sport with his parents, two nights before he left home. They ate mutton stew, potatoes and leeks and a greasy gravy made tangy by herbs Clarry gathered across the creek. ('Don't run off now,' he said, and danced over on the slippery stepping-stones.) Piles of stew. As Nigel tucked into the chewy mass on the black plastic plate on his knees, Clarry knocked the bung out of a wine barrel. It proved thick, sharp, fruity as no other red Nigel had tasted – was it a peach with a hint of bubble-gum? – and strong.

Before the dregs of sun in the trees had vanished, Nigel and Clarry were drunk as senators. From then on the night felt like a view into a moving train, a series of vivid grabs of tenuously connected events from other people's lives.

The first must have been after they finished the cheese. Clarry got into his head that Nigel was a good bloke who didn't deserve to die and, swearing, he *heaved* at the granite to which Nigel was secured. The stumpy little fellow was strong. But his face went redder in the firelight, sweat beaded on his high brow, without a hint of success. Yet Clarry kept yelling, 'Think I got it then!' and, 'Whup! Just a little bit more, I reckon!' At last his grip failed and he tumbled backward down the creek-bank, bottom over bean, ending with a plonk! in the dark of the creek. He came stalking back wet into the firelight with a yabbie in his mouth, its claws drawing blood from his blobby nose. (Genus *Cherax*, and a fine crayfish it was too.) He had set it up of course, but he stood there looking disgusted all the same, dripping, while Nigel snorted uncontrollably.

'The universe thinks itself!' shouted Nigel, possibly after Clarry decided Nigel wasn't a murderer.

'Universe can't think,' asserted the gaoler with a swoop of the head across the fire. He had already burnt the right side of his beard away; some feeling had been taken by a 'spirit of iron' during an experiment eight years back, he'd told Nigel at some stage. 'WHAT'S TWO AND TWO?' he demanded of the smoke whirling into the darkness. 'See? No answer.'

Nigel went, 'Ha,' and so banged his head back against the tree. 'Th'universe is God because the Bible says God is omnipresent. Tha' means he's everywhere.' He rattled his chains, hands far apart. 'So are you sayin' tha' God doesn't *think*?'

'It doesn' say that in the Bible!'

'Bloody does.'

'Bloody doesn'!'

'Bloody fucken well does.'

'Bloody fucken shitten well fucken bloody nubba dinga whatsit fucken *doesn'*!'

'Nubba dinga?'

'My fucken oath.'

'You're sure?'

''Course I'm fucken sure. M'dad was a priest – useta know alla my bubble, every borin' bit – all by heart.'

'*All* of it?'

'Yep.'

'Either people here can do things we can't do any more, or you're not as stoopid as you look, Clarry.'

'I thank y'kindly.'

'All of it?'

'Every bit. Even the bits wrote by Shakespeare.'

'Shakespeare, ay? I guess that blows that one then.'

'Youze talk funny, Donohoe.'

'Talk fucken funny yourself, sport. It's okay. I understand ya.'

'There yer go again. "Okay," y'say. What's this, "okay", ay?'

'"Fine", it means, "fine, good, yeah, no fucken worries, budgie". Anyway. *You* talk funny. You put it on, don't ya. Can't fool me.'

Clarry hissed Nigel quiet, waving a hand. He fell on to his side and lay there, curled around the fire, looking up conspiratorially at Nigel's knee. 'I can speak as well as you can, old son. Better. One thing you learn in the colonies is if you speak like a woman you are treated like a woman. England's different. The struggle goes on there, and transportation's part of that, used by both sides and has been since Raleigh discovered America. It's what I said before.

The military. They run the show here. So you speak like them or you speak like me, but you don't speak like a holy English darling of the diocese. You – you speak strangely, but it's possible they won't hold your fancy turns against you.' He coloured: he had realised it wouldn't matter how Nigel spoke after dawn.

'Aaagh,' he said, pushing himself up on one elbow. 'I've talked m'self sober – this's no good. I wish yez could get me a drink, old son. I'd unchain yez in a minute if I had the keys. Yer a good sort. Yer – yer *olkay*.' He scrambled to his feet. ''Nother drink?'

Nigel drained his plastic mug. 'Why not?' he said.

'Exactly,' said Clarry. 'Why the fuck not.'

Nigel put his arm around Clarry. The poor old bugger was inconsolable. Tears tripped one over the other in their eagerness to find refuge in what remained of his beard. His big head hung low. His shoulders quivered in sympathy with the sobs in his chest. He pounded the granite beside him with every second word. '. . . And he didn' even let me see her when she died!' He shook his head like a bear covered in bees. He sniffled. 'He knew it was wrong. Better 'an anyone else, he knew. A boy has gotta get his goodbye in t'his mum, his old mum, when she goes . . . I hated him. I wanted to kill him that night but I was olnly twelve years old an' I didn' have the thingamybob. I didn' even have the thingamybob! Oh, I'm a poor excuse for a son. Poor bloody bad excuse, that's me . . .'

Nigel decided, patting Clarry's shoulder uselessly, that Clarry's father had made a mistake in attempting to protect his son from death in a world where it was rampant. He didn't sound like an evil father, merely a stupid one.

'Poor bloody excuse . . .' sobbed the gaoler. Nigel squeezed his upper arm. There wasn't much else to do.

> 'I believe in miracles!
> Where you fro-om
> You sexy thaing?'

Nigel clanged his manacles together above his head and gyrated his hips to the beat. It sent Clarry cacking himself in the dirt. Nigel sang snatches of the Hot Chocolate song, bits of Bee Gee numbers and old Slade tunes. It was the last thing Nigel would have wanted to dance to back home, but when Clarry had asked him for a song he'd leapt to his feet and it simply forced itself out of his mouth. He stomped in the dirt and rattled his chains, he banged his head with his plastic plate – he enjoyed himself. It wasn't something good music was supposed to do, was it?

Clarry had never snapped his fingers – never heard of it. Nigel taught him, and the words to Gary Glitter's 'My Gang'. They sang it together; the clouds raced over the moon, and the troopers were armed silhouettes against the sky-glow, but Nigel and Clarry drove away the fear of death utterly for a time.

Afterwards, the gaoler stood with his back to Nigel and sang into the turbulent night sky. The moon was like a flickering light bulb on his bald pate. 'Here's a history lesson for yez,' he told Nigel.

'One Sunday morning as I went walking, by Melbourne
    waters I chanced to stray,
I heard a convict his fate bewailing, as on the sunny river-
    bank he lay.
I am a native of Erin's island but I fought for King and the
    English flag,
I found payment in the Gold Rebellion: my children
    hunger and I slave in rags.

'Captain Logan was then our tyrant, he took our women
    and he made them weep,
The men who fought back he called bushrangers, and
    with horse and musket drove to mountain steep.
Man cannot live on only desperation, he must have food
    to remain so bold
And as I foraged for a grub one morning, I uncovered
    nuggets of the purest gold.

'Now Governor Logan he found out about it, and in his
    greed turned against the King,
But those of us who had been bushrangers rode to keep
    him from this monstrous thing,
And the only friends of the British Empire in this fatal
    planet were the highwaymen,
At Ararat and in Maryborough we gave our life-blood,
    one against his ten.

'And when the fleet had come and the war was over, and
    English troops had restored the peace,
They clapped us all in the selfsame irons as Governor
    Logan and his lackey Reece.
My fellow rebels take this education and never trust what
    marines may say.
For the British Empire has grown old and evil, the King is
    innocent but he's lost his way.

'Like the Egyptians and ancient Hebrews, we'll be op-
    pressed by the English corps,
Till a man is born who can face the devils – the day will
    come when we shall rise once more.
Australia's children be exhilarated, the military their
    deaths shall find,
And when from bondage we are liberated our former
    suffering shall fade from mind . . .'

It was sedition. Nigel could see it in the defiance on
Clarry's soft flushed face. It explained why transportation
had not ended: the English judiciary, and possibly its
parliament, if such existed, was corrupt. If not totally, then
enough for the military – necessarily a strong one in an
empire which included much of North America – not to feel
threatened. Nigel watched the firelight stammer and wink
and thought aloud that he'd rather have a gang of incom-
petents in charge, the way they had back home, than out-
and-out bastards. Clarry, as he returned to sit by Nigel with
the fire throwing high shadows on his forehead, agreed.

'The rebels in America have leaders like yours,' he said. 'Jimmy Carter, that lot. Supposed to be great there.'

By sunrise they had drunk themselves sober. On the embers a billyful of water rumbled before boiling. Outside the fire's warm ring the ground was wet with dew. Magpies gargled in the day. The air smelt full of promise.

As the first lip of light curled over the horizon Nigel and Clarry fell silent. One cuppa, then –

Then the guards stationed discreetly around them (according to custom) would rise and close on Nigel for the final walk. The gallows stood a mile down the track, on the first crossroads out of town. A factory in Melbourne knocked them out by the dozen. All a town had to do was plant them.

The billy boiled. Clarry took a stick and shifted it carefully to one side. From his tucker-bag he pulled a tin of tea. He cast dispirited leaves upon the water and fastened the billy's dented lid. He sighed and sat back next to Nigel against the red gum.

'Never know. They may commute yer sentence,' he offered.

'To what?'

'Lashes and life hard labour maybe. Never know. 'Course you'll olnly go to *biggle* later, then. Now where's yer cup?' He began to rise.

'Clarry?'

'Yes, son.'

'Here – the bracelet.' He unclipped his watch. 'Take it.'

Clarry cocked his head thoughtfully at the gift.

'Nah,' he said.

'Why not? I won't need it.'

'I'll get it later!' He grinned and stood, with some effort, and fetched the mugs, then waddled down to the creek to rinse the lees out of them.

The footsteps crunching down the track from behind Nigel sounded loud and final to him.

Clarry raced back up the river-bank as fast as his pins
would carry him.

'Hay, youze bastards! Youze are too *early*. Can't yez even
leave us to have the Last Cuppa in peace? I dunno, twenny
years ago there was some *respec'* for whatsisname, tradition.
Ya never –'

The guard held out an envelope. 'It's been commuted,' he
told them in hoarse cockney. 'I heard Sir Todd dictate it.
Lashes and life hard labour up the coast. His sister had him
awake all night, apparently. Arguing. She said he didn't
really rob anyone or even touch her, only tried and the patrol
scared them off. So it's *'tempted* robbery, just. Besides, the
hangman's got the shits this morning. Ate a manky chook last
night. Then he's got holidays.'

'Well fuck me,' said Clarry.

'No,' said Nigel, 'but you can have the watch anyhow.'

Nigel did not fall into uncontrollable joy – leaping about,
linking arms with Clarry and the trooper, tangling them in
his chains, tripping, bouncing up again, kissing Clarry,
pounding the man's back – because he was going to live.
Although he had travelled some way during the long night
toward accepting his death, he would have struggled and
cried and shouted and pissed and wittered all the way to the
noose. He still didn't believe completely that he would ever
die. No, what lifted his sleepless racing heart and set his toes
and heels to swinging and tingling was the possibility that no
matter what hell awaited Nigel in whichever miserable
corner of the colony, at Emu station there lived a woman, a
single person in this whole crude world, who (perhaps)
cared.

Nigel, Clarry, and the messenger danced and yodelled in
the new day, the *next* day of Nigel's life, until their legs went
wobbly and their heads giddy. The magpies shut up in
surprise. The tea stewed in the billy. The three men cavorted
in the bright promise of life.

Then Clarry and the messenger marched Nigel off for his
lashes.

Ten

The Nourished Road

The lowest point of a life can be a dream. Especially when you are Nigel Donohoe and have all but made a profession out of swapping one for the other. He had no doubt that this punishment would be the most painful event he had known so far. But very possibly this was his last event altogether and so an urge to remain in a life fallen to dream status dogged him. He drifted in and out of the moment and the two states swapped atmospheres as well as names, dream for life, life for dream. Until he could no longer tell them apart.

Although these people called themselves Catholics, they used masks and dance as much as they used crucifixes. The dancers at his flogging wore masks of moulded fruit-bread; they took bites of one another's faces as they manhandled Nigel toward the triangles. This was fortunate for the scourge, since his 'eyes' were two apricots which needed eating before he could flog Nigel. No Latin was used this time. Instead, during the simulated sex there was an Arabic commentary, so beautiful Nigel immersed himself in its music and managed to forget for a short time where he was.

For minutes. Soon the ritual was over, the scourge buttoned up his fly, and Nigel entered the system through what they called 'Mrs Agony's Bead Curtains'.

Naturally, it wasn't as simple as the name made it sound. The first few lashes were painful, more so than anything except perhaps the time when as a youngster he had tried to piddle like a grown-up and the lid had fallen down on him. He clenched his teeth on the bat-wing they'd shoved in his mouth. He swore as if he'd bumped his head on a lintel. He could feel his skin open like an orange under a thumb-nail. Then, with the first trickles of blood reaching his jeans, the world (or at least the rough post before him) went a red dark and his cluttered memory came to his rescue. It was the mental equivalent of his pocket billiards in the face of worry.

The pain removed itself as he recalled his first love, Marlene White, his fourth-grade teacher's arch-enemy, a tall intelligent girl who pushed Nigel over in the playground seventeen times before she spoke one word to him. Once, her third-grade teacher, Mrs Barstow, had punished the girl for showing her a page of equations she'd solved for her teenage sister. 'Don't you *ever* lie like that to me again, Marlene White!' Mrs Barstow had shouted, an inch from her face. Marlene could not convince Mrs Barstow the solutions were hers. Mrs Barstow's fear of Marlene's intellect puzzled her. But then everyone's fear of her puzzled her. Although gifted, she was still nine years old and wanted to please, so she regularly provoked her teachers and allowed them to reduce her to tears. And something stubborn in her stopped her from hiding her mind, unlike Nigel.

It was after the maths incident that Nigel got the seventeenth shove to the ground. It was the first time Marlene hadn't had an audience. So they spoke as Nigel picked the gravel out of his knee.

'You're a dumb little squirt,' she told him.

'I love you,' Nigel told her.

She ignored him. 'You come up to me again I'm gunna squash your face on the wall.'

'You wanna come to my house after school for some ice-cream?'

'I'm gunna kill you.'

When the bell rang the two walked (a safe distance apart) down the back streets to Nigel's house. It was the best time of Nigel's life. As the whip slapped and flayed his back Nigel returned to this as a dog does to its favourite dead sheep: to roll in it. In his mind he went to a box marked *This Stuff Counts*, and he pulled bits out and dived on them eagerly. His pain passed from one region of sensation into quite another. Besides wanting to experience death fully, if that was what life had in store, he was unsure of whether things normally went this way or were merely transcended because of his retreat into happier times. Nigel wavered between a morbid fascination with the fall of the lash upon him and the days of stretched childhood summer when he first found peace.

(Sometimes he thought he might die just from the pain. People died, he'd heard, but usually afterwards, septic. Nigel suspected he might die and stay nine years old for eternity. He plunged into his memory.)

That ice-cream afternoon, when they peeled the thin plastic back from the three colours of delicious forbidden territory, turned into an orgy. The first hard peelings they tasted virginal, feeding one another off the spoon. It was so cold it made them jump and hold their teeth. Nigel's mum was at the factory cleaning for his dad, so in order to distract Marlene from her gruesome intentions towards him, he broke out the bowls. Nigel flared creative. He grated orange ice-blocks on to the first serves, sprinkled Aktavite, chocolate and crunchy, raided the cake cupboard for glacé cherries.

Marlene and Nigel grinned at each other, brown rings around their mouths, death threats forgotten in the softening afternoon which flooded from the backyard. The Donohoes' kitchen was cool, the part furthest from the windows was always dark. On the edge of this darkness the two lingered over fat mouthfuls. Each tried to outdo the other with moans of ice-cream pleasure. The first bowl finished with tumbles from chairs and mock death beneath the Laminex table.

(Someone was crying. Nigel could understand it. To watch an organised uneven thrashing would have Nigel ashamed of his humanity. He had felt so, merely passing by, in Milton Keynes. He began to feel so now, sympathising with the crying person – woman. Poor woman. No, sympathy was another retreat. Better to give in to memory.)

The second bowl was outrageous: peanut butter, anchovies, Bovril. They tested them individually with the three Neapolitan flavours and together. The idea was to pull the right face for the flavour. Several they had to spit out. Tomato sauce and chocolate tasted the best. Mustard, chopped cauliflower and strawberry ice-cream produced the ugliest face: they called it Hot Maggots.

'You're incredible, Nigel,' Marlene said when he suggested it.

He had never heard her compliment anyone at all. He decided to remember it for ever. And he did.

(*One hundred and thirty-seven*. The number seeped through his agony. While his back seemed twice its normal size he couldn't judge the depth or intensity of his wounds. Surely they were past one hundred in their countdown. Perhaps he'd misheard the hundred part. Something cool – water – splashed him, and a fact surfaced in his mind, overheard or read he didn't know where: people had died under less than one hundred lashes. *One hundred and twenty-five*. He heard that one distinctly. Oh, no. His eyes opened on a grey glare and a carved face of spattered wood and the present spun sickeningly away again into cool darkness.)

Stomachs like small bowling-balls strained both Marlene and Nigel's belly-buttons. The big girl rolled on to her side and placed her hand with surprising tenderness on Nigel's bowling-ball. They lay on the rag rug in the laundry at the end of the sun-room which would later hold Nigel's fish. The afternoon was still too hot for birds to call; the only sounds were the distant grumble of Hoddle Street's multiple lanes, and shallow breathing.

'We got there,' said Marlene. She referred to the sink, where they had washed the sticky gunge off their faces and hands.

'Mm,' Nigel agreed.

With a circular motion, Marlene began to stroke Nigel's stomach. This brought a little nausea, and a tingling. She unbuttoned his spotty grey shirt from bottom to top, then kept on with her strange caress.

'You're preggo,' said Marlene.

Nigel giggled, tried to raise his head, fell back and replied, 'So're you.'

'If you put your dicky in my raspberry split we could have a baby,' said Marlene. They both laughed at her childishness.

'We're not old enough,' said Nigel. Why, he was not sure.

'I know that,' said Marlene. 'You got to have hair on your penis and I got to have hair on my vagina.'

'Penis. Vagina.'

'They're horrible words.'

'Fuck.'

'Fuck fuck fuck – know what that means?'

'What dogs do to your legs.'

'It's what a man does to a woman with his penis. Then you get babies. I don't ever want to have a baby. It makes your bosoms saggy.'

'Neither do I.'

'Boys can't have babies.'

'I know!'

'Yeah sure.'

'I'm not dumb you know.'

'Show me your penis.'

They wound up in the bath together; it made instant brother and sister of them, the only children of foolish but loving parents revelling in too much bubble-bath. Marlene hugged him and hugged him, frighteningly. He slipped out of her arms and under the water. She fished him out and kissed him, with tight-closed lips. Then she pushed him under, into the dark.

(He came to, screaming. His voice gave out but he kept on, gasping. He was sure he would die. It was incidental. He heard his name called and wasn't sure if it was Marlene come to save him or his imagination or his ears. His mother must be worried about him by now.

Seventy-seven, he heard. The totem's eyes wept blood. Whose blood? He blacked out again.)

Two weeks after their bath the new principal learnt of Marlene's genius via Mrs Barstow's husband. In spite of their class-teacher's objections, Marlene White was transferred to a special school, not exactly for the gifted but a privileged environment, equipped for her needs. In two weeks Marlene and Nigel had shared their favourite books and TV programmes, elaborate fantasies about a simpler place where everyone but them had disappeared, and a lot of doing nothing. On her last day at Nigel's school, Nigel approached her across the asphalt, not knowing what to say. She pushed him to the ground and went home.

(Days of travel. Nights of strange dreams. He heard Eden mentioned and wondered if it was the Eden he knew on the south coast of New South Wales. He slept a great deal. Perhaps he might yet die in one of his dreams of plates and pointed hats. He hoped so. He decided he rather liked pointed hats.)

At some point during the indefinite period surrounding his lashes Nigel realised the actual punishment was over and what he was feeling was a kind of echo of the pain. Each lash-mark screamed its story. Snippets of the world beyond his pain fluttered in but Nigel had little interest in life any more. While Clarry nursed him on the road to Melbourne Nigel went over the countless times he had tied his shoe-laces, all of which felt precious to him. While he listened to Clarry instruct and bribe the bullockies (contracted to take Nigel's group to their assigned penal station) and finally say goodbye to Nigel when work called him back, Nigel recalled spitting out his first glass of beer – and he could actually remember its sour yeasty reek for the first time in years. While they rolled down the Carthage road into Melbourne's outer suburbs Nigel had sun-baking experiences: oil smells, grit between the toes and other places, surf walloping away heat and grit alike with a chill right to the back of your teeth.

Nigel's being was a labyrinth built by a jumble-sale Daedalus out of cardboard and twine. In his random grabs from this wonky disposal of memory and values he upset what order there had been and, in the spinning confusion of surf and shoe-laces and discoveries of boyhood, the position of his very nature, his soul, was changed. Not settled. What he had come to think of as a pistachio nut was sent skittering across the floor of his mind; it wouldn't come to rest for some time yet.

He surfaced in his senses. He was in a stable. It was night. He was in Melbourne. Where were the other prisoners? Locked up for the night. Nigel tried to move and discovered why he hadn't been moved as well. The pain was fierce. Under the stiff bandage was raw flesh. He lay watching the strong moonlight descend from a small barred window above a loft, while the pain diminished to a throb. It couldn't be more than a few days after his flogging. Clarry, Nigel deduced from his meagre recollections, had nursed him on the road until Keilor, then paid for decent nourishment and gentle treatment until Eden. What a man. Light-headed but clear, Nigel lay listening to the shouts from the

street and from inside the building attached to the stables.
Horses whuffed and stepped about. An Irish jig strayed
from a nearby pub, an Arabic drone from another direction.
Gradually he passed into natural sleep.

In the morning his back burned fresh. He felt feverish and
longed for the clarity of the previous night. When the other,
mobile, prisoners were chained to the side of the cart Nigel
parted reluctant eyelids. Nightmarish, a pallid beaky face
loomed close to his. They began to move. Nigel's coming
delirium mixed with the bullockies' bawled curses. The cart
moved into bitter sunlight. Again Nigel forced his lids open
a crack.

St Paul's Cathedral. Painted a pale pink and the domes were
plated with gold. It was certainly not a Christian church as
he knew it. A chain-gang worked on the paving before the
pointed doors, covered to their knees in gutter mud. A
couple of clerics in fezzes and rich purple tabards stepped
from a coach to the paving protected from the filth by white
velvet rugs put down before them and taken up after them
by a group of chained children in white smocks.

Later: more mud. Acres of it beside a wide, slicked, *green*
Yarra River that smelt terrible. Sprouting from the mud's
middle was a grid of polished brass tubes shaped suspiciously like the Eiffel Tower and, fitted to the top, huge
enamel portraits resembling Barry McKenzie in a turban.

The shanty town spread over the hills for as far as he could
see. Naked children and bedraggled chickens ran everywhere. There were no trees. *Narrow* laneways totally at
odds with the broad Australian sky snaked up low hills into
the clamour. Incongruously, on one hill recently cleared of
all its iron-roofed shacks, judging by the plaster chunks and
other rubble, the Shrine of Remembrance squatted in grey
cut stone, a little rougher but otherwise the same as in

Nigel's Melbourne. Nigel could not tell if this was fever or reality. Which war-dead did it honour? Nigel could not maintain control long enough to ask. He tumbled back into delirium.

A billboard read, *YOUR useless children can have a 'wonderful' life in KENNETT'S WORKHOUSES. 'Treat' them to the 'luxurious' standard's only 'lord's' and 'ladie's' can afford. Save f f f f f ENROL 'NOW'!* For those not up to the sign's high standard of English or its flowing cross between Gothic and Arabic (?) scripts, there were cartoons of happy children being greeted by the workhouse proprietor. Some things do not change.

His last view of Melbourne was of swamps. The jumble of dilapidated shacks gradually gave out here, replaced by woeful farmhouses nestled in bulrushes and long yellow grass. Soon afterwards they turned north and following another bout of unconsciousness their way grew mountainous.

Nigel's fever worsened, but before he descended completely back into legless walking gumboots and rolling mackerel he experienced a time of intense and far-reaching clarity. He knew. He *knew*. The road beneath him, that wound up between bald eroded peaks ahead, was a fat snake fed on blood. It was. Once begun, roads demand nourishment and are seldom satisfied. This road, however, had taken about as much blood as any road could. It was fat, though ill-cambered and pot-holed. A road like this wanted nothing more than silence, and the racket made by the foul-mouthed bullockies, by the crunching wheels and by muttering convictism drove the road a little loopy at times. So it gave way and let a team of bullocks off its edge, or a cartload of men, to splinter on the rocks below, merely out of temper. Not for the blood. It swallowed wheels and snapped axles tit for tat until the men who plied the roads developed consuming superstitions. They gave libations to certain corners; they chanted over certain fords and bridges.

Listening to some of these rituals, Nigel's mind envisioned with the energy of delirium all the convicts who had died to make this road. Their numbers appalled him. His own world's crimes ought to have appalled him already, yet they had not. They had just frightened the bejeesus out of him. Nigel was joined to this Australian holocaust by a knowledge of how close he himself lived to this blood-letting and coping with blood-letting by ritual. He could have denuded these mountains. He could have forced this road through here. He could have flogged. Nigel Donohoe.

His interest in such knowledge told him he would live. His mind was leaving stuff for him to claim when he returned from fever. One day he would deal with the part of him that could become a Nazi or build such a bloody highway. His soul was still pinging and careening about inside him, waiting to be fastened to new attitudes. But not yet. Hardly right now. Soon. He would wrestle with his own share of the world's mess, soon.

For the rest of the long trip north Nigel hovered in and out of febrile unreality. Only when the swift odour of the sea struck him a couple of days out of Eden did he emerge into a world of weak commonplace sensations. The sky – no not the sky – above was grey canvas. Trees passed, real, blackened trunks, on the slow downward slope to the penal station. His mouth tasted of sour gruel and he wished he had a toothbrush. Once again, he thanked Clarry for his care, and for providing money to the gruff but not heartless bullockies so Nigel could rest in the only cart with shelter from the elements, so his wounds were washed and his dressings changed, so he was fed enough to recover from the inevitable infection. Otherwise he would surely have been claimed by the road.

Eleven

Pickles up the Arse

The convict overlooker told him, 'For a bushranger you're a weed, my lover. Don't you worry though. Plenty of time for fixing that. First yu'll want yer pickle.' He held an object over Nigel's head. It was indeed a pickled onion.

... *mark my terms: the dance or the pickle.* Uselessly, Nigel recalled what the bullocky had told him in the bar in Milton Keynes.

Nigel let his face fall back on to the rough canvas stretcher. He groaned. Then he screamed.

The overlooker laughed as he wiped the pickle juice on his trousers then poured the hot tarry substance over the back of Nigel, who merely twitched. 'Works every time. Take him to the hospital boys — make like rabbits, come on!'

Nigel had avoided the dance part of the large woman's warning but the pickle had found him at last.

The 'hospital' was a bark hut. Or at least his ward was. A minute was the longest Nigel could raise his face and strain his neck looking around, so he saw the room in stages. First he grew aware of the insects infesting the walls. Swart spiders loitered in the corner nearest (the small smooth deadly kind rather than the big hairy harmless ones), huge black moths squatted unseen until a sudden move broke their mottling from the putrid bark, fat cockroaches brandished feelers right up his nose and when he jerked away his hand smacked squirming *things* that scuttled off too quick for his glance. He raised his head to scream – and noticed another patient, an Aborigine.

Like most whites Nigel had passed by Kooris on the street with the averted eyes of one whose distant family has feuded reasonlessly with the other's. If you spoke to an Aboriginal Person you admitted you were guilty. If you were lucky they might not notice who you were. Modern white Australians reckoned it had nothing to do with *them*. Best hurry by.

However, Nigel wasn't a modern white Australian any more. He wasn't sure what he was, but he wasn't what he had been. He had had strips torn off him. Literally. Curious enough to ignore his pain (which hadn't lessened for a while, it'd merely grown ordinary), he uttered, hoarsely, the first clear words other than curses since his punishment.

'Gudday,' he said.

Nigel, typically, seldom thought of the Koori. He had met one, an historian who had scared Nigel and everyone else at the party with jokes altogether too sharp for guilty middle-class Europeans. As an inner-city lad he had seen others. It didn't encourage him to contact them. Seeing as the genocide of the rightful owners was all but over, the history of the time was skimmed as a sad and brutal happening with nothing to be done for it now. This merely strengthened the view of Kooris as what they stood for, at best the one in an adventure movie marked for a sentimental death, rather than as the person in front of you – or across the room.

'Gudday,' replied the man.

'What's wrong with you?' asked Nigel. His directness surprised him. Did his suffering bestow virtue equal to a Koori's? No, but it had raised everyone else in his eyes from less-than-fish to human being. Simply that.

'Ah . . . running shits.'

'Oh yeah,' said Nigel, continuing his new-found boldness. 'My hangman had that so I got off.'

'Yeah?'

'Actually, one of the witnesses against me changed their

evidence, but it was that too. Too much trouble. Hangman was off on holidays the next day.' He attempted a laugh. It hurt a lot.

His room-mate joined in at Nigel's obvious pain. 'That's the worst thing, ay? I remember once this cunt started tickling me. And he was a mate of mine, too.'

'Huh,' said Nigel, by way of appreciation. He was warming to this new brotherhood of ordinariness. As a clever idiot, he had never fitted in anywhere before. 'Me name's Nigel,' he offered. Just like that – me name's Nigel. How often had he said so before, so easily? He amazed himself.

'Frank.' The man rolled off his bed – a shelf in the corner opposite Nigel's – on to his feet. He took careful steps across the dirt floor. 'Howareya,' he said, briefly clasping Nigel's hand.

'Howareya,' said Nigel.

'Yeah,' said Frank.

'Yeah,' said Nigel.

There was no need for explanations about their states. They were in Eden penal station. They were ill.

'I know where I belong – Macka's place down the road.' Frank was not an Aboriginal man, in his own eyes. His mother's eyes had seen otherwise; although taken away from her own mother – herself taken away from *her* mother, Frank's great-grandmother – she had picked up enough before Toongabbie female factory to have some idea of the tens of thousands of years of continuous culture behind her. After four generations of forcible assimilation you struggled to see the faintest spark of the great light which had once filled his people. Not even nostalgia remained.

'Gets them people into trouble,' he maintained, 'such ideas. A man's a man, and he's better off without them.'

What?

The holocaust here was almost complete.

A few questions confirmed it for Nigel: Frank among thousands of children had been sucked into the huge convict-dumping. Less high-souled than the state kidnap in Nigel's Australia, it at least saved a fraction from worse fates. The Europeans in this universe were more frightened of the land, every forest shadow terrified them. Every Koori. With only drudge-paced convict labour they had settled hardly any of the continent, but their creeping horror at the alien landscape was so intense it drove suicidal but relentless expeditions deep into Australia's heart – for butchery. A hysterical war without provocation. Tribes were slaughtered, bush fires set, water-holes were poisoned and diseases sown deliberately. For less than nothing. The surviving colonial corps fled after bravely mass-murdering. Only the green south-east was occupied, and that not densely. Whole penal stations died of starvation regularly through lack of bush knowledge. More arrived, and died. The continent lay almost empty; a nail-paring of Europeans clung to its edge, and those Kooris who'd escaped slowly regrouped in its heart . . . Over a million true Australians had died for this paradise.

It certainly took Nigel's mind off his own pain, anyway.

Frank said, 'Yer a strange one.' He had finished his sixth stint on the slop-bucket for that morning; as he spoke he wiped his arse with the soiled rag thoughtfully provided.

Nigel had grown used to the pong by now. 'How do you mean?' he asked, hardly gagging at all.

'The way ya fought the pickle. Everyone knows it's the next best thing to crystals for keeping ya healthy in this place. Keeps ya from going septic and it keeps ya from the pox.'

'Superstition. It just distracts you from the pain of the bandage stuff they pour on to you,' said Nigel.

'Bloody fact. Half ya disease spirits get into ya body that way but ya pickle blocks the way,' said Frank. 'By the by, ya can take it out now.'

After a few moments Nigel reported, 'I don't think I can.'

This set Frank off. 'Ow!' he said, part-way through. 'Oh!' He ran to the bucket, tugging at his loose trousers. Squatting, he continued to giggle, though grunts broke it up.

Nigel smiled for the first time since his flogging. He realised that since he'd regained his senses, two days from Eden, he had wallowed in self-pity. And why not? he rationalised. Someone has to pity me; we all deserve it. Yet if he followed the kind of notions he'd developed back home, his disbelief in everything except fish, nobody deserved anything, good or bad. Justice wasn't supposed to figure in blanket disbelief. But beneath the fashions he followed lay a childish rage against the unjust world his generation had inherited. Same as every other generation. The sixties had proved you couldn't change it. The late seventies were an attempt to just pull it apart. Beginning with your own soul. Destroy and make different. Out of self-pity masquerading as careless youth. The will to live was too strong, however, so what would this shift in concern give birth to?

More to the point, now he had left behind a world flirting with suicide where would Nigel's knocked-about soul come to rest?

Compared to every other decent human being here he owned a possibly unique ability to step outside his morality for the sake of argument or change or defence, to think laterally, to use his imagination, and not get snared by evil. Only the swine like Todd reserved the right to do that here, because they were happy with swinishness, or didn't believe in *biggle*. So they had the tools to advance but did not use those tools for the common good, merely for themselves. Normal people like Clarry were constrained by their all-smothering church: the meek did not inherit the earth, they inherited Auschwitz country, Terror Australis.

There must be a way to really alter human nature as it stands here, Nigel told himself. To free people from the limits on their souls. We should be able to *rearrange* the building-blocks of our deepest selves . . .

With a pickle lodged stinging in your sphincter you find yourself driven to Deep Philosophy. Nigel pondered as Frank's merriment gave out. Sweat built on Frank's forehead; his bowels voided nothing whatsoever. Nigel scarcely noticed: he was filled with the reasonless conviction that if he could figure out how to trigger such a rearrangement on this tyrannised, superstition-bound shore, it offered a way out of this fine mess.

These unlikely notions he stored carefully in his mind, amongst the rubble next to an unimportant-looking object that resembled a cutlery box, but tagged clearly for later consideration.

In the matter of the pickle, Frank eventually came to the rescue. He was gentle. And complimentary.

'You got a nice arse,' he told Nigel, nodding sagely.

It was the first time anyone had ever told Nigel this – or anything like it. Because he had no gay friends he had never tested his (assumed) prejudices about these matters. The correct line at university involved grave thanks and no action. His mind, though, was too busy examining itself for either shock or revulsion to put together any answer. He found neither.

'Sorry if I hurt you, but I gotta stick me finger in to flip it out.' He gave a short laugh. 'Always looks like a blind eye to me.'

Nigel tensed.

Frank slapped him lightly. 'Now don't do that. Could get painful if ya resist. Just imagine I'm a woman, like ya do when ya wank . . .'

Nigel had imagined many things, but never – bottom stuff. He tried.

'That's more like it. Now —'

One of Frank's finger-nails on the fresh-cracked scabs served to distract Nigel. He yelped.

Frank thrust a finger inside and it was done. He tossed the pickle into the slop-bucket as he returned to his bed. Sitting down, he observed, 'You never been had by a bloke, ay?'

'No.'

'I'm gunna haveta tell ya a few things then.'

Nigel found himself grateful.

Frank made an offer. When Frank got back to work ('On a chain-gang?' asked Nigel. 'Nah, that's only for desperate beginners and desperate felons — and I get enough.'), he'd spread the word about Nigel: the two of them had fallen in love in hospital. It was the only way, Frank maintained, to defend Nigel against rape.

'Those fellas are hungry for new bum. Killed five neweys last time, they did.'

In return, Nigel would sleep with Frank. 'Just to cuddle, nothing rough. And when the time comes, give it a go. I'll be gentle,' Frank assured him with a half-smile. 'Never know, ya might like it.'

Nigel had to admit this was true. He might. Frank's whole stay in hospital Nigel spent approaching, hedging around, arguing over Frank's offer. All subjects led to it. In spite of his quick liking for the wiry little bloke Nigel distrusted Frank's motives at first. 'You're right to distrust me,' Frank told him. 'If I don't give myself the crippling shits to find arse, I do look when I'm here.'

But what did Nigel know about the real conditions of a penal outpost? Only what Frank told him. From the look of the hospital, he could believe life here was primitive. The dirt floor, what with half-digested meat and grains dried into a solid carpet all over it, the nameless deep red and yellow patches like malevolent tomato and creeping mozzarella, brought wistful memories of his local pizza joint. Everything smelt as putrid. He had found a severed

finger in the blanket hem. The insects continued to flicker at
the edges of his vision. Of course most of these weren't so
stage-shy. They can-canned by on the joists, brazen
extroverts on their way to talent quests to sing 'I Don't
Know How to Love Him' or the insect equivalent thereof.

But as to his idea of the rest of the station, he remembered
scraps of *Papillon* and the egg-eating scene in *Cool Hand
Luke*. Too young to understand the adult references at the
time, he never came to believe Steve McQueen capable of
sex of any flavour. When told by his right-on history teacher
about 'widespread homosexuality in the Colony of New
South Wales' he had against his will imagined thousands of
Paul Newmen rolling boiled eggs on one another. These
factors conspired to cloud his notions of prison society. He
never did trust boiled eggs.

'You can't tell me everybody here is gay.'

'Nobody's gay about it mate, but we get by.'

'I mean, there must be some – probably a lot who can't –
who won't –'

'Who won't take it up the fart-box themselves. Some like
a blow-job. And the lucky ones find love. Then it's what ya
mate likes most. Often nothing much.' He snorted.
'Marriage!'

'In love? How can they be in love if they weren't gay – I
mean, like that – in the first place? Did they send a lot of –
them here?'

'Shirtlifters? Call us what ya like. Call us something, any
rate. No there weren't a lot of blouses transported.'

'Blouses.'

'I don't think it's what they call a transportable offence.
Now they've got rid of us and England's turned into Lovely
Land they reckon there're more blouses than ever. It's just
girls in female factories and boys in the stations that does it.'

'I know. You said. Segregation.'

'It's not a church service but it is bloody horrible here –'

'So why love? Romantic stuff . . .'

'Some of it ain't that romantic, believe me. Anywar, I was getting to it. It *is* a bloody war here. A man will stave in the next fella's head in the chain-gang just so as he'll get hung and shot of the place, it's so bad. Bloody Kern wants us utterly under the thumb, he'll do anything to get us there. Blokes jump into the gorge regular, but if the crew catch ya or think ya gunna – lashes, or the Tin Box. You'll see Stupid bloody tasks on top of our regular work clearing or on the roads for no reason but to grind us down. We're turned against each other; mostly by getting us to spy on our mates. Love, though, love they can't stop. It's the untouchable part of us, love, natural endless and wonderful. See, a lot of us here are good blokes, sent here for no reason. There was nearly twenty years this century when judges conspired to turn around the Great Purification set up under King Barnaby the century before. It's happened heaps of times, but this was the biggest. They wanted to take over. Military coup. Would have too, if not for Margaret Thatcher.'

'Hay?'

'Young lawyer. Brilliant. Cleared out the whole legal profession under Harold Wilson, before she went bonkers.'

'Oh.'

'Anywar, so a lot of us here weren't born lags, we've been made into them in penal stations. But part of us remembers, and it's that bit can be tender. Amazing, isn't it? I've known men to hack off their own foot and bleed to death over a broken heart. Wonderful, ay?'

'Great.'

'So whaddya reckon? You know I like you.'

'You could be lying your head off about this place just to get me into bed.'

'If I was like that I'd take it by force. Besides, I'm not bad-looking. Got all me teeth, shee? If ah want shex – wewll, ah'm fofular. Why lie?'

'Virgins! Men like you *like* virgins, I've heard.'

'Men like me. It's overrated.'

'Then you must keep count! To you I'm a conquest.'

'Possibly, but –'

And so it went on. It did distract Nigel from the flies on his bandages, from the painful cracking of the scabs on his wounds with every minute shift of his body, from the ordure. The next morning, over tea like petrol and burnt weevil-cakes, Frank told him he had raved to Nigel for quite a while before he had realised Nigel was asleep.

'What did you say?'

'Don't remember. But I must like ya. I don't know why, ya one insulting bastard.'

Three days it took Frank to overcome his gut-walloping shits. Frank ran to the bucket, rested and tended Nigel gently; when he wasn't actually grunting or eating or sleeping he argued the whole time. The two of them plumbed every attitude Nigel didn't know he had about homosexuality. In truth, he had received lots of half-arsed views without knowing it.

He didn't feel the need to explain where he came from. Suddenly it didn't seem relevant. And although Frank looked oddly at him at times, he never asked. Convict etiquette? It turned out so. Nigel packed as many questions into Frank's recovery as possible, his thirst for knowledge of this delimited society surprising him. He never even read the papers at his parents' place. It might be simple loneliness, he thought.

He did feel a pang when Frank left.

The station doctor and priest, a bald bearded man shaped as much like a duck as it's possible to be and remain human, called in once a day or so to check for gangrene and to make sure Frank wasn't feigning his illness. On the third day he drew back and punched Frank in the stomach.

'Urrf,' went Frank, authentically. He rolled his eyes at Nigel.

'You're orright,' the doctor rasped (there was something seriously awry with his throat which Frank explained had provoked several theories amongst convictism, all involving donkeys).

'Yep,' agreed Frank, ruefully.

On his way out, nimble yet still delicate, the bony convict cast a questioning glance at Nigel.

Nigel made an uncertain noise, part sigh, part moan. He nodded at Frank.

With a wink, Nigel's ward-mate dodged past the doctor into the blaring whiteness outside. The rough bark-and-timber door swung shut on its leather hinges slowly enough for Nigel to catch the duckish doctor's leer at the convicts' exchange. Nigel dropped back on to his stomach. He closed his eyes and thought desperately of home. But he couldn't remember what his fish-tanks looked like. He couldn't recall even one fish's name. In his mind's eye he stared at an aquarium's wall and saw not fish, nor his own face – he saw Frank's deep-set brown eyes, glinting, wanting him. Nigel had to admit it. They were – damn the rotten little things – attractive. He swore he would never tell Frank so.

Twelve

Silver Spoons and Whoop-de-doo

Healing is blissful. Every cut, every viral or bacterial attack, every strain or break or bruise or boil produces a miracle. The body mends itself, and the brain, being wedded to it (except in certain fowl), joins in the general party atmosphere, convalescent. This may perhaps be explained by scientists – armed with secreting glands, regenerating cells, genes selfish or merely never taught to share their toys – but the mystery of our born-again love-affair with nature, the little springtime in our soul, makes theory the obligatory dickhead who hijacks the party's sound-system. Real decisions, ideas, affirmations, rise from these periods. Where do they come from? Should you dip your tender portions into this question they'll be chopped off, hey-I-was-only-asking-thwock! Take the fresh fruit and scarper back to the party.

One morning, Nigel woke – better! He had lain on his stomach and on his side for variety and relief from the aches of a single position; now for the first time in over a week he ventured to test his scabs against something other than the soiled bandages which clung to them. Whatever the muck the doctor had painted on his wounds, it prevented infection. It definitely hadn't been his pained incantations. A delicious itching crept across his unflayed skin. As he carefully pulled his stiff body over he felt sure the scabs beneath their hard black casing would not crack: *whoah* he felt lucky today.

The doctor had planted the idea the previous morning. 'Yer bloody lucky to have weeks skylarking around in this luxury, son,' he had said. As if Nigel had spent his time carousing with a hockey team and a bathful of German shepherds. 'I told the commandant you were such a weakling you'd kark it for sure if we put you to work after the regulation two days humane leave, and for some reason he took notice of me. Then he forgot about you.' He shook his head in disbelief.

It was the one time the doctor – whose tapering legs, thick middle and narrow shoulders gave the impression he had been centrifuged as a child – had shown an iota of humanity.

'Pray the commandant never does remember you,' he had finished, and waddled on regulation humungous feet into the blinding sunshine of the unknown world beyond the door.

Only one word had soaked into Nigel: 'lucky'.

I am lucky, he thought, straining to haul himself on to his back. Lucky, lucky, lucky.

The world is suddenly part of you and you are a part of the world. Day follows day and every one is different. No matter which world you live in, there is that.

His scabs cracked but held. Even the stinging invigorated him. The very vomit and bloody excrement carpeting his 'luxury' was proof of wonderful, animal activity. I am not a human being I am an animal, he decided. And as one he could withstand much more inhumanity than he had previously thought possible. Then he became human once more. Let them chuck it at me.

A moted sliver of sunshine he had seen before yet never examined from his prone position curtained half the room with a triangle of gold. Nigel blinked twice: everything in the hut's other half seemed luminous viewed through this glory. He longed to get up and cross into that divine zone.

However, he had struggled to his feet twice a day to use the bucket and it was a major operation of great delicacy not to bend any part of his back; as well, he knew he would disappoint himself once actually on the other side. So he lay and watched the promised land, ecstatic, letting his mind fill with confidence.

His feelings were based on little. Bugger all, in fact. Every word Frank had said to him about life in the station went against Nigel's ebullience. But if he was to come through this period intact he had to store some ebull away for the times when it might be all he had.

This was how people got religion, he guessed. Death, pain, adversity, cockroaches singing Andrew Lloyd Webber songs, they pushed you through to where illusion took on power enough to sustain you, anywhere.

Nigel had a life sentence here. The ugly reality of it didn't matter one teensy bit. He bower-birded this knowledge, a collection of shiny or interesting nonsenses, this faith: he would get along in Eden penal station, a man with his twentieth-century knowledge; not only that, he wanted to learn everything about everything here; he wasn't a shy boy any more, had already begun one friendship; he was *alive* – and, someday, he would get out of here. But more, much more than this:

He would bring something new, perhaps wonderful, into this world.

Whoop-de-doo!

His last days in hospital passed dreaming what shape his wonderful new something might take. Would it be pink? Naturally, the time went too fast. The doctor – proof that eating too many pears does make you look like a skittle – noticed his patient had made it on to his back and decided to check Nigel's progress by more than asking, for a change. He rolled the new chum on to his stomach, ripped the disintegrated Woolworths' check shirt from his back, and in one sudden action stripped the hard herbal casing of black gloop from Nigel's wounds.

'AAAAAIIIIEEEEE!' Nigel's armpits were denuded in one short and brutal attack.

'You'll do,' said the doctor. 'Tomorrow you're going to work for His Majesty.'

He applied slightly less soiled dressings to the cracked and welling scabs, muttering about the pain in his feet and the bloody stupid tradition of huge bloody shoes for doctors, then toddled off.

Nigel swept the fragments of his imagined wonderfulness into a back corner of his mind. He packed them together, kneaded them into a solid ball, spat on them for luck and popped them into an old Tupperware lettuce-crisper he found there, which he thought would keep them truly fresh. He shoved the crisper under the case of sterling silver spoons he had borrowed with Mario Denuncio from Mario's parents and buried in the backyard then lost the treasure map. It was, beside the memory of his first orgasm, where he knew it would lie forgotten until an occasion arose when he'd truly need it.

Under the silver spoons, he reminded himself, that's where it is. Silver spoons.

Then he steeled himself against the torrid realities of hard labour and prison ways.

This is an ordinary crapulent hut where blokes have certainly died, he told himself. As Frank had told him, it was the sick-room where they put those with fairly serious injuries or illnesses, only one better than the hut called 'Death's Brothel'. You might call this place 'Death's Adult Cinema Live Acts on Stage.' You got to smell death here. Frank had recovered quickly, a tribute to his toughness; they had pitched him back into the camp before he had fully recovered. Nigel was far from recovered enough to work. It was simply the order of things from now on and he would have to accept it. He girded his loins, except his loins felt like superannuated junket from disuse.

The cockroaches chorus-lined across the joist nearest his mouth, mean ugly prison-hospital vermin that'd eat their ordinary three-inch Sydney relatives with taramasalata and a crisp white wine.

'Yrrrr!' he snarled at them. 'Your mothers are boll-weevils and your fathers are butterflies. Your sisters fuck dung-beetles! You come near me and I'll grind you between my teeth until you're fucking *Kit-e-Kat*, hear me?'

The insects Sondheimed on. But Nigel, with a bundle of irrational secret weapons in the attic of his mind (under the silver spoons), was not fazed. He spent the final hours of light of his final day in the prison hospital chewing his mangy shirt into balls and spitting them at the cockroaches and millipedes.

'Take that, mouse-fuckers!' he told them.

'Whoop-de-doo!'

Thirteen

New-Chum City

The Captain assigned new chums to 'snug' work for the first week. 'Easy stuff, like,' Pitcher told him. 'Gives you the place's layout, know what I mean?' It seemed the rat-like cockney was the one man who'd speak to Nigel. All the other new chums in the tent moved their bedding a respectful distance away on his first night there. He wasn't sure why. Nigel recalled Pitcher from his feverish days passing through Melbourne, although at the time he had assumed that the pointed pasty face was one more nightmare image. Nigel accepted his eager company, and Pitcher was useful, if you could stand the irksome mannerisms. Should just a fraction of what he burbled about prove true, then you needed a guide. There was no sign of Frank.

Just as well, thought Nigel.

Rock-carrying was considered snug work. The men from Nigel's tent carried baskets of rubble slung from poles across their backs starting before dawn and finishing after sunset. They paused only for a tea-and-damper breakfast and the afternoon smoko, an unofficial break offered to the non-dangerous in return for good behaviour while out of fetters. (No one worked faster for it.) Nigel's half-healed back was rubbed raw by the pole, and by the sweaty new prison browns on the lips of his scabs; his feet became pounded lumps of dead flesh; his every bone ached from keeping his ill-balanced loads level. But he kept his pace steady.

For a mere stumble and a few rocks spilt he saw a man sentenced to three days and nights in the Tin Box, whatever that was. (Pitcher's quick mime as he passed Nigel down the hill suggested punishment by heat.) A man on Nigel's gang was taken away by the Captain's men in blue, his fucknuckles, for no reason. He did not return. And each new chum felt the convict overlooker's axe-handle upon his legs or back, on one pretext or another.

In the twilight Nigel staggered dizzy to his bed with the desire for simple peace alone to digest his heavy supper, and his first working day. He lay in a stupor too exhausted to tell Pitcher to shut the fuck up, though the second-floor man's squeaky self-importance drove him spare.

'That Clyde gets right up my nose,' Pitcher confided. Never mind Clyde the overlooker, you could get a double-decker bus up Pitcher's nose. 'Fancy calling his stick Geraldine. I'd have given him fucking stick if it wasn't for the punishment crew. Reckon they don't call them fucknuckles for nothing, ay? Ay?'

Pitcher babbled on, hawking intermittently to clear the dust from his throat and licking his lips loudly. Nigel determined that he would kill the bastard later, when he could stand. Instead he fell asleep.

The next day was worse. A vicious sun beat them. Their aching bodies seemed to compress more with each load they staggered under. Men wet themselves beneath such burdens. It was no shame. Their rough clothes continued to chafe and today, suddenly, the men from Nigel's tent had fleas. Nigel hunted the beasties, cursing, but decided he had been lucky to escape a major assault of parasites for this long. There were worse things. He fared better than most in the sun, too, because of his days outdoors and his tanned Australian skin; a fair few, fresh from England, already had blistered necks which the carrying poles opened . . .

Water was a problem. Those who fetched the plastic bucket were forced to stop by each thirsty overlooker on the way. The overlookers' favourites drank their fills as well. Judging by the swearing from Nigel's own overlooker, this was illegal but difficult to enforce when you were at the end of the line – and were a weedy whinging sort of cretin named Clyde. 'Fuck my nostrils with a pickaxe-handle!' Clyde yelled, stamping his little feet on the broken earth in complaint.

'If that's what yez want!' called Dwyer, the next over-looker along, brandishing one beneath his gaunt face.

For Nigel the worst bit was the trot to the rock cart. Loading, though cruel, was short. You squatted, inserted your poles into the basket's handles, then turned to stand. This took place along a semi-cleared front near the logging area. It resembled a neolithic bowling-alley. Stumps stood in clusters, some partly uprooted by the tree's fall, rubble piled untidily near by. Once as erect as you could get with two baskets of stones on your back, you had to *run* across seriously wonky half-baked half-cleared sloping ground. Nigel hadn't fallen yet, but the effort taken to shift so much momentum in the downhill plunge strained his ankles and killed any chance of taking care of his lower back the way his father had taught him. It would have been better to take it easy now and then, to trip and whack the hard dirt with your face, except the punishment crews were always ready with whips.

Stock-whips. Long and slender with intricately seared handles and bevelled, well-kept leather that cut your clothes and skin at a stroke. Blinded you. Castrated you. The punishment crews responded to a whistle from your overlooker. So nobody whistled while they worked, no matter how chirpy the friendly teamwork made them.

'Come on ya blouses, we'll have you, and you and you. *Get* here!'

On Nigel's third night the men of the convict suburbs raided the new-chum area. Pitcher huddled close to Nigel as man after man was dragged from the tent. They returned beaten, grim, and withdrawn. Some returned completely hairless. Pitcher spoke to one and got a blank stare. Nigel offered a drink and the shaved man curled terrified into a ball, squatting, rocking, hugging his knees. Was it the cup or the water that scared him?

As the dreadful routine played itself through, it became clear that for some reason Nigel wasn't due the rape and savage initiation the others were getting. Pitcher knew it, but if he knew why he wasn't saying. He sat on his blanket in the back corner next to Nigel and taunted the baldies in the opposite corner with his plastic cup, cackling nervously when they cringed, and in his own fear he blathered on about the penal station.

Eden station sprawled, from the dangerous Hub, to the bark-hut suburbs, or Skirts, to the fringes of Cholmondeley; it was packed, bustling well past curfew, and in places almost prosperous.

In the Hub dwelt the eldest and toughest convictism, in quite solid buildings of mud and logs, of precious sheet metal and bark, of whatever came to rough hand. So far, Nigel had visited the area once. During the cart trip to the hospital he had spotted a building off the main road and down the hill made entirely from what, at that distance, looked like eyes. Pitcher informed him they were really glass bottle-stoppers, but that the place was indeed called Eye Lodge, and in it lived the cunningest felon in the station, one Herbert Braithwaite, Macka to his friends. Pitcher winked mysterious at Nigel and waggled his cup at the baldies across the lamplit tent. 'Yah!' he said. The baldies cringed, hate in their reddened eyes.

The Hub housed not only the evilest criminals, but also the old bastards, lifers not part of the inmates' leadership and too old for useful labour yet retaining enough nous to make themselves indispensable, usually to the station authorities, or fucknuckles. Mostly this involved grassing in some form. Blackmail networks built and renewed themselves around the station, over decades. The retirement plan here was usually death. A man was worked until he fell. The single way to survive until old bastardy involved forward planning. You had to do your backbreaking work as well as trade successfully in the underground economy, and all the while accumulate favours or, better still, filth. It took a sort of genius to survive at all. A murderous one when crossed.

Braithwaite was apparently one such old bastard, Nigel discovered. His Majesty's Penal Station Captain John Kern had been outwitted for years by the sly survivor. He stepped lightly between execution and riches by salting away food and during times of famine had rescued the whole station in one deal – and Kern's reputation as well. Nobody else could resist the short-term riches available from traffic in food. Kern had thus to weigh the possibility of drought against the old bastard's not terribly flagrant breaches of discipline. It infuriated the commandant and evoked admiration if not affection from the prisoners.

But why should Pitcher wink at Nigel when the old bastard was mentioned? Pitcher acted mysterious about the smallest scraps of knowledge, as if they were explanations of Special Relativity or where ball-point pens went or something. It was both the reason for and the consequence of the cockney's general despicability. It meant nothing. Simple as that. Yet he did have a secret.

Nigel hit his limit of frustration and puzzlement. He slapped the cup from Pitcher's hand. Pitcher checked himself in mid-gabble, mouth open, his fearful gaze on the cup in the red dirt. Slowly, glancing at Nigel, he reached for the cup and stowed it by his bowl.

'No, *no*!' another man yelled from the front of the tent, as two thick Skirt-dwellers dragged him out.

Pitcher turned to Nigel and tittered in his knowledge of shared security. Nigel realised he'd get no sense from the man tonight; he stretched out on his bit of earth, pulled his blanket over his face, and closed his eyes. He did not sleep. There was no sleep that night in Cholmondeley.

It was close to Down Tools. The sun had swelled to fill Cunt Gap, the remotely vagina-like break in the hills. Men reeled back and forth with their loads swinging. A rumour had spread during smoko: tomorrow they would shift across the valley to the other row of hills. Light-heartedness made the overlookers jokey. Dangerous games with the convict labourers peppered the afternoon. One of their favourites was to hold an axe-handle parallel to the ground in the path of a new chum. A man might hop over three such obstacles but when half a dozen convict overlookers got together it always finished with a convict labourer with his face ground into the dirt. His rocks sometimes bounced from their baskets and hit him. This, and seeing who could invent the most condemning reason for the fall to tell the punishment crew, was the object.

Today's final game centred on a thin, slug-white cockney whose sloped forehead and chin emphasised his monstrous pointed nose. He had provided great sport for the over-lookers, arrowing forward despite three tries using seven axe-handles. His tiny feet blurred as he hopped the obstacles. The overlookers made his path ever more dangerous. Rocks, roots and bloated dead wombats were dropped in his way; they dug trenches deeper and wider each time. As Nigel trembled by the scene of their jolly japes he thanked his lucky stars they hadn't chosen him to toy with. Their victim might have been as wicked a criminal ever to have faced a judge, but the overlookers were convicts too. And if they themselves hadn't been nasty as bowls of strychnine soup when transported, Captain Kern's divide-and-destroy policy had made them so now. And anyhow, Nigel knew their victim was only a small-time thief. Just a thief, just stupid.

On Pitcher's fourth trip down the hill the overlookers dropped a half-dead wallaby in one of the trenches. They then buried its head. It wobbled there, kicking with its powerful hind legs, suffocating. Approaching, Nigel saw his own overlooker throw back his head and hee-haw at the demented sky. This signalled the start of the vilest time of Nigel's life so far, a series of grisly snatches of action, heading for a single incvitable result:

A glimpse over his shoulder at Pitcher. The man's eyes widened when he saw the wallaby; he took three steps to the right but that gangling murderer Dwyer tapped him back on track with his axe-handle. Tonk.

The first obstacle course, a trench of horseshit and two men with axe-handles, took the cockney almost to his knees. Frantic, he pulled one leg then the other from the dung before his baskets continued without him, which forced him to hop in double-quick time over the next two axe-handles. Yet he made it. The three overlookers involved cursed simultaneously and ran to join the next set-up. Dwyer's gang cheered, and those with chains rattled them. They had dropped their baskets, to wait.

Fascinated and appalled at once, Nigel slowed so he wouldn't outpace the thin Londoner. He cast a glance sideways and caught a look of sinewy determination on the blistered burglar's face. His narrow lips had disappeared altogether and his black eyes darted around in calculation of the next manoeuvres. Faced with simple stones and axe-handles, creases of triumph spread around his eyes as he swiftly hopped the barriers.

By the time he reached the carefully prepared series of dead wombats, overlaid twisted roots and the tortured wallaby, all triumph had vanished. Nigel veered away from a pot-hole, so close now he could smell the acrid sweat of panic and concentration rising off the poor bloke. It smelt like the Casa Denuncio kitchen.

Nigel had to look away. Before he managed another glance Pitcher was down. On top of the wallaby. Nigel passed the group of overlookers in a rush to the rock cart. They swayed in agonies of mirth. The cockney lay in a burlesque of bestial sex, his groin bouncing up with each terrified powerful kick from the marsupial.

*

When Nigel had tipped his baskets on to the cart he turned
to view the sadistic scene. Eight overlookers surrounded
Pitcher, gasping with laughter, trying to whistle and failing
miserably. Before Nigel reached the edge of the group the
cockney had fallen off the wallaby. His trouser front was
torn and bloody. He was partly disembowelled. His eyes
boggled with pain.

Finally one of the overlookers managed a wheezing shrill.
The punishment crew answered with their own. When they
emerged from the nearest copse the overlookers shouted
their prepared witticisms excitedly, dogs barking their
masters' home-coming.

'The lazy bludger's knocking off early for a bit of the
other!'

'Disgusting what he'll do for a lie-down. Disgusting
Haw haw haw.'

'Whip the daylights outta him, the bastard chum's
dropped his load!'

'Watch out for his dong, you'll have half the roos in the
district on to yez – they're in love with him!'

'Nah don't hurt him, he's the King's official stump
jumper.'

'Whip him soundly lads, don't listen to them. He was
taking a *sticky beak* up the roo's arse when we wasn'
looking.'

'Yeah, he's built for it all right. Nose like that – he's
probably a emu in disguise. Yez can have him for tea once
youze've flayed him.'

'My oath – bignose! Bignose! Bignose! Bignose!'

This last was Clyde. He chanted as the punishment crew
twisted their mouths in distaste at the overlookers. Never
theless, regulations stated a punishment must be meted. The
overlookers were not strictly fucknuckles, but they had the
ears of the crew's superiors in their roles as informants and
if the crew held back merely because of a set-up they'd face
disciplinary charges.

So they laid into Pitcher. Nigel, panting, wiped the dust

and sweat from his forehead and stood dumbly by the thrashing with the other men. This was Pitcher, whom everyone hated, who mumbled about a goose named Henrietta in his sleep. Only two nights back Nigel had wished the man dead himself. It was as though Nigel had caused this. In Pitcher's efforts to escape the singing leather he flailed wildly, banging his head on his scattered load of rocks. His squeals grew ever more feeble, until he lay still and took it. He did not pass out. He did not even whimper. And Nigel could not look away.

After his regulation twenty cuts, Pitcher moved not at all. Nigel and three others were ordered by Dwyer to carry him to the infirmary, to Death's Brothel. Before they could respond the head of the punishment crew, a tall and clean-shaven corporal with a lean look of self-loathing, knelt by Pitcher's head. There was no pulse. The corporal glared up at Dwyer.

'Don't look at us mate,' whined Clyde.

The corporal shook his head.

'A man doesn't die off a flogging,' put in Dwyer, innocently.

'You know they can,' said the corporal. 'This one didn't.'

'So they can,' put in another of the crew, a private. 'So what? Let's go, Parker.'

'Ought to be an inquiry,' said Corporal Parker stubbornly. He stood, whacking the dirt from his uniform. 'A doctor's report.'

'Right, let's do the decent thing,' said another corporal, full of sarcasm. He was mustachioed and immaculate. Since when has that ever happened here? Are ye gunna ask the Captain y'rself?' He rolled his eyes.

'He had a weak liver, probably,' offered the private, who seemed used to standing between the other two in arguments. 'Couldn't stand the effort.'

'Yeah,' said Dwyer, loud.

Parker sighed and grunted resignation. He knelt again, closing Pitcher's eyes.

'Call the priest,' the mustachioed corporal ordered Clyde.
'Take him away,' said the private.

Dwyer leered down at the corporal in triumph. The bell on the hill tolled Down Tools for the evening.

Nigel had never seen death close up before. He had imagined it would sicken him. The pictures of bodies filmed in Vietnam had strung a taut cord of anguish in his chest, but this did no such thing. Pitcher was now an object, to be lugged with aching muscles to the mortuary. He felt guilt because he had wished Pitcher dead, more guilt because he resented the extra task given after Down Tools, and still more guilt because he felt nothing else. He found himself able to recall clearly for the first time since his flogging the firm round shapes of Catherine Samuelson's face. He disgusted himself.

But perhaps it's natural to think tenderly when reminded of how fragile we are, he speculated. Or it was simply mental hands playing pocket billiards in the face of reality. As usual. Whatever, it would be ridiculous to pretend grief for someone you hardly knew. And Nigel was beyond despair at this fatal planet now. This was not a decent place. Yet decent people lived here: Parker; Frank. Of course they were powerless. The idea of transportation made them so. For the system to have survived into the twentieth century, it would have to be controlled by crocodiles as Frank had said. From England's point of view it worked, though it needed periodic clean-ups. Here, authority was obviously rotten by nature.

So you made yourself look away and survived. For what he had no idea.

Work on the far side of the creek began the next morning. There were delays, indecisions, laughs – it was like a session at his father's factory. You could believe Pitcher had never existed. The following night Nigel decided he had been fortunate to get such an easy day; otherwise by now hi muscles would've seized. It would have brought a visit from the crew on only his fifth day on the job, murder in his still delicate condition. He had never known work as hard as this. As it was, with a stomach full of leavened bread and fatty beef-offal stew, he lay back on the slope which fell away from Cholmondeley's edge to the creek and gazed at the violent wash of stars with something akin to satisfaction. He had begun to drop into the station rhythm. Though the fresh scars on his back remained tender he had padded them by rolling down his collar and they seemed in no danger of infection. He'd pace himself. He'd cope.

At last he realised what – or rather who – lay behind his mysterious protection from the nightly skirt raids amongst the new chums:

Frank.

It had to be. But no further contact was needed. No. The rumoured connection between Frank and himself was for his protection until he grew used to life here. A favour from one invalid to another. They might meet and have a laugh about it, months on. Remember when you said I had a nice bum? Ah, what a joker.

Beyond the pebbly verge behind his head the convict settlement pulsed fitfully with small cooking-fires and the odd candle or lantern cast a warm light through the tent walls visible between scattered trees. Upside-down, it appeared nearly friendly; you could forget it was a slaughterhouse. It smelt of men and burnt eucalyptus. It reminded Nigel of a school camp. Nigel eased his tender neck straight again and once more contemplated the impenetrable patterns of the stars.

'Yu'll get a chill if ya fall asleep out here.'

Nigel's eyes flickered open. Fear jolted him fully awake. A dark shape loomed against the Milky Way.

'Ya know yer out past curfew.'

It was Frank. Nigel ought to have guessed he'd be back. Wake up, Australia. Nobody did simple favours out here.

He hunkered down beside Nigel and told him what to expect. Chains of protection operated, either paid or linked by friendship. Hitching, it was called. Frank himself, unlike many others, was only hitched to one person. Tomorrow night he'd return to take Nigel to the Hub to meet his hitch. For the moment, it was enough to know his protection was real, not merely some freak product of the grape-vine. Nigel could count on it. Even against the overlookers, in a pinch.

'I shouldn't a left it this long to see ya,' Frank admitted. 'I been busy on the trade these few nights.' He patted Nigel's upper arm, his hand a warm surprise. 'I heard what happened the other night with your overlookers and the crew. If them or any fucknuckles try that on you just show them your arse and tell them you're hitched to me. Then if there's a real problem their hitching and mine'll have to settle it between themselfs. Life in the big city,' he said. Nigel could see the man's broad grin in the shadows, a grey blur of face, and those eyes.

'Thanks,' said Nigel.

'You know why I like you, don't ya.' It wasn't a question.

'Mm.' Did he? Was that it?

'Well, I'll be gone. Work to do. Back tomorra.'

Frank straightened. His boots scrunched off into the darkness. Nigel got up to go to bed. Although exhausted, and although there were no raids that night, he took hours finding sleep. Trust and fear warred in him over Frank. In the bitter light of his first week at Eden penal station, fear won.

Fourteen

A Sly Old Bastard

Three more days passed before Frank reappeared. Nigel was standing in the new-chum line, wooden bowl and spoon in hand, waiting for his evening stew-lumps, when he felt a touch on his shoulder. He turned to see – nobody.

'Ha!' Frank grinned from the other side at this ingenious prank. He gave a low chuckle. 'Let's go get some real tucker.'

'Whereabouts?'

'Macka's place. Eye Lodge.'

Braithwaite. Oh, fuck. Oh fuck. I should have figured it out, he told himself. Wake up Nigel!

'Well come on, wake up, don't stand there like ya tongue's melted. Let's go.'

The two of them set off in the twilight down the hard-packed dirt road toward convictism's desperate centre, the Hub.

His first good look at it filled Nigel with despair. Here was a forcible reminder of the permanence of his situation. To build so solidly meant resignation to a lifetime of physical slog. You could become a tree-feller, a sawmiller; you could wind up in charge of your own small factory making, say, belt-buckles or nails – but you were still in prison. Nigel took in the carved verandah railings, the bottle windows and patterned wattle-and-daub of the six or seven blocks which formed the convict village, and although it told him that decency and care survived the brutalisation it made him wonder how he could have been so naïve as to think he might change things. At least it shoved aside his dread of Braithwaite.

'Does anyone ever get out of here?'

'All the time mate,' said Frank, surprised.

'Don't they get caught?'

'No reason to catch 'em when they got a ticket of leave. Hay Mohammed,' Frank waved businesslike at an especially gruesome set of teeth in a beard going the other way.

'I mean . . . doesn't anybody – break out?'

'Heaps.'

'But they get caught again.'

'And flogged. Them that survive out there.' Frank nodded at the forest darkness inland beyond the Captain's house on the hill.

'Can't they live off the bush?' Through an open door Nigel glimpsed a man in a tin bath down a hallway. Two younger men scrubbed his back.

Frank watched him watching, then shrugged. 'Some *eat* each other,' he said for effect.

'Yeah, I remember they used to – I mean, yeah.'

'After all, how's a bloke gunna catch enough to eat out there?'

Nigel had no answer to this. He had always assumed the convicts in his school history books were idiots not to have worked out some menu other than their fellow escapees beforehand. In two hundred years of settlement *some* kind of bush knowledge should have grown up, he thought.

They turned off the main road. Under the awning of a larger hut two men kissed passionately, hands exploring. Nigel was at once moved by their tenderness and apprehensive about Braithwaite's intentions. Frank had not mentioned the old bastard in his friendly deal.

'Anywar, if you're thinking of escaping, don't,' said Frank. 'We're leagues from anyplace.'

That shouldn't matter. Nigel almost said it aloud. The only drawback was pursuit . . . It was their religion held them back, he realised. Compared to the Europeans who had settled his Australia they were much more superstitious, with their carved faces of their gods everywhere, as if to ward off the inconceivably ancient native spirits they suspected in rock and tree. Still, survival in the bush wasn't easy, and there were real, antagonised Aborigines to worry about; he'd have to think it through before he attempted to escape himself.

He stopped. He hadn't put it so before, but he did intend to escape. He was going to escape. The word had crept up on him, yet he realised the notion had flavoured his new improved pistachio nut since his arrival. It was escape or give in to this place. A fundamentally new attitude. If he gave in he'd die.

Well what do you know? Every day *is* different.

'Come on,' said Frank from the entrance to a side-track a few metres on. 'Don't stand there grinning like a fool. We gotta meet me man.'

Eye Lodge was the last on a path running alongside the main road then falling away down a steep slope. Surrounded by piles of rubbish, reinforced by what looked like tea-chests and propped up by an assortment of logs that could have gone most of the way to building a new wooden house, everything about the place spoke of an old man whose days of regard for appearances and comfort were long gone. From near by you could see many of the bottle-stoppers had been replaced by pebbles or root vegetables. Nigel spotted a rat's head stuffed in one gap. The large vegetable garden offered the only sign of exertion. It looked weed-free. But the darkness could have hidden a great deal.

When Frank knocked and the door opened, Nigel was surprised to see a neatly dressed convict with combed whiskers and hair; clean, too, as far as the feeble candle-light revealed. Braithwaite waved them in. A strong eucalyptus tang mixed with an equally powerful stench of horseshit met Nigel inside. As Braithwaite shut the door

Nigel turned. The old man held out a hand. Nigel took it firmly, though not too hard, and straight up and down.

Braithwaite opened and kissed Nigel's palm. It was all he could do not to wrench away from his protector's grasp.

Braithwaite laughed, a hoarse animal sound. 'Mm,' he said to himself. 'Ahh mm.'

The old man stood about a half-head shorter than Nigel. He had, perhaps, once been a powerful figure. His red beard and bald pate shone in the wavering glow of the fire. Chest rising and falling at some speed, he stood for a moment eyeing Nigel with amused, piggish eyes. When he stopped being amused he looked abruptly sad. His knees faced one another slightly below his baggy crotch, but otherwise his legs looked as thick and as powerful as policemen. He wore bright red knitted bedsocks.

'Get yer shoes off,' he commanded. 'Mm.' With everything he said came a grunt. 'Stick 'em by the fire. Be nice and roasty-toasty when yer leave. Let's have some rum,' he said to Frank.

'Righty-o Macka,' replied Frank.

Macka grunted dismissively, like a steam train on its first chuff forward. 'Siddown son,' he told Nigel, gesturing at a pile of hessian bags on a bench.

Nigel sat. They waited in silence (apart from the odd rumble) until Nigel appeared out of a dark corner with three heavy bottle-bottoms on a tray. Checking its contents as he took his, Nigel thought it treacly, but it seemed thinner once below his nose – and smelt of liquidised flies.

'The King,' said Braithwaite and Frank.

'The Empire,' said Nigel hastily, jerking his glass to his lips.

'Fuck the Empire,' said Braithwaite, 'how's the rum, hm?'

Indescribably repulsive. Nigel pressed his lips tight together but shook as it went down.

'Good ay,' said Braithwaite.

'Mmm!' went Nigel. 'Mmm – good, thanks, uh –'

'Macka. Me name's Macka, son. Good, mm,' he went, 'good.'

They sat savouring the stuff. Macka lit a pipe carved from a root in the shape of a fat mackerel and sat puffing forth the smoke equivalent of cat's urine, restlessly.

'Mm.' He sounded like a bull in heat. 'I been watchin' yer work,' Macka said.

Doesn't he work too? wondered Nigel. Where did he get the time?

'Yer different,' Macka went on. 'Me and Frank, we like that: different. So far, since I hitched with Frank, we been alone. Ah. But I'm gettin' to be a bloody wreck now, gettin' old. Just about had it, me. Need Frank to take over the business side and one to do his job: gettin' about, carryin' stuff – argh – keepin' an eye open. Stuff. Mmm.' Macka leaned forward on his stool, fixed Nigel with undimmed green eyes, grunted like an emu and said:

'We don't have to fuck yer but we do have to trust yer.'

Frank leant across the couch and patted Nigel's knee. 'Remember in the hospital?' he said. 'What I told ya?'

Nigel shook his head. He realised he ought to have nodded.

'For the first while,' explained Frank, 'you're with us all day every day. That's because we can't let you see our operation an' get away to tell the Captain's fucknuckles. Fucken spies are everywhere. So you sleep with either Macka or me. The idea is, once you get what kind of good life you can have with us, ya won't want to go to the Captain even if yer are a spy – which I don't tally you are.'

'Mm,' said Macka. 'What yer are is – different. Dunno what yer are, but yer don't act like one o' the Captain's bloody ferrets.' He made a sound like a rabbit being choked. He spat at the rough flagstone fireplace, missing; the gob joined a graveyard of spots around the little fire's edge. He looked expectantly at Nigel.

Nigel squeaked, 'Well!' He cleared his throat.

'Don't worry,' said Frank. 'Macka's like me. There's no enjoyment in rape, not for either one.'

Macka made the sound of a two-stroke lawn-mower on gravel. 'My dong wouldn't rise its head if a bloody snake bit it anywar. Don't worry 'bout me boy.' He jabbed his mackerel pipe at his hitch. 'It's Frank what's built like a pickaxe!'

'Fuck off,' said Frank and pushed the old man off his stool.

Later that night, drunk on Macka's rum (which tasted less of blowflies after the first time and more of rat's jism), Frank and Nigel wove down the main track on their way to collect Nigel's meagre effects. An insanely whopping moon cruised the trees lopsidedly near Cunt Gap. By its orange tint it gave the countryside a more alien feel than it already had. Suddenly, it occurred to Nigel to ask how many people lived in this convict Australia.

'How many people live here?' he asked Frank, loudly.

'Shush mate, it's after curfew.'

'How many?'

'Ya wanna get us flogged?'

'All right all right,' whispered Nigel. 'Shshsh,' he told the moon, finger held to his nose. 'But how many?'

'How many what?'

'Dogs, cows, bloody possums – *people*. What's the population?'

'Whatulation?'

'How many live here?'

'Where?'

'Australia!'

'Shush!'

'Okay, sh. How many?'

They heard accordion music played far away, probably from the Captain's Residence above Cunt Gap. A dog barked. They passed through an odour like beeswax and porridge, then back into the normal bright gum smells.

'Thousands I expec'.' He ticked colonies off on his fingers. 'New South Wales; Kingsland; Alfonso; Mendanaland,' whispered Frank. 'Thousands and thousands' – as though he had contemplated each one. 'Not a lot.'

'Crapola! Yeah I know: shush!'

'It's not funny, Nige. You saw what they did to that bloke the other day. Happens regular.'

'Pitcher . . . Pitcher Martin! Great book. You know, sometimes I don't care if they kill me too.'

'Ya would if they did. But I know what you mean. Me neither. Sometimes.' Frank looked inward.

'Is that a death-wish?'

'Ya got some funny ideas, mate. In this world it's only the evil buggers who care so much about their own skins. There's not one of the rest of us who hasn't wanted to give their life for someone they loved . . . like Macka an' me.'

'There you go about love. Tralala . . . you love him?'

'Sounds sick to you ay?'

'No no!'

'Shush up!'

They walked on.

'It woulda sounded sick to me,' Frank explained, 'when I first got here. But now I tally it's the best. See, the Captain and his lot – they want to turn us against each other like *pikun* with their fucken shadders an' grassers an' privileges for some and that. But they can't kill our natural feelings. A man has to love someone, if there's any good in him. Somebody. So we do.'

Somewhere in the dark convict camp a dog was being beaten. It yelped, and fell still.

'I'll answer the door Mum,' said Macka, with the innocence of a choirboy, in his sleep.

But the noise was no dream. It came again, twigs *shifting* instead of snapping outside. Nigel slipped out of bed, while beside him Macka said, childlike defiance in his voice now, 'I don't care if you do come back, we shan't pay your poll-tax.'

The stones in the dirt floor chilled Nigel's soles. A nervous moon shifted to and fro across a rag rug. The noise came again. It was definitely not Frank returning from his mysterious 'business' somewhere in the night; Frank would have given the code knock by now.

Nigel eased the bar off and the door open.

Sitting in a patch of moon by the compost heap, a barred bandicoot cleaned itself. Nigel lowered the door-bar to his side. The animal bolted into the darkness. Nigel sighed and shook his head. He could have sworn the bandicoot had winked at him before it ran.

Quietly, he crept back to bed.

As he slipped under the rough blanket he nudged Macka's elbow and the old man raised his arm and flopped it across Nigel's chest. Nigel froze.

Macka said, 'Don't worry about me, son.' Nigel heard wakefulness in the old man's voice now. 'I'm too rancid to get the old stick even up, let alone whack it into yer while yer lookin' the other way. Yer done good then. Yer done right. Coulda been anythin' out there. I got enemies. I'm glad to have yer about.' He gave Nigel's breast a pat.

Nigel's neck prickled with embarrassment; his whole body heated. Macka hugged him in a gruff way, immersed him in his sour-milk and tobacco odours, scraped his neck with ribald beard-hairs. A thin limp dick squished into the small of his back. Bony knees jabbed his thighs. It took a fair old time for Nigel to relax in this easy grip. By then, snores whiffled his lower jaw and ear, night versions of the self-made animal chorus which went with his words, a chorus children and dogs understand but which we forget. For what seemed like hours the penis nudging his taut spine occupied all his thoughts. Other penises he had known zigzagged through his frightened brain: his dad's tired stump of uncircumcised cactus; an array of high-school dicks worn with demented pride or shame in showers; Todd's permanently semi-stiff tuber; his own plain tissue-smudger, too small from above but in a mirror – more distressingly – average. The parade exhausted him, till he could no longer tell the venous purple horror once flashed at him in Exhibition Gardens from the white baby's pisser Mario Denuncio maintained was like Michelangelo's David's; he kept seeing one or the other or Todd's in the middle of his third-grade teacher's forehead.

He drifted into dreams of buttercups with Macka's rummy grumbles giving reassurance that the man was well past the point where sex ruled every action. The only disturbing element in his dreams was his third-grade teacher, Mr Waller, dressed as a hot pink marshmallow telling the buttercups a new kind of algebra Nigel didn't understand. Nigel slept easy. So it shocked him out of bed and on to the floor to find the morning erection in his grip was Macka's knobbled member. The sly old coot laughed and laughed. The old bastard.

Fifteen

Pecking Orders and Nut Priorities

For seven months Nigel rode the carts to the land-clearance areas with the other new chums but returned to take his supper at Eye Lodge. As long as he showed on time the convict overlookers did not care where a lag slept. Besides, the fucknuckles knew where he was, their shadders and grassers told them. For seven months Nigel found no time to think about escape plans or how to alter this country's fundaments, he was released from Deep Thought for a time. By exhaustion. Slowly, though, he learned to cope.

In fact he grew strong. Although Nigel never did so well that the overlookers thought him underworked he did learn to carry a normal load of rocks or wood without pain. Macka rubbed an obnoxious fish-oil into Nigel's neck and the sun left him alone. As did his fellow workers. But a few rubbings gave him a tan which deepened before winter. The gangs laboured without a break in the mud, except for King Rupert's birthday, yet Nigel found a perverse satisfaction in his triumph over his body's weaknesses.

The time arrived when a mob of new new chums forced the old new chums out of Cholmondeley into the Skirts. Out of snug work too. Macka bribed and wrangled Captain Kern's houseproper into giving Nigel a job in his kitchens. It didn't take much wrangling actually. Nigel had a rare asset: he could count. He became the Captain's Official Egg-timer.

This was not the jolly reefer-party with naughty-shaped

balloons and dancing anthropologists the title makes it sound. He also had to hack and peel and pound and knead and stir for hours together. He had to keep his eyes open as Macka's shadder. And much worse on top of that.

But released from the more than random whacks (aside from those of the tuber-throwing chef) and heavy loads, given lunch and the varied game of dealing with the Captain and his guests, Nigel felt a foot taller and the muscles he'd developed so painfully lost their stringiness. He gained weight. Macka licked his dilapidated chops, put egg-white on the daily kitchen wounds with deliberately shaking hands and called Nigel his 'beautiful boy'.

Nigel blushed to his toe-jam. He had seen himself in the creek a month back on wash-day; he knew he was a different man. It had snuck up while he was occupied with reality. The tight edginess was rounded, full now. His pitted face was softened by a haze of bum-fluff. A brown young man built like a footballer blinked back up at him from the wrinkled water; only the shilly-shally bluey-grey eyes told him this was himself. No matter if he did feel the same total drongo inside his head.

Inside his soul, even.

However, the luxury of the odd spare moment eventually allowed Nigel to do something about his pistachio-nut soul as well.

At first it was a minor revision or two.

With his eyebrows shrivelling as he scooped loaves off the oven's brick floor, or up to his knees in duck feathers and guts in the boiler-room, and once mid-elephant as he counted to one hundred and fifty elephants by the eggs (he overcooked them, which earnt him a backful of short lashes), Catherine sprang to mind.

Damn Catherine. He still felt betrayed by her. So she had pleaded for him. So what. Had she testified in court in the first place he wouldn't be sitting here covered in half-digested duck spew and gizzards, high in the summer heat. What had made her change her mind? Her conscience. She wasn't in love with him. No possibility. He had to wake up to himself. She wasn't a vengeful social climber like her brother – ready for any atrocity which advanced his standing and so his pathetic sheep 'research' and thus his level of knighthood – but she had not returned, she had not even *looked* for the love in Nigel's eyes.

He could not forgive her for it. Of course this tied him to her as much as any possibility of love. He couldn't stand the way she swallowed her vowels so cutely, he thought it was dumb she was so proud of her ability with a banjo, and her nose had a little blobby bit which made her resemble a – a person with a blobby bit. He often conjured her memory to fume at. He always made sure he was alone when he did so.

He had lost most of his self-pity, but he kept this much alive. Never know when it might come in handy.

Eventually a major change occurred in his Deepest Self.

It began when his vague idea of escape revived – out of terror.

The Captain, a weak-lipped man with a redundant dimple in his chin and the watery blue premeditated eyes of a grandmother vivisector under grey curls and a top hat, raged from the head of the table against Corporal Parker, who stood braced forward into the invective as if caught in a hurricane.

'I don't bloody care if ye've married the sister-raping bastard, I want his donkey-fucked arse stripped bare on this table tonight after my frigging supper! Ye hear me?'

The Captain's tirade concerned his paranoia about his opium supply. Nigel and his soup-tureen had to be prodded into the dining-room with a long fork by the cook. If the screeching wasn't enough, *the man had a little pointy Vandyke beard!*

Parker bided his time. 'Sir? Dwyer will think I have

grassed him to you. The man already hates me; this will make him murderous, may I suggest – '

'Blast your petty uncle-rogering feuds with the over-lookers, cunt, the pisspocket has been pilfering my wedge and I don't give a pool of dead monkey's cum for what he thinks or doesn't. Sort your own pecking order with him.'

'But he won't just think, sir – '

Kern slammed the table. 'I don't give a shit in *biggle* about it!' In his fury he cast about for victims. He lit on Nigel. Nigel began to step back but Kern grabbed the tureen of scalding soup from him and flung it at the corporal.

Parker screamed and grabbed his soaked thighs, dancing his excruciation.

'Get out!' bellowed Kern. 'Get the fucker and ye fetch him here or yer both for lashes! GET OUT!'

This kind of thing happened often.

Yet in itself it was not enough to convince Nigel that he needed to escape.

By no means the cruellest turn the Captain had, but certainly the creepiest, was his engorged pursuit of rapists and initiators. Most real crime brought summary punishment from the more powerful hitchings. The attacks on new chums could not be controlled. The Captain, however, according to the Regs of HM's Penal Inspectors, was supposed to combat such wicked abominations with 'a moral vigour suitable to the horrors such bestiality inflicts upon its victims.' He did so with relish.

He blamed the victims. The usual tactic was an attack on the raiders which did no harm but spoiled their night's frivolities. It was easy to find them. Gang rapes were held in the Cleavage, a ferny gully between two cleared hills so misshapen now that convictism had not the heart to say their name any more. Into the Cleavage a couple of Kern's fucknuckles dipped and brought out some kicking chums who became examples of the Captain's diligence.

He shaved them.

Screaming with wrath he had the chums strapped to a special plastic table, where he corrected the new arrival's misapprehensions about what they could get away with in penal Australia, as if they had received no instruction from the Captain's seafaring brothers during their months aboard the hellish prison ships. He raged at the chums for their own good as he washed and oiled them, applied hot towels, and stropped his cutthroat razor. He told them what to expect if they so much as mumbled about mutiny, so much as thought about it. He ran a tight ship. A tight, tight ship.

So bellowing, he brought the razor glinting down upon the prisoner's white flesh. The Captain shaved quickly; he could denude an average man in ten minutes. Nigel knew it, because he had to count elephants for him and enter the times in the Captain's log. And not once in forty-three and a half separate instances did Nigel see a naked man emerge with the shallowest nick on him. It was the best shave of their lives, if the Captain did say so himself. It explained the men who, although tripped regularly and brought lashes by it, did not trim their facial growth again.

To start with, the desire to escape from prison had replaced the tried method of coping (hysterical despair) within Nigel's basic make-up. This was change enough in Nigel's pistachio nut as it spun gradually to a halt in a new position, after brushes with death and hard work. Nothing is of course as simple as it seems, though. The impulse *to remain* became the strange new force in Nigel's pistachio nut. But not in hysterical despair. Far from it. Fifteen months into his life sentence, two things happened to kill the idea of escape in Nigel. First, Nigel was admitted into Macka's business. He had already picked up lots of clues. The man would chortle over a little coup – the next day there was a jar of coffee which couldn't be roasted except by Nigel at the Captain's where the smell wasn't unusual. Things came out during little barneys between Frank and Macka. At last they let him in formally, after a bigger row, one that almost took the roof off Macka's hut.

'Ya don't buy stuff I haven't told ya to buy!' said Macka, his beard a-wobble, his grunt gone to the place grunts hide in times of crisis.

'I did it for you ya mug,' Frank told him.

The two stood just about on one another's toes. Frank's normally gentle brown eyes were dark pits. He loured where his ancient mate incinerated. Both puffed as if making love. Macka's ears wagged as he spoke.

'I don't mind if ya did it for the Holy Blessed Child of Blackpool, son! I give yer orders, right enough – an' if I send yer out for beans you don't come back with a barrel o' gunpowder.'

'We done business with the man before, Macka, he's safe I tell ya.'

'He's bloody not!' he turned and hefted the small keg. He ripped out the bung with his teeth and spat it at Frank's feet.

'Macka!'

'*This* is how safe yer bloody shit-draggin' fieldmouse is, he's frightened of rubbing he's own arse the bloody wrong way, give alone the bleeding Captain and he's fucknuckles!' He up-ended the keg. He waved it about like a watering-can.

Nigel leapt backwards into the wall. A sulphurous taint rose into the room.

Macka looked delighted. He danced from foot to foot while Frank tried to right the keg by lunging at it.

'I'll fucken learn yer,' shouted Macka, '*I* give the orders round here!'

They were all lucky it was past midnight and the neighbours were out of earshot. Someone might have complained.

Frank chased his capering hitch around, shouting his name and much more besides.

Nigel grew uncomfortably aware that the wood-stove was still alight. He made for it and arming himself with a whisk broom stood sweeping frantically in a mist of sparkling flecks.

Tzat! Szat! went the gunpowder. Macka only cackled and waved the keg.

Finally Frank punched it out of Macka's hands. He hugged the old man tightly. 'You *fucken* old fool!' shrieked Frank. 'Ya coulda killed us all ya know, it's not just you and me now, there's Nigel too – or don't yer care about ya "beautiful boy" no more, yer getting too old and fucking doddery to think about anyone else, ay? *Ay?*'

Macka did not answer. They stood wheezing for a minute, then relaxed. Macka pulled out of Frank's embrace.

Frank muttered something, staring at the floor.

'Ay?' said Macka.

'I'm sorry,' murmured Frank, with a classic boot-scuff at a trail of gunpowder.

'Ay?'

'I'm sorry,' Frank said. 'I didn' mean to yell at ya like that, and I'm sorry I didn't click to the risk about the gunpowder. He is a cowardly bastard, that bloke, he wouldn' stand up for a second against the Captain. It was stupid of me. I'm sorry. I won't do it again.'

Macka made the sound of a drain being cleared of gunk. 'Yer bloody right ya won't.' He grinned at Nigel. A few of his teeth were black with muck from the stopper he'd pulled. Trails of explosive stained his clothes and beard. 'As of tonight, son, yer in the business. You two can keep an eye on each other. Stop this one getting into mischief.' He took a handful of Frank's hair. The younger convict tugged out of his reach, surly but smiling.

Macka grunted like a vicar deflowering a choirboy. 'Yair, it's about time,' he told Nigel.

Nigel shrugged and nodded. Anything. He just wanted to get the keg out of the hut and buried somewhere away from these two maniacs. He saw enough insane tempers at work.

So he learned the smugglers' ways. He learned how to slip

out of the station at night, and where all Macka's stashes were. Each penal station was supposed to be quite a distance from the nearest free town, but in practice ticket-of-leavers gathered near by the government ports: they felt the risk from convicts was less than that of possession by native demons. Exorcism was expensive, and messy. Nigel helped lug booty from secret deals to the stashes for burial. The work ate into his sleep, but it was exciting.

They would chew maize cakes and drink rum by the fire after a deal and watch the sun rise, filthy and exhausted – and alive. The maize cakes tasted buttery, sweeter and richer than any bloodless equivalent his own world had to offer. The fire was the most warming he'd met. The dawn was fresher and crisper here. The Melbourne he'd left, with its ribbons around old oak trees, frozen alphabet-shaped vegetables, détente, ex-Nazi tropical fish bootleggers, Henry Kissinger, those psychedelic lamps filled with oil which glooped up and down, seemed unlikely, the memory of some rubbish science-fiction tale read and discarded when he was a young boy.

Why bother to escape? Not only that – who gave a whoop-de-doo for the unopened parcels of ridiculous Deep Thoughts invented in hospital and so carefully stored in his mind (beside some cutlery box), that might (or might not) change his pistachio utterly? What was so bad about his life here? At last his soul was fine as it was. By golly he felt better than he ever had. At last Nigel had more than fish, he had *company*.

And more.

Following a day spent scrubbing the mould from pantry corners that had left him cut by brushes and splintered by shelves and puckered by the wicked herbal cleaning-fluids, Nigel sat with Frank awaiting news about a deal struck with the Captain.

Kern was notorious for entrapment. He'd bargain long,

some useful piece of information would slip out in the tiring process, then his fucknuckles would swoop on the contraband and smugglers both, arrest and confiscate. This way he assured his reputation as the strictest commandment and potted the goodies for free at once. Most convicts, especially the old bastards who had learnt through bitter experience, did not trade with Kern. All kinds of methods had been tried, from burying the stash to dealing anonymously through a ticket-of-leave man, but the Captain had caught the skirts who tried it and punished them in novel ways. Legends built up about them, like the one about the man whose arms had been fastened for a week around the neck of a bullock, which had mangled him . . .

Macka only traded when he knew Kern simply had to have his goods, and he made sure the Captain would never receive the whole amount if any harm came to him or his. Greed, he maintained, had undone the rest. Yet there was a history, that not even Frank had learnt more than hints about, behind Macka's success. Kern and the old bastard had served in the Navy together, were in one of the secret 'coalitions' rife throughout the Empire – Macka could be punished but not killed.

'Unless of course the Captain chucks a fit one day,' said Frank.

'But other than that he's safe,' said Nigel.

'No way. The Captain wants him badly. He'll try him through official channels, but. He'll crow about it. You'll see, Macka'll haggle till dawn with this one. Kern's not past inventing some crisis so's to fool Macka into bargaining. An' Macka'll wanna suss that out just as much as Kern'll wanna bargain long hoping for a slip. Which won't happen. The old bastard may be senile but he's not stupid.'

The fire spat. Frank leaned forward to shove the wood back into place. He looked worried. Nigel, who had seen the Captain throw a fit several times by now, knew why. He worried for his friend.

He had never had a best friend. Unless you counted

Mario Denuncio before the great sherbet-packet plastic Donald Duck ring débâcle. No, he wouldn't count Mario.

He smiled at Frank. Eye Lodge seemed larger in the soft firelight, Frank seemed part of it. He belonged here. The rich glow defined the muscles in Frank's arms, made the knees which opened and closed nervously smaller, his thighs wider. Frank took a sip of his rum. Nigel did the same.

Nigel spread his arms and rolled his head to work the kinks from his exhausted shoulders.

'You look a sight better than when you got here from down south, mate. You know how they say a flogging relaxes a man, well never mind it you were a bloody len'th of tight rope back then.'

Frank was right. Nigel felt drunk and warm enough to break his resolution and explain his origins to his friend. Then he thought: 'Why should I? If it comes up I won't lie, but what does it matter where I've been? His own world had become irrelevant, certainly nothing to boast about. If you forgot about the brutality here for the moment, could he *ever* have felt as easy before the accident with the fish? Right now, life felt too good to alter with strange news from a complicated country a lonely dream away. He'd let things rest.

'Hay. Nigel.'

'Mm?' He looked up. He smiled broadly.

Frank's grin was anything but his usual cynical one this time. 'You were away with the angels,' he said. He leaned toward Nigel, hands on his knees. The lump of wood he used as a stool rocked slightly. 'Hay – seeing as you're in such a good mood, how about it?'

'What?'

'You know: I like you, you like me, an' we got hours and hours till dawn, mate.'

The automatic refusal parked in Nigel's chest and didn't budge. Frank's breath was sweet and round with rum near his cheek. The fire rolled pleasantly in on itself, and up. The usual insect company appeared to have discreetly left the two of them alone for the night. Nigel said, 'I . . . '

Sixteen

Doing It

It happened all the time. From a cliff-top beyond the cleared areas, where the slopes grew too steep and the boulders too large and too many to clear, in a break in the virgin forest littered with wildflowers and lush spring grass swishing above your knees, at the end of half an hour's walk after you dropped from the work cart while it queued for the bridge and minutes before the guards missed you – freedom.

'Will it hurt much, Zak?'
  'Not so much as a whipping.'

Such a glorious day, it faded the usual horrors to monochrome. Nigel had been sent up here with basket and string and scissors to gather wild herbs for the cook. Nigel obeyed willingly, singing. It was an unusual request. The most hated lags were not sent into the bush on their own. Ah, but you couldn't fear spirits on this kind of day – and the Captain had a gibbering, murderous need to impress his visitors that night. Nigel had not collected herbs before and carried the vaguest descriptions of the right sorts from the cook, seeing as the cook had only heard it was possible in a letter from his daring mother in Carthage. Should he take the bristly one with the yellow flower or the smooth one with the greenish bloom? The cook's mother had said nothing about bristles, and the green blooms were yellowish at times. The one might prick the throat, the other had the milky sap of a poisonous plant. Still, who'd get pelted with

potatoes for taking both on the first kind day of the season?
It cheered everyone.

'Ya sure it won't hurt, Zak?'
  'Cross my heart.'
  'Sure you're sure?'
  'Yes, Terry.'
  'Sure you're sure you're sure?'
  'I'm sure I'm sure I'm sure.'
  'Sure you're sure you're sure you're sure?'
  'Yup. Alla them.'
  'Sure you –'
  Thump.

On the clearing's edge, Nigel tripped. As the long grass
rushed at him he caught sight of two figures across the
clearing. Baldies. He then came face to face with a frog.
'Whoop,' went the frog.

'I'm afraid.'
  'Of what comes after, Terry?'
  'No. Of the spider on ya shirt.'
  'Uuurgh! Where?!?'
  'Here, here, I'll –'
  'Eeee! Aaieee!'
  'Hold *still*!'
  'GET IT OFF!'
  'Yeah, yeah – there.'
  'Ah thank God. Thank God for you, Terry.'
  'You're the strong one, Zak.'
  'Not me, Terry.'
  'Yeah you are.'
  'No I'm not.'
  'You are fucken so.'
  'You're the one, dickwit!'
  'Who're you callin' dickwit, fuckface?'
  'You, ya deadshit.'

So it went on, and on.

Struggling to his feet, he saw the two figures resolve into people. From near his ankle the frog went, 'Nurrds.' Nigel ignored it; he pushed through the grass into a world of pollen and bright scents wafted by the breeze. The people at the cliff's edge dropped to their knees almost at the same time. The wind shifted, bringing their conversation to him.

'I don't think I'm strong enough, Zak.'
   'I got a idea, Terry.'
   They stood. Zak, the taller of the two, pulled a couple of snot-encrusted rags from his trouser pockets. Terry caught on and did likewise. Nigel stopped and stared as they tied their wrists and ankles together. He had seen these two somewhere before. Their recently shaved heads made them as anonymous as any of the Captain's victims, though. Terry had tied his wrist to Zak's ankle. Zak clouted him and untied then retied them.
   They knelt once more.
   'Waugh!'
   For a moment they teetered at the edge. Below, Nigel knew, a stream threaded through nasty pointy rocks. Yet still he did not move forward, their familiar faces perplexed him so.

'Now I lay me down to sleep – '
   'Ya can't say that.'
   'What do I say then, smartarse?'
   'Repeat after me, Terry.'
   'Yeah.'
   'Dear God – well, you never did much for us, in fact I can't think of one thing except for porridge in winter – anywar, dear God – '
   'Do I have to repeat all that?'
   'Yes!'
   'Then do it a bit at a time.'

Zak did so. Terry repeated most of it.

'Dear God – and all your minions – we're just two fuckheaded numskulls – '

'Skulls.'

'We never had nuffing – excep' maybe fruit; some lime juice and apples, but with worms – '

'Worms.'

'Sometimes we had cakes and once a bowl of cream that Terry didn't get none of 'cause I drank it all, and of course that was pinched – '

'Pinched.'

'And one time, remember Lord that goose?'

'Goose?'

'That was delicious, Lord. Good one. Oh, and we found a tenner once. You remember, the one I carried around down my under-drawers till it fell apart to smithereens?'

'Smithereens?'

'So I don't guess that counts because we couldn't never spend it. Anywar, as we been in prison of one sort or other – no thanks to you Lord – since we was nippers – '

'Nippers.'

'You know our conditions a been bloody awful pits o' vomitations.'

'Tations.'

'And seeing as we on'y ever had each other and things don't look like gettin' better even a little tiny smidgin – '

'Smidgin.'

'We decided to come up here on a lovely day, say our prayers to You an' splatter ourselves all over those evil rocks an' go to heaven or one of the other good places in the sky if we're allowda.'

'Louda.'

'See ya soon, Lord, or one of ya minions.'

'Onions.'

'I told ya to repeat everythin', deadshit.'

'Deadshit.'

'No you, ya bastard!'

'I did!'
'No ya didn'.'
'Yes I did.'
'Not the last bit.'
'You were just sayin' goodbye.'
'Well – all right.'
'Yeah.'
'This is it.'
'Mm.'
'Less go.'
'Mm.'
'What're ya doin' *that* for?'
'I'm just kissing ya goo'bye – in case.'
'Good idea.'

It was as they kissed – it was something about the petulant puckers on them – that Nigel finally placed the pair. He rushed forward shouting, 'NO! *Wait*!'

Zak and Terry were startled and, taken aback, began to slide over the edge.

'WaaaaAAAAUUUURRRGHGH!' they both yelled.

Nigel replied in the same lingo. He missed them by inches. His momentum carried him helplessly toward the drop.

So beautiful, it was. Delicate rivulets split from the main cascade and tumbled into mist, a dream until it touched the pool below. A host of ferns convened along the pool's spill. Although they swung sickeningly beneath him Nigel never forgot their lush variety: tree-ferns, doughty herring-bones, maidenhairs which glinted in the refractory mist, and crow's-nest ferns with liquid eyes at their centres as blue as the sky. As he gasped towards his death he fell in love with the scene. It came to mean the afterlife to him. He *wanted* to be down there, two hundred metres below. Splintered bones and spilled innards seemed a bargain price for this heaven. He could see a sand-trout in the pool!

*

Yet it would be a pity to throw his life away today, after losing his virginity last night.

Sort of. Nigel had said, 'I . . . '

A wave like nausea but more pleasurable had swept from his toes to his penis' tip. Was this homosexual desire? 'I . . . ' he started again, to say something, anything. He heard himself explain:

'Frank, I've never had – done it with anybody, a man or a woman, and basically, I do like – I do *want* women. It's not the way I thought it'd be.'

Frank was undeterred, certainly not offended. He said, 'You don't have to think of it that way. This is a bad thing, I know, and it leads to becoming a bad man – '

'I wouldn't be too sure of that.'

'It's obvious. We're dooming ourselves by this.'

'No we're not. That's the problem with this place. Bloody superstition.'

'Anywar. It's not like I'm asking to fuck ya or for you to fuck me. Hasn't anyone touched ya, Nige?'

Nigel thought of Marlene White, of ice-cream afternoons. He nodded.

'Well let's play around a bit. Might die in the arse, might not. Won't hurt. And ya can't say you haven't wondered about it.'

'No. I can't.

'And ya can't say ya haven't touched your own body.'

Nigel shook his head. The fire took care of itself for a while. They played, as boys will, and like best friends, they were gentle.

A hand snagged the seat of his trousers. His flight reversed. As he flopped into the grass he saw the one with the quick reflexes – Zak – shoot past him, carried by his own powerful wrench toward the abyss. Zak was, however, tied to Terry, who flung his weight backwards. The two suicidal convicts fell in a pile on top of Nigel. Knees and elbows

thumped Nigel's back. The knees and elbows so much like
Fatguts's and Knacker-Eater's, the skinheads who in
another life had tried to mug him with a sockful of pistachio
shells. Funny they should be baldies here. The other Zak
and Terry had wanted to beat him up as well. Funny.

Winded, it took Nigel some time to speak. By then his
wonder had faded somewhat.

'You fucking mad bastards,' he said into the dirt. 'What
sort of game were you two playing at?' He wormed from
under them. He crawled away a pace and sat up, pushing his
fringe out of his eyes and brushing bits of grass from his
face.

Terry (Knacker-Eater) began to cry. His skinny body
heaved. This carried him up. So, balanced on his forehead
and toes, he bawled. Zak (Fatguts), beneath him, joined in.
And tied to each other as they were, every time Zak
pounded the dirt or kicked a grass-clump it raised one of
Terry's limbs. Soon Zak toppled on to Nigel's lap. They
wailed and snivelled and beat Nigel unknowingly with their
whipcord limbs while Nigel gave them tentative pats on the
shoulder or sandpaper head. His anger turned in, rose as
sadness and then bitterness, as he considered the reasons for
the skinheads' desire to – to do it. The boys were rabbit-soft
by nature. Even Nigel was harder, now. Like Frank and
himself they were best mates and righteous convicts spat on
the pea-green love of best mates. These two open comic
books were prime for brutal rape in the Cleavage. The
Kern.

He placed either hand on Terry and Zak's misshapen
skulls, a useless benediction from St Nigel the Confused, but
it shut their sobs like a tap-twist. 'I know,' he mumbled, '
know . . .' to the warm eggs that pulsed beneath his
fingertips. Nigel did know: if they were anything like the
skinheads he had met in his Australia they were insane by
standards here, or worse.

*

Said Zak, 'We're gunna get flogged for sure.' He wound the rag he'd taken from his ankle around his thumb. Wound it up and unwound it again.

'So jump,' said Nigel.

'Can't do that now,' protested Terry.

'Why not?' asked Nigel.

'It's neally tea-time,' answered Zak as if it were obvious. Terry nodded sagely.

An opera-singing tree would have puzzled Nigel less. The word 'tea' reminded him of his original task. It set him thinking about how he could help the two escape their punishment and dodge his own at the same time. Late back with the herbs when the Captain's fiancée was visiting meant twenty cuts on the back, as well as painful blows with root vegetables. And for Zak and Terry suicide might be the best alternative to the kind of punishment baldies got.

'Why don't ya mind your own bum-fluff?' said Terry.

'Yeah, fart-sucker. Blokes like you get silver spoons and tie bits of string to 'em and tinkle them with *ottots* at Christmas-time.'

Nigel grinned. How good it was to know their counterparts back home had nothing on these two as far as idiocy went. And in this country where the bad were bad and the good were hoodwinked it was wonderful to meet people you couldn't classify. Even if they drove you barmy. They were either proof that stir-fried morals were possible here, with their blathering about silver spoons, or they were mutants. This gave him an idea. The notion sat on the edge of his memory and it would take time to recall it, but he resolved to tease it out. He was definite silver spoons rang a bell.

Why silver spoons, though?

(In a season of self-satisfaction he had all but forgotten his idea about freeing these people's minds.)

Silver spoons?

Never mind. Right now, he had to stave off the consequences of saving these two dorks.

'Fucken stickman,' said Terry, wrenching at the weeds and flinging them over the edge. 'Fucken Empire laddie with tinkly spoons in ya bag.'

Nigel stared at the grass in Terry's hands. Suddenly he knew what to do. 'Listen,' he told the would-be suicides. 'I know how to get you out of your flogging.'

'Yeah,' said Zak, raising the skin where his eyebrows once lived, 'eat prunes and shit our way outta here.'

Terry collapsed sideways with laughter, fortunately away from the edge. Zak made farting sounds and cocked his fingers like pistols.

Nigel could see this was not going to be easy.

'There,' breathed Nigel, taking a step back from his handiwork. Not much time now. Soon the punishment crew and the other fucknuckles would close on the missing convicts with dogs. They must have been missed by now. But this had to be done well or forgotten. After he had dissuaded Terry and Zak from the Auld Pledge (one convict would agree to murder the other so he'd be executed for it), it had taken surprisingly little effort to convince them to try his plan. Once they'd shut up. It was, after all, just the sort of moronic thing they might have invented themselves.

Except the execution of it was all Nigel's.

Against a tree which had been blown down yet continued to grow along the edge of the cliff there lay three figures, twisted, broken. Pathetic, really. Entrails seeped like sausages from one gut, the neck of another was obviously snapped. The third was a frog. The human figures wore Zak's and Terry's new convict browns. They were as ugly as crushed snails. They deserved their fate. Nigel was about to heave them into the gorge beyond living reach. Out of loving-kindness. If you wanted to decay in peace this was the place to do it.

Naked, the real Terry and Zak pranced in the carefree spring sun, giggling.

It would be difficult to drop the grass-stuffed effigies so

they landed plainly dead but not damaged enough to give the game away. Since nobody bothered to retrieve suicides it would be weeks perhaps before the trick came undone, if at all.

Zak and Terry, every inch Fatguts and Knacker-Eater, thought the plan brilliant. Nigel had raised himself several notches in their estimation, from silver-spoon-toter to 'bung man' (whatever that was). Had they tried it on their own they would have taken up hours with epoch-shattering art. Also, they'd have lit out for the bush straight away, in their god-forsaken hides, to be picked up within days by the fucknuckles, bald nudists hardly reaching plague proportions here.

Nigel said, 'Come on boys.' He gripped one dummy by the belt and scruff, checked its clay-smeared underwear face was firmly attached to its shirt, took aim, and heaved. The fake dummy sailed into the gentle air.

'Yes Mama!' said the real dummy.

A perfect shot. Terry wedged between two rocks near the waterfall's base, obscuring most of one side and not sticking up unnaturally. It looked like a good old-fashioned blood-stained corpse. Nigel forced his breath out and turned to the other one.

'Twenty-seven-gauge beauty!' shouted Terry, in a rumba with the bloodless frog. It put Nigel off his throw. For a sickening moment it seemed the dummy would crash into the waterfall's face, where it would surely disintegrate on the rest of the way down. But the breeze gusted and it sailed safely clear and fell flat on its lucky face below its mate.

However, on impact the herbs inside burst through the string seam near the eye. Broad leaves unfurled slowly, a corsage above the ear. Nigel swore. There was nothing for it. Still, the swearing helped so he did so again. For good measure he nabbed Terry's frog and hurled it into the gorge.

He turned back to Zak and Terry. The two wagged their bald heads in admiration regardless of the Zak dummy's unnatural growth. Terry waved goodbye to the frog.

'Come on,' said Nigel, anxious. 'Let's go.'

Now he had to hide them.

Nigel fled into the blessed bush. Hands over their goolies against organic clash, Zak and Terry tippy-toed after him.

Seventeen

And Getting Done

How do you hide a couple of bald naked nincompoops?

Darkness seemed the best bet. Sunset was a good two hours off, though. He might nip back to Macka's and pick up some clothes. They'd surely be caught before he returned. No, he had to cover their trails as planned then smuggle them to Eye Lodge. Frank and Macka would know what to do next. Unfortunately his original plan for getting the boys there gaped under questioning. No way would none of the lags notice them, dark or no dark. But to hustle them through in broad daylight'd be suicide.

Nigel laughed, a gruff bark he recognised as similar to Macka's. Suicide. How many murders and accidents had he witnessed since his arrival? Ten? Fifteen? Others had left for Death's Brothel for the slapstick doctoring which either spat you out pale and weak or disappeared you. Why should Zak and Terry matter? They were not the skinheads he'd met in Collingwood a century ago. Arguably, Nigel was not the same man either. That his own counterpart in this world was a villain no longer surprised him. He plunged angrily into the twilit entanglement of branches and creepers careless of the clear trail he left.

Then he stopped. He heard Terry run into Zak but didn't turn. He had to be more careful. Two lives – three lives – were in his hands. Nigel wasn't angry at Zak or Terry. The life that shoved so many at suicide infuriated him. A hunger for more than stupid dreams had gripped him whole and abrupt, just when he'd felt settled here. Perhaps it had actually been set off by his tender initiation last night. This stuff opened you. You dawdled through the new-born spring droning, 'I Have Loved Me a Man' . . . and here lay an opportunity to let love spur you. A foolish opportunity. The only kind. Now at last he turned.

Zak and Terry ogled him expectantly as if he were the nudist. He glanced past them at their trail. Pliant branches swung gently back into place in the stippled bush twilight. They hadn't done so badly. And they had gone far enough for now.

'You wait here,' he ordered the pale stick-figures.

They nodded, grave; their hairlessness lent them age and infancy at the same time: a pair of grotesquely circumcised bumpkins. Smiling, Nigel shook his head.

'Get down,' he said, with a stern gesture.

They squatted.

He left them.

The nearest thunderbox was the officers' one, built on the edge of the small plain on which the Captain's house stood at a distance where you'd get the irrits if you had to return when decorum prevented a quick crap behind a tree. It was a short steep climb through a wooded patch from the spot where the skinheads (hopefully) squatted. An ugly thought struck him as he picked his way over a rotted log adorned with orange fungus: a guest loo often went weeks without use. Clearing the hump before the rain forest ended, he heard a whipcrack. He threw himself flat.

Voices. Hooves. The whicker of a horse, then another. They drew closer. Nigel made out the Captain's brusque tones, and a woman's voice. It was well-known the Captain was unmarried. Though not through lack of trying. He was a cruel, petty-minded man who normally wore an absurdly tiny top hat outdoors owing to his extreme sensitivity to noise (other than his own). It was his magic hat, everyone knew, activated by prayers whispered into it of a morning.

Anyone who snickered at the sight of him dressed thus was flogged. But he couldn't flog a prospective bride.

Kern's voice rose, assenting to something. A horse galloped. Nigel listened carefully for a few moments. Birds tweaked and tisked in the forest. Slowly, he rose to his knees. The Captain was gone. The clearing seemed empty. Nigel stood, and made for the rear of the thunderbox.

The green-painted loo faced the clearing. It had a red plastic roof and rear hatch. Nigel flipped the unlocked hasp, swung open the hatch and reached in for the can. As he heaved it toward him he noticed two things at once. A horse snuffled from beyond the thunderbox; it must have been tethered close to the front door. And above the toilet seat there was poised a fulsome bottom.

He nearly screamed.

In a wild panic he glanced up. Above the toilet lid a top hat tossed itself backwards with relief.

There came an elaborate fart then a groan and a stream of rather too healthy turds. He had not entirely removed the can so the ordure tumbled into it. Forced to watch the Captain void his bowels, Nigel froze outwardly but inside he squirmed with disgust. After a minute Kern began to wonder aloud to himself, 'Fuck me, the bitch wants it for sure; she'd never fondle her horse's neck so brazenly otherwise. You're in this time, Johnno. You'll never have to pay a florin for box again as long as you live. Fuck me, ay.' He giggled.

Nigel wondered obscurely whether he spoke in this intimate fashion to his fiancée. The poor woman deserved pity, he thought. Someone should warn her, at least about the baldies. Would he shave his own wife?

Another burst of bumfire interrupted him. Kern sighed as a short dribble of urine followed. Lucky for Nigel it was short, since it missed the partially removed can and spattered the crushed yellow weeds beneath, pooling under the toe of Nigel's boot.

Then finally, without the faintest sketch of a wipe, the

Captain rose and fastened his clothing about himself. Nigel's chance arrived. The door scraped on the gravel patch outside the thunderbox, he wrenched the can toward him, closed the hatch at the same time as Kern closed the door, and was off.

Hugging the can to his chest he pelted down the slope into the rain forest. The fetor made him gag over and over. The can wasn't entirely empty but it wasn't too heavy either. His biggest problem was to prevent himself from stumbling. Odds-on he'd fall headlong into it if he did.

In minutes he gained the clearing where he'd met the skinheads, safe. Panting, he placed the can at his feet.

A faint baying rose above the bush sounds. It came from the road to the worksites, below. It grew louder. Distinct barks could be heard. Nigel pulled Zak's handkerchief from his pocket. He tore it in two easily, it was so threadbare. One half he wiped delicately across the pile of fresh turds inside the can. Then he took it to where Zak and Terry had told him they'd entered the clearing and dropped it there. The other handkerchief half he used to pick up a whole turd, which he dropped by a tree at the edge of the gorge.

By the time he had arranged a convincing pile near the trunk the hounds had taken on a more frantic note. They had a scent now. Quickly, he tossed the soiled hanky over the cliff's edge and took up a stick. Bending the stick then letting it go he was able to fling the flecks of faecal matter around the clearing. The dogs would keep their masters here long enough to notice the dummies below, mixed as the strong odour was on Zak's snotrag with Zak's smells, yet they would drag their masters around all over the place in their excitement so no one would get a good look at the dummies in the remaining light. Even if they smelled Zak and Terry's trail away from the clearing they would be distracted by the numerous turdlets scattered hither and yon. When they didn't drag the guards anywhere but around the clearing no fucknuckles would have cause to doubt what his eyes told him.

This was the theory.

Enough. Careful not to step on his false trails, Nigel put the stick in the can, hefted the can and ran back to the thunderbox. Behind him the hounds gave hoarse disruption to the gentle afternoon.

Now came the biggest risk. The Captain's house nestled in a broad wound cut in the forest just below the highest point in the area. From above the house revealed its full size. It really was a mansion, made with convict blood. Nigel and Zak and Terry stared down at it from the lengthening shadow of a massive ironbark at the forest's edge. Lights already burned at the mansion's rear, in the kitchens. Occasionally a convict would zip through the doorway to fetch some-thing for the cook or the houseproper. Nigel knew he would have been missed long ago. He would not be punished tonight for a late and empty-handed return – but tomorrow he'd cop some stripes at least. Yet the prospect didn't worry him. He was too focused on the task ahead and –

And silver spoons. (No time for that now.)

Terry whined, 'Let's go. When do we go? Nobody's come out for a while.'

'Shut ya gob,' said Zak, not unkindly.

'Shut up both of you,' said Nigel. 'There's someone at the window.' He pointed. The house's whitewashed walls shone violet in the sunset. 'See?'

The enormous silhouetted blob that was the cook lumbered away, further into the house.

'Okay,' said Nigel.

'Hay?'

'Let's go – now!'

It was then they heard the dogs bark behind them.

We're going to die. This is the finish, an hysterical left-over of the old Nigel wailed. He was going to snuff it here in this awful place where by rights life should have been sorted and civilised well before his own uncertain world got it together but where in fact the villains spent religion for control. It was his familiar panic in a hairy situation, rising through him.

Oddly, it had little effect.

He ran. Not in his pell-mell stumbling sprint but in an almost measured burst of adrenal energy. Down from the forest he purled towards the coal-cellar's entrance on sure feet. He leapt rocks and grass-clumps, ditches and rabbit-holes, master of his panic rather than the other way around. The twin baldies ran surely too, perhaps inspired by his swift straight effort.

A calm part of him marvelled at this.

He reached the cellar doors well ahead of the skinheads. Mindful enough to control his quick door-swing so he didn't bang the house walls, he gestured at Zak and Terry to hurry. They balked at the dark rectangle at their feet.

Nigel whispered fiercely, 'These are steps – see?'

The wooden rungs appeared to give out a few paces into the black hole. The naked convicts shook their heads.

'Get *in*,' commanded Nigel.

They got. As soon as he could safely do so, he eased the doors shut on their unavoidable noises of descent. On his way to the kitchen porch he heard a dull thud and a muffled 'Shit!' There was nothing for it. The dogs were definitely headed this way for some reason. He left them.

'Ya bloody took ya time,' growled the cook, dangerous. His sweaty blubber positively clapped against itself in his fury at Nigel.

'I couldn't find the right herbs –'

'Never mind the flaming herbs, ye bastard lag, I used normal ones already. Get yerself inter ye serving gear right this minute or I'll double ye lashes tomorrow. *Git*!'

The man made Elvis Presley seem anorexic. Nigel ran for the linen cupboard, followed by a disgruntled hiss and the whomp of a hefty carrot on the door behind him. As he shucked out of his browns and picked a pair of white trousers for the night's service he noticed his boot was still wet with the Captain's piss. Was this why the hounds had followed? As if in answer their frenzied belling grew audible within the house. They were directly outside. Great slavering man-eaters. Nigel wrenched his ankles heaving his boots off without undoing the laces. He tugged on some gumboots – they'd just have to do. With his new certainty he dumped his own boots into a sinkful of soiled clothes, grabbed an apron and headed for the dining-room.

Through the warped french windows he watched Captain Kern and his fiancée pull up on their horses. As a stable-boy led their mounts away the Captain laughed con-descendingly at some remark from the woman. He was a short fat man whose curly grey hair frothed gently cherubic, the sort who like to think of themselves as 'portly' but whose stomachs and florid facial features resembled the cuts made in a frying sausage where the filling blurted forth insanely. His eyes were pale blue ferret's buttons. His bride-to-be was petite, a lively shape; not at all a match for the Captain if weren't for the hollow, drugged look to her eyes. Those eyes were capable of anything.

The dogs' cries must have been a lot louder outside, because Kern's fiancée turned several times to make its source and once on the side-porch she stopped in dull appreciation of the team's approach. Captain Kern halted beside her politely and turned with a smile on his cankerous face; perhaps his magic hat actually did block out most of the noise. His smile remained but he looked death at the search-party, here, on his doorstep. He waved a pink, imperious finger, telling one of his lackeys to take care of it.

However, the dogs had their own idea. The pack of six huge beagle-ish hounds paused only long enough to lull their wranglers into a false sense of security then plunged forward spilling the men into the dirt. Since the dogs had to drag the wranglers a good six feet Kern had time to raise his arms over his face.

It was not his face the dogs were after.

They ripped his trousers off his legs and while half of them fought over the tatters the other half went to work on his underwear. Two dogs then fought over these silken lovelies and the final most adventurous hound nuzzled the Captain's flapping accoutrements, in search of the aroma he remembered so well from the clearing. Kern's screams could be heard clearly through the thick plate dining-room windows. He was a pair of pink legs flailing on the verandah, his hat fell over his nose but held by its chin-ribbon it blinded him. His fiancée's shock turned into giggles; she bit on her knuckles and pressed her crotch with the other fist, doubling over.

Nigel's shock, too, turned into something else. The dogs would never enter the house. Having seen the effigies from the cliff-top the wranglers must have followed the dogs out of curiosity. Sorry wranglers now. Any attempt to sniff out Zak and Terry would be stomped on in Kern's usual heavy way.

Nigel sighed. In his relief he leant on the table and his hand sank in the sauce-boat. The sound of titters emerged from successive rooms as the story spread to Kern's staff. Licking his fingers, Nigel joined in.

The meal was sombre. The servants knew what would happen if their eyes so much as glinted anywhere near the dining-room. A re-trousered Captain Kern drank even more than usual and his fiancée feigned exhaustion after he lapsed from angry grunts into a brooding silence during the sweet beans and cream. She went to bed. Kern took coffee in the library, where he summoned his most slavish fucknuckles. To detail the dog-handlers' extinction, presumably.

At least in the evil atmosphere nobody had noticed Nigel's gumboots under the apron. Before the cook or houseproper could make him put away the scrubbed pots, he slipped out into the night and headed towards Macka's, whom he resolved had to help with some clothes for the fugitives in the coal-cellar or he'd throttle the old bastard.

He could not shake off the unease generated in the dining-room. It followed him home, more intense by the instant. It's simply Kern, he told himself, the man can't be trusted not to vent his spleen at random, violently. His staff knew it and stepped light.

But if that was all, the feeling ought to have left him as he headed down the hill. Instead it got worse.

Curfew was about to descend, so Nigel's hurried trip home was excusable. Only new chums and shrivelling scrotums kept curfew hours strictly. Nigel was still sort of new. Other convicts wandered about the night's last legal business with their usual easy disregard. Men sat on porches along the main road chatting with plastic mugs of moonshine in their callused paws. Past the huts' rough bark shutters games of chance continued by soft whale-oil lamplight. Lovers strolled in the first balmy evening of the year holding hands or with arms about each other. Old ones provoked obscene comments; younger couples brought dangerous stares. On the other side of the penal station whistles sounded: a fight perhaps or random victimisation. The Captain would be restless tonight, thought Nigel unhappily. Normally Nigel's pride would have made him saunter like the rest but tonight he didn't care if he was called a shrivelling scrotum. He almost ran. And not just because of Zak and Terry. His confidence had vanished. His unfocused worry had blossomed into nameless dread.

He had never known true cold sweat before. Whoever had invented it didn't tell you about the light feeling in your

limbs, as though your bones had filled with laughing-gas.
Or the heartburn when you hadn't eaten since lunch-time.
Or the wavery tremors which didn't resemble shakes, more
like a nausea that never quite hit. Was this a premonition?
No, it was an unfounded anxiety attack, premonitions were
shorter. He had no reason whatsoever for nerves.

Ah, but you do, a sinister monkey whispered in his belfry.
Love.

There was that.

And the previous evening Macka had returned crowing
from his dealings with Captain Kern, laughing that he had
stitched the Captain up good and proper, because the
Captain had already sold on Macka's green tobacco to
other station commandants for his honeymoon (trip to
England) money. Macka had guessed something of the kind
from the man's nervous manner and had extracted a
humiliating price. But of course not too humiliating? He'd
made a derisive sound at Frank, like a goose at a pig-opera.
'Whaddyer bloody take me for?' he'd said. Then he'd
grunted (an old banger changing gears) and crowed again:

    'Ook-a-rook-a-roo!'

There was that, too.

Kern was capable of anything when incensed. Which didn't
take much. Perhaps he wouldn't find the dog-handlers'
excruciations satisfying. Perhaps the new-chum haul from
the Cleavage was thin. Perhaps he had not merely called his
fucknuckles into the library for the dog-handlers but had
already sent someone to Eye Lodge while Nigel was
scrubbing pots . . .

You're a serious deadshit Nigel, he told himself. He
forced himself to slow as he turned into the path to
Macka's. The lamp burned to the left of the window, brassy
with the fire's added lick, a signal that all was well. Frank
would know for sure why he was out of breath. With love

came fear. He'd laugh and slap Nigel's cheek a few short times the way he did, affectionately. Macka had dealt with the Captain heaps of times before and never once had anything gone wrong.

But that was before the dogs ripped Kern's hose and trousers off.

Nigel shook his head against his fear. The bottle-stopper walls of Macka's hut gleamed ever so faintly. Smoke corkscrewed a foot out of the chimney before it disappeared into the night. By the time he reached the door Nigel had done away with worry; what Terry and Zak would need exercised him more. Those two dags could never be oversupplied – and still they'd fuck it up and get caught. He smiled. Maybe he should go with them. No, he couldn't leave Frank. Macka would think of wha—

The door was not half open when Nigel realised something really was wrong. A more potent tang than the usual cabbages-and-eucalypt-and-pipesmoke-and-milk-and-rum-and-urine crashed through him, bringing a weight to the pit of his stomach ahead of the smell's name. With the room's contents in full, obscene view, the odour identified itself.

It stank of blood.

In a surprised pose, leant back against the bark wall above the bed, arms spread wide mocking welcomes for ever after, eyes wide too as though some wonderful surprise awaited, sat Frank. Macka rested less tidily. He faced one knee; both hands were clenched by his left hip (the sore one); a foot was planted close to the stump he sat on, the other lolled as far as his gangly leg allowed.

Nigel's first thought was about one of those terrible movies: *Where the token poof, the token nigger gets it for the sentimental value* – he shamed himself with his tawdry commentary, but thought it anyhow. *I'm in one of those movies* – and he hated himself.

He despised himself.

Whoever had done this was long gone. Nigel stepped over the threshold. He closed the door behind him without turning. His chest rose and fell with a rhythm that soon broke, and, having caught for a moment, it heaved, then fell as far as it went. It heaved again. He walked in small steps towards Macka, he turned towards Frank, circled, reversed and circled again, then stopped. He put his fingertips to his forehead. His forehead was still there. His eyes stayed dry.

'What?' he said. '*What?*'

Fears don't come true this way. And all love is supposed to end right now. But, horribly, it continues. The sun rises tomorrow and so shall I. Not wiser. Not even brutal. Simply alive.

His only friends in this world were dead.

He sat on the log opposite Macka and frowned.

He had never felt even vaguely like this before.

He would never be rid of this feeling.

He did not want to be rid of it.

Never. Never.

His only friends in this world or any were dead. There were pornographic holes in their heads, in their chests . . . *that chest, that brow, those lips* . . . cold summary execution . . . *cold soon* . . . cold blood. They were dead. Macka and Frank were dead. The fire crackled gaily in its flagstone hearth, a honey moon smeared the hut's distorted single window. Nigel sat so long and so still a moth landed on the back of his hand, he sat until thought returned with the ache in his arse. When he stood, he knew exactly what he would do.

Eighteen

Nicky Whoop

He didn't like to do this to an innocent corpse. But then, he decided, if the corpse minded – who cared? A haunting would improve life here immeasurably. Dark rage steeled Nigel's muscles. Grief simplified his thoughts. He went about the gruesome task of digging up and washing a fresh-murdered corpse with an inexhaustible vigour, a steady heart. Despite the fact that he had to exhume three corpses before he found one the right size. When he did he sat back in the comfortable turned dirt and tittered. Quietly of course. The corpse was far from innocent. It was Dwyer. The overlooker had been killed by Corporal Parker in a fair fight the day before. Fair on Parker's side. Dwyer had been beaten by accident, had fallen on his own knife. The fucking bastard.

Nigel wiped the tears from his filthy cheeks. He stood and checked for patrols.

Clear. None too carefully, he filled in Dwyer's grave. Now to wash the fucker. He hoped the corpse would bleed. Yet, when he came to it, who cared? He didn't value his own skin much; this was all to give two clowns in the Captain's cellar a fighting chance. He pictured fighting naked clowns as he lugged Dwyer's corpse from the cemetery to the river. Whoop-de-doo what a laugh.

What a night the Captain would have. First, public doggy fellatio. Now a cracker of a surprise. If the first did not destroy him, the second would. You couldn't hide these things from the other commandants. Just as well, he decided; he didn't have time for revenge. Captain Sir John Kern, I sentence you to live. He chuckled, pouring the last of the rum on the bed.

Something by Macka's leg caught Nigel's eye: the mackerel pipe. He pocketed it. You could tell the old bastard didn't approve, but it was a bit late for a spanking. Nigel chuckled some more.

Frank stared at an infinitely distant point above Nigel's shoulder. He didn't seem to mind the laughs. Nigel reached out and for the first time touched the convict's – *ex*-convict's – body. The cheek was cold. The head did not move. Nigel twitched a smile at him.

'Okay,' sang Nigel, as if he were baking a birthday cake. He wagged a finger at his handiwork as he mentally ticked off tasks done. '*That's* over there, that's in *there*, the pretty boy is at the table – ' he nodded politely at Dwyer. 'The rum's all gone, the clothes are outside, the keg's in place!'

He began to sing to himself, 'Echo Beach', by Martha and the Muffins, patting his pockets to make sure he had put what he put in there and not dreamed it.

For reality seemed very far away, tonight.

His pats turned into a dance. Singing the guitar noises through puckered lips, he pranced about for a minute, jerking his head to the beat. He forgot the words and sang, 'Whoopy doopy whoopy doopy whoopy whoop-whoop-whoop,' then the chorus. He grinned at his clumsiness. He subsided.

From the fireplace he took a burning stick and set it to the fuse and ran out the door.

The explosion behind him was all he had hoped for. A crack and a fireball, sparkly and splintery, a shove high, high at the moon which pushed air past him and nearly reached the hard knot in his chest it was so exciting. 'Goodbye Dwyer,' he whispered, pelting sure-footed, ears ringing through the night.

*

At the Captain's house, lights were out, for the moment. He made straight for the coal-cellar. No problems with the watch; they were probably inside waking those not already startled by the bang. Nigel didn't bother to try for silence; he flipped the doors back and clattered down the ladder.

'Waaugh!'

Two absolutely grimy, frightened faces retreated into the darkness.

'Come on you drongos,' he told them.

'Errr . . . '

'Nicky *whoop*,' said Nigel. It was primary-school language. Just their level, he thought. As he followed Terry's blackened, coal-dented cheeks up the ladder he realised that the Terry and Zak he'd met in Melbourne were psychotic as well as childish, whereas these two were dodgem-heads, plain and simple. It separated his world from theirs.

They dressed in the glade, now slivered under a hard and fast moon, where they'd staged the suicide. None of the clothes fitted properly – or even remotely. The trousers were designed for water-buffaloes, thin-legged and enormous-waisted. Nigel had forgotten belts. So they took his own and sliced it in three lengthways. Terry's shirt had apparently come from the body of a one-armed man: they had to cut a hole in the sealed sleeve. Worst of all the clothes were, for some reason, orange. But Nigel couldn't afford to be seen in prison browns and the sight of Terry and Zak in the buff was the second most offensive in Nigel's memory. In any case, the leather jackets hid a number of faults. Nigel remembered Frank dressing to trade in a nearby town, how he had cursed the holes in his various jackets on winter's nights. Until he'd found the oversized brown one into which Nigel shrugged himself now. Dry-eyed, he smiled briefly at the cloud-cut stars. It was his first hint that softness was possible after this terminal night.

*

Next they went to one of Macka's hidy-holes. A great deal
of the wealth stashed in camouflaged pits and caves around
the penal station was too bulky to be useful. This cache,
however, contained money. Nigel and Terry heaved a small
chest out of a hollow on to an outcrop by a tributary to the
station's stream. The three knelt on the silvered rocks and
broke and tossed the bundles of worthless American
currency above their heads hissing their laughter at Jimmy
Carter's smiling faces. Then they had to clean it up. Luckily
beneath the republican money they found some guilders.
Fivers. They folded them into a more practical size, put
them in their orange shirt pockets, and were off.

Nigel decided to skip the two nearest towns. Their first stop
was Cann River City. It meant a night's slog away from the
coast and at least another couple of days' walk again,
south-westish, but then nobody was after them, they could
take it easy.
    That was the theory.

We're desperate fugitives from justice, thought Nigel as he
tramped through the long grass between the two gawking
skinheads. It made him chortle. His rage, his enabling grief,
was stretched by travel into a steel cord which reached
through his chest to – where? His companions' curiosity
about his laugh (rapidly overcome by the still mountain
wonder) he ignored. What to do? That was it. At the very
moment he had settled into life here – any life in fact – it had
fallen apart. (. . . *That chest, that brow, those lips* . . .) If
inside he had previously resembled a garden maze made
from old socks and junk window-frames, now – now the
bloody fruiting vines and flowering creepers holding it all
together had been blown away. By four bullets. With shock,
with punishment, with hard labour, his whole being had
been up-ended and rebuilt. Four bullets later it was a
scattered mess again. Below the loony assemblage had run
the ground-water thought, *a man can get used to anything*.

Well this man could not. It had been a mistake to try to get used to it. No, not a mistake. Never. But the cruelty here – it was too much. Sooner or later he would have had to deal with his basic sense of displacement here. Knowing it without admitting it, he had put away his notions about this world for later.

His only friends were dead.

So on a bleak hillside, later began. His friends, either one of them, would have ridden such a blow. Would have gone on, sadder, yet because that was simply the way things went here they would have gone on. Would have. If only – Nigel could not go on. *Things* had to change.

Silver spoons.

He now remembered the nonsense about the silver spoons. In the wreckage of his mind, by the memory of a treasure map and the Denuncios' silver spoons buried in his backyard so long ago, he had stored two conclusions:

1.   What decent people needed here was to step outside the paths fixed in stone by a church that accepted oodles of ways of staying virtuous – yet nothing outside the book. *Imagination* allowed you to cope with the Todds and Kerns, who used it themselves and ran the show, but if you tried it you were damned. *Biggle*. Even Frank had thought himself damned. That attitude had to be changed. If possible.

2.   Nigel possessed an indefinite wonderfulness, a feeling that he was worth something, although he was not sure what. Perhaps a wet mackerel.

These two thoughts stored away while in hospital he clung to with the desperation of a man who has nothing else.

He had nothing else. His only friends were dead.

But what to *do* with himself and his precious conclusions? He needed help. Definitely, the fiasco at the cliff-top had tied him to Zak and Terry. Besides, he couldn't leave them yet: they'd get picked up doing something daft for sure. Then there were the Serbs. Briefly, he prickled with shame for forgetting them for so long. They were hundreds of miles away though. Out of the question. Yet a mile further down the mountainside, Pixie, Charlie, Johnno, Doug and Wal were on his mind again. He couldn't sensibly say why. He checked his pace. It was nearly a full minute before Zak or Terry missed him. Nigel tucked in his short orange shirt. His skin was chilly but he was far from it.

Nigel had sprawled dead to the world during the long journey to the penal station. The names of towns here were similar at times but they were in different places, given the lack of wool-growing and continued convict settlement, the aborted gold-rush and no railway system. So he didn't really know where he had come from. Convicts were purposely settled in penal stations either out of the way of ports or far from their Australian homes, or both. And Nigel had to admit it did disrupt any plans he might make to hide.

He set off once more. His memories of the Serbs stayed with him. They thought themselves damned too, but more than anyone else they'd have a willingness to act on what he had to offer. However, to get to them, he told himself, they'd have to skulk at least two hundred kilometres along the populated coast, and cross way the way over the high plains between Mount Bogong and Mount Buller to avoid Melbourne, then it'd still be an almost hopeless task to slip unseen through the Goulburn Valley (or whatever it was called here) and across the Goulburn River. Once west of Seymour (he was fairly sure Milton Keynes was in the area) he could hardly ask directions, since the danger of being mistaken for his double would increase as they neared Todd's farm.

No. It was an absurd scheme. And then what? Chew the fat with Pixie and Johnno and face arrest again? And what if they didn't help him act on his brilliant idea of stoking people's imaginations?

'Ahh,' he said, before he caught up with the skinheads. A ghost gum loomed out of the dark at him. 'What the hell? I'll do it,' he informed the tree.

Well, he had worked out a possible route to Todd's farm.

Some concrete plan to put to the Serbs might yet come to him in his sleep. He yawned and clapped the skinheads on the back as he passed them. Time to find a spot for a kip before the sun rose. Leave world-shaking, mate, he urged himself; things to do.

A densely wooded creek curled round the hill ahead. This was the spot. They had left behind mountains for the moment. He increased the pace, then busied himself making sure the area was safe, letting the steel cord in his chest drag him about. They camped on the soft meander. Lacking bedrolls, they slept head to toe, hugging one another's calves. The creek gurgled. Birds began to sing. The three desperate fugitives pulled their hats down their foreheads against the grey false dawn, and slept.

Nineteen

Bush Whackers

'Get up.'

In Nigel's dream his mother was divided into four parts. Each one of her wore a long black beard. Fake-oh. *You've chucked away your lunch again*, said one of his mothers, the short one. *Fish-paste is brain food, how do you expect to grow up and change the world on a diet of chips and Chiko rolls?*

I am a grown-up man, complained Nigel. I know the world can't be changed.

Bollocks, his mothers told him. They pulled hard on their chickens' reins and the birds reared into the air, flapping dust at him.

'Get up, yer arsehole.'

There is a wisdom in dreams, but it's because any weird combinations thrown together from elements of our lives are bound to bear fruit if we apply our noggins to them while they're in such novel arrangements. A change is as good as a tram ride.

The different mothers (orange acrylic fur suits) in Nigel's novel arrangement made it clear they operated as a team. It was the reason his lunch was so colossal. The suckling pig made him drool. He ached to sink his teeth into the cantaloupe slices, and once again wondered at the point where orange could become green near the skin without going the pukey browny colour of kids' paints. The guacamole beckoned, as did the steaming Turkish bread and souvlakia, with little hands. You hoo!

What his dream had to 'say' wasn't apparent. He hadn't imposed his thoughts upon it yet. But his mothers made it abundantly clear that what they had to say was important, to remember it when he woke.

Which meant of course he would not.

They told him the secret of success, satisfaction, happiness.

Hi-ho, chickens away!

They galloped off across the plains

'Get the fuck up, cunt.'

What a dream. Nigel's eyes were glued with sleep. He was hungry as anything. An iron-capped boot nudged his ribs. Drowsily, he flopped a hand on to it. Yes, it was a boot.

Hmm, he thought. There's someone here.

Abruptly he remembered his situation. He rolled on to his back. His hat fell off his forehead and his eyes struggled open.

The ugliest face he had ever met bar none stared down at him. It was slit-eyed, smiling and nodding, and there were distinct wisps of roped hair plastered across the spotted skull above it. It was a jowl on a neck.

'Oh shit,' said Nigel.

'Stand, dickfabrains,' said the face. 'Now.'

Zak, Terry and Nigel stood back to back to back, facing outward at the group of bushrangers. Nigel had to revise his rating of the ugliest face he had ever met. Quantum ugliness, he decided. The bushrangers' horses cropped quietly on the river-bank. Even they were ugly. Irrelevantly, Nigel recognised them as the source of the four dream chickens.

'Turn out yer pockets,' said the balding one, waving a pistol which resembled a beetroot with a handle.

'What if we don't?' said Zak, defiantly.

'We shoot yez,' said the ugliest one. Definitely, he was the ugliest; probably his unfortunate thyroid condition had driven him to crime. That, and the fungus.

'You're a big fat stack of pig's knuckles,' Zak observed, astutely, 'An' if you reckon we're gunna do anythin' for youze, you're, uh . . . '

'Cat's balls?' suggested Terry.

'Nup,' said Zak.

'Orange pips.'

'Nup.'

'What about that spit that goes all ropy around the back of ya throat sometimes?'

Good idea, thought Nigel, glancing at the hair remnants.

'Shut the *fuck* up!' screamed the least ugly one, disfigured only by a protean wart complex on one eyelid.

'Nah,' said Zak. 'These stickmen aren't so tough. Just ugly.'

Nigel had to concur there, but Zak didn't have to verbalise it. He told the lad as much.

'Don't get upset,' Zak said. 'If they're gunna kill us they're gunna kill us, and I don't think they will.'

'Yeah, I've owned a worm more tougher than youze,' Terry chipped in.

The bushrangers took aim with their beetroots. It appeared to Nigel that Zak and Terry had underestimated their assailants. It didn't faze him much, the thought of death. He had been prepared for it throughout the previous night. But he hoped it wouldn't hurt. And he wouldn't have minded some brekky. The bushrangers cocked their pistols and fired.

It was a hopeless gesture, but all three had the same thought at the same time, to duck and fend off the flying shot with a forearm. At that very moment, Nigel knew exactly what he would do to change this world; his dream helped him do it.

The pistols cracked. Bodies fell with grunts. The horses made nervous equine nostril noises. Though, used to gunfire and mayhem, they didn't bolt.

So, thought Nigel, being dead is just the same as living only you can't move. He could still smell the fresh creek smells (to his regret he hadn't checked the stream for fish before he'd died). So when his body rotted he'd stink. Yick. A blister on his foot still hurt – would it go on hurting through eternity? Most of all he wondered what would've happened had he lived to try the scheme which had been inspired by the two conclusions stored by the silver-spoon memory; he had a good reason to find the Serbian assigned workers, and now what could have been a grand idea was wasted. He was crouched here for ever. What a boring afterlife.

Someone groaned.

Behind him, Zak or Terry stood. At least one had survived.

A hand patted Nigel's left shoulder.

He was alive! Then why could he not stand? He tried – and could. It must have been the terror which had paralysed him. But what terror? He had not been afraid of death. Shock, then. Anyhow –

He was alive. Around him lay the bushrangers, in various poses of pain. They looked less ugly, dead. The four had neatly shot each other. It was a lucky thing. Bugger me, thought Nigel. It was incredible.

Nigel, Zak, and Terry turned in silence on the sand, gaping at the fluke, at the bodies scattered round them. Four dead highwaymen. Nigel's gaze caught Zak's light blue eyes; he then sought Terry's simple brown ones. They glanced back and forth between one another breathing harder and harder for as long as they could possibly stand it.

'YeeeeHAH!'

'Yip yip yip yip yip yip yip!'

'Whoop-de-fucken-doo!'

They linked arms and crunched the sand. They jigged and reeled and do-si-doed. Nigel surprised the other two with his virtuosity and strangeness in an a cappella version of 'Let's Twist Again' complete with spastic foot-waggling dance. They scattered the birds in the gum-trees. They drove off the fish in the creek. The bushrangers' horses shifted from foot to foot, their ears twitching in vain attempts to shut out such uncouth hullabaloo.

Presently, their exuberance left them. The three collapsed on the sun-warmed meander, panting, still grinning fit to bust.

'Hay,' said Terry, after they'd wasted some more time.

'Mm?' said Zak.

'We got horses,' said Terry, 'We got great big hairy living snorfling ugly fucken horses we can ride anywheres we want,' said Terry. 'We got horses coming out of our bloody ears!'

So they did.

The ride across the high plains was never easy. Nigel had never ridden a horse. He felt there were secret signals the horses knew but had suppressed under some equine thirty-year rule. His own horse looked at him that way, anyhow. He called her Mrs Pimlott after his father's arthritic secretary. Brown and slim and young she showed no trace of arthritis, but the human Mrs Pimlott was so secretive his father's office was a Pentagon among glue factories. Terry of all people gave Nigel his one horse-tip: Mrs Pimlott's previous rider must have been quite a horseman, because she responded to Nigel's slightest twitch of the bit. Usually when Nigel had no intention of turning.

At first, since they didn't possess pass papers, blessed or otherwise, they avoided the roads. Impassable cliffs or gorges blocked their way. Forests were bad enough. The horses seemed to delight in dismounting them where branches overhung. (Zak and Terry became quite good at dismounting and leaping back on straight away.) So they stuck to the sketchy convict-built gravel roads but took the less travelled ones whenever possible. And to avoid pain in the early weeks they kept their rides short. Which grew into a habit. What with so much cooking to do. And getting lost. And sightseeing. And getting lost.

It took them almost two months to cross the high plains.

The countryside astounded Nigel. Very gradually, he grew less conscious of the steel cord tugging him forward. He talked to Zak and Terry more, but no matter how much they badgered him he never mentioned the night of the escape and why he had left them in the dark for so long. What he spoke about in the beginning concerned practicalities, and the mountainscape's beauty.

Stands of wind-wrought snow gums dominated as the three climbed higher. The first wildflowers of the season dotted the meadows of native herbs with delicate colours. One night at camp Nigel spotted something moving underneath a rock's edge and tipped it to reveal a fluttering mass of Mount Bogong moths, granite-coloured, gentle and fervent as prayers at midnight. Not even the skinheads could remain afraid of these. Nigel stared, remembering the moth on his hand as he had sat by his friends' dead bodies. It was the second time he had allowed himself to think of them. He heard one of Macka's grunts (like a sheep on acid) and swayed, weak on the edge of tears that wouldn't budge.

Amongst the bushrangers' effects were bags of flour, tea, salt, sugar and dried beef. These provisions allowed the three desperadoes to avoid towns for a fortnight. Although the wildlife in the mountains was plentiful the pistols – and their users – didn't manage to hit one rabbit or wallaby the whole slow trip. Partly because the pistols bucked like rutting foreign ministers and because Terry loved telling stories of pistols exploding in the face. One look at the beetroots confirmed this for Nigel; he cringed every time he fired. It helped to imagine he was shooting Kern.

The trip brought the three young men together. Nigel discovered the skinheads did indeed make love at night, not so much from stumbling across them as from their indecipherable arguments over mechanics. He grew readier to talk to them by the day but he assumed it would be a long while before he could mention anything that mattered so he contented himself with questions for his companions. Terry and Zak regaled him gladly, with squalid tales of their childhood together (they had met when rat-hunting, Terry had fallen the length of a Melbourne grain silo on to Zak, asleep inside), dubious stories about their ancestors (Terry claimed descent from the man who had invented skipping) (Terry was a world-class skipper, you had to give it to him), and wildly improbable theories about how the universe functioned (gravity affected objects more which had a K in their names). Ah, why had Nigel never bothered with the country before? He grew to know Zak and Terry, quickly, following his cord of grief across the mountains. Finally he woke one morning and the cord was gone, out into the scenery, or carried away on Zak and Terry's harmless babble. The grief was still there, but he could take it most of the time. At last he was riding toward definite people instead of on some mindless way away from pain. He was going to see the Serbs. For a reason.

On the night before the three descended toward their first populated area and the danger of capture, they lay by the fire with their heads against a weathered log, chatting into the early hours. Above, the glittering floods of summer stars wheeled from east to west against black infinity, as usual. Snow sat grey on the higher ground. An owl swept along the nearby forest's edge. Leaves and twigs clicked and cracked inexplicably every so often, as did the fire.

'You guys gave me a great idea back when you tried to jump off the cliff,' said Nigel, his hands laced over a stomach full of damper and the last of their dried meat.

'Or rather you helped jog my memory, and this idea's gotten better with a little ageing in me scone.'

'Yeah? That was funny, that,' said Zak. Till now, the two young felons hadn't mentioned their suicide attempt, though they had discussed every other square millimetre of their lives with Nigel. And they hadn't shown any curiosity about Nigel's reasons for this mountain holiday. They had accepted him as their mother. They loved him unquestioningly.

'You neally went over into the drink yaself,' said Terry. He had taken to chewing a grass-blade as he rode; he chewed one now, sagely.

'You saved my life,' Nigel told them.

This struck Zak and Terry as hilarious.

'We're real sorry,' said Terry.

'We didn' mean ta.'

'It was a accident!'

'I wouldn' of only I wanted to smack ya up for being a Nosy Parker,' explained Zak.

'But we're glad we did, ay?'

'No worries.'

'Nup.'

'Never.'

'Not even when your horse stepped on my foot yesterday.'

'And not even when you cooked those berries and neally poisoned us.'

They went on.

Perhaps to them saving a life wasn't an obvious choice, yet neither was letting one slip away. If so, they were freaks. His idea might appeal to them then. Since the morning they had been bushwhacked, he had known what he would do. Like his several mothers on chickenback in his dream he would provide food for thought. There was nothing like an example. If the books here said you could not transgress into the abundant fields where imagination cross-fertilised ideas without losing your soul, then the books had to be proven false by people who transgressed pell-mell full-on all over the place *yet didn't do harm*.

The accepted channels for new ideas here, the cynically controlled ecclesiastical moil of research described by Clarry which destroyed more ideas (and idea people) than it fostered would not work. You had to step outside the law. It was a notion as foolish as male nipples: bushrangers who delivered imaginative shocks but did no harm. But he had to try it.

There was nothing else left for Nigel Donohoe. He had to change himself or he had to change this world. Temperamentally, he was just not suited to accepting this all-saint-endorsed law that said you would get your reward in heaven. By the look of them, neither were Zak and Terry.

He waited for the skinheads to finish taking the mick.

'What I want to do after we get down from here is find some people I know and train ourselves up and start a war.'

They nodded. It made perfect sense to them. How reassuring. Let's start a war!

Although it wasn't literally a war, more a forceful advertising campaign for an idea: silliness. Or, he told them, insanity; so it would seem to ordinary people. Naturally he did not mention his alien origins for the moment because it would have led utterly off the track with these two. The fixed ideas of right and wrong people had, he went on, might come down to some gland – well, they would find that out, the war would fail in that case. But it was such fixed ideas that allowed the nasties into the driver's seat. An education in uncertainty couldn't hurt. Others. 'It might mean death for us,' he said.

They pooh-poohed death. They were not afraid. Nigel believed them. He continued.

When the eight met at Emu station they would form a gang of bushrangers. Together, they would hold up travellers on the highways and give them something to think about. Something seriously ridiculous. Together they would ride. It came to Nigel as he spoke that he was a kind of genius of uncertainty in this world, possibly in any world; he felt it coursing through him, part of every sinew and bone and blood cell and piece of belly-button lint which formed him. This was what he had been born for. *Yes*. The confidence he'd found recovering from his wounds in the prison hospital rose in him, another parcel he'd put away for later. Possibly unfounded – more likely, cretinous – though his guesswork about this world was, his spirit soared. Against all likelihood and reason he was fizzing with success. Trembling. *We can do it. Yes*.

'I can see it in front of me,' Nigel said, fists clenched by now, sitting forward, his blood up. 'We're going to be – conquistadors of confusion! Knights of numskullery! We are going to gallop like fools and shout like nongs about a new order, and nothing will stop us. We'll be a pack of bloody galahs and I can think of none more dopey to have by my side than you Zak, and you Terry. What do you say boys? I need your total commitment, right now. Put it there.'

'Hay?' they said at once.

'I – I want your oaths. I want you both to swear on – ' he looked around for something sacred, a meaningful object the three of them could always respect, a symbol of their quest. He patted his pockets, and found a lump.

The mackerel pipe. Perfect.

Standing, he drew it out and held it high in the firelight. The fire chose this moment to sling a million sparks into the air, but Nigel did not flinch. Bravely, he held his ground and gestured for the skinheads to rise as well. And when the gust died back the entire firmament seemed to spread out here on the top of the Australian continent, all the universe behind this simple mallee-root pipe underlit so its deep wavy grain seemed to shiver like a live fish. It was everything his army could want in a symbol: fleet and hardy and sharp and good to eat.

'This is it,' he said. 'Will you swear?'

'Fucken oath,' said Terry.

'Bloody fucken oath,' said Zak.

'Bloody fucken shitten – '

'Yes,' said Nigel. 'Now swear this: I . . . go on, say it.'

'I . . . '

'In the name of *Scomber scombrus* . . . '

'In the name of – of – what was that?'

Nigel repeated it. 'It's another name for the mackerel,' he explained.

'In the other name of the mackerel,' said Terry and Zak.

'Most solemnly swear . . . to ride in hard . . . attack all certainty . . . and disappear like thieves into the night . . . but we shall not steal! . . . nor shall we seek to gain in any way from our missions . . . we shall bumble on the beaches and up the trees and in the gardens and the duck-ponds, we shall never surrender . . . and we shall not cease until we have changed this planet for the better.'

' . . . for the better.'

'In the name of the mackerel!' shouted Nigel.

'Scumbag scumbarrel!' hollered Terry.

'No mate, it's Scumbag scumbrains,' said Zak.

'Fuck off, it's scumbarrel.'

'It's bloody not.'

'Yes it is.'

'No it isn't.'

Nigel decided they'd be impeccable as soldiers in his army. Or perhaps actors . . . He watched the two tussle on the grass, kicking them when they rolled too close to the fire. A Movement was born, a Legend begun. He wished he had some tobacco, for a ritual smoke of the mackerel. I better not, he thought, because the taste'd make me ill; besides, we have all the strength we need within ourselves. And with that the wind rose and the fire gushed sparks again and Nigel felt a rush of what at first he assumed was Destiny (was Destiny like wind?), but then, shuddering, facing the sky, unaware of the skinheads' fingers up each other's noses, to his open-mouthed surprise and with an intensity of anger and loss and sheer cleaving anguish that he had never in his life experienced for another, Nigel wept.

Twenty

Budimir for Ever

Todd had put the Serbs to good use. Good, that is, if you were Todd. The whole property had a renovated look to it. In the – was it as little as two years? – since Nigel's arrest the house had been painted, all the nearby sheds except the Serbs' own quarters had been demolished and rebuilt from solid brick. Right down to the chicken-coop, which was a puce palace with Greek columns on either side. There were new fences, water-pumps, tanks, dams and irrigation ditches. The depressed and scrawny sheep appeared to have undergone psychotherapy and although they were no more suited to tough Australian conditions they languished in the shade of trees now, in grassier pastures. Transplanting the trees alone would've proven impossible with normal convicts. Nigel shook his head in wonder, distracted from his bold ride down the drive.

A little Serbian know-how had taken Emu station past 'farmhouse' into 'garden cottage' territory. It was still the same low, cream, broad-roofed structure, red plastic on top and wooden verandah all round. But a lick of green paint on the window-sills, a drop of water near by and some seeds had transformed the place. In the early morning sunshine, below freshly emptied summer clouds, the simple beds of marigolds, nasturtiums, wild violets, pennyroyal mint, alyssum and geranium, the rhododendrons and hydrangea, creeping jasmine, roses, lavender and fuchsia, along the paths and around the walls, showed Nigel the first spot he had seen in this universe nurtured with as much care as he had given his fish-tanks back home. It was a kind of aquarium for humans. It produced homesickness as well as a boundless admiration for the Serbs in Nigel's newly determined breast.

However, tying Mrs Pimlott outside the (new) stables, he twinged: why had they done all this for Todd? Not another premonition, surely. No.

A chicken interruption. The important part played by chickens in Nigel's story cannot be overstressed. They may be creatures as moronic and as ill-natured as Ku-Klux-Klansmen (though not even chickens set burning crosses on their fellows' lawns or go around in childish ghostie outfits) (perhaps only because they can't light matches or buy pillowcases) but without them he would have undoubtedly been caught again and hung.

Nigel had sent Zak and Terry to Milton Keynes for supplies under orders of strict silence. How'd they buy the food? they had wanted to know. Quietly. He'd meet them well away from the Samuelsons'. With or without the Serbs. He knew it was foolish to come here in the daytime, but he told himself if he saw Todd he'd deal with him one foot forward at a time. Perhaps two in an emergency. He was confident. And if he saw Catherine –

He put her out of his mind and through the murmuring chicken flock strode toward the labourers' door. He had no intention of seeing her. She had nothing to do with the great distance he had travelled or the trouble he had gone to finding the place. Her memory was another untidy event he only ever thought about now and then. At the very most. In fact, hardly ever.

So when before he could touch the polished brass handle, Catherine Samuelson opened it, he just smiled faintly and leant against the porch rail. Unfortunately there wasn't any rail.

'You . . . ' She took a mere instant to recognise him, despite the scraggly beard and long hair, the filthy orange clothes, the hat and weather-worn skin. She helped him to his feet.

'Um – gudday,' said Nigel.

As though her cool hand had delivered an electric shock, waking him, he felt – friendly. What do you know? he thought, I don't hate her.

She looked past his shoulder in the house.

'Quickly,' she said, 'get in here!'

In the sweep from boot to hat she made as she shut the door, Nigel caught the way she saw him. How he must have changed! Apart from the dark brown hair now at his shoulders and his weather-worn face, he fancied his grey eyes gave a glow of determination. His bearing showed him transformed from a hapless ditherer to a man of action. Uncertain action, true, but definitely uncertain, no longer tense or gawky. What were broad hips for a man of his build were now the right size for a torso toughened by labour. He was proud of the fluffy patches to either side of his mouth and chin, no matter what Zak or Terry said about them.

'You need a shave,' said Catherine. 'And a bath.' She wrinkled her slightly upturned nose.

Ah well. Out of mind, he thrust disappointment. Down to business. 'Where are the Serbs?' he demanded, manly.

'What has happened to your voice?' She stepped back as if he had a disease.

'Never mind. Where are they?' He hoped they still lived here. 'You know: Pixie, Johnno, Wal and the rest?'

'That is Budimir,' came a voice from behind him.

Nigel spun. Further down the corridor stood the Serbs. It was Wal who had spoken, the big young rebellious one.

'I am Budimir my friend,' he said in quite good Australian, grinning as he approached. 'I hate these herbal Anglo-Saxon names. Budimir – for ever.'

Then they were upon him. He had forgotten how dangerous their affection was. Of course he stood up to it better now. He was pummelled and squeezed until he felt like King Kong's toothpaste tube. Their long beards seemed made of the same stuff as cats' tongues. Still, how would they shave? Chisels?

'Nigel, *sihi*!' they shouted as they bashed him.

Johnno, shy dark Johnno, his scars more a part of him with a deep tan, punched Nigel's stomach (lucky he had a manly stomach) and cried, 'Hay! *Idi ugrizi svoi dupa!*'

'*Ugrizi moi dupa!*' replied Nigel, pointing to his buttocks.

They fell against the narrow corridor's walls laughing, pounding their knees, each other, any flesh would do. They slapped one another like queens.

All at once they stopped. They turned, sheepish, towards Catherine. Then, seeing the amused incomprehension on her face, they erupted into belly-laughs again.

'*Ugrizi moi dupa!*' they repeated with endless simple pleasure. Tears rolled into their beards.

I love these blokes, thought Nigel. I love each one of them. They loved him back. And that wasn't all.

A posy of freesias gave delicate scent from a bottle on the polished jarrah table between them. The assigned labourers' tiny coat-bath-tea-sitting-tool-provision room had, by a miracle of efficient storage and renovation, been transformed into a comfortable parlour. Here the seven filled each other in on the past two years over the Serbs' favourite sweet black tea. After much polite you-firsting, Pixie told Nigel about life here.

Todd was one of nature's *bêtes noires*. When the Serbs arrived here they had found the pathetic signs of their predecessors scattered across the property. Blood-stains. Unmarked graves. Once, a boot with a foot in it. He worked men on minimal food, with ancient and sometimes token ritualistic tools, allowed no spare time or sugar and, worst, planned nothing. Should one of his mates mention, say, a sagging fence on the station's far side, he would pull the whole team off an essential task to mend it. Appearance reigned. The farm meant only his ticket to a new class of knighthood. He made more than enough from fines and kickbacks. The Serbs had at first suffered his whims and random cruelties. Budimir showed Nigel some ugly scars not made by whips.

Then love had changed everything.

On sight, Catherine had become their goddess. They had had much of the religion knocked out of them over the years. They had settled on her. She went unaware of this for some months. However, inchmeal, the five prisoners of war made their devotion felt. Pixie spent his every waking second for weeks composing an ode on her delicate ears. He made ink and a quill and calf vellum himself during the long winter nights. When he slipped the verses beneath her pillow he had not slept for a week.

'It frightened me,' Catherine confessed. 'I expected a stranger lurking around my bedroom at night. Perhaps you had escaped. There had been odd reports from Kingsland,' she said to Nigel. 'And this was some kind of ironic torment for the wrong I had done you.' She lowered her vivid blue eyes to the table between them.

Budimir (back when he was Wal) had gathered dainty wildflowers and pressed them. These too had appeared beneath Catherine's pillow.

Charlie had whittled a scrimshaw in the shape of Catherine's long, fine fingers clasped in prayer.

Johnno fashioned a kite for her, its luminous panels showing the story of St Alice, the maiden who had metamorphosed into a butterfly.

By the time Doug's *kecak* was ready Catherine knew the assigned labourers loved her.

'We drank tea,' Catherine filled in, 'just like this. Doug unwrapped the cheese as though it were Queen Claudia's crown jewels. He cut me a piece and as I raised it to my mouth their eyes followed it, just full of fear.' She smiled at the blond cheese baron. 'Doug was in tears. And when I told them it was delicious they rolled their eyes so I thought they would faint. It was then, I think, I fell in love with them.'

Five grown men blushed like choicest pippins.

Life on the station grew easier. Because Catherine blackmailed Todd on the convicts' behalf. His affairs with various women, animals and helpless inanimate objects would ruin him should his legal 'friends' discover them. She made him give general kind concessions to all he met so he wouldn't suspect her relationship with the Serbs. 'I suppose I am a wicked woman,' said Catherine.

'No, no!' the Serbs protested.

'You know I am,' she maintained, smiling sadly. 'You can't do bad to do good.'

Reluctantly, they nodded.

Although Nigel was sure the love the five men shared with Catherine was entirely spiritual, he fought a jealous rage which built until his ears went scarlet. It surprised and annoyed the hell out him. He had thought himself over his childish crush on Catherine. She had, after all, betrayed him.

Catherine's hands lay flat on the table. She spread her fingers, staring at them, and closed them. 'Nigel,' she said, gently, aware of his mood but not its reason.

He hmm-ed at her, unable to speak.

'Nigel, forgive me,' she said. 'You can see it; I'm wicked.'

'Oh shut up about this wickedness!' Nigel snapped.

The Serbs feigned invisibility, confused.

Catherine nodded. It infuriated Nigel all the more.

'I did speak for you to Todd,' she told him. When he did not respond she added, 'But when I saw you whipped, half naked, humiliated, I knew it had not been enough.'

She had been the weeping woman. Catherine had wept for him.

'How could I have believed your story? After I returned from court the houseproper asked me what to do with your things. I—I looked through them. I found a picture of the boys here, and you. A fantastic picture. After I got to know them, I found all you had said of them was true, and they told me what you had told them. You are from another place. Another world. I — ' she stood ' — I've kept your things for you . . . I'll fetch them later . . . I don't know what else to say. Forgive me.'

Nigel thought of Macka, and of Frank. He said, 'Forget it. You don't know what you did for me. And besides,' he went on, brightening artificially, 'I escaped. So it's over now. Sit down; you don't know what you did for me.' But Nigel did. She had woken him up.

The early sun streamed through the neat new windows behind Catherine Samuelson. Her brushed-out hair fell a lustrous jet about her sturdy shoulders. She looked less prim than when he'd last seen her. It might be possible, he decided. The simple deep blue skirt and white blouse and loose-laced yellow bodice were worn with easy vigour. She *was* different. Like a girl who has found the company of other women. He had forced her out of her normal track as well. He and the Serbs. Well, mostly the Serbs. They were the other women. Mothers and sisters. Yes, she might go. Nigel had realised that the Serbs would never leave her on a hare-brained jaunt with him. So he'd have to convince her to come too. Drats.

He forced himself to begin with Pixie.

'My story's quite involved.' He glanced from face to Slavic face. They were ready for a long tale. He was sorry to disappoint them. He could fill them in later. 'It's got everything to do with how I came up with this idea, but I think the idea's gotta be explained first. See, if you like it we've got a lot to do today.'

Doug looked blank. Budimir blinked, surprised, an act which involved his eyebrows and ears as well. Charlie and Johnno gave crooked smiles. Pixie nodded, ready for any strange balderdash Nigel might utter, ready to love it. And Catherine? He didn't look at her.

'This world,' he went on, 'this colony, as far as I can tell, this Empire. It's all – *wrong* to me!' He gestured wildly. 'The people like Todd have control. They've destroyed this country. Who knows what's happened in America? If the scientific community has to pander to what the church says, well, no pool of agreement can be settled, no basics are sorted out before research begins. You get hundreds of conflicting schools and most of them justify superstitions to serve whatever slimy goatee happens to be in charge. In my world there are more religions to begin with and the church has a say in your personal life but it's divorced from the state, mostly, well, in a lot of cases. We've got a lot of problems, but here, at least in Australia, the Todd creatures make it every bit as corrupt outside the penal stations as in. And you guys know how bad it gets in there. I've seen horrible . . . horrible stuff . . . some friends of mine saw there was no escape, no place to go if they survived their sentences except more of the same brutality, and they decided to kill themselves. Two – two other friends were shot *just because the station commandant had a bad day*.

'Now. I used to go through life without any idea of how lucky I was, how many choices I had. Some ways, I was spoilt for choice. There were heaps of things needed to be done and I had the intelligence and the energy to do 'em, but I let myself get confused by theory when what was good was obvious all the time: people need food and shelter and care when they're sick and art and love when they're low. Pick one and go for it. Some damned thing. Doesn't matter if you can't logically justify virtue. Here you have the opposite, sort of, you have it all mapped out for you. Except the totally good are guillible because the Todds can appear to do what the book tells them and really do otherwise. So: *you* have to do things you might not approve of, too: to combat the Todds you guys have to step into moral complication, possibly compromise. You found that out,

Catherine.' He ventured a glance at her. Did her eyes shine or was it merely the sun? '*You are not evil*, not *lost, if you step outside the laws*.

'You only imagine you are. Now we can prove that you don't have to either roll over or turn mean, but it takes stirring up people's *imaginations*!

'How can you do that? Just look how long it took Catherine to outwit Todd! I'm not trying to have a go at you or anything, but I mean – *come on*. You could have done that *years* back!

'No. There's a better way to give ordinary people the power to imagine things their religion doesn't say. I woke up one day in hospital and realised I was special. And not just special here, special everywhere. It took pain to show it to me. We all are special, but you must have strength to do something about that. Now I – ' For a second all he could think of was Frank's dark eyes. He shook his head.

'Now I do. I hope you do too, all of you.' He looked at Catherine again, and she was definitely with him.

'Because we are going bushranging.'

Puzzled, but with him. He spoke fast. 'We have to ride out of here and show people what we are, and what we are is not damned. We can be outlaws – but stir up minds at gunpoint! I can do it. Come with me; it's gunna take every speck of energy, of thought and of courage, that you possess. It's quite possibly suicidal in this country. But imagine it! A world where no matter how terrible a ruler might be, there's a confused *splendour*, a *multitude* of opinions jostling and scrapping and never settling down, so every cabal and clique is finished before it begins! It's split by doubt, by people whose *imaginations* have given them the tools to fight for themselves and recognise hypocrisy, so evil can never act in concert, or if it does, never for long, always with people at its heels if not downright opposed to it. Imagine a world where every child rebels as he or she grows older, and so examines life, love and knowledge from a fresh perspective. Imagine what we can *discover* that way! In my world it's a truism that the greatest discoveries are always made by young people. We can *fly*, literally.

'I have this in me.

'Where I come from, we threaten to kill millions one way or another with our science and belief is a total shambles. Yet we've got hope. Hope is itself imagination. It's a form of doubt to you. One day war might end, we might live for ever, and nobody starve.

'One day,' Nigel whispered.

He was aware he was on his feet. And that he hadn't told them what he actually proposed to *do*, just a load of sentimental half-baked claptrap, American style. Catherine, across the corner of the table to him, stood also. He had been looking – he wasn't sure where. Into the rafters probably, carried away with his wanking. So he hadn't seen Catherine leap to her feet, eyes fierce, face radiant, mouth open every bit as imbecilic as Nigel's. He hadn't seen her chest heave as he spoke, orgasmic, neither had he seen the tears mount in her eyes then patter on her breast.

It was because it hadn't happened.

What she had done was make a smile mixed from equal parts of frown and quizzical grin, she had hugged herself clenching her fists on her thumbs, and when he had risen she had stood herself, and held on to the table's edge, knees just a little weak (at his tone more than what he'd said) (or possibly at something else).

But Charlie and Johnno and Pixie and Doug and Budimir had wept. Great walloping garlic tears into their tea. Not at Nigel's incoherent rave; they hadn't heard a word. At Catherine. They hadn't looked away from her except to check for sure it was Nigel who'd taken her out of herself, given her one step past what they had given, inspired her. They had noted the small signs of emotion they had learnt to read in their years of attentiveness. They were with him. They'd leap into pits of finger-nipping chihuahuas for Nigel. They would endure an intimate evening with Telly Savalas (had they heard of him) for Nigel. Because of her.

Okay, Nigel decided, I can handle that.

Behind him and down the corridor the door slammed open. Nigel turned.

Todd Samuelson stood on the top step.

Even this far off you could see his nostrils were flared with rage. His Vandyke beard quivered. His eyes bulged until they were painful just to look at. Between and around Todd's feet, hopping up the steps and tracking cautiously into the convicts' quarters in jerks, were dozens of chickens.

'CATHERINE!' he boomed. 'What in the names of the kabbalas of blood and piss is going on here? If ye want to run this farm yerself, fine but the convicts – ' Then he recognised Nigel.

'*YOU*! By God I'll skin yer alive this time, Donohoe, I'll have ye eat yer entrails in a public place!' He pointed at the largest Serb he could see. 'You!' he commanded, derisively. 'Take his arms. Bind him, Wal, and bring him out into the yard.'

The young former goatherd rose slowly. Quietly, he said, with a painstaking dignity, 'I am Budimir.'

'Ay?' shouted Todd. 'I don't care if ye've got the pox – '

'I am Budimir. Budimir. Bud-ye-mirr. That is what I was christened in the church of Sveti Kliment, that is my name. Not *Wal*.' He made it sound like a species of grub. '*Budimir*. For ever.'

'*WHAT?* !?' Todd advanced two steps into the corridor. The chickens came with him. 'You Slavic potato,' he said and reached for his pistol. 'It's you behind this,' he told Nigel, taking aim at him.

Budimir did not flinch. Perhaps Nigel's speech had worked on him after all. He made for Todd at speed down the length of the building. Todd cocked his fat unwieldy gun. Budimir barrelled towards it, but Nigel saw Todd's fist clench as he took another step forward. There was no time to duck.

The gun went off.

Todd fell. The bullet whacked into the door behind Nigel. Budimir ran full pelt into Todd, knocking him into the yard. Todd did a quick bowling-pin-like spin in the air and landed on one foot. With a wail of pain he crumpled amongst the chickens. Budimir carried on, tripping over the station-owner and stumbling for some fifty metres before he regained his balance.

The chicken Todd had stood upon clucked angrily at a chair-leg.

While Pixie set Todd's ankle and leg in mud, the others readied themselves to leave. Catherine looted the farm's pantry. She persuaded Todd's wife and the houseproper that the convicts held her hostage and that all their throats would be slit if they went for the troopers. Remove Todd's gag or untie him and they would hear. Johnno and Charlie, wearing their best scar-faced, gap-toothed grins tied the women securely.

By the time the group set off on Todd's best horses, the sun was low enough to redden the whole horizon. They galloped, heads held high, toward it, shamelessly theatrical.

Twenty-One

The Weird Colonial Boy

How do you change the world? Roll it over, whip off the old epoch and dump it in the bucket, lift it by its teensy-weensy peninsulas and wipe its cute little volcano, cream and powder the South Pole, bung the new era under and fasten its *Zeitgeist* round the Equator, good as new, there we go never mind? Sure, if you're in the cartoon business. But if you're an escaped convict elephant-counter teamed with five Serbian sheep therapists, a gentlewoman farmer whose father gave her poison to carry in memory of him, and a pair of right dills, it ain't that easy.

You have to use your strengths. Even if they're weaknesses.

Chickens could not get them out of this one. Unless they were very large and numerous and equipped with machine-guns. At least they had a day's grace before anyone called at the station. It'd be just possible to reach the foothills by then. But a huge search-party would set off for the mountains – and finito benito. Victoria (Alfonso yet) was too small to hide a rabble of non-horsepeople.

Nigel did have a spot picked in which to hide. Pixie, however, commandeered the get-away by force of extravagant confidence. He *knew* this was the best way out of an impossible situation. He told them, 'I feel it in my bone.'

And so because of Pixie's bone they were detained in Milton Keynes.

By popular demand.

Not an hour's ride away from Emu station, they made their plans. Such as they managed. The Serbs took immediately to Terry and Zak. When they met, the two escapees were filling in time with a game: Who Can Stay in the Saddle Upside-down for Longest. The horses didn't like it one bit. As the company rode towards them, down a path off the main Milton Keynes road which forded a tributary of the Goulburn, Zak tumbled from his mount into the water. Terry slapped his knees. 'You should try my horse,' shouted Zak, 'Fatguts is more harder than yours.' Fatguts snorted angrily from the river-bank, wishing he'd trampled Zak.

Their polemic led to a brawl over whether Fatguts or Knacker-Eater was the more dangerouser horse. It was some time before they noticed Nigel and his friends.

Soon after the smooches and back-bashes the Mackerel Gang held their first formal meeting. Zak and Terry wanted them all to swear on the mackerel. Nigel assured them they would, later. Pixie spent half the evening convincing the others his idea would work. Eventually he wore them down, since there was no alternative less foolish, and they set a fire and ate.

Over damper (which Nigel never did get used to since it crunched on his fillings) and fresh mutton (stringy and scrawny but heaps better than anything Nigel had eaten in weeks) Pixie set everyone tasks for the next day. Afterwards, while the Serbs and the former baldies filled one another in on their histories, Nigel and Catherine wandered down the creek a way.

'I am sorry,' said Catherine.

'Look I told ya – ' Nigel snapped. 'Sorry. That wasn't the way I was gunna say it.' He sighed, tugging a willow-leaf that wouldn't break off. 'I'm harder now, ay?'

She laughed! 'You . . . you were so . . . I don't know . . . innocent when we met.'

'Prison's knocked it out of me.' The branch snapped and fell on his head, snakelike.

'Not exactly.' She sat down on a tufty overhang and dangled her legs over the brown water. 'More . . . substantial.' She offered her hand to him, then when he stood staring at it, pulled him down beside her. 'Have I changed too?'

He sat. Not knowing what to do with her hand, he patted it. 'Yes,' he said, almost falsetto. 'Hgm – yes. You're less strident, and more confident and – but – you're just as beautiful.'

She took her hand from him and punched him with it.

'You are!' he insisted.

'I know that, ninny. Well, I know how I look. The boys are always telling me, *advising* me rather, on how to dress and so forth, but they do always manage to slip a compliment in. You either grow to have a ridiculous idea of yourself, or become realistic. I know how I look.'

'Okay, fine. I just wanted to say I liked you.'

'Thank you, Nigel. I . . . like you too.'

'Ta muchly, I'm sure,' said Nigel, chuffed.

'Or I wouldn't be swanning out breaking the law with you, hmm?'

'I've got some idea why you're here,' said Nigel, disappointed, recalling the story she had told him about her father.

She got up. 'Well maybe someday you will tell me.' She brushed the grass from her moleskins and walked away.

After half an hour, Nigel followed.

Early the next morning the Mackerel Gang readied themselves for a foray into Milton Keynes. It took hours. Their make-up was appalling, mostly flour. But the Serbs and Nigel had shaved their heads as well as their faces; they wore plain white Serbian church clothes without the shawls or bells. Budimir was dressed as a woman. Terry and Zak had refused to shave but with a little lard had spiked their hair into brown fishy shapes. Catherine's hair was cut short and she wore a pair of Todd's moleskins, riding boots and a large white shirt. Pixie's skill with make-up did help sharpen her soft lines, but there was no way she could hide her breasts so they eventually settled on an enormous fake stomach.

Even with Catherine's Passover lip-paints and coloured shading the Gang's disguises seemed transparent to Nigel. Catherine's moustache kept falling off. Budimir walked like a seagoing bear. The blue cosmetic dots on Zak and Terry's rancid orange clothes had already smeared and looked merely pathetic. Despite the fact that seven had ridden away from Emu station and nine walked into Milton Keynes, despite the boldness of *not* scrambling for the hills immediately, despite Zak and Terry's successful suicides and all Pixie's earnest reassurances that he had done this a thousand times, Nigel worried. Albino sand-loaches had marked the limit of his previous responsibilities. It was my idea, he reminded himself as they neared the outskirts of Milton Keynes. Stick up for it, he told his over-active digestive system.

He had performed only once in his life, in a school pantomime. (His stomach went, Reep.) Everyone – well, his mother – had loved him, but Nigel put his good acting down to just doing it and never thinking about its details. (Rumble – gulp – gurgle . . .) Like audiences. What did they do here if they hated you? (Sploodge.) People were already staring suspiciously. (Gloomp wroop – urp.)

Pixie, though, Pixie was unflappable.

As soon as they reached the town centre, with its dingy pubs, prayer-tower, decorated court-house and statue of King Rupert's father, Rupert XIV, atop an elephant, Pixie halted. He surveyed his potential audience. A lone trooper swept the cop-shop's verandah (urgle); two old women in cheap plastic skirts tottered along in a natter; a mangy dog slept on a pub's verandah. Most of the town was at lunch.

Pixie ran a few paces. He stopped again. 'Step up!' he called. 'Step up you every one and all!' After three years in

Australia his accent had softened; what remained, rolling 'R's and heavy plosives, he made into showmanship. Grammar was not the strength of this kind of drivel. 'Step UP, peoples! Here fresh from their tour of Allied Europe, from the blessed heart of ENGLAND and acclaim in HOLY BLACKPOOL in the companies of KINGS on their way to MELBOURNE and EXCLUSIVE performance for the VICEREGAL PLEASANCE in a RARE opportunity to see the CELEBRATED DUMB-SHOW that has STARTL-ING THE WORLD, I bring you, for two nights only, the PERSPICACIOUS, always SPONTANEOUS and occasion-ally EXTEMPORANEOUS, not to mention PUSIL-LANIMOUS, the EIGHT the ONLY, the filling up your face with ASTONISHMENT, the filling up your gobs with GASPS, the filling your kiddies' hearts with JOY AND GOOD BEHAVIOURS FOR HOURS ON END, I give you the SENSATIONAL, the OVATIONAL, the PRO-VISIONAL, the ABSOLUTELY – '

Pixie stopped. Nigel's stomach cha-cha-ed with his spleen. In all the discussions nobody had thought to name them. Now, with men emerging from the pubs in curiosity, women rolling up their aprons as they stood in doorways, children hopping up and down under restraint from their elders on the porches, Pixie balked.

He temporised:

'The PULCHRITUDINOUS, the PURULENT, the PRODIGIOUSLY – PURPLE! Never before WITNESSED in the WILDS of this COLONIES – ' His voice rose, frustration creased his wide forehead, a dreadful silence spread from his open mouth for a long moment. Then inspiration made him laugh out loud.

'*THE WEIRD COLONIAL BOYS*!!' he boomed.

Budimir ran forward and performed a circuit of surprisingly graceful cartwheels, considering his great size. His dress, an ill-fitting spare of Catherine's, did not flop down to expose him, such was his speed. But his hirsute limbs lent his turns comedy. The children giggled.

'AND now . . . ' continued Pixie, 'for your DELECT-ATION, RECREATION AND TINTABULATION' – which oddly produced applause from the gathering crowd – 'we present a FREE AND GRATUITOUS sample of tonight's EXTRA-CURRICULAR EXSANGUINA-TION! Step up. Step UP! Gather closer. Watch and learn what the holy *habised* CROWNED HEADS of Allied Europe and Britain have risen to their feet for. Gather ROUND my friends!' The crowd jumped back at his shout. 'Do not be shy . . . do not MISS the chance to see for YOURSELVES . . . '

Now he whispered. The crowd strained forward to hear, then crossed the dusty square almost boldly to form a semicircle about the troupe, which had halted by the elephant statue's feet.

'See for *yourselves*,' he continued, 'a tale of love and magic which will make your bellies swell with *tears*, make you hug your eyes with *laughter* – ladies and gentlemen and shiny-headed nurselings, I give you, *The Adventures of Rajiv Rompastillio*.'

Recognition laughter and scattered applause. The audience appeared to know the story. Pixie had assured Nigel he knew thousands of narratives perfect for dramatisation from his days as a spruiker, but Nigel had worried all the same about their translation for an Australian audience. No, Pixie had said, there were only so many western tales and they were all religious in one way or the other. Now Nigel saw it was true: the audience knew what to expect and appreciated the surprises Pixie threw in, as well as the old favourite parts. His stomach shut up; his nerves subsided so much that when a suitable cue arrived Johnno had to shove him into the circle. As he stumbled on the audience roared with laughter. This was coarse theatre indeed. Nigel made a virtue of his incompetence. Pixie played up to this, setting Nigel difficult events and concepts to mime, like 'blasphemed' and 'greenish'. The group crudely but inventively adopted the roles of animals and spirits, villains and heroes in the morality tale. It worked, and it was going to work tonight.

As long as nobody saw through them.

The door-chimes tinkled in the wind and Nigel hastily closed the door on the children capering with excitement on the verandah. In the gloom at the rear of the general store a red face which obviously hadn't heard the buzz from the town centre hovered behind grain-bins, suspicious of Nigel and Catherine's streaked make-up and odd attire. The canvas was nowhere obvious. Catherine would have to ask. He nudged the side of her false gut. Gruffly, she cleared her throat. 'Excuse me, sir,' she said, as if she had a dead rat in her mouth. 'Canvas?'

The proprietor hmfed. Nigel could see him debate with himself the pros and cons of calling a trooper.

Nigel said, adenoidal, 'Uh, we're from the travelling – '

A girl burst into the room, sending the door-chimes into dull conniptions. She skidded to a halt, panting, in a shaft of floury light. 'Dadda, there's a playing company in town and . . . ' She followed her father's stare to Nigel's face. A finger gravitated toward her lower lip. She kicked a heel. Abruptly, she ran around the counter to the protection of her father's legs. 'It's all right,' her father murmured, bending. The girl whispered to the proprietor. 'Oh are they?' he said. She whispered again. 'Yes, love, you can go. Now run along out back and you can tell me all about it when I'm finished. Go on. Go!'

He turned to face Nigel, smiling. 'So what can I do for yez? Canvas was it?'

'Yes,' squeaked Nigel, 'and some rope and . . . '

It was the curiosity and discussion that scared Nigel. The news of his raid on Emu station didn't reach Milton Keynes until the late afternoon, when a bunch of troopers thundered out on horseback to head off the escaped convicts' obvious flight to the mountains. Further excitement then

coursed through the town and Doug, who was careful not
to open his mouth since his accent was the strongest and
was thus forced to listen politely to every booby on the
street, heard from a trooper that the 'six savage fiends' had
'surely headed for the high plains' the previous day. 'Ye
better guard yer takings well, boys,' he informed Doug, who
mm-ed and nodded.

Catherine propped near by, hand on her wilted
moustache. She seemed rigid with fear. The trooper must
have been one of Todd's cronies. Nigel hit her with his
canvas roll as he passed, accidental-like. She threw a furious
glance at him but did not move. The trooper finished with
his saddle and strode over to Catherine. He took a rope-end
from under her arm between his fingers and rolled it
critically. 'Can I give ye a piece of advice, son?' he said,
clapping a hand to her shoulder.

Catherine pursed her lips stoutly and nodded.

Nigel edged back towards them, ready for violence.

'Stay a while. The wilds out there are dangerous for
unworldly folks such as ye are. Stay a fortnight! We like ye
here, and ye'll do well.' He turned and strode to his horse,
spurs rattling. Before he mounted he winked and clicked his
tongue at Catherine.

As he galloped down the road to guard Todd on his way
to the infirmary Nigel closed his eyes to offer thanks to
whoever had made their luck. *We're glamorous*, thought
Nigel, astounded. The trooper had hung about giving Doug
and Catherine the goss' not from suspicion but out of
admiration. A thrill made him want to heave the canvas in
the air, to cheer, to kiss Catherine square on the lips. The
tension drained from him.

Tonight's performance would be just fine.

It was more than that.

It was balderdash, Nigel had to admit it. Yet it was
charming balderdash. The thinly disguised Serbian folk-

tales filled with suspense and comic opportunities when acted out. Pixie, in his role of Magnifico the Narrator, could hold a crowd on his own, which was lucky since Johnno and Doug acted about as well as legless pigeons, even after some practice and rehearsal. Pixie drew an audience through what he called 'A thousand cunning mensurations'. Usually the stories involved plucky goatherds recapturing their rightful inheritance from their evil half-brothers or they were apocryphal religious numbers, themes so familiar as to bore anyone with a mental age above three, Nigel would have thought. But Pixie made a crowd forget their age. He wooed the most sceptical punters with friendly cajoling and the rest of the audience joined these exchanges on Pixie's side. He had a particular magnetism for women over fifty: the lust fairly oozed into the grass from them as they followed his every cocksure step around the stage.

Budimir revealed a natural talent for physical comedy, and he rioted with Zak and Terry. They rolled, slapped and double-took like heroes. Charlie had a gift for uncanny animal impersonation. Because she was known in town Catherine played bits of landscape, and marshalled Doug and Johnno whose stage fright often threatened to scupper the whole event.

However, it was Nigel who tipped the balance toward adulation that first night. And during the next six as well.

After Nigel's show-stopping début as the Blind Butcher in the town square he was given the lead role in two of the three pieces programmed for their marquee in Prince Tarquin Gardens. The audience couldn't get enough of him. What he had this world was starved of. It proved, Nigel decided, that these humans were genetically just like him. Yup. One organisation in charge of right and wrong had won, a fundamentalist syncretism had sucked up all religions in its path like a philosophical drunk. This world craved the ridiculous. It was a bridge back out of stagnation for those who 'knew' the truth and so couldn't argue their

way into a sceptical righteousness that would let them fight
the beards of evil. *And the fool shall set ye free*, he said to
himself.

Well, perhaps a little bit, maybe, after a while, without a
north wind, and not on a Tuesday. With luck.

So in the last performance Nigel went berserk.

Six days of confidence, founded on adulation and experiments which seemed to work every time, surged in him. The
final tale concerned a farmer King (Zak) who promised his
canny daughter (Nigel) to whoever could rid him of his
fleas. Budimir played the hapless peasant loved by Nigel and
Terry played the evil warlock who had cast a flea spell on
Zak. Six performances old, the tale had found its natural
pace and the comic business was well worked out. Until the
confrontation scene between Nigel and Terry.

' . . . and Princess Geoffrey went away and conned magic
in the forest with Stomach, the good witch, for four days
and four nights,' narrated Pixie. 'Meanwhile the King's
itching grew frenetic. The Royal Scratchers worked around
the clock but could never find the exact spot which satisfied.
They worked *under* the clock but still he found no joy. By
the time Princess Geoffrey was ready to battle the Warlock
the King was beside himself with lack of sleep. Scratcher
after scratcher was disembowelled and drawn and quar-
tered. The King fretted over his beautiful daughter's
disappearance. The Warlock, in his disguise as the King's
Chancellor, encouraged the King to suspect Our Hero of
kidnapping her. On the fourth day just as Jack was about to
get torn limb from limb by the King's ravening newts,
Princess Geoffrey returned from the forest and unmasked
the Warlock and challenged him to a contest of magic.'

So far, the play had run as planned. The Royal Scratchers
had outdone themselves, the Warlock's scenes with the
King had given a man at the front a honking fit, and
Budimir's Hero had stumbled about so nervously clumsy
three girls had wet themselves but wouldn't leave; the
mature women in the crowd squirmed with lust for Pixie.

Then, weaving the spell which would finish the Warlock once and for all, prancing about uttering a nonsense incantation, Nigel outdid himself. He ranted. At first he did not connect his energetic babble with the vision suffered on the night he had tried to convince Clarry he was insane, when he'd raved like this and seen the Excelsior Hotel floating in the air; he certainly did not connect it with the jumbo jet seen in the cemetery when he'd raved, in shock.

Nigel ranted, inspired.

Reality disintegrated.

Out of the cloudless night beyond the marquee's supports there appeared a massive Mack truck loaded with sheep. It was about three metres off the ground. Nigel threw himself to one side shouting to Budimir to do likewise as the metal behemoth swooped down from the sky. The truck farted and squeaked to a halt, safely above centre stage, its driver blinking and rubbing his worn eyebrows, clearly convinced he'd had one red too many. The door opened and the blue-singleted beer-gut stumbled from the cabin. He dropped startled by the gap on to his feet, then his knees.

'Oh my God, oh my God!' shouted Nigel in a panic. If the performance went badly the town would fall back on its natural suspicion of strangers for sure. Then their tat and slap would all be seen for what it was – and they'd be lynched. Badly! Oh what had he *done* to this poor innocent stoned truckie?

He grabbed the stunned driver by the belt of his jeans and tried to hoist him back up to the truck. 'Get out! Get outta here!'

The audience shrieked with laughter.

Nigel stopped. He stared at them.

They laughed again.

The driver had had enough manhandling by now. He removed Nigel's hand from behind him and pushed Nigel away.

More laughter. Some applause.

Most of the short fist-fight that developed between Nigel

and the driver drew happy hysterics from the crowd. As did Nigel's screams of frustration. Slowly, the truck, the stinking sheep and the belligerent driver began to fade. By then Nigel had realised the audience had seen nothing of the big Mack. He stood and panted, remembering the night the Excelsior Hotel had drifted in from the sky, thinking, Is it because I'm homesick I've seen these things? He did not feel homesick. I babbled then and I babbled now, is that the connection? But anyone can babble.

Can't they?

Not the way Nigel could. Heaven knew what the audience thought. What he had done was very weird to them. Some of Nigel's actions fitted with the casting-a-spell routine, some not. Several people were scratching their heads. It's about to get very ugly, Nigel thought.

Pixie covered for him.

'This was the most awesomeness of spells,' he said hurriedly. 'The Princess had conjured a spirit to combat the Warlock which was so strong even she had trouble controlling it. "Phew," she said, after getting it into the bottle.' He looked at Nigel.

'Phew,' said Nigel. The audience laughed, as relieved as Nigel that the story was back on track. Nigel mimed picking up a bottle. He wagged a finger at it.

'Finally, she launched the spirit upon the evil Warlock.'

Terry didn't need a hint. He leapt into the new gag with an idiot will. His struggle with the spirit was a masterful piece of lunacy; he slapped himself and hopped and twisted his face exactly as though someone else had a hold of him.

What, Nigel wondered as the pantomime drew to a close, would have happened had the truck remained? Certainly a disaster, but would it have become visible to the audience? And *why* had it happened in the first place? After the last bow Nigel heard one farmer say to his wife, 'That Prince Geoffrey's the weird colonial boy if y'ask me. He's neally *too* funny'. His wife had nodded absently, her eyes on Pixie's departing bottom. 'Never seen anything like it,' she said. 'Yairs,' said the grazier.

It was definitely time to say goodbye to the Milton Kennelers. This kind of surreal event would reveal them one way or another. In any case he was getting keen – more than keen, ravenously excited – about his plan for world domination. Should his revolt provoke more eruptions of trucks and pubs (and aeroplanes . . .), he had a quivering feeling that he might not have to die to bring some imagination into this world.

If people and things could roll into this universe because of whatever he had done, he might step through the other way himself. Jubilant, he ran after Pixie, wondering absently why he didn't want to tell Catherine since out of all of them she'd best understand his brainwave. Never mind. They'd strike the tent while the Kennelers slept and be far away by dawn; with Todd still incapacitated and the search for Nigel now diverted toward Melbourne it was time to head for the mountains again!

It was time to get into some heavy-duty stupidity.

Twenty-Two

Rampant Ice-cream

It was the night he heard the news about his double's death. Too bad you can't save everyone. It would have been interesting to meet the man. Very interesting. But it would have been a distraction. Can't involve yourself now. Important work to do.

Yet he could not sleep.

He rose for a leak. It was around three a.m. Never mind summer it was colder than Baal's balls out there. Cold enough for ice higher up. He pulled on his trousers. Snores filled the air. A muttered tune from Zak.

As he unbuttoned his fly he caught sight of a white form squatting on the bushes' far side. The form stood hastily and slipped back down the hill between the trees to the hut. Leaves crackled. When he returned he found Catherine on her knees by the fire's embers. She fed it twigs. He hunkered down beside her. She took her time talking. It was no problem. You developed tough hunker-muscles in Donohoe's line of work.

'Nigel. He was your brother.'

'No. He was me. Not even that. A stranger.'

The fire caught. Flames licked logs.

'Before Milton Keynes you said you knew why I was in this.'

'I know you better now.'

'What do you know?'

'You're good at organisation. The best. And you just

wanted out of Emu station. I know you love the boys. And I know you've been fighting what you told me about your father and the poison all your life. That's a lot.'

'He was not a bad man. If anybody deserved a knight-hood for services to sheep it was him. He and my mother struggled through droughts and bushfires and *pikun* for those sheep. Nothing ever came of it. He had no imagina-tion. Now I've met you I can see that. And Todd . . . he took their deaths his own way. He wasn't born evil. My father's strangeness gave him a brilliance a little like yours, but here – he found himself damned to *biggle* and what else was there to do but revel in it? He learned the delights of revenge early. He discovered its rewards. It's a disease in our society. Perhaps it's a sign life will gradually change anyway without you . . . You know should he ever discover you're still alive I tally he'll hunt you till you drop.'

'What if he drops first?'

'You don't know him! He has no scruples. He will find you and kill you.'

'You've forgotten. I'm the man who can do dodgy things and not believe I'm lost for ever. I can de-scruple with the best. I thought you'd learnt something about that.'

She smiled at him. One of her front teeth was crooked. He loved to see it.

Together they watched the fire for a fair while.

At last she said, 'I'd best go to sleep. Lots of work hunting for ice in the morning.'

And with that she rose and kissed him on the cheek. A hard and short but affectionate kiss.

'Dance with me?' he said. And he was thrilled that he was not nonplussed into speechlessness by her kiss.

She nodded. She had danced with most of the gang at one time or another. But never without music. Or alone.

He stood. In his orange undershirt and trousers and without shoes he took her in his arms. In her white cotton undershift she stepped to one side. They shuffled about for a minute. She smiled again. Nigel would have done harm for

that smile. She bade him goodnight and left and crawled
into her bunk. It was around four a.m. He went back to his
pallet.

He still had trouble getting to sleep.

Stars. Up here the Milky Way was enough to see by. They
creaked out of bed in the starlight. Every one of them
cursed. Catherine too. But even a fool knew timing was
essential in an operation like this so the evil moods weren't
personal. Just part of the territory.

A solid breakfast was essential as well. Eggs and steaks
and fried bread and strong black coffee. With plenty of
sugar. They were well supplied. Whatever they needed they
bought. Disguises weren't necessary. Zak and Terry picked
up supplies because they were supposedly dead. Nigel could
have gone as well but he kept Catherine's warning in mind.
Nigel's double had been executed two months back.
Regrets passed but not fear. That was the game he was in.

And what a game. Some of the preparation had to be
finished that morning. The ice collected for weeks on end
from frosts and mountain peaks wouldn't last a few minutes
out of the vault. Charlie unscrewed the hardwood door
with quiet pride. Mist flowed out. Charlie winked at Nigel.
Nigel gave a laconic nod. Then he slipped on a rock into the
freezing water. At least Charlie did not laugh. They stepped
into the vault in silence and hefted the ice and carried it up
the hill from the stream to Doug in the hut. And his ice-
cream churn.

Budimir broke the churn-handle. They had to improvise
one with a spade.

Dawn. A wan wrinkle of blue under a string of baby-pink
and straw clouds. The air was sharp in his passages. So were
the birds. What a racket. The horses stepped sideways on
the wet grass. They tossed their heads. They knew what was

up. So did Nigel Donohoe. And he wasn't in the mood to take lip from a horse.

This did not go for Terry however.

'Fuck my tits to smithereens you bastard horse.' Terry picked himself off the dew then squared off with Knacker-Eater. The horse walked forward. It stomped. 'All right all right.' Terry held out skinny hands. 'Just let me on?' The horse sent vapour jets at him. 'Pleeease?'

It was not a good morning to be Nigel Donohoe.

Half an hour later. The sun had a definite place booked on the horizon by now. It wouldn't be late for the party. And Nigel was determined neither would he.

He gave the signal.

Johnno waved his own flag from his cart on a saddle in the next line of hills and flicked his reins. Soon he was just a line of dust in the pale first rays. He was a good man. He'd be ready on time.

Nigel turned to the others. Budimir. Pixie. Doug. Zak. Terry. Catherine. They were all good men. Except Catherine. Suddenly he felt fine. It didn't matter how many more things went wrong this morning. He smiled.

'Let's go,' he said.

Their horses' hooves made breakneck ruckus in the quiet mountains. The operation had begun.

Riding through the platinum light he remembered Catherine's kiss. Two months later and she had not touched him again. Courting was different here. He had to accept that. Tread carefully. Sometimes he thought frustration was what their courting was about. Pixie had implied that when asked. Never stated. Just implied. Nigel thought of Kern. He wasn't as frustrated as Kern. Or as mad to start with. In fact his memory of the kiss jogged him out of pessimism about the raid. A little.

*

The first ambush was simple. It was set for an hour after dawn. They would attack and execute then ride away. Back to their hidden valley to lie low and prepare for the next one. It would be a test of their organistion. If nothing else it would test whether or not their little mountain valley was hidden enough to conceal them from reprisals. There might not be any. What Nigel planned was so outrageous they might be ashamed to relate what had happened that morning.

But they might not.

It would be a shambles if they went on like this. After Terry's tumble from his horse one stupid mishap led to another. First they got lost. This took a good half an hour. Then Zak and Terry decided to make up with each other over their previous night's tiff. This meant creative falling off horses. Budimir lost his patience and roared. Fatguts and Knacker-Eater bolted. It would have been a laugh but Johnno had orders to begin when the sun cleared the trees behind his location and if he went in out of the blue on his own he would be caught and gaoled.

Finally Charlie exclaimed that he had forgotten the cherries.

'Never mind the cherries,' said Nigel.

'Don't speak to him like that,' said Catherine.

The two glowered at one another. Zak giggled. The horses twitched their nerves.

'Okay,' said Nigel. 'I'm sorry Doug. But we can't go back for the cherries.'

'It will not be the same,' said Doug.

'We shall think of something,' Catherine assured him.

Doug nodded reluctantly. 'Yes. We think.'

'We think as we ride,' said Nigel.

They rode.

The spot picked for the ambush was bordered on one side by a river and on the other by sheer cliff. The dirt road ran along the river's old course on gravel piled above the floodline by convict gangs years before. One third of the party would attack frontally. So to speak. Another three would emerge from behind simultaneously and the remaining three would be saved for surprise events during the raid. Their victims would thus find themselves trapped on open ground which sloped violently on their left and almost as steeply down to a deep rushing part of the brown water on their right.

It was a pretty spot in the early hours. Thick forest grew across the river. Daisies and green pea stuck out of the cliff. Once Zak and Terry and Budimir had scouted the area for unwelcome guests the group split and stationed themselves at their starting-points.

Nigel and Catherine and Pixie would begin the event. They waited by the side of the road behind a copse of poplars. Some convict overlooker's whim. Catherine looked as nervous in her costume as Nigel felt under his. Pixie appeared calm. With a loaf of bread over most of his face you could tell only by the smoke puffing calmly from the mouth-hole. Nigel needed a piss. Too late now. Never get the feathers back in place on time. He caught Catherine's eye. She smiled. There were no hard cherry feelings then.

He still had not told her about the possibility of his going home. Pixie had nodded when Nigel had told him. He had sworn himself to secrecy. It had been easy. He had not believed Nigel. It was one thing to believe a story of television and atom bombs you had never seen but it was another entirely to doubt the evidence of your own eyes. Or lack of evidence.

Well Nigel would get evidence. In about ten minutes from now.

It began with hooves thrumming and tackle rattling and the rumbling crunch of metal rims on gravel. Nigel accepted the mackerel pipe from Pixie. The fuse took too quickly. It singed a feather on his hand as it zipped down to the rocket. A colourful Charlie special.

Fssst. Whistle. Crack.
The show began.

Later he remembered only slices. Thin slices. And since not
all of it could be rehearsed at once and some of it never he
recalled his own astonishment at the total effect of his plans.
Its main purpose was a shock to the imagination. Living
proof that 'unconventional' did not mean 'evil'. If a reality
break occurred he was too busy to notice. What he did recall
was his own voice. A happy unstoppable burble in words he
could not speak in this world which though it conjured no
Mack trucks or Excelsior Hotels drew him apart from the
hectic action around him and above him and to a place he
now recognised as the space between worlds born of what
this universe had lost (or never had):
   Flapdoodle.

The horse's muscles shift under her flanks (Nigel thought). I
think Mrs Pimlott's moves therefore I am Mrs Pimlott. We
swing sideways before we pull up. Surprisingly easy to do
backwards under pressure. Practice. We might not convince
them we're serious about a new mind-freedom with our
silliness alone but even here obvious expertise counts for a
lot.
   The fearsome clatter and breath behind my head then at
the carriage and I might swing off and fall on them as we
stop or not. Not. Mrs Pimlott's cool (he reckoned). And the
carriage team has decided not to panic even if it *is* faced with
two chickens mounted backwards and a man with a loaf of
bread for a head. 'Spring with indelible passion!' I cry. My
actual written first line is forgotten.
   It's a day like the day when I tossed my crutches aside in
the park (he recalled). I could walk without them. I crowed
I actually crowed with joy to see the insignificant pinking
clouds troop by above the rising sun. My leg was whole. The
sky is just like that. It's magic as Pixie bellows his
introduction. They stick to lines these people but it's a

birthday celebration planned by an alien and it's strange enough to inspire a stone if Pixie deviates not one whit.

The passengers flip the heavy windows down on their leather hinges. They sticky-beak startled from the cushioned dark. A viceregal head emerges wigless into the cool to face the attackers who are clip-clopped backwards a pace at the Lieutenant-Governor's horrific eyes. Stark evil. Malevolent liquid green. Here is no stone. No convincing him. Or perhaps it was his suddenness. In any case he looks like my third-grade teacher Mr Waller. He had a rotten-potato nose that seemed to store up spite. It had stored for twenty-four years and allowed him to mutter, 'Now now children,' instead of, 'Shut the fuck up or die, little shitbags!' Does this man see his colony so?

'Look here!' he calls.

It might be him. Memory plays tricks. This might be my old teacher's double.

No time. I'm shouting things such as 'Up with your feet you slimy propeller-hungry double dissolutions! Hand me a cabbage so I can feed this man my beliefs.'

Catherine although she's learnt a lot stammers her disquisition on the mating habits of slugs. They climb a tree and circle in each other's slime until it builds strong and thick enough to suspend them on a string of it and at its end they twine in a double helix swapping sperm. She gets involved. Heart-rending as she falters through the lonely outcome where one drops off and the other climbs up and the two slugs never see one another again. Slugs in the night.

Woo! The passengers are bombarded by words and fireworks on all sides. When at last the driver pulls his gun he's hesitant and my flower soaked in EA 69 adhesive seals his barrel in time. He plucks at the petals in a kind of love-me-love-me-not frenzy and tumbles from his seat. His gun skitters across the polished wood. It explodes! Lucky he's not hurt. But he's up and running.

I gesture. *Let him go*. Pixie breadloaf agrees.

Then Johnno dives from the cliff.

His enormous kite gives a creak. It falls. We've done this before but we're all scared silly every time he does it. Some of us hide it better I see. Budimir dismounts coolly. Sawing the rear carriage wheels into kindling nearly takes his thumb off.

Johnno drops for elongated moments. He noses up. Before the weak thermal takes him he begins to stall and we all stop raving at the passengers. This is more frightening than anything we could have made up. When we begin again as Johnno soars the Lieutenant-Governor starts and his neck bangs the window-frame.

'Oooh!' we all go on cue. We point at Johnno's spiral descent out of the salmon light. His angel's robes flap ecstatically. I see as he nears that the headband base of his halo has slipped over one eye. Arrr. He's a pirate of the Lord's buccaneers.

Our choral accompaniment rises to Johnno. It seems to buoy him. His minutes above the carriage grow longer for it. This world knows no medieval glory. The Abbess Hildegarde was probably never born here. Heaps of rehearsal went into this. And it's probably as inaccurate as my memory for music ever is. Johnno balked at the angel's dress but the music convinced him. Now he sings louder in praise of a humanistic God than anyone here bar Pixie.

He passes over the trees. Will he make it to the rendezvous point across the river? No time to wonder we restart the carriage's decoration. Two chickens and a loaf of bread and the God King Emperor of Britain and a snake and a hammer. Us. We paint and saw and glue. Most of this is scripted.

The passengers cower within yet they can't resist a glimpse at our maniac labour. A child begins to sing along with Catherine's 'Whoopty-whoop-whoop-whoop' song and there is a smack! And quiet.

Finally it's ready. I glance at the horizon. The sun flows weakly but fresh over the clefts in the hills. Soon it will grow warm. And we will be far from here.

'In the name of Kenneth Kaunda, glorious king of the African Realms,' intones Pixie, 'ruler of rivers, monarch of mountains, palindrome of plains, this buggy of joy is *COMPLETE!*'

The last cue. Through the hole in the carriage's roof Budimir pours his insulated saddle-bags of ice-cream. Then the chocolate sauce. Then in honour of Marlene White my lost love my genius bathmate: Hot Maggots! Tomato sauce and mustard and chopped cauliflower topping yum yum yum.

'Mackerel Gang, let's *go!*' I shout.

Budimir is the last to his horse. We gallop away down the side-track to the river ford. Exhilaration races our hearts faster than the hoofbeats along the road.

(Nigel wondered:) How will these well-off travellers limp into town? Will the public laugh or will they seek revenge with the help of some bearded Todd creature?

Who the hell cares? Whoop-de-bloody-doo!

So went Nigel's mind as his guerrilla band rode back to their mountain hut. He imagined the most likely outcome. The passengers would leave their decorated transport and brush down their clothes. They'd await a passer-by. They would not admit their weird encounter. Stories would spread regardless. The coach by the roadside would lend credence to the fabulous accounts of the child and driver.

A seed . . . a seed of revolution!

Nigel and the Mackerel Gang celebrated that night with rum and dancing round the tiny shared room. Zak and Terry kissed shamelessly until their foreheads clunked. Budimir kissed everybody. Charlie's eyes glittered with dreams of what else he could make with Nigel's strange ideas. Doug cooked the most delicious wild nameless birds whose meat fell off the bones into the sweet peppery gravy. He was thrilled with the Governor's burbles in his Hot Maggots and stuff the cherries. Pixie wept.

And Johnno. Johnno walked dazed into door-jambs and

once into a wall. He had flown. He had raced a sparrow. He had startled a flight of rainbow birds from their warren by the river. Their tiny forms had swept across the rushing brown and settled to watch their clumsy cousin fall. Once again it had only been a short flight from cliff to field beyond the water but he knew something no man had known before him. He knew what most chickens have lost with our interference. His dangerous practice had paid off. He had flown.

Catherine tried to join the party. Nigel thought her speechless with joy at first. When she smiled a strained close-mouthed smile he smiled back as he whirled at the end of Budimir's arms around and around to their mates' clapping. He got no time to see. When she hugged Pixie a little too hard and wiped his tears from his new beard with her checked sleeve-end under a tight frown he was amused and he let Doug drag him outside to take his turn at the ice-cream machine. When he returned and found Zak knocked out on the floor after a leap and a whoop which had carried him clear to a rafter he volunteered to run down to the creek for cold water because he didn't see Catherine in a shadowed corner clutching a blanket-edge (thumbs held in her fists).

He didn't see. People think differently.

And when finally the party had died down and she gripped his wrist like it was the last branch before a plummet to death and took him outside it had crossed his mind she wanted finally to kiss him the way he wanted to kiss her. Later he scolded himself for not seeing. He shook his head wanting to hit himself for his self-centred careening about.

Outside she said:

'Nigel. It's wonderful your plan worked. It was magnificent and I wouldn't have missed it . . . never. Perhaps it'll do all you say. It may be a beginning. And I'll follow this with you all until the end.'

He caught her mood. After four hours of celebration. He had not seen. 'I can hear a "but" coming,' he said.

'Yes. Oh, Nigel, I'm afraid of my brother! I know it's miserable. What you say is quite believable about the child and the driver spreading the word, but I can only see Todd hearing of it and although he may not decide that it's you at first, and he'll want proof as to who it was they actually executed in Melbourne, perhaps not straight away but soon and certainly, he will connect you with this and because he doesn't know you had a double he'll think it was a mistake or a trick. You will be identified and when you are he will come after you with every effort. He's a powerful man, more powerful than you think – no! Let me finish! He's in more secret coalitions than anyone knows. People owe him favours for the revenges he's taken on their behalf. He lives for revenge. When he decides it wasn't you they hung he will exist only for your torture and death. I'm mortally afraid for all of us. Most of all . . . I'm mortally afraid for you.'

Nigel was touched. But he was not so daft or self-centred not to be chilled as well. Her eyes had grown large her jaw was clenched shut now and he wanted to kiss it soft but it was the wrong moment. It might never be the right moment. He believed her fear. He hugged her but he could not reply. All at once her strong body and his new-found toughness seemed fragile meat on thin bones. Like Doug's wildfowl. Like pathetic chickens.

Twenty-Three

Fiends at Large

'All we have to do is keep moving.'

'Nigel, we must end this eventually! You know it's more than death now if any one of us is captured.'

'I know: Todd will pull our little toe-nails out and have them for brekky. My punishment for coming back from the dead. Zombie man must die. Zak and Terry showed me the poster this morning. It doesn't include you though.'

'I'd confess.'

'Oh Cath . . . don't be silly.'

'Look who's talking. I am not being silly. You and the boys wouldn't be charged with kidnapping if I blobbed.'

'Hay? Oh, that's blabbed; you're picking up my stupid turns of phrase. Anywar, I don't intend to be captured. I – I would lose you. I can't have that.'

'Then we must end it. I agree, it is working the way you said it would. Although no one's copied us yet, I will admit people are intrigued because they're not being robbed by us. I do believe what Zak and Terry tell us about the buzz in the towns. But it's also working the way *I* said it would. You heard them. Gunmen have been hired to roam the countryside and capture you or kill you. You are safe nowhere. At least change our permanent base. I've got a friend in the east, she's lonely and absolutely trustworthy – '

'I have a theory.'

'Oh, I'd hardly heard of that word outside astrology before I met you. Does everyone in your world have theories?'

'Coming out of our ears.'

'The way you talk. I'm sure you have trouble understanding one another in your world.'

'Yup. Look: if I'm right we only have to stay at large for a while longer. The last two raids proved it.'

'Proved what, Nigel?'

He couldn't tell her. It was not that he didn't know. Rather, the way she might react to his idea gave him twitches. 'I'll tell you tonight,' he said to her, letting Mrs Pimlott drop back a tad, eyes locked on the far horizon past the edge of the high plain, where the tall yellow grass dipped away and hazy air replaced it. The layered chinoiserie of distant hills soothed his overworked nerves.

After a while he ventured a glance at her. She wore her fine brows high in that half amused, half puzzled way he often provoked in her. But she was focused far off, and the expression was fading. A rush of affection for her almost forced his answer then and there.

No. He'd tell her after tea. Wait for the right time.

He didn't though. She didn't force him. Yet when he kissed her ever more gently good-night that evening the tenderness in her blue eyes gave him hope.

Another raid went by before the right time arrived. Their fifth raid. A taunt from one of their victims impressed Nigel more than Catherine's arguments. By repetition their impact had faded and Nigel had begun to wonder if she had some reason besides the Todd threat for wanting an end to the Mackerel Gang's raids. He could not think what. The taunter, a white-haired matron wrapped in crinolines and black lace, threatened in a low, Liverpudlian voice, 'Ye'll regret this son – ye'll rue what yer doing to me with yer filthy fingers.' Tied to a burly wood-feller by one foot she managed to berate Nigel non-stop while he glued lemons to her, right up to the moment he stuffed her mouth with fairy-cakes. 'I know Todd Samuelson!' she shrilled, amongst other more colourful things. 'He's on yer trail and he'll catch yez before long, *mark my terms*.'

Nigel did so. That night he lay awake and decided there was not a right time to tell Cath his plan. It didn't matter whether he had imagined her feelings for him or not, he had to let her know. It meant explaining why, and there she might reject him. From what he had gathered, these people were direct with affection yet slow in – in marriage. There, he had said it to himself. Marriage. He was quite the grown-up now. A leader of men. He could take a knock-back. He leapt out of his bedroll. The moon was old and hard in the sky. He skirted the fire barefoot on the dewy grass, dressed only in long underwear. He knelt and touched the lump Catherine's sharp shoulder made in the bedclothes. Oops. Wrong lump.

'Waa?'

'Cath,' he whispered. Quickly he moved his hand to her shoulder.

She seemed to wake fully.

He gestured.

She got up.

She wore a petticoat identical to the one he'd first seen so long ago, when he had woken on the rock ledge in ignorance of so many kinds. He tried not to stare as he led her by the hand away from the campsite.

'The grass is wet,' she whispered.

A knobbled white snow gum corkscrewed from a mound just before the level ground ended. Far enough away not to disturb the others. He placed a hand on either of her white shoulders and took a breath of crisp air. A breeze rose and died. A smooth damp root pressed into his heel as he talked.

'So you see. People can go through. We can go through. If you want.'

He thought he had finished his explanation.

'I'm sorry – '

His heart sank. He clenched his jaw against disappointment and swallowed.

'I'm sorry,' she said, 'I didn't quite understand what you told me, I suppose I was still asleep.'

'Ohh, Cath.' He rocked back on the slick root so his toes pointed up, unwound. 'When we um – attack people, the way we do, strange things happen.'

'Yes. I should say so.'

'I mean really strange. I *see* parts of my own world floating in the air. It seems to be related to how weird I get because so far aside from the one time when we performed in Milton Keynes and I really went overboard – remember? – they've only lasted moments. But they're intense. They've happened four times now. Remember when I started dodging around near the end of the last raid, yelling, "Duck!"?'

'Yes.'

'I thought for a second I was on an army training-range. I was being shot at. It happens when I get carried away, when I do something unplanned, completely insane by this world's standards. It was so real if I'd only kept raving and climbed a tree I could have jumped into it. At Milton Keynes I saw an enormous – a kind of cart and driver but they faded away because I stopped.'

'Yes.'

'So you see, *I think I can get back home.*'

She stepped back from him. In the sharp moonlight her bare arms, her fairly pale round face, her white shift and her legs, almost glowed. Her long hair had come adrift; as she paused in thought a wavy strand drifted down to touch her nose. An impulse to suck that strand shot through him.

'Oh Nigel.' Hurt filled her voice. 'I'll never see you again.'

She was mistaken. But since she stepped forward and took him in her cool strong arms he let her live with that mistake for a time, and felt only a little like a cad.

One calf touched his shin. It was a powerful, furry calf that had never been shaved. One hip pressed into his lower groin.

A bony hip. Through his unbottoned top a nipple tickled his chest. A hard nipple. Her belly's taut muscles pressed back, but were not tense, against his erection. A flagrant, whopping erection.

He examined her sad face, found darker speckles in her eyes which he chided himself for never having noticed, and said, 'I told ya, sleepy noggin. You can come too.'

'To your – universe?' She shifted slightly; he gasped. 'How?' she asked him.

'I'm not certain how. It's always quite high in the air; I'm convinced that if I can climb up to it I can just hop in. Either reality is at least partly based on consensus or space-time in this universe is sort of allergic to imagination. Or I'm a loony. But if I'm right and my world intrudes into yours when I next get into a good strong roll during a rave, we link hands and leap right into my vision. Into my universe, yes. We escape! We can all escape! Will you come?'

'You know I'll come.' She smiled. It woke her face. Even her high round forehead seemed to radiate her happiness through its wrinkles.

Nigel smiled back. He knew it was a less graceful sight. Downright ugly, in fact. But he couldn't help it. He felt his lips pull away from his gums to give her a big pink flash.

It didn't appear to put her off. She kissed his teeth. She kissed his heavy lower lip. And she moved against him. Not intentionally, and Nigel was careful not to try and start something, but enough for exquisite tension, anticipation. He kissed her too, still smiling on top of his smiling, kissed whatever offered itself, neck, throat, collarbone, freckled shoulder. Eventually he did get round to sucking parts of her hair.

It was difficult riding Mrs Pimlott the next day. He was sure he'd rupture all over his saddle soon. Messy. Nevertheless he soldiered though the next guerrilla action without being crippled for life.

They had chosen a convict transport for this one. The trick was to disarm the fucknuckles as quickly as possible. Then down to work:

Charlie and Budimir had built a whole replacement wagon for the convicts. It stood three metres high on papier-mâché onions for wheels. It was a lovely pink with an orange paisley pattern. It had fairy wings courtesy of Johnno. Charlie had designed a clever mechanism which played a tune as the wheels turned, tonk tink tank tunk. No tenks. He hated tenks; they meant something in Chyrian. Bags of green custard would be catapulted at the fucknuckles as they rode off, tied to their steeds with yellow ribbon.

It was a smooth disarmament. By naked yodelling Serbs who dropped from the trees.

'Second-hand bivalves *lift* yourselves in song!' Nigel addressed the fucknuckles, who struggled beneath their hairy attackers as Terry and Zak and Catherine (his Cath) tied them, eyes averted. 'Bake your childhoods in comforting lime and beeswax for all I care, you brassy drake-pushers, gargle-hunters of the night. Rouben Mamoulian greets ya sassy windjammers all over. Greet. Greet-greet greet-greet-greet. Give me pork booties and the rest is mere monkey cabaret. Pshaw! Pshakespeare!'

He persisted while the others swapped the wagons and Terry pulled one of his body stunts.

Sure enough, the Melbourne Cricket Ground shimmered into view in the air. A house-sized slab of a Victorian Football League match, like a three-dimensional movie projected into the air. Hawks battled Saints in all their brawling glory. How the crowd cheered as the brave thirty-six punched one another (and one of the umpires) out. Almost horizontal winter rain pelted barrackers and gladiators in tight shorts alike and made the ground a quagmire. Funny, it was late summer here, thought Nigel.

He broke off his harangue. 'Look! Look!' he shouted at Catherine. Immediately the vision faded. Nigel pleaded with her but she had her shoulder to the unwieldy winged chariot and by the time she made it to Nigel's end the footy match had vanished.

He took up his rave again but there was no football replay. He would decide on a signal with Cath, he vowed, so he wouldn't have to stop next time. She'd see it. She had to see it. Next time.

Months passed. The trouble was, he needed to get worked up before anything happened. Which usually kept him from giving any signal. And the visions themselves prevented him. Once he saw a long polished tableful of media executives at a restaurant deciding how they'd rubbish a Labor Party election campaign, both blatantly and otherwise. While the rest of the Mackerel Gang dressed the workers at an isolated supply-post in clown costumes complete with grotesque orange fright-wigs and scary make-up then manipulated them like puppets through a scenario about a huge hairy pope of turnips (played by Terry) that licked you to death if you mentioned *boeuf bourguignon*, Nigel raved and stared at the dozen or so fat, self-important journalists trying to make a mockery of democratic choice three metres above the post's dirt floor. In the end, so fascinating was their assumed power over a public they despised that Nigel's inspiration withered and the executives disappeared.

Nigel persisted. The flashes of Nigel's world were usually short, they came perhaps one raid in three, and raids often took months to write and build. Yet it wasn't difficult to wait because the Mackerel Gang raids were the best fun. The best.

Zak and Terry had developed a nice line in silly songs and sight gags. As well as, of course, verbal abuse. 'Yaah!' Zak'd go, faced with a woman in a net hat. 'She's tryna keep the flies inside her head. Lemme stick some flypaper in ya ear lady!'

It went down a treat.

Since they weren't known here, Nigel taught them card-games, and these featured in the sight gags. While berating his captives about their ignorance of canasta Terry might reach into his trousers and after a painful struggle appear to pull off his own testicles. Here was proof of the need for balls in card-playing, he would groan.

Charlie built these tricks for Terry. He nodded seriously whenever Terry told him about another idea. The others rolled about the campsite in fits but Charlie took notes. He made drawings. He sent Catherine out to buy what he couldn't make. The finished organs throbbed and spurted blood, wind-up masterpieces. Terry's teeth-jarring screams did the rest of the work. Grown men fainted. A woman split her corsets laughing. Another vomited. He removed his brain and bounced it around, splot, splot, splootch. He impaled his eyes on a knife and ate them. He pretended to batter Zak to death with his own leg. His victims never failed to be impressed.

Altogether eighteen months passed dodging Todd, travelling all over the colony of Alfonso, getting better at their various skills. Having fun.

It was when Terry tried to inflate himself through his own untied umbilical cord that he came a cropper. The whole operation fell apart.

Nineteen eighty-two finished hectic. Nigel didn't manage a personal appearance on a raid for a month, and it was a month more until he got another view of home (a drunk standing on a tram-stop singing highlights from *Aida*), owing to two heavy doses of the flu. It took his complete concentration not to fall from Mrs Pimlott on the long ride north to Botany Bay. But they wanted to distract Todd with more raids across the border. Perhaps some of his support would fall off if they left his district alone. Besides, rumour had it that he'd teamed with some Cro-Magnon thugs so vicious they'd murdered each other for first molestation of a motherless little golden retriever puppy. Survival of the vilest.

On retreat from turning the Carthage water-supplies pink, Terry persuaded Nigel to stop a lone traveller and show off Charlie's latest invention, a fat suit made to look like skin which inflated through its belly-button and ripped Terry's clothes apart as it went. Terry secretly hankered after fat. Despite Todd's puppy-molesters the Mackerel Gang was headed back to Alfonso after the Carthage raid. Not to their mountain hideaway though. That night Catherine was going to write to a Todd-widowed schoolfriend who owned a farm in the eastern hills beyond Cann River City. The isolation would allow them to try some truly splendiferous ideas. Nigel was keen to get to the farm but all he had thought about during his illness was the chance to show Cath proof of his theory so they could set a date for departure. Lately she showed puzzling signs of an impatience with the Gang's aims. Perhaps it was sexual tension but it was her adherence to custom which produced this and nobody else would tell him about these *biggle*-damned things. Some really strong taboo about talk of marriage. He grew more impatient to make an intense enough vision to show her his world. To take her there.

Nigel decided to join Terry on that sunny afternoon amongst the cacti. He insisted that Cath come without telling her why. A surprise.

They rode down a lonely road through impenetrable prickly-pear in southern New South Wales. An American tourist was the troupe's victim this time. On the First Person We Meet principle.

As they drew closer to the lone horseman, marked as a foreigner by his chaps and ten-gallon hat, Nigel noticed something strange. Yes . . . near by the resemblance was uncanny. The bobbly nose-end, the beady hooded eyes and delicate lashes, the jowls and permanent shadow. No, it wasn't Richard Nixon. It couldn't be. But it was uncanny!

It turned out he wasn't the ex-president's double. At least that wasn't his name. Catherine's mouth dropped open and the look-alike's mouth twitched at the corners out of his usual frown. In his own amazement Nigel thought no more of this, to his cost.

As instructed the wrinkled wanderer tossed his pistol into the blighted field beside the road, but after removing his clothes he took advantage of Nigel and Terry's relaxed guard and Catherine's struggle for the babbling Nigel's attention. He gazed with unfazed American seriousness at Terry's expanding form and the pimples which exploded as he inflated, then ignoring Nigel's rant he removed a tiny silver pistol from between clenched buttocks, stepped over his bound wrists and shouted, 'Drop yer weapons or the fat boy gets it!'

Nigel and Catherine let the pistols by their sides fall to the ground. Nigel had counted far too much on Terry's ability to stun. Catherine groaned as if she should have known it was coming.

'Right,' said the naked Californian. With one foot he gave Terry a shove into the cactus field. He took fresh aim at Catherine's chest. 'Walk,' he commanded, waving his little gun.

Nigel knew the gun shot only one round, but he saw no way to draw the man's fire safely. He walked.

Without waiting to dress, the *doppelgänger* mounted and rode after them. 'Hup, Spiro!' he told his horse.

Behind, Terry wailed in the prickly-pear patch. He could not move. His false body wheezed its air away. Soon he would feel the cactus spines.

Under a sun which had grown fierce in its old age Nigel and Catherine tramped along the road. Had the Yank walked them the other way they would have passed the Serbs and Zak. As it was, they'd reach the nearest town soon.

Then the court and tooky. Todd and the villains who went around raping defenceless pets would make Nigel's lashes seem like a candle-light dinner with Barry Manilow, not easy to stomach but fine as long as he didn't sing. Now there was someone Nigel had not remembered for a while . . . 'Copacabana' flooded his mind. It prevented any constructive thought about escape.

But Catherine wasn't disabled by pop. She began to giggle.

'Quiet,' the dead ringer said.

She tried. The laughter snorted through her nose.

'Quiet you!'

'I – ' she gasped. 'I – ' she began again.

'Quiet I say. I want no' (expletive deleted) 'explanations from ye.' He was obviously not a follower of the revolutionary but altogether too reasonable Jimmy Carter.

'I – !' Catherine dawdled to a halt. She pressed her hands to her face, seemingly unable to help herself.

'I warn ye!' said their jowly captor. He levelled his pistol at Catherine.

Manilow or no Manilow, Nigel saw his chance. While the pale rider had his eyes on Catherine Nigel stepped back and jerked the man's ankle. His gun went off.

The shot went wide to heaven knew where and Nigel jerked again and the tourist slipped out of his saddle. Before he regained his feet Nigel was on top of Spiro. Catherine scrambled on behind him and they circled and rode away.

Half an hour down the road they met Terry, who sat on the verge very scratched and bleeding, pulling needles from his plastic clothing. 'Me fat suit,' he wailed. 'The bastard's ruined.'

Catherine dismounted. She had not spoken till now but Nigel had sensed her anger. At least it had driven Barry Manilow from his head. He kept to himself as he tied Spiro to a fence. When he had finished he looked up and found her waiting for him.

'Do you know who that man was?'

'I'm really not sure. It seems so unlikely I – '

'Not unlikely at all!' With a boot-heel she let fly at the gravel track in the middle of the road. She puffed frustration. 'His name is Karyl Robut. He's been used by His Majesty's Intelligencers against Jimmy Carter's officers for the past decade. Publicly, he's a minor official in the Arkansas adminstration, but I've read descriptions of his handiwork in the war there and though he denies it he's responsible for some of the most successful espionage in the American colonies. Nigel, he is Todd's friend. I've seen letters from the man to my brother with these very eyes!'

Terry got up, sucking on a wound on his hand. He said as he approached, 'He's just a old stickman who had one good trick.'

'Tricky!' Nigel couldn't help himself.

'It's not funny! He's old but he's still cunning and ruthless in pursuit of his aims. I don't know what Todd has promised him for your capture, but it's no coincidence we found him along this lonely road so soon after our attack on Carthage. He is definitely after skins. Or worse. We were lucky today,' she told Nigel, who nodded, 'but we won't stay lucky if we continue our raids. At least let's rest for a while.'

Nigel nodded again. 'We do need a rest,' he said. 'But the raid on Murray Town is still on.'

Exasperated, Catherine growled.

Terry said, 'The boys'll be diskappointed if we don't do it. Charlie's got three new wind-ups and Doug's already bought he's ingredients.'

Catherine inhaled deeply. 'I can't stop you,' she said.

Nigel put a hand on her shoulder. It was hot beneath her heavy shirt. She twitched but did not draw back. 'We'll be really, really careful,' said Nigel. 'Murray Town's not anywhere near our new base. We just need a couple of raids and then we can finish.'

'Finish!' said Terry.

He turned to the bleeding ex-convict. 'We have been at it or a while now, mate. If it doesn't catch on soon we'll have to hink of something else.'

'But it is catching on!'

'Rumours. Look, maybe we'll start our own colony. The Empire's wasted this country. I know spots so far from anywhere they're . . . well we'll think of something.'

But Terry turned and started away, a cut knuckle in his mouth. Nigel threw an annoyed look at Catherine and followed. 'What Cath's saying is right. The important thing is we're all together. I know you're having fun and that will go on for a while. It will!'

Terry stopped. He gave a nod and put a boot into Knacker-Eater's stirrup. Nigel patted his sharp shoulder-blades. He returned to Catherine. 'You are right,' he admitted.

She raised her eyebrows but gave a troubled smile.

'It honestly won't take more than a couple of raids to test my theory,' he told her. 'You'll see. It'll work out fine.'

'I hope so,' she said. She mounted. Her horse stepped back a pace.

He went to gather Mrs Pimlott's reins, suddenly washed out again by the flu.

So ended the best two years of Nigel's life.

Twenty-Four

For Love Alone

In February, by a large brick fireplace in the sitting-room of a farmhouse in eastern Alfonso, accompanied by Pixie on a rather lumpy harmonica and lots of stomping and clapping:

''Tis of a Weird Colonial Boy, Nigel Donohoe his name.
We may guess about his parents, no one knows from where he came,
He'd be his father's only hope, his mother's pride and joy,
And probably did his parents love their Weird Colonial Boy.

'He was scarcely two-and-twenty years when he left his fish at home,
And through Australia's fucken hot clime he wandered all alone,
But when at Emu station, mistaken for a villain,
He was clap't in irons and flogged and generally nastified so bad he thought that it would kill 'im.

'In nineteen hundred and seventy-nine he begun his weird career:
He bailed up Lieutenant-Governor Waller, he rode in front to rear,
Dressed in feathers and a chicken's beak he had bags of ice-cream pourn,
Topped with cauliflower and tomata sauce – it's the way a legend's born.

'O come along me hearties we'll ride the mountain peaks,
Together we'll be morons together we'll be geeks,
We'll get lost in all the valleys and get bucked off on the
    plains,
and bugger up this slavery, we'll screw their iron chains!'

Zak had invented a verse for each of their attacks. He sang it to a familiar air. The little twerp's changed, thought Nigel, pleased. When we met he could hardly put two sensible words together. He's got a purpose he's willing to die for.

The idea bowled into Nigel's pleasure. He put his drink down slowly on the flagstone beside him. The version of the song *he* knew ended with the death of the Colonial Boy. How would *his* song end? Although they attacked less frequently these days, Cath's friend had told them that in town today she had heard more stories of his exploits. Others were using his name. Other songs were sung, at inns, at night, after official closing. Thus the celebrations. He was growing famous. But in Australian history your fame usually arrived shortly before certain doom. These Australians loved a battler as much as his own did.

On each of the last few attacks he had seen fragments of his own world. The more weird the attack, the more outrageous his own contribution, the more defined his visions became. Yet Cath saw straight through them. As did everyone else. And the risks were straining life here.

Still. He took a sip of his drink. He had developed a taste for this horrible muck. He tried to take some heart from the stories Cath's friend had brought them. More than rumours. Perhaps it was really taking off. At some point it might become unstoppable. A republic of silliness.

At what point, though? If only there were not equal and opposite rumours of a new task-force put together to crush the attacks. Headed by Todd Samuelson. Of course. He was supposed to have sworn to 'bring the murderous rogue to justice' from the steps of the Viceregal Mansion in

Melbourne. Heavy-handed opposition was a form of victory for them in itself, he had tried to tell Cath, it was the moment when the whole population might get militant. 'Very well,' she had said. 'We can stop now.'

Cath was settled on some cushions at the far side of the candle-lit party. She appeared small there, with her knees drawn up in her arms, breasts squashed. She was smiling at her friend Eleanor, thinly, an ear cocked at Zak's happy drone. Nigel noticed she had dark rings beneath her eyes. He wanted to stand and shout, 'You don't know how important this is to me! Men I loved died when I should of, so it doesn't matter what happens to *me*, I'm not doing this for my health you know. And you're not the only one who's afraid of losing someone else. I love you. I love you Catherine, and it'd kill me to hurt you.' But of course he didn't. The image of pointy-bearded, denim-crotched hordes lurking over the horizon continued to twist Nigel's gut. He continued to blame Cath irrationally for giving him the image. He broke out in a sweat. One last time, he told himself. It didn't do any good.

This feeling crept in now and then as he worked, too, the slickness in his armpits, the hair raised on his nape. It passed. He took it as another sign that he had been in this business for too long. Over a year now. He busied himself. The troupe prepared for what was to be their crowning glory, as it were, an attack on the nobility. It was the boost they needed. But although Terry's disappointment over the ambush vanished at this prospect, the others took their lead from their Weird Colonial Boy, so Nigel couldn't talk about his spells to anyone but Cath. And while he and Cath were closer than ever physically (as close as you could get to a gentlewoman without marriage), their opinions had shifted further apart. He no longer mentioned the times when he felt the way she did. The ambush by Todd's hit-man had scared him at the time, and he did have his moments, but generally he believed they could go on as long as it took to

get home. And why not take all of them home with him?
Sanding, or sketching for Charlie, or painting a kite with
Johnno, the feeling would come and he'd tell himself that if
they took the usual precautions and checked the area
thoroughly beforehand, nothing could go wrong.

Then he touched his forehead. Touch wood, he thought,
and smiled humourlessly.

Taking Budimir's lead, Charlie reverted to his real name,
Slobodan. Doug became Veljko, but the scarred kite-maker
preferred Johnno or J.G. to Ratomir Guljvic, and Pixie
maintained he disremembered his christened appellation.

Each of them brought their own expertise to the project.
If Nigel or Terry could describe a mechanical idea,
Slobodan the ex-handyman could build it. There were of
course some heroic failures. Like the marshmallow-gun
which backfired pink gloop on the user each time. For this
attack he was working on a huge number of wind-up
rabbits that either hopped or humped until they wound
down and gave off odoriferous smoke as if they'd worn out
their little vitals. He divided his time in the shed behind the
farmhouse between these stinking cuties and a gross new
outfit for Terry. At the end of each day Slobodan returned
smelling of various repellent natural substances. It made
Nigel wonder how he collected them.

Veljko, the cheese-maker, never offered his cheeses for
the troupe's use. Cheese was sacred. But he cooked gallons
of custard, baked cakes in the shapes of dimpled spiders and
hairy bottoms, and during the past two weeks he had raised
the art of moulded jellies so high that he could make a
convincing mackerel which spurted unnatural blue fluids
when you bit into it or threw it or squeezed it between your
knees. 'Blue bloods. What a joke, heh?' he said.

Besides being the bravest man Nigel had ever met,
Budimir was magic with horses and whichever other
animals the troupe decided to use. He drew the line at
cruelty, though. He would have beheaded anyone who

threatened his Catarina, cheerfully, but break a mouse's whisker and you knew his wrath.

Pixie wrote the scripts. He spent hours each day muttering to himself on the front verandah of the farm, fat leather dictionary by his side. Then after dinner he'd write it all out in a neat, tiny hand.

And when Johnno couldn't fly during an attack he sulked for a week. This time he was as happy as a snake in a mouse plague. His glider was sky-blue. Given the right weather he would seem to float unassisted. Nigel learned to predict when Johnno would leap out of his chair and race around the long dinner table, a beatific smile shoving aside the scars, to hug Nigel and blubber thanks for giving him the idea of the hang-glider.

The weather continued mild although summer was well past its prime. There was talk of drought. As the day for leaving on the raid approached, Nigel's tension grew. His anxiety attacks hit more often, less rationally. Once, checking a shadow, he got stuck for hours in a hollow tree.

Four days before they left Cath surprised Nigel. It wasn't difficult with a man like him. But Cath was increasingly unpredictable; she'd say, 'It's your fault, you know,' which was not absolutely true, but wasn't a lie either. Like the world, she was changing, but not in the way he had guessed.

From what he'd heard and seen for himself here, Cath was outrageous in her casual dress, let alone that she allowed kissing, sometimes in public. On this nothing Sunday, while Eleanor took the boys out for a morning off, fishing, she leaned from Eleanor's bedroom window and called him in. They had rowed the night before, in whispers, in occasional drizzle that refused to be rain. He dropped his paintbrush in a bottle and went inside.

With her straight back to him in front of the looking-glass, Cath sat, hands at rest on her lap. She was dressed in one of Eleanor's plastic gowns. She did not move as he entered. 'Sit down Nigel,' she told him.

He parked himself on the very corner of the satin bedspread. He waited.

'Sometimes, man, I want you to undo me, button by button, take the collar of my dress and peel it off my shoulders until it hangs below my breasts, unlace my shift, pull the lace out of its eyes and don't – ! Do not get up. Sit down, Nigel. Don't touch me.'

The eyes in the mirror brooked no disobedience.

'Do you know what – how do you put it? – turns me on?'

He nodded.

'No you don't. Your lanky legs turn me on, when you scissor around on a raid, your words move them about – I think you don't know you do it, do you? It's your strange combination of absolute immaturity and livid rage I can't resist. You were angry even when I first met you, you know.'

'So were you.'

'Good. That's what I want to know. Tell me more.'

'Well um –'

'How did you see me? What did you see? Did you want me?'

'Yes. Yes I wanted you. I've wanted other women, I've wanted some badly – I've wanted every woman badly some-times, but you I wanted to *fight*. No that doesn't make sense.'

'Yes it does.'

'Really, I wanted to argue. When I saw your back in the kitchen, then, you were so *unrepentant*, although you hadn't wanted to hurt Melinda, your back was so strong-looking, like it is now, and then in the sitting –'

'No. What did you want to do with my back?'

'I've had no experience at this; it was only a second.'

'No tell me! There's a lot in a second.'

'Well.' He scratched behind his head; his ears were hot. 'Like you said. I want to do it now. I want to fold back your dress and tug it slowly down. I want to – are you sure you want to? – okay, I . . .'

Hesitantly, he told her about how her breasts might feel cupped alive in his thick hands, against the lines in his palms. He told her how he imagined the crease through her belly-button as she bent sometimes and the way he looked at the lines in her wrist as he stroked it, how he wanted to pick her up under knees and shoulders, so that she doubled, his Cath, naked in his embrace and wanted to stroke her so that she turned as she did in his dreams and gripped his waist with her knees, fluid and powerful and wild.

She spoke to him of her longing for him behind her . . . she grew much, much more explicit than he could have imagined. Oddly, he wasn't embarrassed. He contemplated her as her words drummed out and his lap sizzled and then his legs as well, their breathing grew deep and open and passed desperation into sunlight. Or had the cloud cover merely broken?

Abruptly she stopped. 'See you at lunch,' she said.

He did nothing. He didn't know if he could stand.

'Please?' she said.

He rose. He went to kiss her.

'No!'

'Just a kiss.'

'We would – I would have to tell you I – '

'What's wrong with that?'

'We can't say it. Bad luck.'

'You are so superstitious.'

She said nothing.

'Thank you,' he said.

She said nothing.

He left.

On a golden afternoon two days before they left, Cath returned with a cart-load of supplies from the nearest town. Ordinarily, Zak helped Nigel with the sewing in the parlour. Today he was behind the stables with Terry and Slobodan testing Terry's new practical joke. So when Cath entered for help unloading she found Nigel alone.

'Fuck it!' He gazed in fury at the blood swelling on his pricked finger.

Cath raised her eyebrows. She repeated her request for help.

'I heard you the first time,' Nigel told her. He shoved the fingertip into his mouth.

'Yes. I understand,' said Cath patiently.

In her ticket-of-leave-man's trousers and shirt and waistcoat she looked more beautiful than Nigel could endure. Especially now she'd removed her false beard and let her hair down. Her plump cheeks glowed a little from the sun and wind. It made Nigel all the more feral with anger. He couldn't help himself. 'I bet you do,' he said.

'What does that mean?' Her indigo eyes shone steely in the bounce off the hardwood furniture. Her hands went to her hips.

'You *don't* understand what it means leaving your home for ever, everything you know and care about, find yourself in this hell-hole possibly for the rest of your days. You don't understand one bit.' He dropped his needlework on the chair beside him and stood.

She stepped toward him. 'Don't I? You're not the only one who's given up a life for ever. You seem to think simply because your world's so full of wonders only you could have sacrificed a thing. I was happy until I met you, Nigel Donohoe. I lived in comfort and people listened when I spoke. I felt no need to drag myself around the evil bush, nor to defend myself against mosquitoes by night and assassins by day, nor eat rotted meat, nor defecate in bushes. There was *never* sand in my bread before I met you!'

'Oh you poor thing.' While they were two feet apart the space between them stretched with each word. 'You were never sentenced to death, flogged, trundled off to a fucking murder academy and left to – you never. You just dobbed in suckers like me. You never gave a damn.'

His words sank through the gap between them. He wanted to stab himself in the throat.

Tears dribbled over her lids. One plopped on the rug. Cath banished them with both hands at once.

'I gave a damn. I gave two damns. You might have been the bushranger and rapist you resembled but I begged for your life. What will you do for me? my brother asked me. I told him – anything, rather than hang an innocent man. *And he made me do things to him.* Disgusting – I – ' She whacked her eyes with both palms and heaved. She spun, and ran outside.

Nigel stammered into the divine afternoon. He looked for her, his Cath – he looked for Catherine. She was nowhere in sight. He went to the wagon, to unload supplies for the long trip west.

The quiet, almost autumnal roads let them brood. The Serbs were visibly torn between their love for Catherine and their loyalty to Nigel. Even Zak and Terry sank into silence. The weeks across the penal colony toward Milton Keynes seemed an epic slog. Horses developed the farts. Slobodan cut himself wood-chopping on night, so he was useless repairing a broken axle the next day. Zak, normally indestructible, gave himself concussion in one of his falling-off-the-horse competitions and Terry fretted over Zak's dizzy spells. The fields, trees, penal stations and towns passed monotonously; strangers' faces appeared depressed, and while worry at a possible drought might have explained this, Nigel took each gloomy look as a sign of his own failure.

When they reached the selected ambush area, a small lake near the Duke of Ballarat's country retreat, the first rain of summer hung heavily above. Its curdled mass was set to break any possible drought, which was a cheery thought, but the close air shortened tempers all round.

They camped in a dried-out valley a few hours' ride away from the lake. The water-supply Catherine had told them was a pretty, tinkling brook proved a string of stagnant pools. Budimir found a spring on a hill after an afternoon's nervous tramping through yellowed bush. They breathed

sighs of relief and drank deep. They unpacked and began
final preparations.

Imagine you are Henry Belt, Duke of Ballarat. Descendant
of kings, defender of the Empire, cardinal, the younger
brother of one of the most powerful men in England. You
are wide and bald. You are pugnacious. You wield power
comfortably. England is easily duped by those prepared to
follow the forms; it's the way it has always happened.
'Eternal bloody law,' as you father, Rupert, used to say, and
as you say now yourself.

Into your audience room after prayers comes a gross
example of the more obvious scoundrel this colony has
spewed forth. He's masked, but you know who he is. You
are the Weird Boy's next victim, he informs you. You thank
him and release his lip. You stroke your chihuahua. He will
capture the Boy, the scoundrel boasts. Capture? you holler.
You demand his blood, his head, his tender morsels in a
plastic cup.

I have it in hand, the scoundrel offers, wagging his pointy
beard, all I need is your permission.

Permission? For what?

He tells you. Even you are taken aback. And there is
danger to yourself. No, no danger to anyone but the villains,
the pointy beard assures you, he goes on and on until
eventually you nod and wave him out. It's time for your
guppy-bath.

*The bushfire sprints through the forest exploding trees,
skipping ahead of itself on the wind, sucking, trembling
before it rushes, screaming its desire, performing casual
feats of singular vandalism in the most vibrant colours it
can find. The starkest black. The chipperest orange. The
profoundest crimson. It is a jostling pack of great big
psychotic children on day-release from the depths of your
soul, and it wants to play so badly, so badly. It knows all the
games there are.*

*

One moment the raid was a lift from the trudge of tired lags about a drab country into a zone altogether different, a light place where songs without words made perfect sense and love was all you did anything for.

One moment they had the Duke and his fucknuckles bailed up on the forested road from his country retreat to Hepburn Spa, and Nigel was telling the Duke, 'This is lysergic acid diethylamide, a hallucinogen personally recommended to me by one Todd Samuelson whom, in a way, you know. It was invented in 1943 by one Albert Hoffman and today comes courtesy of one delicious sticky bun. Happy Turnips! Not what I'd recommend myself, ordinarily, but you – sir? your grace? your corpulence? – you more than most need jogging out of your ways, titular head of the church here as you are. Eat it.

'I'm a nun. Go on, you can trust a nun can't you?

'Go on, *EAT* IT!'

One moment, Johnno floated above the trees, his glider painted grey for the sky's dull metal, his bags of moth confetti tumbling about him. Zak sang a song about unmannerly eating of asparagus with the fingers so it drooped and dribbled butter in your lap. Pixie rollicked his lines on the red dirt road, dressed as a nun like the rest, a machine-gunnish pitch for Golden Magnificence Peter-warmers the Sweet Suit for you Toot-Toot. Veljko and Slobodan and Catherine were shrieking, 'The world still lives by imagination and passion. You eat your enemies' brains and become smart only if either one of you was smart in the first place! Howzat!' – and hurling jelly mackerel at the Duke and his fucknuckles, whilst Slobodan tied them with a giant lemon-yellow eel. Terry was beginning the tirade which would end with all his facial features falling off, his legs melting into gelatinous slag and his hair erupting into a cloud of live Mount Bogong moths to match Johnno's paper storm. Rabbits glued with EA 69 all over the fine ducal carriage as well as the nearby paperbark gums humped for all they were worth, stinking their friction.

Nigel delivered a free-form fulmination, and what looked like one of Melbourne's many gardens had begun to shimmer in the air above the cavorting nuns and below the hovering Johnno.

One moment this raid was the stuff of future song and film and future happy post-structuralist tenure-driven history spats between unfettered academics.

The next it was apocalypse.

Of course Johnno saw the bushfire first. He waved his arms and shouted in his native speech. The Serbs had never seen a real bushfire before and Catherine was still terrible with such an excited rush of the Chyrian tongue. He reached up and ripped part of his cradle out and impaled his kite. He began to drop. He slid temporarily out of the fire's line.

This kite-destruction was either inspired, thought Nigel, or –

The fire roared down the road.

Terry's nose and lips dropped off in surprise. A mackerel popped in Slobodan's fist mid-throw. Pixie screamed.

'Your horses!' Catherine shouted, cool. She had done something like this before. The men woke slowly from their funk and stumbled arms outstretched toward their mounts, half of whom had already fled, but Nigel went on raving:

'. . . finger-snapping mementoes of love gone sour rumble over my Aunty Beryl, um – give me your wounded your crippled insane, give me your water-buffalo. Yes! Look out down the road everyone it's Todd Samuelson and his hungry rippling goannas!'

The lawns, flower-beds and bronze statues in the air firmed at last. Nigel shouted and Catherine shouted more or less the same thing at the same time, 'Catherine, come on! Budimir! Veljko, Slobodan, Terry, Pixie, Zak, *follow me*!'

A carnivorous grin splitting his greased facial hair, Todd Samuelson rode hard through the growing corridor of flames and detonating trees and levelled his pistol at Nigel. Behind him, Catherine had gathered the rest two-a-horse, and she screamed at Nigel to stop and get on to Mrs Pimlott, whose reins she held.

But Nigel went on shouting, ' . . . pickled elephants in corsets take me whole! Everybody please follow me, please come, I don't have much newel grace in my Bible left . . . '

Todd's men fired at the troupe and they all save Catherine took off, toward the attackers. Nigel glimpsed Pixie passing, a bloody hole in the small upper arm, holding Budimir's back despite it, then they were gone and the troopers circled Catherine and Nigel, smoke billowed in and everyone was coughing, the fire was on them now. Nigel flung a gesture at the shimmering vision above the ducal carriage and scrambled for the carriage's roof.

Catherine did not follow. Nigel turned. He remembered the small surprise he'd saved for the Duke's flunkies and reached into his pocket; he had found the liquid incense among the things Catherine had saved for him. Now it'd give the boys a chance. And Catherine. He now knew Catherine wouldn't come. Raving still, he twisted the top and flung the amyl nitrate at Todd as the gun went off and just before he dived out of that universe he turned. Lit by flames, wide-eyed with fear, she stood behind him on the jouncing leather hood. He opened his mouth. She opened hers.

Something splattered his face.

Rain! The sky was opening, too late.

'*Go!*' cried Catherine.

She pushed him.

Watching her turn slow-motion and leap for her horse, he fell, watching her back. His Cath. No.

Flames, rain, Todd falling from his saddle, humping rabbits, burning paper moths, smoke, and a nun galloping off on a terrified horse, it winked out of being at once.

He fell. It took eternity. He dropped and landed.

Alone.

Twenty-Five

Simple Pleasures

Alone.

It must have rained during eternity. The grass he woke upon was wet but his clothes weren't. He knew at once he was back in the Australia of Anzac bickies and fines for jay-walking. Automobile fumes crinkled his nose. When he tore the grass from near his sooty face in a hopeless tantrum he saw it was machine-cut. Slowly in the pre-dawn grey, it occurred to him he had been wrong about three things. This wasn't Melbourne, too many birds gossiped and carolled self-importantly for that, the street along this park passed too wide and too relaxed even for so early in the day; it was some country centre. And the way through had never opened for the others. When he left off blaming himself for a second he realised the only way to his world from the other was a Fool's Gold swordtail.

At that idea he lurched to his feet; he couldn't recall the third thing.

Images, of Todd's face reared in too much ecstasy before his hands found it, Pixie's arm punched open, Catherine's eyes unreadable except for pain, the possible madness and bastardisation Terry and Zak and the Serbs would suffer if the puppy-rapers caught them, images so violent and immediate they were certainly more real than the park which swam and dribbled behind his overflowing eyes, drove him forward. He tripped as he wrenched his bandeau away, the veils and grubby linen of his habit. He moaned lowly without knowing as he made for the street.

A hearse passed, shiny in the gathering light. He bawled at it. Dropping his nun's robes, he spied the large wooden crucifix and at the last second he grabbed it and tore it free. Wooden beads skittered across the footpath on to bitumen. He stuffed the cross into a back pocket of his tough orange trousers. He didn't know why. Perhaps he'd meet a vampire on his way back to Melbourne.

The city woke around him. From the sign on a chip-shop window he discovered he was in Ararat. A day's hitch from Melbourne. Good. He wiped his eyes and walked more purposefully toward the outskirts of town.

The man in the Toyota didn't want to speak. He flipped on the radio. From the look of him he'd set out from Adelaide late last night. He ground a fist on his stubbled chin now and then and thumped the wheel as if to keep himself awake. The man chain-smoked short Escort filters. He drove foot to the floor.

The radio hissed, all disc-jockey talk anyhow. Then out of the dreamlike white noise a phrase popped clear:

'. . . death of Sid Vicious in Greenwich Village in 1979 . . .'

No. Sid Vicious was dead.

The driver thumped the wheel.

Nigel listened hard to the static, he reached for the dial and turned but lost the station altogether. It slipped on to a country-music programme and when he tried to change it the driver thumped the wheel, very hard indeed. To his surprise Nigel found the wailing soothed him.

Blither's shop was no more, not even a building. He stood in the gutter nearest the concrete rubble, hungry, footsore. There was nothing for it but to go home. Surely *they'd* still be there. Deciding to put off the tearful reunion with his mum and dad – none of his fish would have survived to cry over – he had hopped a tram in the vague hope that Blither might have more swordtails. Now he turned to cross the street again, turned back, turned once more.

Blither had moved across the street.

The peeling sign read (did he buy them pre-battered?), *AAAAAAA Chicken Sexing Agency and Secretarial College*. Someone had spray-painted arrows reversing the secretaries and the chickens.

Inside, the familiar cocktail of chickenshit and panic struck him. The reception desk beneath the stairs was as tiny as before. He pressed the doorbell by the payphone.

A door opened down the corridor; from it drifted anguished squeaks. Blither emerged from the gloom, blinking rapidly.

'Remember me, Blither?'

'Blit-er. It's Blit-er. No I to not remember.' The ex-Nazi pulled at his pointed nose then examined his fingertips. He peered over his steel-rimmed bifocals at Nigel once more, absently wiping his hand on his lab coat. Something like recognition followed by suspicion shifted in his blue eyes. 'You . . . you are dteadt.'

'I came back.'

The thought alarmed Blither. 'What to you want,' he snapped.

'Fool's Gold swordtails.'

'Hm? Ah, those.' He made breathy contempt. He turned to go. Nigel took his shoulder and held him there. The action seemed natural yet somehow strange for him in this imaginary city. Too simple, too forceful.

Blither felt likewise. His eyes widened with offence and shock. 'Let go of me,' he whispered.

'Shut up. What about the swordtails?'

'There is no life from where they came! The pollution has the whole stream extinct made. This is five years ago. Let me free.'

Nigel let. Five years. He demanded against all likelihood, 'You *must* have tried; perhaps there were some taken, were *en route* before everything died there.'

To his surprise, Blither nodded. 'Yes,' he admitted. 'I have receivet another shipment. They tisappearet.' He threw a glance over his shoulder. 'One tay I check the tank, they are gone. I train it, I fint nothing but chicken poo-poo. Going home I fint the fishes in the gutter. How they get there – ? Some kids I suppose. Hey, where are you going?'

'Customs and Excise, Immigration and the RSPCA, the ACTU and the Israeli Embassy.' Nigel left. He now knew how Carmen the swordtail had jumped universes. And the others apparently too, though into the gutter. Chickenshit as well as chemicals. Five years it had taken for Nigel to work it out. Wonders of science. A lot of good it did him.

The day passed slowly. Nigel walked. He noticed nothing, nobody. He bumped into people without apology. They didn't seem to expect one. He did apologise to walls and lamp-posts. His boots filled with sweat. The horribly clear bright day darkened and cooled. He felt it incidentally. A restrained excitement filled the autumn streets but he wandered through it, his stomach a distant vacuum, now and then mildly surprised that the people he crashed into considered his clumsiness a joke. Something important occupied their minds. He didn't give a damn what. Guilt pushed everything aside. He wished he had perished in the bushfire, over and over, until the words lost meaning: I swore an oath with Terry and Zak, I want to die, I didn't keep my part of the bargain . . . Then he prayed his friends had escaped: they had a chance, a good chance, Todd might be overdosed and he's the brains of them, and it rained on the fire, they'll continue because they're best together . . . That lost meaning also.

C.A.S. He stared at the initials for a long time before he worked out what they were. Letters. Capitals. Embroidered initials on a handkerchief sticking out of someone's sleeve. Now how did the alphabet go again? Someone sitting on a stool on the other side of the trattoria window against his forehead. The coffee-jockey appeared, waving him away. I look like a derro, he realised. It was his first rational thought for hours. Even when he understood that these were Catherine's initials, he dwelt on the fact that he and she had parted without making up, rather than on the rather fanciful person sipping a cappuccino a few feet from him.

His first impulse on seeing Catherine's face, on recognising her, was to rush in and apologise for killing her. He got as far as the door before he thought: She did escape, thank God she escaped so who cares if she'll never change, if nothing there will change? He pulled on the handle.

There was a Catherine Samuelson in this world too. And he looked like a derro. He had no money for coffee so he was a derro. He turned away from the trattoria. He propped.

If there's anyone you can tell about these past years, he decided, it's Catherine. She had wanted to believe him at Emu station when he had burbled at her about fish and space exploration. This Catherine might believe him now. Or at least suspend her judgement. Of course his own double had been a murderer, so she wouldn't be the same as his Cath (no), but he tucked his shirt into his trousers, shoved his unruly hair to one side with splayed fingers, and went in.

'Um – excuse me.'
    'Yes?'
    'I used – I used to work with your brother.'
    'Oh, fucknuckles.' She rolled her large eyes.
    'Can I speak to you?'
    She looked him over, direct. 'Yeah. Sure. Pull up a seat.' She gestured with a smile at the stools fixed to the floor. 'What's he done now?' Catherine flicked the fringe out of her eyes.

The Catherine Nigel knew had never worn a fringe. He recalled a longer strand by her nose that she had never touched, but which he had. He felt faint.

    'He doesn't owe you money, does he?'

'Hay? Oh, no. I – ' He looked down at his filthy clothing. At a loss, he shook his head.

'Do you want a coffee?'

He mmmed emphatically. Suddenly he felt the weight of Melbourne's cappuccinos.

'Crème caramel? Let's celebrate.'

'I haven't – ' Nigel patted the hand-sewn pockets of his orange jeans. He had some florins, a stiff card of some kind, a rabbit's foot, the mackerel pipe, the wooden cross; he actually felt it all as if he might have missed something.

'It's all right, I'm a rich student, I'll pay. Not every day you get a Labor government.'

'What?'

'Bob Hawke?'

'Oh. Yeah.'

'Wake up Australia. Crème caramel?'

'Fine. Thanks. Thank you.' He smiled.

And he bathed in the smile she flashed back at him as she turned to the coffee-jockey. Until he noticed the calendar hung on the mirror behind the till. The month was March, 1983.

Where had the rest of February gone? How long had it taken to get here?

Now he felt guilty to be relieved. Whatever had happened to his friends was a month gone. Finito benito. He took a deep breath. Nineteen eighty-three. Bob Hawke. My parents think I'm dead. Right. He needed a cup of coffee.

When she had finished ordering (she was a regular here; he would have met her had he visited Carlton more often, but he'd thought Carlton was trendy) he told her, 'I've got a story to tell you about your . . . about your brother, and – sort of – about you.'

She raised unplucked eyebrows. 'Good-oh. I love stories. You can take the simplest things and by the way people think about them, they get – ' Catherine shook her head ' – beautiful, complex.'

The coffee arrived. He sipped. It needed sugar. Funny he had never taken sugar. By heaven, it was delicious! 'Thank you,' he said, holding the cup in both hands.

'It's just a coffee.'

He put the cup down. 'I'm Nigel Donohoe,' he said.

'Catherine Samuelson.'

They shook hands. He bit his lower lip. It occurred he had munched on the lip before, since his argument with Catherine: there were chunks out of it. 'I've been away for the past few years,' he began.

'O.S.?'

'No. In the country. Sort of.' He bit his lip again, decided against it, and said, 'Look: I might as well tell you the whole thing. You're not going to believe this.'

'Let me decide that.' She sipped.

He nodded. He sipped. 'Okay. I mean, call it an acid trip if you like.' She laughed. Just like the real Catherine's, he thought. How he had worked for that honk! He wondered if she'd snort. He decided to find out. He started to tell her what a dope he'd been, with his fish, his life with his mum and dad, his university non-career. She warmed to the game, showed him the crooked front tooth he loved, and flirted a little with him. He caught himself thinking that she had gotten more actual for him, then reeled at the grotesque idea that the other Catherine must therefore have gotten less so. They are different people, he told himself.

Yet Catherine sat in front of him and he knew what the inside of her arms felt like.

'And what are you now?' she asked.

'Mm?'

'You said you used to be a dope.'

'Yeah. Well. I suppose I still am. As much as anyone. Sad, ay? I think I'm more prepared to do something with myself. You may not be able to change anything, but if you don't try you're just a – ' he waved a hand ' – you're just dumb. A headless chook. There is such a thing as evil.'

'Too right. So what about this story?'

He took the plunge. 'Catherine, I've been in another universe for the past couple of years.'

'Call me Cath. So have we all. But the Labor Party's gunna get in for sure this time. You can feel it on the streets. That's why I'm here tonight. It's *fabulous*.'

'No. I mean – yes, but – I've actually been away.' He pushed his hand up at the window. 'Prince Planet, you know?'

She snorted. 'You're having me on.'

'See, it was all because of this fish.'

'All right, when does Todd come through the door, huh?'

'I told you ya wouldn't believe me!'

'All right, keep your shirt on, darling.'

'Don't call people that if you don't mean it.'

'I'm sorry, I'm sure.'

'No I'm sorry.'

'I am.'

'I bloody am.'

'Look I fucken am, all right? Don't argue!'

He gave her a shy, sidelong smile.

'You dag,' she said. She had lots of fillings.

'I needed that,' he said.

'I'll say. Was it good for you?'

'Can I say what I wanted to say now?'

'Okay, you ate this fish.'

'Carmen the swordtail. And I didn't eat her. She was a Fool's Gold swordtail. A rare tropical fish, to the plebs.'

'Thanks.'

'Right. No more interruptions. Anyhow, forget the fish, the fact is I went to another universe, who gives a flying fuck how. Another earth, like this one, but not quite. Believe me?'

She put her head on her hand and her elbow on the counter. 'I'm not saying anything,' she said.

'Good.'

She poked her tongue at him. She remained jokey and sceptical, but as Nigel submerged himself in the telling she brought a hand up beneath her breasts and hugged the ribs beneath her blouse, fascinated. She narrowed her eyes when he mentioned the initialled handkerchief. She pursed her lips when he told her about meeting her other self. She looked away at the smoked mirrors, then back again, into his eyes, as if telling him she knew there was more to Nigel's emotions about the other Catherine than he had mentioned. She was intelligent, and involved. As he covered her betrayal of him in the courtroom she shook her head. She might have laughed at the idea of Todd as a judge, but she didn't.

By the time he'd finished she wore a mask of grave uncertainty. He couldn't tell what she was unsure about, besides of course his sanity. Probably she was guessing whether he was dangerous or not. He finished his second coffee, and recounted his feelings on coming home.

'I don't think I can get back. All my fish must be dead now. I don't want to go home, possibly ever – no, not really, well . . . I made myself into something there, Cath. I want to stay like that. It finished in a mess, maybe a bloody one.' He took a deep breath. 'I suppose I'll finish my degree. I want to be useful. I'm strong and I can work. Hard.' He shrugged. 'What do you think?'

'Dunno. Do you reckon you're dangerous?'

He laughed. 'Okay, just make believe it is true for a second.'

'It's a corker. If only you had some proof . . . it's like one of those dream stories where they wake and there's a real coin under the pillow or whatever.'

'Mm. But it doesn't matter if you don't believe me.'

'It does to me, busta. I like you.'

He looked at her. His awkward pleasure at her remark was shoved aside by inspiration. 'Hay! I do have a coin!' He thrust his hands in his pockets. He stopped. He had used to do that a lot. He pulled out the cross, Macka's pipe, the rabbit's foot, then the coin. It tumbled on to the counter.

Cath snaffled it. She read the back. 'King *Rupert*?' She snorted. 'Good one.'

For good measure he pulled out the final object.

A Polaroid photograph.

She took it. Her lips parted as she absorbed its contents. Nigel remembered what it was now, a group shot of the whole ratbag bunch: Budimir, Veljko and Johnno loomed before a stand of paperbarks; in front of them Slobodan wore half a pineapple suit and Zak and Terry had hands on one another's rough-cut fuzz; Pixie lay in the foreground, his gruesome gums shining in all their glory from his rampant stubble; behind Pixie, at the centre of her admirers, stood Catherine. Thinner than this one. No henna. A strand of long hair curled past one eye. She wore a leather apron and carried a blacksmith's hammer.

He could now believe there were good reasons why the Mackerel Gang should have escaped and perhaps under Catherine's guidance settled down together at Eleanor's, where he'd taken the photo. But the photo was proof they were gone. He was gone.

Catherine hadn't wanted to leave with him.

Nigel attacked the tears on his cheeks with a shaking hand, too late.

'You – ' said Cath.

Nigel nodded miserably. The fevered emotion under his shock and his recent forgetfulness had broken out.

Cath took him by one shoulder and pulled him across the space between the stools. He leant at a strained angle. But he felt better, deep in her perfume.

'Could I have some water please?' Cath asked the waiter. 'My friend's just heard some bad news.'

After a time Cath paid the bill. Together they went out into the warm, tense street to join the other people at loose ends that night. They bought gelati and watched the election coverage through a shop-window. Nothing yet. You couldn't tell until the Western Australian votes came in. 'Could be the end of an era or it could just be a blip. Could be both,' Cath told him.

'You never know,' said Nigel, empty, 'but you have to try.' He looked down at the convincing pavement.

'Hay.' Suddenly she shot him an unreadable glance. 'Howabout we go back to my place, hm?'

He raised his head at her.

'Oh you drongo, you don't have a place to live . . . well we are friends in a way, anyhow. Come on, big eyes. I don't think you're dangerous and I am curious about you; I tell you what: while we watch the election we can get to know each other by making some bread; it sounds dull and obvious, but it's great therapy.'

'Maybe I can become a baker,' said Nigel. All at once it seemed the most solid, wonderfully fulfilling job on earth.

They caught a tram to her house in the northern suburbs. As Cath opened the front door a chicken slid down off the green tin roof. It fluttered to her feet.

'Great daggy thing,' Catherine Samuelson told it. She flung it over the side gate. 'They do that all the time, the thickheads,' she said to Nigel, crossing the verandah back to the door. 'Well, come in.' She disappeared down a dark hallway.

The smell of proving dough on his mind, Nigel hesitated a moment on the cocoas mat, then followed. Electric lights flicked on behind the windows. A television crackled to life. The indignant chook trotted down the side path back to its coop, after the simple pleasures of water and grain and a place to roost with its mates.